"Hearing our old names brings back the memories of a life we can't return to. None of us can stand the walk down memory lane, so we just kept the numbers. Blue prefers the Spanish numbers, so we use them."

IMMORTALS:
The First Ten

by
DC Sargent

This book is a work of fiction. Names, characters, places, situations, timelines, and incidents either are the products of the author's imagination or are used fictitiously. Any resemblance to actual persons, living or dead, businesses, companies, organizations, events, or locales is entirely coincidental.

TRIGGER WARNING: This book contains elements that may be disturbing to some readers, including violence, torture, foul language, stereotypical dialects, police brutality, and other sensitive topics. Reader discretion is advised.

From the Department of Realistic Far-Fetchery
Cover Art: Ken Koeberlein, Koeber Designs
Consult/Content Editing: Madison Sargent Schuler, Celeste Sargent, Tracy Homan

www.dcsargent.com

ISBN: 978-1-957071-01-5
10 9 8 7 6 5 4 3 2 1

This one is for you, Daddy.

PROLOG

In a patch of autumn woods within sight of the crackling campfire, tow-headed Pherall Maurice knelt beside her twin brother Korbin and watched him collect fungi from the base of a fallen tree.

"You see these?" asked the seven year old boy. "These funguses can be used to start a fire. You blow on them and tuck them under a log. Then you have a campfire."

A billow of smoke wafted by.

"But Daddy already started a campfire," observed Pherall with a point.

Korbin dropped the fungi. "Did you know trees bleed?"

"Nuh-uh," Pherall scowled, wrinkling her nose and plopping her hands on skinny hips.

"They do." The boy stood and, using a small pocketknife, scraped a section of bark away from the trunk of a nearby pine tree. "Give it a minute. It'll bleed."

Pherall watched smelly sap ooze from the tree. "Is that tree blood?"

"Yep." Korbin tossed fine, board-straight blond hair from blue eyes and scooped a drop. "Sap is tree blood. If you're bleeding, you put this on the cut and it glues it shut. See?" He touched the drip to her finger.

"Eew. It's sticky," she said, pressing and pulling her fingers apart.

"It holds the skin together."

Pherall smeared the glob of sap onto Korbin's cheek. "Blood is gross."

"Aaargh!" Korbin shrieked. "You got it on me!"

"Treeee bloooood," Pherall wailed, coming after him with sticky fingers. "You better hide!"

Korbin braced to run. "You'll never find me this time. I've been here before. I know the perfect spot."

"I always find you."

"Not this time," he vowed. "I'll hide good. Wait two minutes."

"If I find you quick, you have to wear my pink pajamas … again."

Korbin screamed and took off.

Pherall turned back to the tree and removed more pine resin with the tip of her finger, giving her brother time to hide. "Ready or not, here I come!" she shouted after a bit and turned toward the wooded campsite.

Through thick trees and under bushes, she searched, but Korbin was nowhere to be found. For a few minutes, she followed her nose, peeking here and checking there as she walked. Suddenly, she stopped. A glint narrowed her blue eyes. Korbin was near but wasn't on the ground. The smile dimpling her cheeks was certain of that.

He was also to her left.

She followed the familiar sensation to the base of a gnarly tree and, with puckered lips, looked up into the empty branches. "You're in that tree, Korbin."

There was no answer.

Pherall crossed her arms and smiled. "I win. You have to wear the pink pajamas."

IMMORTALS:
The First Ten

CHAPTER 1

Twenty-two year old Pherall Maurice turned away from the violence on the screen and grimaced at the terrified shrieks blaring through the theater. Heat flushed her cheeks and breathing grew suddenly difficult. She looked at the exit, longing to be outside. The movie was almost over; thirty minutes tops. She could make it.

Blood splattered the screen and a mangled body slid down, leaving disgusting streaks. The sensation continued. An exit sign twenty feet away glowed green, beckoning to her, and she shifted in her seat.

Thirty minutes.

Creepy music thundered again, warning of more to come, and a knife glinted in foreshadow. Growing antsy, she looked again at the door and tried to breathe deep, but it didn't work. A character screamed and she was done. She didn't care about the movie anymore. She needed to go.

As if pulled by a magnet, Pherall rocketed from her seat and rushed for the exit door, nearly tripping over spilled popcorn in her haste. She exited the theater with her hand over her mouth, unsure what in the world was wrong but desperate for air. Nauseated, she let the heavy exit door to theater Number Four slam shut and leaned against the dark, graffitied alley wall. It smelled of sour soda, stale popcorn, fresh blood, and garbage, which didn't help her twisting stomach at all. Through the metal door at her back, horrid shrieks and creepy music thumped noisily, blending with sounds of city traffic, a distant siren, and the roar of heartbeat in her ears.

The movie wasn't *that* gory, was it?

Scattered strands of fine, board-straight blond hair got caught in the wads of gum and sandy bricks that made up the outer walls of the building, but she was too dizzy to care if she lost a few. Gore usually made her queasy, but she had never reacted so strongly to a horror flick before.

The overwhelming feeling had come upon her suddenly and, even now, was raging. Despite the cool autumn night air, a fine sheen of perspiration dampened her forehead. Her heart was racing. She could smell the sweet iron stench of blood from the movie, and it was gross.

A few deep breaths later, she opened clammy fists and pushed herself away from the filthy theater wall. There was no way to get back inside, but she was okay with that. Even now, as the alley slowed its spin, she could not only still smell the blood but could see it. A glance down at the toe of her black suede boot earned a confused grimace. She was standing in it. Everywhere she looked, she saw it—fresh blood—and lots of it.

Her stomach lurched.

After a small pep-talk, she braved a closer peek at the ground and examined the splatters. The blood was real. In fact, a trail of it passed the door she had just exited from and disappeared into the shadows of the movie theater alley. The magnetic pull returned. As if on autopilot, she gripped the wall and followed the drips toward a row of dumpsters perched at sloppy angles throughout the alley. Sound effects and movie dialog buzzed through each door she passed and, somewhere far away, a siren wailed, but Pherall barely heard those things. Careful not to step in the disgusting splatters, she maneuvered through the labyrinth of garbage dumpsters, following the trail straight to a pair of occupied work boots just visible behind the bin.

Pherall stopped short. One boot was a dusty brown, the other dark and shiny and soaked through with fresh blood. Every common sense alarm she possessed buzzed in her head, demanding she back away, but she tiptoed toward the gore anyway. As she neared, the bloody shoes scraped the ground.

Pherall jumped back nervously, expecting a masked murderer to jump out just like in the movie; but then she noticed a puddle of blood pooling beside one leg. The thick smell, heavy with the potent notes of the garbage bin, nearly buckled her knees; but she fought off the wave of dizziness and rounded the smelly dumpster. On the other side, she stood over a young, twenty-something man lying crumpled on the ground. "Oh my God!"

Startled, he looked up.

The overwhelming sensations that had plagued Pherall shifted abruptly from repulsion to good Samaritan, and the odors vanished from her attention. This man was in trouble and needed help. Hurrying, she dropped to her knees beside him. Only, he didn't want her there. Grunting softly, he struggled to push himself up but fell heavily onto his hip instead, exposing a patch of dark blood that had soaked the fabric of his white t-shirt. It glinted wet in the poor lighting.

The man wobbled and fell onto his back. "Go away!" he gritted through clamped teeth.

Pherall ignored him and lifted his shirt to see the damage. Blood gushed from a small hole on the right side of his abdomen. Her stomach jumped sharply and she nearly retched at the sight. "Have you been shot?" she asked stupidly.

Without waiting for him to answer, she pulled her pink shirt off and thanked the stars that she'd worn layers tonight. Wearing a black spaghetti strap tank top, she wadded the pink cloth into a ball and pressed it firmly into the bleeding wound.

He winced in pain. "Get ... away from me!" he grunted, trying to push her hands away.

"No! You need help."

"Let it bleed."

Ignoring him, Pherall pulled her cellphone from her back pocket and started to dial. "Hold still. I'll get an ambulance."

Like a snake, his bloody hand seized hers, crushing her fingers onto her phone. Deadly serious, he yanked her forward. "You have to leave!" he hissed, propping himself into the pale light.

It was then that Pherall got her first good glimpse of him. Messy, sweat-darkened brown hair stood in scattered locks across his forehead. Dark, level brows were drawn in pain over strong, handsome features. His build, solid and muscular, suggested a very active lifestyle. He had a militaristic look about him, as if he should have been wearing fatigues. But his hazel eyes ... they intrigued her the most. They were mysterious, cryptic, and lonely with a magnetic coldness about them. More than that, an aura of danger emanated from the man, even in his last moments. Oddly enough, despite the gore and tough talk, she didn't feel at all afraid of him. Rather, she felt drawn to him.

Pherall moved a lock of dark hair from his lashes. "What is your name?"

He didn't answer. Instead, he passed a quick glance over her squatting form, then snapped his attention back to her face in a puzzled grimace of pain. His brows flickered, and, for an instant, it looked as if he might ask who she was. The words didn't form, though. Instead, his expression darkened sharply. He jerked away from her touch, wrinkling his brow, and snatched the phone from her hand. "Leave me!" he warned, his tone taking on a note of urgency.

A gush of blood soaked Pherall's fingers, reminding her to keep pressure on the wound. "No. You're bleeding. Let me get an ambulance."

Scooting further away, he jerked a pistol from his waistband and pointed it at her. "No ambulance!"

Pherall pushed the point away and tried again to add pressure to his wound. "Be still," she bossed.

He shoved the pistol hard against her chest, forcing her to stop. Cold, deadly eyes glared in warning. "You never saw me," he whispered with difficulty. Freeing himself from her, he searched for a handhold and finally made it to his feet. Then, clutching the putrid dumpster, he staggered away.

Absentmindedly, Pherall stood. Dizzy and more than a little confused, she watched the dying man stumble away with her cellphone and wadded pink shirt. Then, like a big dummy, she wiped her hands on her jeans. She didn't realize it at first. She was too busy wondering what to do next.

Just then, behind her, the exit door to one of the theaters popped open and a chattering flood of people poured out toward the parking lot. Disgusted with awful movies and grumpy dying men, she turned toward the noisy movie-goers, unsure of her next move, and saw her roommate Mia's dark head poke up from the other side of the crowd.

With a crooked smile, her Korean friend swam upstream across the dim alley, fighting the throng of people, and hurried sheepishly to the dumpster. "I can watch this some other time. I've already seen it twice—Pherall! Are you okay? What happened! Why are you bloody?"

Pherall glanced at the blood smeared on her jeans, only then realizing what she'd done. "A shooting. Some man," she babbled, pointing to the blood on the asphalt and nodding toward the end of the empty alley. "I wanted an ambulance, but … he wouldn't let me call. He took my phone," she finished, still flustered, still unsure what to do with her hands. "I don't want to be here anymore. Can we go?"

At the sound of a scrape, the girls looked at the roof above. A shadow moved. Both frowned in alarm and faced each other.

Mia took Pherall by the elbow, visibly agitated, and ushered her toward the parking lot. "You know what? Yes. Let's go," she agreed quietly. "How about to the police station? I can take you there."

Pherall nodded, eager to go.

More than a little unnerved, the girls stepped into the rush of still exiting movie-goers and headed toward the parking lot. As they neared the end of the alley, a man with short black hair, cold blue eyes, and a five o'clock shadow pushed toward them, moving against the traffic. He looked at Pherall.

Pherall hesitated at the sight of him, feeling the strange pull again. Just like the guy in the alley, there was something about him that seemed to draw her interest, but he didn't slow his speed.

There was nothing visually unusual about him that she could tell, but oddly enough, she found herself staring. He turned his gaze forward again with a snap and hurried by. Without knowing for sure, she had a feeling he was heading for the man in the alley.

Mia and Pherall stepped down onto the asphalt just as a second man, a blond Hispanic with a half-ponytail and dark-rimmed glasses, shouldered through the crowd. He carried a black bag and a fierce look of determination in his light features. He also moved quickly against the current, his attention focused on some distant point. Hard, steel-gray eyes flicked to Pherall with a start as he neared. His gaze held hers briefly before shifting forward again as he hurried by. He, too, was looking for the man who'd been shot.

Pherall slowed her step, sure of this, and stared at his back with a curious expression. There was nothing remarkable about the men besides their upstream course against the crowd that made them stand out, yet her mind had photographed them. The images of all three were now burned into her memory, puzzling her.

A tug on her arm reminded her to continue toward the rows of parked cars. Allowing Mia to pull her, Pherall checked back over her shoulder again. The blond had disappeared into the alley. She looked beyond for the man with black hair, but he was gone as well. They were definitely going to the wounded man—she didn't know how she knew, but she knew—either to help or to finish the job. To help, she decided, resuming her step again, only it would be too late. By now, the man in the alley would have bled to death.

The chirp of Mia's pink beetle-bug car door refocused her attention.

"Are you alright?" Mia asked, hurrying toward the driver's side.

Pherall nodded, shaking herself back to the present. Her fingers were sticky now and smelled, so she concentrated on not thinking about them. "I'm fine, just a bit shaken up, I think," she assured, ignoring a noisy group of teens heading toward the theater. "He took my phone."

"No biggie," Mia said dismissively and paused beside the door. "It's password protected and insured, so don't worry about it. We'll replace it tomorrow."

"It's not just the phone. It was him. He wouldn't let me call for help, and I can't get the smell of his blood off my—"

Mid-sentence, Pherall broke off and whirled, wide-eyed, toward the crowd of teenagers. In an instant, she zeroed in on one—an attractive misfit with a brown backpack at the rear of the group. He was dirty, sweaty, and out of breath, unlike the relaxed teens nearby. He had unruly, shoulder-length, ash brown hair and a

5

slender, athletic build. Intense, dark brown eyes met hers at the same instant and locked there.

Pherall's heart skipped hard, and she stared at him.

He stared back.

Mia watched the exchange. "Pherall, let's go," she called warily.

Pherall heard her name but couldn't take her eyes from the young man. His gaze shifted away in a flash of anger and he hurried by, speeding up to pass the crowd and scanning the parking lot.

"Pherall! Are you coming?"

Pherall's heart was beating too hard to register the question. She glanced mindlessly at her friend, then looked again at the young man. Puzzled by her own behavior, she watched him even after he reached the sidewalk in front of the theater. Instead of going toward the front entrance with the other teens, he turned sharply toward the alley at the back of the building, his attention angled up toward the roof. Suddenly, he broke into a run, reaching into his backpack, and vanished into the shadows beyond the theater exits.

Pherall stood stupidly, watching.

Eeeeeerrrch!

A black van skidded noisily around the corner and screeched to a stop at the end of the alley behind him. Men in SWAT gear leapt down, shouting orders, and spread out. It was the Jackboots, a militarized police force with open jurisdiction and unlimited resources. They wore shiny black boots, leather gloves, helmets with face shields, and rather excessive battle gear. Rapid gunshots and chaos erupted from the alley, instantly clearing the lingering pedestrians.

The girls both exchanged 'oh shit' faces and, without another word, got into the car. Mia put it into reverse.

Eeeeeerrrch!

A second black van screeched to a stop behind the little pink car.

Mia slammed on the breaks. "What in the world?" she muttered, gaping into the rearview mirror.

Pherall spun around in the passenger seat, frowning in confusion. The van doors flew open, and Mia's pink car was instantly surrounded by faceless Jackboots with enormous weapons.

"Out of the vehicle!" screamed one. "Hands where I can see them!"

A horrified look passed between the girls a split second before both were hauled out of the vehicle.

6

Mia slapped grabbing hands off her and shoved one of the agents away. "Get off me. What is wrong with you?" she snapped angrily. "We haven't done anything!"

The agent caught himself with a back-step, then—*Crack!*—smashed a gloved fist into Mia's face. She fell to the ground with a cry of surprise.

Pherall could only gape in horror. She'd heard stories of Jackboot brutality but had never believed it. Stunned, she planted unblinking eyes on the agent standing over her friend and watched him smash his boot down.

Mia shrieked in pain.

Snapping out of her shock, Pherall lurched forward, fighting the hands that held her. "Stop! Stop!"

Violently, Pherall was heaved backward toward the van.

Mia grabbed the booted foot, stopping the next blow. In one motion, she hiked herself up, shoved her shoulder against the man's thigh, and hooked her hand around his boot. With a sharp thrust, she brought him to the ground and the beating to an abrupt end. Crying and bloody, she scrambled backward onto her feet, her hair and clothes ruined, her face bloody.

Several faceless figures rocketed forward, pissed that she had dared defend herself, and she was quickly surrounded by the Jackboots.

Mia went down with a cry.

"Get off her!" Pherall threw her weight forward, struggling, desperate to help. "Why are you doing this?"

Mia was shoved facedown onto the asphalt. She hit the pavement with a sharp grunt, then yelped in pain. "Ow! Ow!" she cried out.

"Kill her!" ordered a voice from inside the van.

Horrified, Pherall yanked and pulled, trying to get loose. "No! Don't!" she managed, twisting to reach her friend.

A pistol pressed against Mia's head. She sobbed in fear. "Daaaaddy!"

Pow!

Pherall jolted sharply, instantly hysterical, and screamed. With the report of the single pistol shot still echoing through the parking lot, strong hands hauled her into the black van in a blur of chaos. A piece of cloth was wrapped tightly around her head, and she was shoved facedown into the carpeted floor. A heavy knee pressed into her spine, pinning her, and a gun barrel dug into the back of her head. There was a shout, and heavy bodies moved in around her as the agents piled back into the vehicle.

Slam! Slam!

The van's sliding door thudded shut. With a jerk, they were in motion.

CHAPTER 2

Pherall landed hard in a wooden chair and nearly fell backward in it. With a yank, the cloth and several strands of blond hair were ripped from her head and tossed aside. She hissed in pain and squinted into a ridiculously bright light aimed directly at her face. An unnatural silence filled the room she was in, which amplified the sounds of movement against cloth or footsteps on the tiled floor. A dark camera lens below the bulb reflected a rounded version of her own image. Her hair was a mess, hanging in medusa-style tatters over her tear-streaked face and around her shoulders. The rest of the room was dark and smelled of fresh smoke.

"You're a pretty thing," commented a puff of cigar smoke. "What is your name?"

"Screw you," Pherall sobbed, ignoring the question. Gone was the mild-mannered, bubbly personality that usually made up her demeanor. Now, she was darkness. She'd never met this side of herself before but didn't care. After what she'd seen, she made no effort to reign in the fury boiling her blood. Glaring into the light, she twisted her wrists in her lap in an attempt to get sensation back to her fingers. Drying blood stains darkened her jeans and flakes crumbled from her hands bound tight with a zip-tie.

A hand yanked her head up, cracking several vertebrae in her neck, and the question was repeated. "What is your name?"

Pherall winced. "Go to hell!" she hissed, glaring past the blazing light. "Why did you kill her?"

"I'm asking the questions here," snapped the arrogant voice.

"No! Fuck you!" shouted Pherall. Her sobs made it hard for her to speak, and she spit the curse words out. They weren't words she used often, but right now she needed them. "You owe me an explanation. I'm not telling you a damn thing until you tell me who you are and why you murdered my friend!"

"I didn't do it."

"It was your voice that gave the order," she growled through her tears. "Over the radio. Yes, you did!"

"Answer the question."

"No! If you don't like it, shoot me and get it over with," she dared sharply.

Suspicion colored his tone. "You do not fear death?"

Pherall scowled at the silhouette. "Are you implying that I'm going to live? I didn't have that impression."

The dark shadow chuckled, an ominous sound. "Alright. You win," he agreed, putting the matter aside in sudden good humor. "I killed your friend to get your attention."

A look of disgust darkened Pherall's wet features. "A simple 'Excuse me, Miss' would have been plenty."

The interrogator's voice shifted to the other side of the light. "Ah, but I wanted your undivided attention."

"You have it. What do you want?"

"Your friends."

"I've seen what you do to my friends."

A fancy lighter flared, igniting the fading end of the fat cigar. The sweet smell of butane joined the putrid smoke already choking her, and the shiny lighter was snapped closed with a metallic click. Pherall couldn't see the face behind it, but she didn't need to. The cigar was plenty. The voice she would never forget as long as she lived, which at this rate left her about ten minutes. A blast of fresh smoke hit her in the face. Moments later, the back of his hand cracked against her cheekbone, startling a cry from her.

"The ones at the theater," he clarified in a nasty tone.

Several seconds passed before Pherall caught her breath, but the slap did not produce the desired effect. Angrier than afraid, she glared through tangled blond strands. "That was Mia, you asshole. You killed her."

"Not that one," puffed the cigar. "The one behind the alley."

An image of herself kneeling over the wounded man flashed in Pherall's mind.

"Yes," said the smug cigar. "That one."

Pherall shook her head. "A man was shot," she said flatly. "I don't know him."

"Are you certain?"

Anger heated the tips of her ears. "If you wanted to know who he was, why did you shoot him?" she railed, unable to think of a good enough insult. "For a blood-thirsty criminal, you don't appear very organized."

The voice went dry. "He was trying to get away."

"Can you blame him?" she shot back.

The chuckle returned. "How well do you know him?"

"I don't know him."

Another puff of smoke. Another slap. "I believe you do," he said, lowering his voice an octave and taking a wad of her hair in his fist. "You know *all* of them."

Pherall yanked her head, trying to free her hair. "I knew Mia," she gritted through her teeth. "That was *it* at the theater."

A black laptop thumped onto the table, startling her, and a small screen appeared. An instant later, a grainy image blinked on, artificially lit with a green glow to show a darkened alley. Right away, she spotted a small image of herself kneeling over the man on the ground. His face was obscured by her back, but the movement of her head indicated conversation.

"How do you know Cinco?"

"Cinco," she echoed. "Number Five?"

"Yes."

"I don't."

"You do."

"No. I don't."

"Then, how did you know his name just now?"

"You said Cinco, you moron. I can speak Spanish."

Another low chuckle suggested her frustration amused him. "You do know Cinco," he accused again, fast-forwarding the image and ignoring the insult, "and apparently you know his friends too."

Pherall laughed through her tears, not because the situation was funny, but because everything about this moment seemed so absurd. She was arguing with a cigar over a grainy video of a dumpster. "Mister, I think you have the wrong person."

"Do I?"

A fat tear slid from the corner of her eye. Despite her best efforts to keep it together, she could feel a tingle of hysteria bubbling just beneath the surface. Instinctively, she knew the only way to keep it contained was to feed the anger. Without it, she would dissolve. "My roommate wanted to watch a movie. I didn't like it. We tried to leave early," she said, speaking clearly to emphasize her point. "I don't know who you are. I don't know the guy in the alley—Cinco, Number Five, whatever—and I don't know his friends. I knew Mia. You! Killed! Her!" she screamed.

The video image stopped just as Mia pulled Pherall to the end of the alley. The tip of an ink pen or pointer appeared over the screen and pointed to the black-haired man. A box blinked on around his head, and the image was increased until his eyes were visible. An instant later, his cold blue gaze shifted toward Pherall, paused for a moment, then turned forward again.

Pherall's heart stopped. Even before the image began moving again, she scanned the crowd for the blond with the short ponytail.

The gesture was noticed.

With an amused huff, her interrogator congratulated her on finding the next friend. "Clearly, you know Blue as well," he chortled, expanding the image to show the next man's face. Frame by frame, the blond's eyes darted toward her, made contact, hovered for a moment, then shifted forward again.

Blue?

An erratic current thumped through Pherall's body. With mounting alarm, she watched a quickened image of herself stop mid-road to stare behind her at the two men. A moment later, the video clicked into real-time and whispering voices spoke together over a radio connection, joining the show.

"... *the girl? She just recognized two of the ...*"

A stretch of unintelligible voices cluttered the audio.

"... *know them?*"

There was a scraping sound, and then the voices continued, all of them talking over each other.

"... *be a coincidence ... He's here somewhere. Do not engage until Uno is ... Watch the girl! Watch the girl ...*"

A gust of wind distorted the chatter, and another voice took over.

"... *until we have positive identification of all four subjects.*"

There was a click.

"*Team C confirm identification before moving in ... Roger that. Team C, standing by for confirmation ...*"

A burning sensation spread through Pherall's stomach. She watched the screen, breathless, anticipating the sight of *him* again as the crowd of teenagers appeared. Instinctively, she scanned the unfamiliar faces, and then ... there he was. The video slowed to half-time and focused on the image of herself standing beside Mia's pink car. Unmistakably, she turned to watch the young man with the messy brown hair walk by. Without being enhanced on the screen, his lingering stare at her was visible.

Even on screen, Pherall relived the physical sensations she'd felt at that very moment in the parking lot. Her heart skipped. Her skin tingled. Her throat tightened at the sight of him.

Who was this guy?

Garbled voices stretched with the slowed image. "*The girl just locked eyes with the guy in the back ... Sir! It's him! It's Uno! ... He recognizes her ...*"

Pherall frowned. Uno?

A female voice broke in. "*Recognition confirmed ... Team C, engage ...*"

A scraping sound preceded a series of footsteps over Maxim's voice. "*I want her unharmed.*"

Another voice joined the conversation, this one speaking in elevated tones. "*Get her! Get her! ... And the friend? ... No, we don't need her ... Engage! All other teams engage. Fire at will ...*"

In an instant, both vans appeared on the video, one blocking the end of Uno's alley and one blocking Mia's car in. Chaotic popping erupted in the alley, and a mix of different voices tripped over the open line. "*... kill shots, gentlemen. Aim for the vitals! Aim for the vitals ... Oh, shit! Uno has a ...* (Boom!) *... Aaaah!*"

The screen flickered and went black, leaving only the voices.

"*Advise subjects have grenades. Flank 'em! ... Female is in custody, Team C ... Copy. Team C, evacuate ... Subjects are exiting north. Team D engage ... I found Cinco! He's dead.*"

Heavy panting and running footsteps cluttered the audio.

"*Team A, moving in for body retrieval ... Incoming! ... Subject in custody, Team A*—(Boom!)—*Oh, shit! Somebody cover us! Uno is coming! ... Team A, get that body outta there! ... Aaaah! I'm hit! ... Help us! Somebody help*—"

The audio clicked off, leaving a loud silence behind.

Pherall stared at the blank screen, stunned by what she'd seen, shaken by what she'd heard.

Shit.

Whatever innocence she might proclaim, she knew now it would do her no good. That she didn't know the men in the video would not help her. She'd seen the footage with her own eyes and looked very, very guilty. Of what, she wasn't sure, but instinct told her she was in serious trouble. The Jackboot teams she had encountered tonight may have behaved more or less like authority while the men in the images appeared to fit the traditional criminal roles, yet she wasn't fooled for a moment. The memory of Mia's execution by these bastards flashed vividly in her head. She was *not* with the good guys.

The room fell very silent.

Wild, panicked thoughts bounced around Pherall's skull, creating a tunnel vision in her eyes and a hum in her ears. She could feel her interrogator's gaze on her but didn't know what to do. The only tangible thought she could decipher was to stop talking and fast. With every word, she incriminated herself further.

Footsteps circled around the table and her interrogator's silhouette appeared to her right behind the light. Gloved fingers gripped her chin, and her head was shoved back hard. "Explain that," whispered the cigar.

Pherall's breathing grew shallow, but she said nothing.

"Explain it!" he shouted, knocking the chair from beneath her and throwing her to the floor.

She tried to catch herself with bound hands but landed instead on her shoulder.

When she didn't answer his question, the silhouette smashed a booted foot into her side. "Answer me!"

Pherall grunted sharply and curled into a ball, her mouth open in a silent scream of pain.

He kicked again.

Immobilized by the attack, she struggled to control her breathing. He struck her again and again, then paced around her curled form, letting her writhe on the floor for a minute or two. A spring appeared in his step that suggested he was enjoying himself, which really sucked. When Pherall could finally draw breath, broken though it was, she focused her thoughts and concentrated on distancing herself from the pain of the beating. Somehow, she had to get her panicked mind under control because freezing up wouldn't help her now.

"Perhaps losing a few fingers would help jog your memory," he said calmly.

Cold fear snapped Pherall's brain back into focus, triggering something primal within her. Flight was no option. There was only fight now because this asshole wasn't taking her fingers. That she would die today was expected, without her fingers was unacceptable. Dead or alive, they were staying on the end of her arms. Through her hair, she watched the black boots approach.

A flashback of her brother teaching her to fight blinked into her mind. "You have one shot at surprise," Korbin had told her. "A man can almost always out-strength a woman. Use your agility and your opponent's weight against him. Try to take him out with the first strike. Catch him off guard ..."

The boots stopped by her head.

As Pherall braced herself for the blow, she watched his foot. He liked to kick with the right. Once he lifted it again, she would have to get the left out from under him before he knocked her out. She would have one shot at this.

Bang! Bang! Bang!

A sharp knock on the small window in the door interrupted the horseplay. From the other side, an alarmed voice shouted through the glass. "Maxim, we need you!"

Maxim exhaled a puff of smoke and shifted his boots. "Excuse me. I have to go kill your buddy again," he told her, then turned to someone else standing quietly in the room. "Get her ready for transport and put a guard detail on her in case her friends show up. The boat should be here any minute."

Maxim walked to the door and paused. "Lock this behind me. If she tries anything, use the stun gun. We need her alive."

There was a grunt of acknowledgment and new footsteps.

Focus. She had to focus.

For effect, Pherall balled up as if afraid of another beating, but her gaze was focused as the new pair of boots stepped into view. She didn't know what he was going to do but now was her chance if she wanted to live. Breathing heavily, she curled a knee beneath her and set her bound hands on the floor. A little closer …

They stopped inches away.

To her disbelief, the bastard reared back for a turn to kick her.

In one motion, Pherall grabbed his ankle with her tied hands and flipped onto her back, spinning her legs toward him the way her brother taught her, and pulled him off balance. As he toppled, she hooked one leg around the back of his ankle and swung the other up toward his thigh, then jerked down hard with her uplifted heel.

"Oof!" He landed on his back, stunned.

With a burst of emergency energy, she charged toward the door. At the same time, there was a *Crash!* and it splintered open by a violent kick to the knob.

A familiar man appeared in the doorway, his level brows drawn low over hazel eyes. They locked on her. Large biceps and muscular pecs stretched the fabric of his ragged shirt, and long, powerful legs accented his narrow waist as he burst inside behind the broken door. His dark hair, short in the back and longer on top, settled in shaken scatters, and his t-shirt, jeans, and the boot that thumped back to the floor were blood-soaked, just like she remembered. She recognized him instantly. It was Cinco, the man she'd met behind the dumpster.

Pherall had too much momentum to stop.

Behind her, the startled guard grabbed his pistol.

Cinco opened his arms, letting Pherall crash into him, and spun with her.

The agent fired.

Cinco slammed into Pherall with a pained grunt, crushing her against the broken doorjamb. With a foul curse, he twisted and fired off two shots of his own, dropping the agent.

Pherall blinked up at him, open-mouthed, then looked at his bloody shirt. "You're alive?"

"For now," he managed, peering out the door.

"How the hell are you not dead?"

Cinco hooked a rough arm around her middle and jerked her out of the room. Two steps later, he back-pedaled, ducking three white darts with red stabilizer fins. They missed him by inches. He turned his pistol the direction they'd come from and fired twice. Another spray of bullets peppered the wall beside his head. He jerked back into the doorway, pinned. "Get the gun," he said with a calm nod toward the dead agent.

Pherall grabbed it and ran back. "But you died."

"Do you know how to use it?"

"My–my brother taught me some," she sputtered.

Without a word, he spun Pherall to face him. Jerking sideways away from another dart, he checked the pistol in her hands for ammo and yanked her bound wrists over his neck.

"I can run," she offered.

"Oh, good. Can you shoot?" Already moving, he pulled her legs around his waist, produced a machine gun, and took off with her, firing as he ran.

Agents fell.

That was her clue. Pherall hooked her ankles behind his waist and twisted, adjusting herself so her shoulder was out of his way and her weight was centered. Bracing her bound arms over his shoulders, she steadied herself to create less bounce as he ran. He rounded a corner into a dark hallway with pipes running along the walls and increased his speed. While he ran, he fired forward and cleared the front. Pherall kept her pistol pointed behind him, squeezing off rounds and shooting Jackboots until her gun clicked.

"Freeze!" shouted an agent from a crossing hallway.

Gunshots peppered the wall in front of them.

Cinco angled his weapon to the right, sliding to a sloppy stop, and fired. Pherall caught the wall, stopping their fall as the butt of his gun thumped her hip in recoil. As the man sprawled, Cinco got his feet beneath himself and redirected, hurdling the fallen body, and darted into the crossing hallway. "Watch behind me," he said quietly and hopped to a stop on the other side.

Pherall's feet hit the floor. Dropping to his knee, he snatched the fallen man's weapon and ammo with quick hands and reloaded the new magazine to Pherall's pistol. The tiniest shadow moved along a far wall. "They're coming," she warned, tightening her arms around his neck.

Cinco scooped her up again and took off. Just as they moved, a round of tranquilizer darts hit the wall, missing them by inches.

Pherall jolted at the sight of the needles, then resumed her cover fire down the hall, giving Cinco time to exit their hiding place.

Cautiously, he hugged the walls, rounding corners and searching frantically for a way out. "This place is a maze," he complained, turning a different way.

Pherall glanced at the floor behind them and noticed a dull path in the sheen of the tiles leading to the left. "That way! Back up. Back up! Look at the floor," she said, squeezing off a few rounds.

An agent grunted and spun.

Cinco doubled back, saw what she was talking about, and ran. "Good eye," he panted, rounding a ninety-degree corner that opened into a foyer at the front of the building. "As soon as we get outside—"

Pow! Pow! Pow!

Gunshots from outside splattered the double doors, shattering the knob and puncturing holes. Light from a streetlamp beyond spilled through the dots.

Cinco slid to a stop, dodging the bullets. "Whoa—hello!"

A moment later, there was a *Kick, Kick!* but the front doors of the building held.

Cinco quickly backed up. "Um ... duck," he warned, looking around for someplace to hide.

Three seconds later, a massive *Ka-Blam!* splintered the doors, blowing them inward off their hinges. Cinco spun, putting his back to the shrapnel, and covered his head with an arm. Through the debris, a slender athletic silhouette appeared behind the smoky crater.

Pherall instantly recognized the familiar young man with messy, shoulder-length hair.

It was Uno.

"God, I love him!" Cinco whooped in celebration. Running headlong, he charged through the gaping hole toward the cab of a pale blue pickup truck. The pickup slid to a halt across the gravel drive. Uno, age young-twenty or so, jumped onto the runner and jerked the passenger door open with one hand while firing a pistol toward the building with the other. At a run, Cinco lifted Pherall's hands off his neck and, without slowing, swung her legs to his right side. With a leap, he hit the running board and slid inside the truck in a single bound.

Uno crashed against her and twisted, slamming the door behind himself. Curling his lip, he fired out the window with his shoulder against the dash and his foot on the back of the seat beside Pherall's arm. "Go!"

The black-haired driver floored the gas.

As the truck fishtailed on the gravel, Jackboots came pouring out of the building, shooting at them. Broken glass from the passenger side window splattered inside the door.

Pherall grabbed her head and ducked. "Shit! Shit! Shit!"

Uno fired methodical shots in return.

The truck peeled out toward the road, throwing a spray of rocks. Holes appeared in the rear glass by their heads, and bullets *tink-tink-tink*-ed into the side of the truck as a machine gun joined the chaos.

"This is not happening!" Pherall promised herself in a tiny voice.

Pop!

The passenger-side mirror exploded.

Uno jerked sharply away from the flying glass. "Blue!"

Blue, the blond with the gray eyes and half-ponytail, sat up with a rocket launcher and fired from the bed. The mass of Jackboot agents vanished in a pile of billowing dust as the truck reached the road. The wheels gripped the asphalt, and the pickup rocketed away in a squall.

CHAPTER 3

The momentum of the turning vehicle jolted Pherall back from her squeezy-eyed hiding place and, slowly, she lowered her arms. Wide tires rumbled noisily over the asphalt, an eerie sound after the chaos. A steady gush of wind blew through the missing windows, but it wasn't enough to hide the smell of dog sweat and old engine oil clinging to the dirty seats.

Nobody spoke.

In the silence that followed, Pherall lifted her head, exhaling in short puffs. She was alive. How she wasn't sure, but ... she'd killed people. Realizing what she'd done, she dropped the pistol onto the seat and snatched her hand away from the offensive weapon. Then, she remembered Uno. She looked up and found his cold brown eyes pinned on her. As if by current, their gazes held, locking firmly into place.

Pherall's heart thumped a Morse code in her chest. Without being told, she knew Uno was the leader of the group. Despite the appearance of one so young, he possessed a strength about him, an aura of authority. Everything about this Uno was downright scary and, instinctively, she cowered from him. Her next move was to reach for the pistol again, but he snatched it before she could and took it away.

He was soft-spoken, his speech unhurried. "What is this?" he demanded with a sharp glance at Cinco.

His gaze came right back.

Cinco untangled his legs from Pherall's. "I don't know," he answered in a low voice.

"What do you mean you don't know?"

"I don't know, Uno!" Cinco shot back. "The Jackboots said she recognized us."

"Recognized us," echoed the unamused Uno, his tone accusing. His lash-lined brown gaze shifted to the driver. "Ocho?"

Pherall followed Uno's glance, startled by another number name. Ocho was Spanish for eight. Why didn't they use normal names? she wondered. What was up with the numbers?

The black-haired driver's apathetic blue eyes flicked toward Pherall for a quick once-over, then turned back to the dark, elm tree-lined road. "This is the first time I've seen her," he answered, his tone flat and disinterested.

Uno's gaze shifted back to Pherall. His features were rigid and unwavering, his demeanor suspicious. Everything about him—his eyes, his tone, his body language—suggested he had severe trust issues. He wrinkled his forehead in memory. "You were in the theater parking lot with a Korean girl," he remembered, narrowing his gaze.

Pherall couldn't even blink.

Up close, Uno's ash-brown hair was sweaty and windblown, giving him an unruly, I-just-ran-a marathon look. It fell over itself into his face and reached his shoulders where it wanted to. His dark brows were bold, with contour that matched his expression. The eyes she remembered well—dark brown, intense, and astute, like a hawk. Now, after a closer look, she suspected they had perhaps a bit of Russian in them, which gave them a pleasant, faintly exotic look. His masculine features were symmetric and quite attractive, with just a hint of boyish, a dash of salty, and a sprinkle of deadly. There may have been freckles.

"What is your name?" he asked in a low voice.

This time, she didn't even consider not answering. "Pherall."

"Why did they think you recognized us?"

A bead of sweat formed on Pherall's temple. Awkwardly, she gave her head a slow shake. "I don't know," she answered, far more frightened of Uno than she had been of the cigar behind the light. The agent Maxim was an asshole and a bully, the kind of person who strutted and barked because he lacked real confidence —a typical coward. This guy, this Uno, didn't have that problem. He was even-tempered and patient. Even his voice was quiet, a characteristic that suggested he wasn't in the habit of repeating himself. "They had a video from the theater, taken from the roof. I looked at you," she said with a light shrug. "Apparently, that was enough."

The dark eyes remained fixed. "At me?"

Pherall's heartbeat pulsed in her throat. He was deciding whether or not to kill her, she realized. It wasn't clear how she knew that, but there was no doubt. "All of you," she clarified, suddenly anxious to escape his disturbing presence. "I was leaving the theater and passed a crowd. I saw Ocho first," she motioned hesitantly to the guy driving the pickup. "He was heading toward the alley behind me. The blond," she gestured behind herself to the guy in the bed of the truck, "was behind him. I saw you in the parking lot."

"And Cinco?"

Pherall glanced at her rescuer, who stared unblinking out the front windshield, seemingly detached from the exchange. "I found him in the alley. He'd been," she dropped her gaze to his shirt, dried and stiff now from the blood, "… shot," she finished in a whisper.

Uno adjusted his back against the dash, preferring his backward position so he could face her. When he spoke again, the tone of his voice had dropped to a chilling rumble. "What caught your attention?"

Pherall clammed up. She'd said something wrong. He was going to kill her. "I don't know."

"Guess!" he ordered sharply, startling her.

Pherall didn't want to answer. She fidgeted her fingers together and, after a moment, braved a look at him.

Uno lifted a brow but, as she had suspected, didn't repeat himself.

"You reminded me," she hesitated to steady her voice, "of …"

"Of?" he prompted.

"… of Cinco."

At this, Cinco turned toward the conversation in surprise, frowned, and locked eyes with Uno. "I don't know her," he swore quickly.

Uno held Cinco's gaze for several seconds before calmly lowering his dark lashes in decision. His tone was curt. "Pull over, Ocho," said the unblinking leader.

Cinco let out a breath and peered aimlessly at the dash, an unspoken curse on his lips.

Ocho pulled onto an empty road and stopped the truck beneath a sycamore tree.

Pherall set her jaw, determined to go down with dignity, and peered ahead out the windshield. This was where she would die, she thought, looking out at the dark field. Despite her resolve, a low tremble worked its way through her body. Her breathing grew shallow, but she wouldn't allow herself to give in to the fear. No matter what happened, she would not beg. She refused.

Uno opened the door and stepped out of the pickup. "Cinco," he said, turning the pistol in his hand so that he held the barrel.

Cinco hesitated for an instant, then pushed Pherall toward the open door. She slid out and watched Uno hand the pistol to Cinco, who took it awkwardly. In the silence that followed, she faced Uno directly, careful to hold her head high. "It was your eyes," she told the leader, paused a moment longer, then turned to follow Cinco to the field.

Uno caught her elbow, stopping her. "What about them?"

Pherall turned her head his direction, eyes averted. "They're cold. Empty," she said, then looked at him again. "Beautiful."

He released her arm.

Pherall took one last good look at him, positive he could hear the erratic pounding of her heart, then turned away. Numb, she followed her killer. Cinco led her to a ditch fifty yards away and chambered a round. She watched him, then looked up into his pinched face. "Why does it matter?" she asked, purposefully holding eye contact.

He fooled with the pistol safety, trying to avoid her gaze. "Why does what matter?"

She angled her head, making him look at her. "Crossing paths with you," she said angrily. "Who the hell are you?"

"It's a long story."

Disgust darkened her features. "And you don't have time to explain," she finished.

A heavy sigh lowered his shoulders, but only for a moment. "I told you to go away," he snapped back with far too much emotion in his voice, in his handsome features, "but you didn't! You didn't listen!"

Surprised by his outburst, Pherall exhaled, discarding the angry reply she was about to let loose on him. Instead, she softened her tone. She hiccupped but managed to maintain her composure. "I didn't want you to die. I wanted you to live," she shook her head and tossed her hands, "but you're already dead, Cinco. All of you are."

Guilty, he looked away, suggesting she'd hit a nerve.

Another wave of tears rolled down her cheeks, but she ignored them. "If I had to guess," she continued, gesturing a shaky hand toward the waiting pickup, "I'd say you have been for a long time."

Unshed tears glistened in his eyes, and a light breeze fluttered a lock of his hair. "We have," he whispered.

Pherall gave him a long look, wondering who he was and why she felt so drawn to him. He was an asshole. All of them were. Unanswered questions danced around in her head, but it was pointless to ask them. The guy was about to kill her. There was no time to worry about his demons now. Determined to go with pride, she turned her back to him in disgust and waited. Several seconds later, Cinco took her gently by the arm and pushed the barrel of his pistol against her spine behind her heart. Trembling, she closed her eyes, dropping tears down both cheeks. After several moments, the barrel moved from her back to the base of her skull. After another long pause, she felt Cinco step closer and take a better grip on her arm. The barrel pressed harder, but the gun still didn't go off. To her surprise, the barrel vanished from her skull, and Cinco stepped abruptly away.

She didn't move.

A few moments later, footsteps approached behind them. "Cinco?" came Uno's voice.

Pherall winced at the sound of it.

"No," Cinco growled, rounding on his friend. "No!"

"Get in the truck," ordered Uno.

Cinco's voice cracked. "Uno, don't!"

"Go."

"No," Cinco snapped in a choked voice. "I'll do it! I can do it."

Uno touched his shoulder. "You don't have to," he said quietly. "I will."

Cinco stood fixed where he was for several moments, clearly conflicted, and lowered his head. Beneath twisted brows, he turned a troubled look to his friend and exhaled a shaky breath. "Uno," he whispered.

"Go."

Pherall remained where she was, which took some effort, but intuition told her to stay out of it. Without moving, she listened, hoping Cinco would argue more … but he didn't. To her dismay, he walked away, leaving her alone with Uno. She tried to exhale in disappointment, but the breath wouldn't come. She was holding it because Uno was being very quiet. Once again, she braced herself for what was to come, but this time there was no barrel, no grip on her arm, no internal conflict.

Pherall squeezed her eyes closed. Had Cinco given him the pistol? She waited, not knowing how he would kill her, then figured it was best not to know. Only nothing happened. After a full minute, she could stand it no longer. Slowly, she turned to face the young man standing at her back.

Uno stood glaring down at her. Her blue eyes locked with his and held. Near his thigh, just below her field of vision, she noticed a slight movement of his fingers as he shifted something in his hand.

Pherall couldn't bring herself to look down.

The silence between them hung heavily on the air. This was Pherall's chance to talk her way out of this, but she refused to plead like a coward. Without being told, she knew it wouldn't work on him anyway. Dignity, she reminded herself, was the only thing she could take with her. But as she held his gaze, her dread and uncertainty were replaced with curiosity. "What's going on between you and the Jackboots?" she asked at last. "What are you fighting them for?"

"Our right to live," he answered.

She laughed in amusement at the irony, then bit back a sarcastic, and rather fitting, reply—the one he deserved. Instead, she gestured toward the truck and spoke without thinking. "If you're fighting to live, Uno," she scolded, finding an unexpected surge of courage, "then you should try to live. You're like zombies. All of you."

"Zombies?"

"Yes, zombies. You don't see it?"

"No."

"Whatever you boys are doing," she assured, acting on gut instinct, "it isn't living."

An eyebrow shifted. "Have you ever lost someone you love?" he demanded, his tone purposeful and unfriendly.

Pherall laughed. It was a sour sound, and it came from a place of fresh darkness. "Mia! Three hours ago," she answered angrily, "because I *looked* at you. They shot her. The authorities I have trusted all my life beat her and then shot her in the head. No reason. No provocation. I asked and was told it was merely to get my attention. Because I looked at you!"

He didn't answer.

Pherall peered past him to the dark field and took a deep breath, unsure what to say next.

After a long time, Uno spoke, his voice so low it was almost inaudible. "Everyone we loved," he said, taking an intimidating step toward her. "Our sisters, mothers, grandfathers. Our girlfriends. Wives. Mentors. Friends. Everyone we knew. The Jackboots got them. And they didn't just kill them. They tortured them. Raped them. Used them as bait only to kill them the moment we arrived. We begged. We tried anything to stop them. We destroyed everything we owned hoping to protect the last of the survivors, but they found them. My sister was thirteen. Without the people we loved, yes, we died inside. For years, we died," he said, advancing slowly. "It was a slow death."

Pherall backed a step away from him. "Why are the Jackboots doing this?"

"To find us."

He took another step.

She backed up again.

"Everyone who crosses our paths suffers this fate. If those bastards even *think* we care about someone, they won't stop. They'll hunt you like an animal."

"I'm nothing to you," she interrupted hotly. "Why should you care what happens to me?"

"I don't," he said in a cold voice. "Cinco does."

Pherall glanced toward the truck and saw Cinco standing with his arms over the bed. His back was to her.

Uno caught her arm abruptly, regaining her undivided attention, and snatched her close. "To keep you alive condemns you to the same end as the others. Cinco knows that," he said, then inclined his head, "and now you know."

Pherall's breathing increased, more from anger than fear at this point. "So what?" she snapped back. "You'll kill me now so they don't kill me later. That makes no sense, Uno. How I die should be the result of *my* decisions, not yours on some whim."

"It isn't a question of whether they will or won't kill you," he reiterated in frustration. "It's *how*."

"Oh," she conceded with a sarcastic wave, "well, having my head blown off in a random field and being left to rot is certainly much better. I didn't realize the delightful opportunity I was about to miss. My bad."

Uno looked past her and narrowed his eyes. "Tell me, Pherall. Does keeping you alive really allow Cinco to live," he asked quietly, "or does it force him to suffer all over again when they get you?"

Pherall took a moment to study him and the different expressions playing across his face. She was irritating him, that was certain, but he didn't simply give in to the emotion and respond accordingly. He controlled it and stayed focused on his topic. His thoughts were entirely unreadable through his features, but … she wasn't dead yet, so something was happening. As she formulated her answer, she glanced down at his hand.

It was still empty.

She chose her words carefully. "If Cinco is willing to risk reliving what you described for a chance to feel alive again," she said, dropping her voice to a whisper to hide the tremble, "how can you deny him that? Why would you?"

It was Uno's turn to not answer.

Pherall shook her head. "I can't say what he needs—I don't know him—but he needs something. You all do," she said, giving him a light jab in the chest. "You boys can't let those asshole

Jackboots dictate how you live and who you love. You live in fear of something that hasn't happened … and you're miserable."

Uno gave her arm a sharp jolt. "They all get caught!" he hissed, finally losing his cool. "Everyone!"

Pherall flinched, certain he was about to strangle her.

For several seconds, he stared at her with an agitated expression, but it cooled quickly, leaving his features stoic once more. His voice chilled again. "They know who you are, Pherall," he said, regaining his composure. "They know your face. They think you know something. Whether or not you do won't matter. They'll hunt you, but … whatever. Apparently, it matters to Cinco. You can either take your chances on your own or," he paused, "or stay with us."

She blinked at him.

Abruptly, he released her. "You're free to go."

Pherall fell to her butt.

He stood over her, glaring down in the moonlight. "You won't survive long anyhow, so the choice is yours. We live on the run. Either way, you can't go back to your old life. I suggest you fake your own death and hope like hell the Jackboots believe you. If not, your family dies."

Sitting on the ground, she stared up at him through tangled, messy hair. He was definitely an asshole, an intimidating one at that. "Do you *want* me to stay?" she asked skeptically.

Uno didn't bat an eye. "I want you dead, quick and painless, now, so I don't have to invest in your death later."

Pherall chuckled sourly and gestured her dirty, manicured hand in the negative. "Then go," she said with a wave. "I'll be fine."

He stared down at her for another moment, then inclined his head. "Okay," he said and spun on his heel. Without another word, he strolled back to the truck.

Drained of energy and throbbing in pain from her earlier beating, Pherall lowered her head to her knees and wrapped her arms around her legs. The events of this awful night had all started with a horror movie she never wanted to watch in the first place. Now, her life was ruined. Mia was dead and her family was threatened. Somehow, she was supposed to fake her own death and vanish, but how? She didn't know how to pull something like that off. And where in the world would she go? She couldn't even go home to pack her things. To withdraw money would give her away. All because she spotted some random men in a crowd.

Seriously?

With another chuckle, she realized she still didn't know why these men were being hunted. She was also surprised to discover that she'd started crying again. With a sniff, she flopped backward onto the dry ground for a well-deserved nap and wiped her cheeks. Lying there, she closed her eyes and imagined living her life hiding from the authorities. She knew absolutely nothing about living off the grid. She'd killed government agents. That was capital murder.

Uno was right—there was no going back.

For a long time, she lay still, coming to terms with her new reality. In her mind, she imagined going back in time and telling Mia no with finality. She wasn't going to the movies. If she had said no, Mia would be alive, and they would both be asleep in their beds. If only she'd said no.

But she hadn't.

When she opened her eyes again, Cinco was standing over her, his silhouette bathed in moonlight. She jumped when she saw him.

He jolted backward sharply when she moved, and his eyes grew wide. "Y–you're alive?"

Pherall turned her nose away to hide her filthy face. "For now," she muttered, echoing his earlier comment. "I won't be for long, I hear."

Composure restored, he frowned. "Why didn't Uno kill you?"

Pherall sat up with some effort. "I don't know," she admitted, running fingers through her crazy hair in a puny attempt to regain control of it. She felt stickers in the wadded mess that dangled over her shoulder and gave up trying to fool with it. "He said I'm either free to go or I can stay with you guys."

Cinco stared at her, wrinkling his handsome brow. "He said you could stay?"

She smiled at him, unsure which emotion to call forth. Amusement raised its hand. "Yes, against his better judgement," she answered, selecting annoyance instead. It seemed more appropriate. "He preferred to kill me now and save the trouble I'll cause but didn't for some reason."

"But … he said you could stay?" he asked incredulously.

Pherall stood up carefully, dusting grass off her jeans and straightening her dirty black tank top. Her voice still shook, but she was determined to appear in control. The best way to do that was to keep her hands busy. "He also said I could go, so I'm going to go. It was a pleasure meeting you, Cinco," she said, extending a filthy hand. "Thank you for rescuing me back there."

He took her hand but didn't shake it. "You can't leave."

"Watch me."

"But Uno said you could stay."

"That doesn't mean he wants me to stay."

"I want you to stay."

"You don't even know me."

"What does that have to do with it?"

Pherall slid her hand from his. "They're waiting for you," she said, motioning toward the others and turning to leave. "Goodbye, Cinco."

Cinco caught her arm, stopping her, then pulled her off balance. As she fell backward into him, he hooked an arm around her middle and heaved her off the ground. "You're staying."

"No, no!" she protested in surprise, kicking her feet. "I'm not staying!"

"Yes, you are."

"Uno scares me."

Cinco high-stepped over the uneven ground, ignoring her.

"Put me ... *down*, Cinco!"

Ignoring her struggles, he marched back to the truck.

Pherall stretched her foot, trying to scrape a toe across the ground. When that didn't work, she threw her arms high, toddler-tantrum style, and tried to shimmy out of his hands. "Let me ... gaaah!"

It didn't work.

Blue's blond head poked up from the bed of the pickup, blinky-eyed from his nap, and he did a double-take. Open-mouthed, he adjusted his glasses for a better look. "Ooh! Cinco gets a woman?" he asked incredulously and sat up fully. "I want a woman! Can I have a woman?"

"No," said Uno.

Ocho shook his head and drummed his fingers onto the steering wheel in agitation. "This is a bad idea, Uno," he warned, avoiding direct eye contact with Cinco's burden.

Uno opened the truck door, ignoring him, and stepped out. Without a word, Cinco climbed in, dragging the struggling Pherall in with him. She hooked her fingers around the door frame but was plucked backward. Uno, wearing no expression on his stoic face, slid in beside her with a sharp bump, ending her struggles. His thigh rested firmly against hers no matter how hard she squished toward Cinco. Uno shut the truck door with a slam, which tinkled the broken glass, and waited.

Ocho glanced uneasily at Pherall. He appeared as if he wanted to argue some more but thought better of it and pulled the pickup back onto the road instead with his lips pursed in disapproval.

"Find an impound lot, Ocho," Uno said, reloading a magazine with bullets. "We need a bigger vehicle."

CHAPTER 4

Pherall watched her four odd companions transform from normal-looking psychopaths to hooded criminal psychopaths in an instant. Cinco, Ocho, and Blue donned dark, shapeless hoodies that hid their faces and heads. Uno finger-brushed his unruly hair into a ballcap and pulled it low over his eyes. Instead of going through the front gate, which was reinforced and video recorded, the men went around the back of the impound lot in search of healthy vehicles and cut through the fence. Uno stayed within sight of the pickup, deterring any thoughts of escape that might have danced through Pherall's little heart. From his position, he gave orders and made decisions through well-practiced hand gestures. The entire operation took six minutes.

Ocho selected a bright red super-cab pickup truck with a hitch and hot-wired the ignition. At the same time, Cinco and Blue discovered a convenient pull-behind camper buried in thick brush near their makeshift entrance. Ocho backed the truck up and Cinco connected the two vehicles. Within minutes, the entire group was caravanning down the road, away from the city. Blue and Cinco rode together in the red truck. Ocho, Uno, and Pherall, sitting stiff and silent in the middle, occupied the blue pickup. Right away she missed Cinco, who was following in the truck behind them, and stared straight ahead at the dark road. Cold wind blew in through the broken windows, blowing her hair around her face. She was cold. Cinco had taken her warm shirt, leaving her in a spaghetti strap top with bare shoulders, but she knew better than to waste her breath complaining. Uno and Ocho talked occasionally to each other, but neither spoke to her, which was fine. Pherall preferred to be left alone. Finally, after what seemed like forever, Ocho found a remote spot to camp for the night. After a nod from Uno, he pulled off-road into a patch of woods and stopped in an undeveloped clearing.

Blue, dressed in a black hoodie, pulled the red truck in and stepped into the headlight beams to prepare the camper. Chatting easily with Cinco, he knocked his hood back, giving Pherall her first good glimpse of him. There was a boyish yet rugged look about him as if he'd aged overnight. The top of his hair was long and pulled back into a ponytail that reached his collar. The sides of his head were shaved, producing a wide mohawkish hairdo. He wore glasses, the cheap over-the-counter kind, which were actually kinda cute on him. His Hispanic features were light in color and more angular than the others, but not unpleasant. He was shorter than Cinco but taller than Uno and covered with scars and puckers over nearly every visible inch of his body. He wasn't a bad looking guy, but there was something in his eyes that gave Pherall pause. Yes, they were cold and calculating. All her new companions wore that expression, which only vanished when they spoke to each other, but Blue had something more. At first glance, she wasn't sure what it was, but if she had to guess, would say he looked ... crazy—not like completely crazy, but maybe just a little bit crazy.

Ashamed of herself for thinking that about a perfect stranger, she slid out of the truck and made it a point to not look at Blue again until there was a reason. The last thing she needed to do was cause trouble by gawking. Keeping her mouth shut, she watched the men busy themselves with the rundown camper and waited for instructions. About a minute later, Ocho had the lock picked and was opening the door to the stolen recreational vehicle.

Pherall was leery of Ocho. Of the bunch, he was the most clean-cut, despite the five o'clock shadow darkening his jaw. His jet-black hair was short and neat. His blue eyes, similarly cold and very intelligent, were pretty and ringed with thick lashes. But there was an unapproachable air about him. He, like Uno, didn't care for Pherall and didn't hide that fact. She needed to stay away from both Ocho and Uno because both were dangerous ... especially Uno.

Pherall shivered. Merely thinking about the strange leader set her pulse on dubstep. Growing warm at the ears, she turned to see where he was and found him standing right behind her. Startled, she jumped backward.

Of course, Uno saw it. Looking at her directly, he slung his backpack over his shoulder. "Inside," he ordered, then went around her toward the camper.

Pherall's cheeks flamed. She remained standing where she was, uninterested in following him, and tried instead to catch the breath pinched in her throat. It was weird, but every time she got near Uno she choked, and it was pissing her off. As he disappeared inside, she tried to decide what her best options were. Should she take off now, she wondered, looking at the dark woods around them, or wait until everyone was asleep to escape from these four strangers? The eerie darkness peering out through the woods encouraged her to wait. Her mind pictured a likely scenario in perfect detail: She takes off, running full-bore into the blackness in a bid for freedom. Cinco sees her and charges after, hot on her heels. Twenty feet in, she face-plants into a tree and is dragged back, minus a nose.

She would wait.

Besides, waiting would give her time to plan where and how to disappear. Where could she go? her mind wondered. Like, to Mexico or something? Europe? Wait, no … she didn't have a passport. How does one vanish to another country without a passport and driver's license and money? People did it all the time, she knew, but how? She was a smart girl, dammit. Somehow, she had to figure this out—preferably before morning—because her mind was made up. The thought of staying with these guys didn't sit well at all. From what she could tell, they seemed just as dangerous as the Jackboots, and she certainly didn't want to be where she wasn't wanted.

"Are you coming?"

Awkwardly, Pherall hurdled back to Earth and turned to see Cinco standing on the camper steps, holding the door open for her. She shook her head and stepped back, having no intention of entering the RV of death. Dark woods surrounded them. The disastrous image she'd imagined ran through her head again, discouraging her. She could never outrun him.

Cinco stepped down from the steps, correctly interpreting her pause. Pherall backed away and glanced over her shoulder toward the road. There were no trees that way.

Cinco reached her quickly and caught her arm, startling her. "Let's go."

"I'm not going in there," she insisted, trying to back away.

Cinco hooked an arm around her middle, a familiar gesture now, and braced to lift her.

"No! No. Cinco," she rushed, twisting free of his grasp and staying his hands.

His brows lifted in warning. "Walk or I carry you."

Pherall stood where she was, braced to struggle again.

"Nothing is going to happen to you," he assured.

Unless Uno had another change of heart, she thought to herself. Her posture straightened somewhat despite her utter disbelief in his vow of protection. She'd seen enough of it to know it was nonexistent against Uno. Cooperate now, she decided, escape later.

Cinco extended his hand to her back. "Come on," he said, giving her a light nudge and prompting her to fall into step beside him.

Tucking her fingertips into the pockets of her jeans, Pherall shuffled reluctantly toward the camper. Against her better judgement, she let him guide her inside, feeling like a chicken wandering into the fox den. Once inside, Cinco closed the door and locked it, which didn't help Pherall's frayed nerves, then moved around the stolen camper opening windows as if this were the most natural thing in the world to him. An awkward fifth wheel, Pherall stood in the middle of the floor, anxious and unsure what to do.

The others ignored her.

The inside of the camper was decorated in blotches of orange and brown paisley. It smelled musky from being closed up for so long, years it seemed like. Dust and old spider webs covered the Formica counters and filled every corner, nook, and cranny. Broken leaves and dried grass littered the floor, mixing with a few bug carcasses, some old, chewed-up dog toys, and a crusty old washrag. Thrilled to see the mess, Pherall picked up the washrag and started meticulously wiping the place clean, taking frequent trips to the door to shake it out and keeping busy enough to avoid her companions. Blue, who chattered happily about nothing, busied himself digging in drawers and cabinets in search of food or fun. A ball of rubber bands nearly started a fight between him and Ocho until Uno snatched it away and put it back in the drawer. Cinco and Ocho moved around noisily inspecting the small camper and making a checklist of things to buy with a broken pencil. Uno sat down at the dusty table and, crossing his ankles on the bench seat, produced a cellphone.

When the place was as clean as she could manage without water and bleach or a blow torch, Pherall set the disgusting rag aside and wiped her hands on her badly soiled jeans. By now, Ocho and Blue were sprawled on the sofa, while Cinco stretched out on the floor near the door with his head propped on a wall, leaving nowhere for Pherall to sit but at the table.

With Uno.

Tucking her grimace away, Pherall sat down on the bench seat across from him with her fingers twisting in her lap. If he noticed, he made no indication. "Aren't those traceable?" she managed, gesturing to his phone.

Brown eyes flicked to her face. "There are ways to hide the signal," he answered quietly, lowering them again. "Do you know your bank account number?"

Miraculously, Pherall did. "Why?"

"If you want your money, you need to get it now. It won't be available in a few hours."

Pherall actually took a moment to wonder if this was all just a bad dream, a melodramatic misunderstanding, or one hell of an amazing scam, but the memory of Mia's execution replayed itself vividly in her mind. A flash recollection or two of herself shooting

Jackboot agents also appeared. No doubt, that was on video. Pursing her lips, she typed in her number and handed the phone back to Uno. Within moments, all her money was transferred into an encrypted account. It felt odd simply handing it over, but she didn't give the sensation time to fester. There were more important things to worry about, like how she would look in a sombrero. "So, what happens now?" she asked the unfriendly leader.

"You disappear."

Pherall didn't know what to think about that.

"Social media?" he asked without looking at her.

"Only one … wait—two," she sighed, brushing dirty fingers through her hair and turning her face away from him.

"Write down all your passwords and where they go, birthday, and security questions."

More than anything, Pherall just wanted to go home. Sighing with fatigue, she stood and searched the drawers for a notepad, then took Cinco's pencil. After a quick scribble, she slid the pad to Uno, returned the pencil to Cinco, who was watching her, then stepped over him and left the camper so she didn't have to see Uno delete her life.

Maybe it was better this way, Pherall thought to herself. Let Uno do the work. She didn't know anything about disappearing. As hard as it was knowing that her life was being erased, it would be one less thing she would have to figure out on her own … when she escaped. That would happen tonight. As soon as the men fell asleep, she would take off. Probably on foot. They would hear the truck if she tried to hot-wire it. Except, where was she supposed to go?

Maybe now was better.

Outside, early birds were beginning to chirp, suggesting that morning was near. No time like the present, right? Unsure which direction to start, she inspected the outer edge of the still, starlit woods and felt lost and alone. She was supposed to be at work in a few hours, she thought, unsure which emotion to attach to the realization. Weary, she turned toward a clank and a curse and watched as Blue and Ocho stepped out of the camper, thwarting her escape. Their heavy footsteps crunched through fallen leaves toward the propane tanks and stabilizing equipment under the RV. Neither paid her the slightest attention, but that was okay. She was in no mood to chat with anyone. Whatever they were doing probably wouldn't take long. Preferring to be alone with her wounded reality, Pherall climbed into the cab of the old pickup to wait and curled into a ball on the bench seat.

CHAPTER 5

The next day, Pherall woke to the smell of motor oil and stinky dog. She moaned and blinked swollen blue eyes open to a blurry seat belt buckle and a wadded old glove. Confused, she lifted her head and cracked it on the steering wheel, earning an unpleasant zap from the hot wires dangling from the ignition, neither of which helped her headache. Her ribs screamed in pain where she'd been kicked, and her cheek was sore from being backhanded. A quick look at her side showed a patch of impressive bruises there. Stiff and achy, she sat up and squinted through the windshield at the bright daylight. The sun was high, so it had to be about noon. The woods were still. Very carefully, she climbed out of the pickup and went to the camper.

It was empty.

Pherall crossed her arms, cold in the flimsy black tank top. "Where the hell did they go?" she grumbled, then inadvertently saw her reflection in a small mirror. Mortified, she dug through the bathroom drawer for a brush. The ponytail helped. Unfortunately, there was nothing she could do about the bruises on her face. Next, she searched for a note. Something. Anything. But there was no evidence there were ever four men here. Again, she wondered if she'd been the victim of an elaborate scam. At this point, especially before coffee, it appeared that she'd just had her account cleaned, her identity taken, and been left in the middle of nowhere in a stolen camper, which was probably worth at least a couple years in prison. Of course, that was if she survived the capital murder charges.

Crabby and sore, she turned on a small dusty television and fiddled with it until a local channel appeared. It was staticky but functional, despite the weak battery powering the camper. Standing in front of the dusty screen, she watched a ridiculous commercial about a man in love with a hamburger, then waited to see what was on.

More commercials.

Irritably, she daydreamed out the window thinking of something else to do, then realized this was her chance. The men were gone. She needed to go … now.

"Terror at the movie theater," a speckled newscaster buzzed in dramatic tones. "Two women were gunned down last night by gang members. Authorities need your help. Story at six."

Pherall turned in surprise, catching just the last glimpse of the screen before the anchor's face vanished. "Two women ... ," she echoed in disbelief and slapped the flickering television off.

Her mind replayed the nightmare: Mia being struck and thrown to the ground, the Jackboot thug standing over her with a pistol, the loud bang. The gunshot echoed loudly in Pherall's head, jarring loose the tears and a wave of horror long overdue. Mia was dead. All thoughts of running drained away with her grief. Crumpling to her knees, she wept for her friend.

After an hour, Pherall had pieced together what she could of the events. It had been the authorities that killed Mia, no gang, and they were the ones who had told the story. The media was simply relaying the lies they'd been fed. The only reason for the authorities to lie about two deaths was because they expected to find her. When they did, she would never make it to prison. They would kill her.

She wasn't safe here either.

Uno had nearly killed her last night and, on a whim, chose not to. How soon before he changed his mind? Cinco certainly wasn't going to stop him. That was clear. She needed to get out of here. People disappeared all the time, she reminded herself, never to be seen again. All she had to do was figure out how they did it.

Korbin!

Korbin would know what to do. Somehow, she needed to reach her brother before the story came out tonight. That was the plan. Her fate would be her brother's decision, not Uno's. With a clear goal in mind, Pherall wiped her eyes and stood. She was hungry. There was no water to wash, and she had no way of knowing where anyone was or how long they'd be gone. She did, however, have a truck with wires dangling from the ignition, she realized, dashing out the camper with a slam. She'd never hot-wired a vehicle before, but—*Zap!*—there was a first time for everything.

The engine started.

Pherall squealed in delight, threw the truck into gear, and headed for the shipyard where her brother worked. He worked the night shift and wouldn't arrive until the sun was down, which gave her a few hours to kill. Right now, time was all she had, so she figured she might make peace with it. In her mind, she envisioned parking on the side of the road near the shipyard and waiting for a few hours. That was the plan. Unfamiliar with the current area, though, she turned onto an old, two-lane highway, unaware that she was going the wrong way.

It was a while before she noticed.

"Where. The hell. Am I?" she muttered in disgust.

Nobody's fool, she turned the truck around and backtracked past a decorated mobile home, intending to take the other direction at the highway junction, then discovered she'd backtracked onto the wrong road. It turned out she needn't have worried about the time because, before long, she was hopelessly lost.

"My life as a fugitive is not going well," she complained, pulling her lips into a comical frown.

Miles and miles of fields blurred outside the window. No stores. No signs. No houses. Nothing.

"I'm an hour in. This is not good," she grumbled. "I'm gonna die."

About then, a rundown hillbilly farmhouse oozed by. Pherall drove right on past as if she hadn't seen it. She wasn't stopping at some hillbilly house. Ever. She'd seen that movie.

Cannibals.

This was precisely why she hated horror movies. Her mind pictured it with vivid clarity: She steps up onto a rickety porch and knocks at a cockeyed door. Some super friendly dude with the shakes answers, invites her in for dinner, and—*Voila!*—her thigh bone in the crockpot. No, thank you.

Miles and miles went by.

"Oh my God. Have I left the country?" she wondered, looking around for a sign. "Driven into a new dimension?"

Finally, a yellow sign appeared around a curve half a mile ahead.

"Yeah, baby!" she celebrated and sped up to read it.

CAUTION: Cattle Guard Ahead.

Pherall's face fell. "What the hell is a cattle guard?" she asked the steering wheel.

Bbbbrap!

Her wheels rolled over a metal grate.

"Oh, come on!" she groaned, bumping along the dirt road that followed.

By the time Pherall escaped the maze of country roads, the sun was going down and she was starving. Her first stop was a truck station she found just off the interstate. There were showers there, and she desperately needed one. After soaping herself silly and washing her hair, she scrubbed her clothes, rinsed them well, and then put them right back on. In a moment of good fortune, she found some cash and a wet theater receipt wadded in the back pocket of her jeans. Soaking wet and smelling of cheap soap, she went shopping. It was enough cash to buy some convenience store food, a long-sleeved t-shirt, a toothbrush, and a few toiletries.

The male cashier eyed her appreciatively as she paid and called her darlin'. Pherall had no interest in single men from this dimension, though, and ignored him. Nursing a nasty cup of coffee, she checked a map on a rack in the store, found out where she was, and was on the road again, this time in the correct direction.

*****

The shipyard was a massive expanse of containers, cranes, and heavy equipment, all perched on the side of a wharf packed tight with ships. Enormous cranes and pulleys lifted and lowered metal shipping containers while men with reflective hard hats marched busily around doing whatever it was they did.

Pherall pulled the truck off the road under a billboard sign and parked behind a bunch of bushes. It would be a walk, but she was smart enough not to head for the parking lot and congratulated herself for her forethought. Sticking close to the tree line so she could hide from passing cars, she hot-footed it to the yard, careful to stay in the shadows. Hopping the fence was easy. The hard part was going to be finding her brother in this labyrinth of metal containers, forklifts, and people. Fortunately, she'd been to the yard before and was familiar enough with his usual work area to point her nose.

Korbin, she promised herself, would know what to do. He always knew.

Carefully, she made her way along the endless rows, looking around for anything familiar and letting instinct guide her. She and Korbin spoke almost daily. Often, he would tell her about his night at work and all the shenanigans he and his buddies got into while the boss wasn't looking. When she found the area he mentioned most, she eased around one of the shipping containers, hiding in the darkest shadows, and poked her head around the corner. Blazing lights lit the loading ramp with almost daylight enthusiasm. From where she stood, she could see men moving back and forth clearly, but the shadows were pitch. Overhead, one of the cranes clanked to life. There was a resounding thud and some barked orders. Minutes later, a container lifted from the ground and swung out over a waiting ship. It blocked a flood lamp when it moved, casting a black shadow over the yard.

40

Pherall used the shadow to get closer. With the container in the air, several men turned away and began readying the next one. That's when she saw Korbin … and he was heading her way! His straight blond hair, identical in color to hers, poked comically from his hardhat. How many times had she teased him about his permanent hat-head hair? This was why. Watching him approach, Pherall realized she'd never been so relieved to see him as she was this moment and thanked her lucky stars for the rare crumb of good fortune. By some miracle, she had chosen this exact spot to hide, and it had been the right one. She wanted to whoop with joy and squeeze his neck tight. Finally! After almost twenty-four hours of hell, something was going right. It took all her willpower to wait for him to reach her, but she bit her lip and forced herself to be still. He had to come a bit closer.

She could hear his footsteps.

Pherall's adrenals fired. "C'mon, c'mon," she whispered, urging him to walk faster.

He reached the end of the row beneath a swarm of screeching seagulls.

Two more containers.

Pherall's hands shook, and her breath puffed in tiny clouds. Twenty more feet. One container away, he stopped, checked a panel on the side, and looked down to mark something into a small computer. "No, no, no," she grimaced, willing him to turn her direction. Desperate, she waved.

He didn't see her.

"Korbin," she whispered a bit too softly.

Korbin jerked his head up. Instead of turning her direction, though, he turned the other way.

Pherall stepped out and—*Wham!*—Cinco crashed into her, taking her off her feet and into the shadows of the next container with an '*oof!*' His hand clapped firmly over her mouth, and she was held still.

Korbin turned toward the sound.

Pherall was furious. Her brother was right there!

As another shadow darkened the area, Cinco peeked around the corner and tensed. There was a crunch of small pebbles against the concrete as Korbin's booted feet turned, then, after a slight pause, the footsteps came closer.

Pherall wiggled to get free, but Cinco's solid arms locked. He held his hand tighter over her mouth, warning her to be quiet, then slipped around the next corner of the container, missing Korbin by inches. As Korbin passed on the opposite side, Cinco gripped

41

Pherall by the ribs and lifted her. She nearly cried out in pain as his fingers mashed her bruises but wisely silenced her grunt. Strong hands grabbed her waist from above, and she was dragged onto the top of the shipping container and pushed flat by Uno. And—Holy shit!—he was pissed!

So was Pherall.

Pinning her with an arm, Uno clamped his hand tightly over her mouth, fangs bared, and dove down beside her on the cold metal. Breathing in choked, silent breaths, she tried to look over the edge as Korbin circled the other side, but Uno forbade the movement. None too gently, he turned her chin, forcing her to look at him, then pointed, lifting his finger just enough for her eyes to follow. At the top of a storage building, high enough to see the entire yard, were a cluster of familiar black helmets and binoculars. Currently, they were looking away.

Jackboots?

Pherall jolted at the sight of them.

Uno pointed again in the other direction.

Another helmet.

Pherall frowned in alarm. The Jackboots were here?

A moment or two later, the end of a weapon appeared and the binoculars swung toward them, clearly following Korbin.

Uno stiffened, signaling for her to be still.

Pherall's blood ran cold. Had they been spotted? Were the authorities going to kill Korbin? She wanted to look, but Uno's grip remained rigid, keeping her head pressed down. Behind them was a loud thud, the clank of some chains, and a nearby container was lifted, casting the familiar block shadow across the yard.

In the flash of darkness, Uno yanked her up and shoved her off the end of the container, moving quickly before the light returned. Cinco's strong hands caught her mid-fall and set her on her feet in the shadows, then curled around one arm tight enough that she couldn't get away. Uno landed lightly behind her and froze. They braced for several minutes, waiting for both surveillance teams to look away at the same time. While they waited, Uno pulled a cellphone from his pocket. "We got her," he whispered and hung up.

"Where's the truck?" whispered Cinco.

She indicated the billboard with a point.

"Go!" hissed Uno.

Like a shot, they took off with Cinco pulling Pherall toward the fence. She was thrown over and they hurried to the road, hugging the shadows.

When a significant distance lay between them and the yard, Uno stopped. In the faint glow of a streetlamp, he turned and snatched Pherall close, piercing her with hard brown eyes. "*That* could have gone badly," he scolded sharply.

She glared back at him. "You said I could go," she reminded, shaken and embarrassed.

A long moment of silence passed between them.

With a jolt, Uno released her and marched away without answering, leaving her alone with Cinco. As he walked away, she saw him tuck the end of a blade into a black band he wore around his wrist and realized that it was the blade he'd held the night before. With it, he would have killed anyone they came into contact with.

A sick feeling swirled in her stomach.

Cinco stopped beside her, clearly unhappy. "Do you *want* your brother dead?"

"No, of course not, but I also don't want me dead. Last night, you and Uno couldn't decide whether or not to kill me," she said with a withering stare. "What happens when Uno has a bad day or if I say something stupid over breakfast. What then? You're not going to defend me," she accused hotly, then jabbed her finger at the yard. "Korbin will."

Cinco shook his head. "Not if he's dead, Pherall!"

She lowered her arm.

"And we're not going to kill you. Uno doesn't change his mind … ever," he assured with emphasis. "The fact that he did last night was a miracle. He isn't going to change it back."

"And how am I supposed to know that?"

"You're just going to have to trust me."

Pherall pointed again to the shipyard. "I trust Korbin," she clarified again.

"Dammit, Pherall," he hissed, struggling to control his irritation.

"Uno said I could go. Why are you even here," she searched for the right words, "saving me?"

"We're trying to stop you from killing your brother!" he said, throwing an arm toward the shipping yard. "You, however, seemed determined to get him killed, despite what we say."

"That is not true! I had no idea the Jackboots would be here."

Cinco looked ready to wring her neck. "We did! Pherall! We made this clear last night. The government knows you escaped," he argued back, spacing his words evenly and slicing his hand in irritation. "The *only* way your family will survive is if they *and the authorities* believe You. Are. Dead. Right now, the Jackboots know you're alive. They're positioned all over that yard, waiting for you to contact Korbin. Did you think we were joking?"

"No. Yes. No," she corrected, then lifted her hand in frustration. "I don't know!"

"You watched them kill your friend. No reason. No explanation. No apology," he said in a quieter voice. "And she didn't know shit."

Pherall frowned at the shipyard.

Cinco set his hands low on his hips and took a moment to reign in his anger. "If you contact Korbin *ever*," he insisted in a low voice, "he becomes bait. Bait doesn't survive."

Feeling like a jackass, Pherall flicked a glance at the blue pickup truck pulling onto the road. "How did you know I'd be here?" she asked, trying to steady her own angry voice.

"Same way the Jackboots did," he answered flatly. "Your social media accounts. Most of your communications are to your brother. Uno didn't get them deleted in time, Pherall. You're already compromised."

"So, where were you this morning?" she wanted to know. "You guys just left me."

His brows lifted in irritation. "We were trying to hide you. We used your bloody shirt and cellphone to stage your death," he said, letting that sink in. "Your things were planted on shore by the bay, and a report was called in about a body in the water. Then we went shopping."

"The news said I died last night."

Cinco nodded, not at all impressed, and softened his tone to diffuse the argument. "That's the official story. When we left, the divers were going into the water to look for you. The longer they aren't sure, the better. They'll check the entire bay, which will give us time to get out of here."

Pherall took one last look at the shipyard in the distance, then exhaled heavily. With a nod, she turned and climbed into the waiting truck. Uno didn't look at her. Cinco got in beside her and slammed the door shut.

The trip back to the camper was made in silence.

CHAPTER 6

Pherall was busily warming a pan of canned stew on the small, freshly cleaned camper stove when Ocho and Blue returned in the red pickup. Blue strolled in with a cheerful whistle, dressed again in his hoodie, and helped himself to a morsel of food from the pan she was stirring.

"Mmm," he said and walked away.

Behind him, Ocho stomped in and slammed the door shaking the entire camper. "Are you always going to cause trouble like this?" he demanded, pulling his black hoodie off over his head and shaking out his black hair.

Pherall tapped her wooden spoon and set it down. "Probably," she replied, fully prepared to ignore him.

Ocho, wearing a green t-shirt now, gave her a dirty look, then scowled at Cinco. "Your little pet has a mouth on her."

Cinco, lounging lazily on the sofa, looked up from the book he was reading and planted an unamused stare at Ocho, then lowered his eyes again.

"She's going to be nothing but trouble," he continued to Blue, who was the only one who would look at him. "Why in the hell did you bring her here, Cinco?"

Cinco turned a page.

Pherall, however, was unable to keep her mouth shut. His contemptuous tone sparked her temper, and she spoke louder than she meant to. "I have enough to worry about right now, Ocho, without you making me feel worse. You've made your point. You can quit now."

"No, I won't quit," he barked back, leaning forward in full argument posture. "I don't want you here."

Pherall's mood veered sharply to anger. "I didn't ask to be here," she reminded him, reaching for a stack of paper plates.

Blue made himself comfortable beside Cinco. "If she cooks, she can stay," he declared.

"What? No!" protested Ocho. "I do the cooking."

"Your cooking sucks."

Ocho rounded on him. "This isn't a joke, Blue. Shit will go south quick with her here. I'm not sticking my neck out for some stupid—"

"Then don't," Pherall interrupted hotly. "I don't recall asking you for a damn thing."

Insulted, he thrust a threatening point at her. "Was I talking to you?"

"Go away, Ocho!" she said in disgust, then turned her back on him.

Ocho slung his pullover hard onto the kitchen table bench and came at her. "You watch how you talk to—"

Cinco launched from the couch and slammed Ocho backward against the wall with a wad of shirt fisted in his hand, rocking the entire camper. "Don't do that again," he said calmly.

"Then get rid of her," hissed Ocho.

Blue shifted uncomfortably in his seat, eyes wide and breathing labored. He acted like he wanted to get up but kept changing his mind. "Where's Uno?" he whispered to himself in agitation. "This is not good. Where is Uno?"

Uno slid the bedroom door open with a snap and, clutching an atlas, walked into the front room wearing only a pair of jeans. He was slender muscular, with sharp definition around his pecs and biceps, and had serious underwear model abs. His chest and arms were hairless, his hips narrow—features not overlooked by the female.

Pherall blinked away from him, embarrassed about the commotion and clearly surprised to see him without a shirt.

Uno touched Blue's shoulder as he passed, calming him, then turned narrowed brown eyes to the others. There was an edge to his voice. "She stays," he said simply and strolled past toward the tiny kitchen.

Cinco released Ocho and sat down again.

Ocho straightened his t-shirt and stood up, his temper temporarily diffused. "Sorry, Blue."

Blue made a 'yikes' face at Ocho and tried to take Cinco's book. "I'm hungry."

Uno set the atlas on the table as he passed it. Besides his partial nakedness, his mere presence in the room was palpable, a phenomenon Pherall noted instantly, and not just by her own response but the men's as well. Immediately, she sensed relief from the others. It seemed odd, considering he was the youngest of the group. Pherall stared at him as he approached. To her dismay, she couldn't look away from him until his gaze released hers. When he did, she discovered a bizarre buzzing sensation in her belly—not butterflies, more like … pterodactyls. Like an idiot, she backed away from him and bumped her backside against the counter, eager to maintain distance.

Though Uno was the smallest of the four, he was still taller than her, which made him even more intimidating. He stopped beside her and peered down into the frying pan, then took the knife she'd used to cut the larger pieces. "Don't ever cut meat in front of Blue," he murmured, careful that only she heard him, and stuck the knife in a drawer, "and don't startle him."

Awkwardly, Pherall nodded, staring up at his ridiculously handsome profile.

He noticed and, with a snap, his eyes met hers.

Annoyed at herself for gawking, she turned abruptly away and handed him a paper plate and the wooden spoon so he could dish up.

After sixty seconds of peace and quiet, Ocho started complaining again. "This is bullshit, Uno," he persisted, heading for the stove. "We can barely take care of ourselves. I bet she can't even use a gun."

"Yes, she can," Cinco offered from the sofa.

"Can she clean one?" demanded Ocho. "Load a magazine? And what are we going to do when the Jackboots find us again—when we're surrounded, jumping off buildings, or ducking RPG rounds? Who's going to protect her helpless ass then?"

"I imagine saving your own ass is high on your list," Pherall said cheerfully, "so let's keep it that way. My ass, helpless or otherwise, is none of your concern." She thumped the paper plates down beside the stove so she didn't have to hand one to Ocho, then turned to organize, arrange, and rearrange the groceries still bagged on the counter … loudly. As tempting as it was to throw a can of corn at the butthead, she reminded herself that she had nowhere else to go and absolutely no survival knowledge against an organization like the Jackboots. That fact was especially evident after tonight's disaster. And Korbin was off-limits, so she bit her tongue and arranged cans, forbidding herself to cry despite the burn behind her eyes.

"That's for me to worry about. She's my responsibility," Cinco said with a note of anger in his voice.

Ocho took a plate and waited for Uno to move away. "You're going to protect her, Cinco?" he scoffed.

"Yes."

"What, from the Jackboots?"

Cinco turned another page. "And from you, apparently."

Not at all bothered, Ocho nodded and piled food onto his plate. "Well, who's going to protect her from you?"

Cinco rested his elbows on spread knees, his book forgotten, and made a face. "What?"

Ocho set the spoon aside. "You'll have her pregnant in a week, Cinco."

Pherall's eyes went wide. Why, that horrible—!

Uno took a bite. "No, he won't," he said, opening an atlas and taking a seat at the table. "She'll sleep with me."

Pherall's can clattered to the counter.

Blue pushed his way toward the stove and bumped Ocho out of the way. "Wait! That's not gonna work, Uno," he said, taking a plate. "You're eternally stuck in your sexual prime. Oh my God."

"Uno? In his sexual prime?" Cinco set his book aside with a belly laugh and elbowed his way to the stove. "I can't even picture that."

Ocho and Blue blinked at Pherall, then at Uno, and burst out laughing.

Uno studied the atlas and took another bite, ignoring them.

"To save a lady's reputation," Blue professed, clutching his heart in ultimate sacrifice, "I'll do it. I'll take one for the team." He swept a chivalrous hand toward the sofa. "She can sleep with me instead."

"I don't think so," Uno muttered without looking up.

Pherall couldn't even …

It was Cinco's turn to dish a plate. "She's mine. I found her. I'll sleep with her," he said, taking a fork. "There's room on the sofa bed for two."

"No," Uno said between mouthfuls.

Blue clapped his hands together and pointed. "I know! We'll take turns. Not you, Ocho. Me and Cinco. Me one night, Cinco the next, and then me for two nights and Cinco on Friday and, when she screws up, we'll stick her with Uno."

"I said no."

"I'm leaving." Scowling in disgust, Pherall dished a small plate and took a fork. Squeezing past the men, she made her way to the door and went outside to eat in peace. They were welcome to argue among themselves, but she didn't have to listen to it. There was no reason she couldn't just sleep in the truck again, she thought in a moment of brilliance. It really didn't matter which of them drew the short straw. She couldn't stay with these men.

As she ate, she tried to think of somewhere she could go. All she had to do was change her hair, alter her makeup, and think up a new name. Perhaps she could join a convent. She could be a nun. They'd never find her in a habit. Or she could join the circus. It couldn't be that hard to ride a unicycle.

Pherall was busily imagining her life with the aborigines and trying to decide where exactly on her face to put her tribal tattoo when Blue stepped out, adjusting the glasses on his nose. He crossed to the truck and took a seat beside her on the open gate of the pickup. Of the four, she knew the least about Blue, only that he wasn't stable, and didn't know what to expect, so she braced herself just in case.

In his hand, he held a pistol.

Without speaking, he turned the gun to the side and began pressing a button with his thumb, popping the clip out the bottom of the pistol grip and bumping it back in again. He did that several times, then handed the clip to her and pulled the slide back, showing the empty chamber. Certain it was unloaded, he gave her the weapon. She set her plate aside and took it, unsure what he wanted her to do with it. A moment later, he touched the clip and waited.

Ah.

A bit awkwardly, she put the clip into the grip and snapped it into place.

He waited some more.

So … she dropped the clip by pushing the button on the side, then snapped it in again. She already knew how to drop a clip but wasn't going to tell him that. To say so would imply she was good with a gun. She wasn't. Her brother had shown her the basics, but that had been long ago. Even then, she'd never been comfortable around them. The exercise was repeated a few more times before he seemed satisfied. With a nod, he took the pistol from her and pulled the slide back, releasing it slowly to show the bullet now in the chamber.

She was watching.

Then, he dropped the clip from the grip again and ejected the bullet. Fifteen minutes later, Pherall knew her way *well* around a pistol. Pleased, he stood up from the tailgate, stuck the gun into the back of his waistband where he'd found it, and went into the camper.

Pherall picked up her food to finish eating.

A minute later, Blue returned with a vicious looking machine gun, plopped down beside her, and began dropping and engaging the magazine clip.

He never spoke a word.

*****

Satisfied with the lesson, Blue clicked the safety on his weapon and slung it over his shoulder, then stood and waited for Pherall to stand too. When she did, he closed the truck gate and gestured for her to return to the camper. She preferred to spend another night in the truck but followed him anyway, quite positive they no longer trusted her alone with a vehicle. With each step, she prayed silently that Uno had lost his first argument, but that was doubtful.

Inside, the guys were busy transforming the camper from day use to night use and preparing their beds. Cinco and Ocho were unfolding the full-size sofa bed, which took up nearly the entire living room, and Blue began disassembling the kitchen table. It dropped down into a single-sized bed, which meant the previous sleeping arrangements stood.

Damn.

Pherall would much prefer to sleep with Cinco than with Uno, who was now busily re-bagging all the cans she'd just set out. Uno hesitated when she walked in, then continued without looking at her. He still scared her. She didn't know why, but he did. She eyed his back, unsure why she felt that way. He hadn't done anything to her, not really. Even so, it was clear that the others were also intimidated by him. There was just something about him that made it impossible to relax in his presence. And she was supposed to sleep in the same bed with him?

Pherall looked down the narrow hall of death to the teensy bedroom pulsating at the back of the camper. It was the only private space besides the microscopic bathroom—not necessarily a good thing. A minuscule full-size bed peeked out through the open door, taunting her. A king-sized bed would be better, she mused, with an electric fence down the middle, or maybe a brick wall, but there was nothing barring the center. The thought of sleeping there with Uno was enough to make her mouth run dry. She really, really wanted to sleep in the truck. That cab was comfy-ish … sorta. It was decided. She was going to say something.

Now.

Satisfied with her decision, she crossed the obstacle course of sofa cushions to the kitchen, trying to figure out how best to politely decline the horrid sleeping arrangement. When she reached Uno, however, he looked at her, and she promptly chickened out. Like a big coward, she moved awkwardly around him to the water bottles on the counter as if that was her intention all along. She was positive he noticed the tremble in her fingers … again. Doing her best to play it cool, she chose a water bottle from the pack and took a drink, trying to build up enough courage to face him. She would have to blurt it. Ready again, she turned to inform the leader of her decision. As she opened her mouth, Ocho squeezed by for his own water bottle, a move Pherall was positive was meant to intimidate her, and nearly knocked her into Uno. She caught herself, avoiding the disastrous collision, and spun to glare at the butthead.

At the same time, Cinco, standing over his side of the open sofa bed mattress across the camper, pulled his t-shirt off and mindlessly tossed it over the arm of the couch.

Pherall saw him and—*Splat!*—her water bottle dropped to the floor and rolled into the cabinets by Uno's feet. Stunned, she gaped at Cinco.

He was powerfully built and bronze with a well-defined outline and large chest. His shoulders were broad, his arms contoured with solid muscles. A small patch of hair darkened his chest between his pecs and trailed down a hard, flat stomach, then disappeared in the low waistband of his jeans, which outlined long muscular legs.

Pherall might have been impressed by such a physique, but she didn't see any of it. The bullet wounds—the one she'd seen in the alley and the one he'd taken rescuing her from the Jackboots—were gone. She'd asked him about it before, and he'd avoided the topic. It had gotten away from her amid all the distraction, but now …

"Oh, great," Ocho grumbled behind her, "she's already in heat."

Pherall spun, wide-eyed, and slapped Ocho hard in the face, surprising herself as much as him. He stumbled back, knocking water bottles from the package, and scattering them across the counter. He caught himself on the edge, glaring in outrage, but remained motionless. "Go to hell," she snapped before hesitantly turning again to look at Cinco.

Cinco had already pulled his shirt back on and, carefully avoiding her gaze, was straightening it around his waist. Blue just stared back and forth between everyone, a slightly confused look on his face. Beside her, Uno pinned cold eyes on Ocho, who'd gone still.

Pherall's cheeks flamed in embarrassment, accentuating the annoyance she felt for the whole bunch of them. Stone-faced, she marched to the bedroom without a word to anyone and shut the door, quietly and with poise. Leaning against it, she exhaled and rubbed her temples.

Crash!

The entire camper shook, then went still.

Silence.

Pherall didn't even want to know what happened. Alone at last, she tried to slow her racing thoughts but was too tired to make sense of anything. She hated it here. Her heart hurt and she missed her brother. She wanted to go home, but she couldn't.

Wearily, she turned to the bed and found a small bag of women's clothes. With a deep breath, she dug into it and withdrew a toothbrush and paste, a pair of pajamas, and something for her to change into in the morning, including a fresh pair of panties. The sight of them brought a thrill of excitement and a pang of sadness, both at the same time. She had a drawer full of these at home, she thought, tossing the bag aside. Clutching her new pajamas, she hurried to the closet size bathroom, changed, and brushed her teeth, then crawled into the side of the bed where she'd found the bag.

Uno came in a few minutes later.

Pherall's pulse thudded hard and pounded loudly in her ears. Dammit, she thought, irritated by the recurring reaction. She wanted nothing more than to hide under the covers and not look at him but forced herself to remain composed, or at least pretend like she was. Bravely, she lifted her lashes, found his eyes on her, and flushed four shades of purple. Heat crawled up her neck and burned her ears. "Th–thank you," she murmured with a catch in her voice, "for the clothes."

He transferred her dirty clothes to the same bag with her clean clothes, adjusted the pistol clipped to his waistband, and climbed into the bed beside her. "Keep it bagged," he said quietly and turned off the light.

Pherall scooted to the farthest edge of the bed, putting as much distance between the two of them as possible to prevent accidentally touching him, and stared forlornly at the dark wall. Questions tumbled around her head. She didn't get it. If Uno hated her so badly, why did he insist she stay? If she left, where would she go? Everything, her whole world, was shattered. She had no home, no family, nothing now. Suddenly, scoring even a kind word seemed hopeless. The familiar burn returned, stinging her eyes, but this time it wasn't for Mia. It was for Korbin and her family, for the happy life she'd just lost, and for the piece of herself that lay dying in Uno's bed. Unable to stop the tears, she buried her face in the flat pillow and, shoulders shaking, silently cried herself to sleep.

Beside her, Uno lay still, careful to keep his breathing quiet, and stared at the dark ceiling.

CHAPTER 7

The following morning, Ocho, sporting an impressive black eye and a foul mood, drove the camper out of the woods. After ditching the blue pickup, they put Pherall's old life into the rearview mirror and left. Miserable, she rested her forehead on the cool window and watched the world blur by.

When they were well on their way, Cinco slid his arm around her shoulders and leaned her against him. It was a small gesture, but it meant the world to her. She snuggled against him, appreciating the strength she found there, and let the hurt melt away. Occasionally, he brought her attention to something outside the vehicle and made small talk which helped. Before long, they were playing childish travel games to pass the time.

Of course, Pherall hadn't yet grown comfortable in her current company and, in her awkwardness, frequently misspoke or would blatantly say something stupid, much to the amusement of Cinco. By noon, he was prompting her. Every chance he got, he made fun, teased her, and made her smile. Soon, the two were laughing together—her usually in outrage, Cinco triumphantly. Blue was quickly attracted to the fun, and, by evening, they were a trio. Cinco and Blue's mission in life from that night on was to gang up on Pherall, and both had a ball doing it. Despite herself, Pherall began to enjoy their shenanigans.

Uno watched the fun but said nothing, never smiled, and didn't join in.

A few days later, they stopped at a twenty-four-hour laundromat. Fortunately, it was empty. Pherall, glad to have something to do, loaded a machine with powder and was busily stuffing all the dirty clothes into one bucket when Cinco rushed out of the men's restroom wearing nothing but a pair of boxer briefs. "Wait!" he called, hurrying toward her, clutching his wadded clothes.

Pherall turned to take his laundry and burst out laughing. "You don't have any other pants to change into?"

"No. I wear an odd size, so they're hard to find," he said, swiping a saltwater fish hobbyist magazine and holding it in front of himself.

Pherall added his things to the bucket. "I'm not looking," she promised. "Where are the others?"

Cinco took a seat on a plastic chair and crossed his muscular legs. "In the men's room," he said, snapping his magazine open in search of an article. "You have all they own too. You like fish?"

Pherall closed the lid with a smile and sat on the machine. "I don't know. Depends on what article you read to me."

Cinco raised his brows, realizing this life changing moment was up to him, and selected an article at random. "Algae Suckers For The Beginner Saltwater Enthusiast," he began in haunting, suspenseful tones.

They drove for days.

Each night, Ocho pulled the camper off the road wherever he could find a campground, rest area, abandoned gravel patch, or empty field. From what Pherall could tell, they had no destination. Ocho merely zigzagged through the states and wound aimlessly along lost highways and rolling hills. The endless drive was the point; isolation was the method. During one of their restroom stops, Pherall bought a deck of playing cards, a ball, and some travel games to help pass the time. These long hours on the open road she spent with Cinco and Blue, who had designated the back seat as theirs, forcing Uno and Ocho to sit in the front seats in all their unwelcomeness.

"Stop hitting me in the head!" barked Ocho. "I'm trying to drive."

Cinco and Blue cracked heads diving for the ball, which had rolled beneath the bench seat. Both clutched their wounds and grimaced in pain, but neither gave up the scramble. Pherall snapped her legs out of the way with a yipe, entirely uninterested in the never-ending mountain range blurring past the windows. The two men fought but, in the end, Blue got the ball. With intense concentration, he dribbled it on the seat, which wasn't as easy as it looked, and scrutinized the targets of his play.

Pherall held her arms open, creating a basketball hoop.

Very carefully, Blue aimed and threw the ball. It thumped against the window and dropped successfully into Pherall's hoop. "Another point for me," he said, forming his own arms into a circle.

Cinco snatched the ball from Pherall's lap, dribbled it while he got into position, and threw it. It hit the window and bounced off, missing Blue's hoop and launching the three laughing idiots into an instant game of keep-away volleyball.

Whack!

"Ow! Stop hitting me in the head!" barked Ocho. "Uno!"

Uno didn't look up from his atlas. "Find a field and pull over for the night."

"Already? We're four hours short of our target for the day."

"Then stop complaining."

"Oh, look! A field."

Three nights later, Ocho dropped Uno, Pherall, and Blue off in some random town to go shopping while he found someplace to park the camper for the night. Pherall needed a jacket, and Blue needed to get out of the truck. He was restless and driving everyone insane.

Pherall actually enjoyed herself in the thrift store and probably picked out more than was necessary, but she was excited for a baggy pair of sweatpants to sleep in. As they moved north, the temperature steadily dropped, turning the camper into an icebox at night. She found an oversized t-shirt to go with her new pants and a super cute pair of bunny slippers with crossed eyes to tie the ensemble together. Tonight, she would be warm.

As Uno paid the bill, Pherall and Blue stood at the glass doors and peered out at the rain. Ocho was waiting in a gravel parking lot across the street. He was alone. The camper was gone, as well, meaning Cinco was somewhere setting it up.

"We're gonna get wet," Blue complained, wrinkling his nose. "I hate getting wet."

"My new jacket will protect me," Pherall bragged, pulling it around her shoulders and showing it off.

Uno handed the bag of clothes to Pherall to carry and plucked a local newspaper from a rack. "Here. Use this," he said, giving it to Blue.

Blue scowled at the paper in disgust. "What?" he said, flipping through the pages. "You expect a bunch of classified ads to keep me dry? There are no comics in here. I want an umbrella."

Uno snatched the newspaper back and pushed him out into the rain. "No. You'll dry. Let's go."

Blue cried out in protest and stomped toward the puddled crosswalk. Pherall hurried to keep up and waited beside him for the light to turn green. Uno stopped beside her. As they waited, an oncoming van sped toward them, sloshing water high.

Blue saw it coming and grabbed Pherall. With a shout, he spun her in front of him and ducked to avoid the spray. Uno snapped his newspaper in front of her.

Pherall shrieked and—*Splash!*—Uno's newspaper folded over her face as a blast of cold, muddy water arced across the sidewalk. When Uno lowered his arm, he was soaked from head to toe in filthy water. So was Pherall. Her face was dry, but mud dripped from her new jacket.

Blue, on the other hand, was entirely unscathed. "Ha!" he celebrated in amazement when he realized this and danced in delight. "Haha! Oh, that worked! I'm not wet at all. You're right, Pherall. That jacket is spectacular!"

"Really, Blue?" she sputtered, shaking her hands off.

There was a scream of laughter from the parking lot across the street. Inside the truck, Ocho slapped the steering wheel in hilarity.

Uno rolled his newspaper into a tube and held it out to Pherall. "Upside the head?" he recommended dryly.

"I'd be delighted." Pherall took Uno's soggy newspaper from him and whapped the idiot with it just as the light turned green. Feeling much better, she handed the floppy mess back. "Thank you, Uno."

He gave her a sidelong look. "Welcome."

"Would you like to borrow my new sweatpants while your clothes dry?"

"Please."

"You want the slippers too?" she asked without looking at him.

"You can wear the slippers."

"Deal," she said, following him into the crosswalk.

In the evenings, Blue found tools or weapons for her to learn about and taught her to use and understand each. By the second week, they were working closer combat. Eventually, the blades came out. At first, Blue used short sticks and pretended they were knives, demonstrating how to strike and how to block. Soon, however, they upgraded. Their first blade was a fake blade—a rough piece of wood Cinco had carved over a few nights.

"It's thick so it won't break, but it's got an edge and has a point, so be careful," Cinco said, handing it over.

Uno spun sharply, whatever he was doing entirely forgotten. Blue was thrilled.

Pherall, not so thrilled, not now that Uno was watching.

Proud of his new weapon, Blue raised the faux knife with a bright smile, using it instead of sticks to recap a lesson they'd perfected days ago. "Just like the sticks. Disarm me. Ready?"

"Ready!"

He slapped the ground with both hands like a chimpanzee, teasing, and came at her with his arms up. "Ooh! Ooh!" he cried, swinging the knife over his head.

Laughing, Pherall braced her feet. Moments later, she was on the ground—dead.

Uno strolled closer, watching, his brow furrowed.

Blue balked at Pherall. "That was awful! You walked right into it. Get up! Get up. We do it again."

Pherall climbed to her feet and stole another uncomfortable glance at Uno. His gaze was steady and focused and pinned right on her ... or them. It didn't matter who he was watching; it was distracting her. She nodded, telling Blue she was ready despite that.

"This time, I'm coming in from the side. Get ready," Blue warned, then leapt forward, slashing the knife.

Pherall successfully disarmed him, peeked at Uno, and was quickly disarmed herself. Before she knew it, Blue had her in a headlock, and the point was to her throat.

Uno stepped closer again but spoke not a word.

Blue ignored him. Pherall couldn't. The moment Cinco handed the fake knife to Blue, Uno instantly became a part of the nightly ritual. He didn't interfere; he merely stayed close and observed. This was true any time Blue had a sharp object. Uno never interrupted, but Pherall would look up to find him watching her. It made her clumsy, which meant more lessons.

From that point on, Uno grew increasingly agitated around her and oftentimes short with the others. Rather than avoid her like Ocho did, though, Uno began almost to hover. When he was near, Pherall detected something coming from him, a curiosity perhaps or a deep dislike, but she was rarely out of his sight. Whichever it was, though, he was careful to hide his thoughts via expression or comment. They rarely spoke. At night, she slept beside him. Not once had he made an inappropriate move, comment, or gesture toward her. He didn't look at her, and he stayed on his side of the bed. Ironically enough, Pherall was entirely comfortable there. Uno intrigued her, probably because she couldn't read him. She became jittery when he was watching, so she made it a point to absolutely ignore him ... unless he wasn't looking. On those occasions, Pherall watched him, but only a little. Her physical reactions to him hadn't changed much, but she'd grown used to them by now.

Ocho left her alone.

*****

By the third week, the group had developed a routine. Before sundown one day, the boys began their search for a place to stop, usually near the road for an easy exit. So, Pherall was surprised when Uno directed them off the beaten path. Ocho pulled into a neglected field flooded with tall grass and parked the camper near a creek behind an old, crumbling barn.

Pherall, dressed in jeans and an old maroon t-shirt, stepped out and stretched her back. Her hair was loose today because she'd lost her ponytail holder at a truck stop shower the night before. "Where are we?" she asked Cinco.

"Middle of nowhere."

"Where are we headed?"

"Coast, I think," he said, lowering the stabilizers on the camper.

Pherall scanned the secluded, tree-lined meadow. "How did he know this was here?"

"Maybe he's been here before," Cinco suggested with a disinterested shrug. "You'll have to ask Uno."

Yeah, that wasn't going to happen.

At the mention of him, Pherall scanned the area to see where Uno was. She found him in the bed of the pickup setting up the new water drum, which was large enough to supply water for two nights in the camper, including showers, toilet, and cleaning. When he heard his name, he lifted his head, still bent. Right on cue, Pherall went into sensory overload. This time, however, instead of looking away, she smiled at him.

Uno hesitated, as if unsure the smile was for him, and dropped a strap. It clanked loudly beside his foot. Irritated, he bent to pick it up and continued preparing the tank for a fill-up. "Blue," he called, hopping out of the bed, "tank's ready. Go fill it."

Blue unhooked the camper hitch from the truck and headed for the driver's seat. "Need anything while I'm there?"

Uno checked the propane tank in the front of the camper, then dusted off his hands. "Sanitary hand wipes for the sewage dumps and," he glanced at Pherall, "take her with you."

Pherall lifted her brows and shot Blue a surprised look, then quickly hopped into the truck with him. "Why is he sending me?"

Blue fiddled with the radio, selecting a hard rock station. "I don't like being alone," he explained, bouncing the truck onto the paved road. "He is acting funny, though. Dropping shit and daydreaming. Not really like him."

"What's he usually like?"

Blue twisted his mouth and pondered before answering. "Focused."

Pherall blinked at him in surprise. If anyone was focused, it was Uno. She couldn't possibly imagine him being more focused than he was now. "I'm probably distracting him. I imagine all of you are having to rewire with me around. It's harder on Uno and Ocho, I think, because they're not really happy about me coming along."

He made a face, indicating an inaccuracy in her suggestion. "Ocho, yes, because he's an asshole. He'll come around sooner or later," he said without concern. "Uno, no."

"What about Uno?"

Blue turned into traffic on a four-lane highway. "You tell me."

Pherall huffed at the very idea. There was no way she would admit what was really going on every time she made eye contact with Uno or touched him by mistake or whenever he spoke to her. "I don't know," she said instead. "He kinda scares me."

Blue gave her a lopsided look. "I don't know about that. Used to, maybe. First few nights, yeah. Not now. You stare at him a lot. That ain't fear."

"Intrigue?"

He cut a sideways look at her. "That's a little better," he supposed.

Pherall's cheeks flushed. It embarrassed her to think she'd been so obvious. Her next horrified thought was that Uno might have noticed.

Blue chuckled, pulling into a run-down gas station, and stopped beside the water hose. "Uno notices everything," he said, correctly interpreting her pink cheeks. "Everything."

Had she made a spectacle of herself? Seriously? Pherall wanted to crawl under the dash or facepalm. Instead, she scratched at an unpainted fingernail. "I don't mean to stare. It's just that Uno is very intimidating. I don't know how else to describe it except he scares me."

"It ain't fear."

"It is."

Blue slid the transmission into park. "When you're upset or afraid, you cling to Cinco, when he's not around … me," he said, angling his head to look at her. "It's Ocho you're afraid of, Pherall, not Uno. When you're around Uno, something else happens."

Pherall blinked at him, surprised that he'd noticed such details when she herself hadn't … really.

He folded his arms lazily over the steering wheel and watched her, knowing he was making her uncomfortable. "So, what is it?"

Pherall tucked a strand behind her ear. "I don't know how to explain it," she whispered, telling the truth this time. "I can't breathe and," she tapped her chest, "my … ," she glanced at him, then awkwardly cleared her throat and turned back to the window. "I don't know."

Blue turned the truck off, dropping the subject, and handed her some cash. "Sanitary hand wipes. Rubber bands for your hair. Bathrobe and fuzzy slippers, preferably with polka dots."

"Puzzle?"

His fingers bit down on the money, stopping her from taking it. "Don't talk to anyone," he warned before letting it go.

Pherall saluted him like a good little soldier and hurried inside.

While Blue filled the water tank, she moseyed through the sleepy convenience store in search of hand wipes and ponytail holders. Blue had been teasing about the bathrobe, but she was disappointed not to find one anyway. Clutching a box and a package, she stood over the magazine rack and selected a puzzle book, then took her things to the counter. The clerk, who muttered a distracted greeting, handed over change and a receipt. Pherall exited with her loot, unaware of the narrowed gaze that followed her from the store. Once she was out of sight, the clerk checked the screen on a computer, then picked up the phone and dialed the number at the bottom of the page.

When Blue pulled the truck back into camp, Ocho was waiting with a dark scowl and a toe tap. "Why didn't you wait for me, Blue?" he barked angrily.

Blue wasn't at all intimidated. "We just went to get water," he said, sitting forward to hug the steering wheel again.

Ocho marched around the nose of the truck and opened Pherall's door. "Out," he said, jabbing a thumb.

Pherall took the bag with the puzzle and wipes in it and slid out without a word to the butthead.

"Where are we going?" asked Blue.

"To get groceries," Ocho said curtly and flopped into the seat. "Next time, wait for me."

"What about the water?"

Ocho slammed the door shut. "We'll fill the camper when we get back," he grumbled without looking at Pherall again.

With a sigh, Pherall went inside.

Uno, wearing a faded blue t-shirt, jeans, and unlaced brown hiking boots, glanced up when she entered. "Where is Blue going?"

"He and Ocho are going for food."

Uno pulled his feet onto the seat with him and crossed his ankles, focusing on his cellphone screen.

Pherall passed him and set the bag on the counter, remembering what Blue said about her not being afraid. Paying attention now, she took note of the thump in her chest and the heat warming her ears. If not fear, then what? Puzzled, she opened a drawer to get a deck of cards and snuck a look at him. Damn, he was good-looking.

His fingers went still, and he lifted his lashes, catching her.

Electricity zapped down her spine, and she nearly dropped the cards. Blue was right. It wasn't fear. It was attraction.

Dammit!

Irritated, she snapped the drawer shut and hurried out of the camper in search of Cinco.

Uno watched her vanish, then stared at the door after she closed it. His heart was hammering hard … again. He breathed deeply, attempting to calm his pulse, and ran his fingers through his messy hair in frustration. After a minute, he smiled to himself and lowered his lashes to the screen but didn't see what was on it. He'd lost interest.

*****

For the next hour, Pherall sat with Cinco on an open patch of ground, still a bit unnerved by her earlier conversation with Blue and then that … whatever … with Uno. Annoyed with herself, she dealt a fresh round of cards. "We have time for one more game before it's too dark to see," she said, tossing her straight blond hair behind her shoulder. It fluttered lightly off her back, reminding her that she'd purchased a new pack of ponytail holders. "Blue will be out here for another lesson once the sun goes down."

Cinco squinted at the sun setting on the horizon and picked up his cards. His brown hair fell boyishly over his forehead but didn't quite reach his hazel eyes. "He'd better hurry. What are you two working on?"

"Disarming, right now," she said, studying her hand, "but I'm not very good at it."

"What are you good at?" he asked, selecting a card.

Pherall tapped her ankles together. "Loading and unloading a pistol."

Cinco regarded her with open amusement and laid a card down. "Well, that's something," he supposed, "because you suck at cards."

She watched him win the round and made a face. "I'm good at puzzles."

Cinco gave it a moment's thought, then gestured in remembrance. "I saw you throwing knives the other day. Blue seemed impressed."

She flashed a sheepish smile. "I need to work on my distance a bit, but I like knife-throwing."

"What else are you good at?" he asked, keeping the conversation alive.

Pherall shrugged and thought back. "Dance and theater. I'm a pretty good actor."

"Really? I used to dance some," he said, laying a mediocre card down. "Hip hop."

"No way! We'll have to do that some time," she smiled and drew from the pile with slender fingers. "Tell me about the guys. Their occupations."

"We're fugitives," he said simply.

"I meant before, you goober." She won a round. "I don't know anything about you. None of you have jobs. How do you have money?"

"Uno has money. His parents left him a fortune. The rest of us are bums. What about you? What was your profession before we so rudely ruined your life?"

"I was a teacher's aide. Mia and I were studying to become teachers. How old is everyone? Tell me about them," she repeated.

Cinco shuffled the cards he'd picked up and bridged them like a pro. "Ocho was a mechanic with a family. Thirties, I guess. He's probably the most normal of us all. He's a good guy; he's just stubborn and kind of an asshole. Blue is a war veteran. Upper twenties. Uno is twenty-one. His parents were KGB. He had a sister."

A breeze blew a loose strand of hair into Pherall's face and caught on long lashes. "He told me. She was thirteen when they killed her," she said, sliding it away and angling into it.

Cinco nodded. "How old are you?"

"Twenty-two. And you?" she prompted.

His shrug was nonchalant, but his expression seemed to tighten ever-so-slightly. It was evident he was uncomfortable talking about himself. "I'm twenty-eight. I was Special Forces."

"Were you ever married?"

"Engaged."

Pherall studied him for a moment, already knowing the fate of his fiancé, then set another card down. "What happened to your wounds? And why are you on the run? What do the Jackboots want from you?"

Cinco slapped another winning card down. "Ha! I win again! I need a water bottle," he said, standing. "Want one?"

Pherall shook her head and watched him walk inside. Frustrated, she scooped up the cards and put them in the glove box for later, then shut the truck door. Cinco wasn't coming back out, and she knew it. He would conveniently get busy, so he didn't have to answer the questions, which puzzled her. Why was he avoiding them? They were legitimate questions. When she'd met him, he was bleeding profusely from a bullet wound to the abdomen. When he'd rescued her from the Jackboots, he'd been shot in the back. Yet, the other night, she hadn't even seen a scab. And what *did* the Jackboots want?

The sun vanished, casting a purple haze over the sky.

Pherall sighed impatiently. Any minute now, Blue and Ocho would return from town with food, which was good because she was hungry. After that, Blue would come out and give her another lesson, which she found herself looking forward to. While she waited, however, there was a barn to explore. She was intrigued by old buildings anyway and needed to pass the time, so she meandered toward it for a quick look. Standing on the outer edge, she held onto a sturdy beam and peered inside.

It was a large building with significant structural damage to one entire side, leaving a massive gap in the outer wall. Old, graying boards fell away from the remaining walls, giving it a rickety feel, and lay in piles around the entire perimeter. It smelled musky and damp, like rotting wood and mud. The last traces of light poked through in hazy rays, casting an eerie feel to the place and elongating the shadows. Crumbling horse stalls and rusty antique farming equipment decorated the inside, often peeking out from fallen boards and rogue patches of tall grass that grew up from the exposed ground below. A second story ceiling sagged heavily over the main room, spilling its contents over the edge into a tangled mess of lumber and rusty nails. Through the planks on the far side of the building, she could just see fragments of the camper hidden behind the barn.

Behind her, tires rolled over gravel, startling her back to the present. Oh, good, they're back, Pherall thought and turned, expecting to see Blue and Ocho returning in the red pickup, only it wasn't them. As she watched, a dark jeep with an extended cab rolled up the dirt road and stopped on the trail behind her.

Pherall took an uneasy step back, unsure if she should play it cool, call out an alarm, or take off running.

A dark window rolled down, and a ruddy-faced man appeared wearing a friendly smile. "Excuse me. I'm lost," he said, beckoning her closer. "I have a map here. Can you help?"

Pherall shook her head.

"Come here," he persisted in a super friendly tone as if calling to a skittish child. "I just need directions. I have a map."

From some distant place in her mind, her alarm bells went off. "I can't help you," she said and turned toward the nearest corner of the building.

"We have a positive match!" said a voice behind the driver. "Capture the girl! We want the prisoner alive!"

All four jeep doors opened at once and seven men wearing cloth masks over the bottom halves of their faces piled out at a run, clutching weapons and rope.

Pherall cried out in surprise.

A gunshot broke the evening calm, startling her, and struck one of the men. He was heavily armed, clutching a machine gun and wearing belts of extra ammunition. With a shout, he spun to the ground and went still. The others scattered, diving into hiding places and dropping into defensive positions. Pherall tried to reach the corner of the building. Another shot splintered a board two feet in front of her. She back-pedaled and spun to go the other way, but a man was charging for her. With a cry, she squeezed through some broken boards and darted into the old barn. Two charged in after her, one with a telescoping baton which he extended with a snap, and the other with a pair of open handcuffs.

Outside, a gunfight erupted.

"It doesn't have to be this way," one man called into the darkening debris. "Come quietly, and you won't get hurt."

Ka-Boom!

A grenade explosion outside burst with a powerful shock.

Pherall stumbled, momentarily breathless from the concussion, and stepped down on an upended board. It rolled, taking several planks with it. The pile shifted beneath her in a loud crash. "Aaah!" she yelped and fell forward with a clatter, missing a jutting nail and a frightened spider by inches. She quickly snatched her hand away.

Footsteps crunched behind her.

"I've got this side. You go that way," one man said to the other.

Pherall leapt to a bare patch of floor and stopped. Everywhere she looked, she saw rusty nails and rotting boards that would surely snap if she stepped on them. Carefully, she moved forward, searching for a stable foundation.

There was a scrape to her left.

"Box her in!"

She turned the other way, reaching for a bowed beam to help with her next step, and scanned desperately for a way out. Shapeless structures surrounded her, blocking her exit. Turning again, she searched for a broken slat wide enough to exit through but couldn't make out a path to reach one in the purple haze of gloaming.

"She's heading for the back. Block her! Block her!"

A board broke behind her.

Pherall crawled across a dark, metal something. Climbing quickly, she reached for the closest piece of solid floor, then stopped, realizing she was about to pin herself inside a stable.

The man with the cuffs was ten feet from her.

Spinning the other way, she spotted an expanse of solid-looking floor across the tangled boards and jumped for it. The man jumped too. Midair, his solid body crashed into her, redirecting her trajectory. "Oof!" she grunted, stunned by the blow.

C-c-crack!

They went through the rotting floor together and landed on a small patch of smelly, muddy ground. She hit hard and felt rough hands grab for her wrists. "Aah!" she cried, struggling to free herself.

An instant later, a board whooshed by and—*Whap!*—handcuff man went flying, taking her with him.

Pherall spilled from the momentum and rolled onto her shoulder in the damp earth beneath the building, scattering a swarm of tiny gray bugs. In fright, she whirled to her back and saw Uno standing over her with a two-by-four in his hands. A sob of relief caught in her throat at the sight of him. "Uno," she managed, trying to get up.

He swung the board again. She ducked, and it broke around the staggering man's shoulders, knocking him to the ground.

Another explosion burst outside the building.

Uno dropped the board and reached for her. "Come on."

Behind Uno, a flash of fire struck the rotting wall, casting a pale yellow glow into the barn and outlining the shape of a man sneaking up behind.

"Look out!" she cried.

He whirled to face the approaching man and, with a balanced jerk, rolled the plank beneath his foot. The plank shifted, redirecting the guy's momentum into a pile of boards, which resulted in a wild flap of arms and a pained grunt. The telescoping baton in his hand clattered to the floor and disappeared.

The first guy leapt out of the hole.

Uno spun again to snatch the handcuffs from his hand. With a twist, he rotated Mr. Handcuff around and sent him flying into Mr. Baton, who was just getting up.

More boards fell.

While they were busy, Uno snatched Pherall out of the hole and slung her onto the small piece of floor. "Stay with me," he told her, balancing calmly on the rickety boards.

Both men were up.

Uno ducked a board and came up with a rounding kick, knocking the plank from Handcuff's hands. At the same time, Baton tried to dart by, reaching for Pherall. Uno completed his spin, bringing the stolen handcuffs around, and knocked Baton's head backward. Teeth clattered to the floor and rolled away. Stunned, the man fell, clutching his face. Uno turned back to Handcuff with a punch to the stomach, doubling him forward. Uno heel-palmed his head back and swept his feet out from beneath him. As he fell, Uno cracked his elbow down on the guy's sternum.

Handcuff landed on his back.

Uno snatched a board from the bottom of a rickety pile oozing down from the second floor and yanked, burying Handcuff beneath a mountain of lumber. As the clatter faded, the silhouette of a third man appeared clutching a pistol. He aimed at Pherall.

Uno shoved her, knocking her back several feet.

Pow!

A bullet whizzed by, passing inches from Pherall's head.

"Don't sssoot her!" shouted Baton without his teeth. "The bounty—!"

Mr. Third sidestepped several feet to the left, his face contorted in anger. "To hell with the bounty," he growled.

Uno dove for Pherall.

Pow!

Uno and Pherall crashed into the side of a broken stable wall in a spray of blood. Pherall gasped in pain, positive her back was broken, then saw Uno's face mere inches from hers, frozen in grimace.

"Uno?" she cried in horror.

Their eyes met.

He exhaled a short breath of air and sagged against her, his hands fisting tightly into her shirt. A gush of blood spilled from his mouth and rolled down his chin. He coughed.

"Oh, no!" Pherall slid down, unable to hold his weight. "No, no, no, no!" she cried, reaching the floor with him. She rolled, lying him back and gripped his bloody face, instantly in tears. "Uno! Don't do this. Please, don't do this."

He choked again, suffocating, and gushed more blood.

"Oh my God! Uno!" Pherall brushed messy hair from his face with violently trembling hands and gripped his head. "Don't leave us."

He caught her bloody hand in his, trying to focus on her face, but his eyes fell away, and his choking slowed. His arm dropped to the floor, and he went still.

Uno was dead.

Pherall cried out and hugged him to her, cradling his head. "You killed him!" she screamed as Third approached, still pointing the pistol. "You killed him!"

The large man snatched her away from Uno and jerked her to her feet. "Get up," he snarled, shoving the barrel against her ribs.

Sobbing angrily, she knocked him off balance and snatched the pistol from his hand, the way Blue had shown her, only she lost her balance when it came free and tripped. The gun flew from her hand as she fell and clattered away. Boards scattered, tangling around her. Third bent to grab her, and she shot upward, ramming her shoulder into him. He toppled over a broken tractor frame with a grunt and went down hard. Enraged, she dove for the pistol. He kicked her shoulder, knocking her backward, and then jumped on top of her. Growling in outrage, she balled her fist and hit him with a shout, then grabbed a small board beside her and backhanded him with it. He rolled away, stunned. Before she could get up, he caught her ankle, snatched her to him, and punched her.

Pherall saw stars. She landed against a board with a cry and tried to get up, but her arms wobbled beneath her. She struggled to stay awake, to focus her eyes. Gripping her throat, the asshole yanked her around and slammed her down onto her back, then jerked a knife from his belt. Her fingers curled into a pile of sandy dirt. With all her might, she slung it into his face and quickly scurried away. He thumped a knee down, catching himself, then growled and lurched forward, shoving her down again. She landed hard on the bloody patch of floor where she'd left Uno, but he was gone.

"Uno?" Confused, Pherall hesitated, then spun to see Third coming at her with his knife. She ducked.

In mid-swing, Third's knife was redirected with a jerk and landed deep in his own belly. He hit his knees with a startled look on his face and crumbled to the floor.

Pherall stared at the man in surprise, then blinked behind him and saw Uno's blurry silhouette against the crackling fire climbing up the side of the barn. Uno yanked the knife from Third's belly, letting him fall, then hurled the weapon at Mr. Baton, just staggering to his feet. The knife thumped into the toothless man's chest, and he fell again.

Furious, Uno, blood-soaked and dirty, hauled Pherall up from the floor, grabbed the pistol she'd dropped, and twisted at the waist. "Drop it," he warned sharply, aiming at Handcuff crawling out from beneath the boards with his own gun.

On shaky arms, Handcuff raised the weapon.

Uno fired, then turned to point his smoking barrel at a fourth man stepping into view at the front of the rickety building. The newcomer instantly dropped his weapon and held his hands out. "I'm unarmed," he called out.

Watching him warily, Uno took Pherall's hand and led her from the burning structure. His voice was cold and exact. "Who sent you?" he demanded, easing her around the man.

"There's a bounty—a big one," Fourth answered, gesturing nervously toward Pherall. "A really big one. We got a tip and came to collect. It's just a job, man."

Uno shot him. "You're fired," he said through his teeth.

The bounty hunter sagged, wide-eyed, and slumped to the ground.

Before the man was dead, Uno had picked his pockets and gathered his ammo. "Cinco!" he shouted, shouldering the blood from his chin. "There's a hitch on the jeep."

Cinco rounded the corner, hurdling bodies, and jumped into the driver's seat of the jeep. In a puff of dirt, the vehicle took off and backed into the hitch of the camper. Cinco hopped out, attached the hitch, and darted to the stabilizers beneath the camper.

Uno moved to another body. "How many were there?" he demanded with a glance at Pherall.

"S–seven," she answered, taking weapons from him.

Uno scanned the bodies on the ground as Cinco pulled the camper around. "That's all of them," he said, standing with his load and shoulder-bumping her toward the trailer. "Get in."

"But Ocho and Blue aren't back yet."

"Get in!"

Pherall hurried inside. Uno dropped his armload onto the RV floor, folded the steps in, and pulled the door shut behind them. Cinco took off with a jerk.

Pherall grabbed the kitchen counter, catching herself as the camper bounced and swayed over the uneven ground. Wide-eyed, she stared at Uno, handsome even through the gore, and alive. He stood clutching the hallway wall across the living room, his big brown eyes staring back through strands of messy hair. Spatters of blood freckled his chin and neck, and a dark patch soaked the entire front of his shirt. A long silence passed between them before a tear rolled down her cheek. "You died," her voice cracked.

He didn't answer.

"I don't … I don't understand," she managed with what voice she could find.

Holding her gaze, he removed his blood-soaked shirt. A black bruise darkened his bloody chest, stretching from collarbone to lower ribs. Purple skin puckered angrily around the edges of the gun blast, knotted but unbroken. He wiped his face with a clean patch of shirt and waited, giving her time to figure it out.

Even as she watched, the exit wound shrank.

Exhaling hard, Pherall clapped a hand over her mouth, then quickly caught the edge of the table to keep her knees from buckling. In her mind, she replayed the moments with Cinco bleeding profusely from an abdominal wound, a fatal shot apparent even to her untrained eye. When he'd rescued her from the Jackboots, he took another bullet but kept going. Now, she stood before Uno, who only moments ago had died in her arms.

The words were hard to form. "That's why they're after you," she said, letting the truth reveal itself. "The government. The Jackboots."

He nodded.

"Cinco … behind the theater. He died," she stammered between breaths. "That's how the Jackboots caught him."

Uno came closer.

Pherall's pulse exploded in alarm. She tried to back away but was already against the counter. "You aren't twenty-one," she said, unable to escape.

His gaze pinned her, rendering her motionless. "I'm not."

"H-how old are you?" she whispered, watching him close in.

"Older than you."

Pherall struggled to wrap her mind around this but couldn't process the information. She grew dizzy and the floor swayed beneath her feet. It could have been Cinco's driving—she wasn't sure. A million questions crashed through her mind, but none made their way out. Uno was too near. Warily, she watched him approach, her breaths coming in ragged bits. Right on cue, her heart malfunctioned. "Uno … ," she attempted, unable to steady her voice.

Brown eyes dropped to her mouth. He reached her and slid his hand into her hair at the base of her skull.

Pherall's breath caught.

A bump sent them into the counter, and his fingers tightened. His other hand slid intimately around her hip and pulled her close. She could feel the weight of him against her, feel his warmth, smell the blood on his skin.

Was he really about to kiss her?

Pressed against his bloody chest, she watched his lips. Three inches from hers, they stopped and hovered there. His heart hammered hard against his ribs, matching hers, and a fine tremble danced through his fingers.

Didn't he hate her?

Breathing in chunks, he came closer, parting his lips to kiss her, then froze again, suspended a mere inch away.

To Pherall's surprise, she wanted him to do it, but, again, he remained motionless.

They were so close.

Hesitantly, she touched his arm, hoping to encourage him. The moment she did, he startled and lifted his head as if realizing what he'd almost done.

"Sorry," he whispered in embarrassment and released her.

This time, Pherall's knees did buckle, and she sagged to the swaying floor.

Uno strolled purposefully away toward the bedroom, leaving the scent of blood lingering behind him. There was a small purple pucker to the left of his spine beside his shoulder blade with a bright red ring around it—the entry wound. In the bedroom, he dug out a clean shirt. Favoring his left arm, he pulled it over his head with a wince and a soft curse.

A wave of nausea rolled through Pherall. That bullet had been meant for her, she realized, letting her head thump against the cabinet door. He'd taken it for her, just like Cinco. Pherall turned her head so she didn't have to see him. "What about Ocho and Blue?" she managed, unsure if she wanted the answer.

"They'll find us," he answered and straightened the shirt around his waist. Clearly in pain, he flopped down onto the bed and closed his eyes.

That wasn't what she'd meant, but Uno was asleep now.

CHAPTER 8

In a rundown camper park, Pherall and Cinco, both freshly showered, sat at a picnic table and watched the sun come up. Uno still slept inside, fatigued after his recent death. "You too?" she asked in a flat voice.

Cinco nodded. "All of us," he admitted, messing his hair up and leaning heavily on an elbow.

"It makes you tired?"

"And hungry. It takes a lot of energy for the body to repair itself. The nastier the death, the longer we sleep."

"So, did you get bitten by a spider or fall into a toxic vat of chemicals?" she wondered. "Aliens?"

Cinco spread his hands. "We don't know. Uno was the first. He and his parents defected to the United States long ago. Rogue spies found and executed his entire family a week before his twenty-second birthday. His little sister wasn't there. He woke up, much to the surprise of his murderers, and was handed over to the authorities. He hasn't aged a day since. Our government and the Russians fought over who had the right to experiment on him. I guess the experiments were really bad. Eventually, the scientists became complacent, and he escaped. A retired KGB agent, a friend of his parents, I think, helped him. Uno trained with him for several years until he found out there was another Immortal. He rescued Blue. The government wanted them back and retaliated by slaughtering the agent. When that didn't work, they went after Uno's sister. It made him mean. Now, he listens, waits for evidence of other Immortals, and goes to get him. That's why we're here."

"To find another Immortal?"

Cinco squinted into the bright sun rays sliding up over the horizon. "Seven. Uno found evidence of a recent transfer, so he's checking all the Jackboot bases. We raided one the night you met me. We found evidence that Seven had been there, but he was gone. We were too late."

Pherall took a moment to remember that fateful night and how mad the Jackboots seemed when they thought she knew the guys. "Are there females?"

"No. So far, he's only found men. Blue told the story of a woman they thought was an Immortal, but the experiments killed her."

"How?"

Cinco didn't know. A gust of wind blew a lock of brown hair straight up on his head, and he bounced a knee in agitation. "You can't imagine the things they did to us. It really isn't hard for me to believe they found a way to make one of us stay dead, but Blue thinks the girl wasn't an Immortal. He met Number Three. I don't know of a Four. They called me Five. Her number was Six," he said, using the tip of a small blade to carve crud out of the picnic table while he strolled down memory lane.

"I was on a mission with my team when I found out about me. Landmine, I think. My team reported it. I was arrested and sent to a government lab. For months, they cut, medicated, electrocuted, drilled holes, and experimented on me. Dreaming up creative ways to make me reset. They watched me die over and over without mercy. I was held in a glass box and watched day and night, my every move recorded," he said through tight lips.

Pherall listened in numb silence, careful to remain still and quiet so he could tell his story at his own pace.

"One day, I was transported. I don't know where I was going, but a few minutes into the ride there was an explosion. The van flipped, and there was Uno and Blue," he glanced at her and flashed a brief smile. "I was pretty messed up by then. Scared of my own shadow, depressed, betrayed by the country I loved. I tried to contact my family, thinking there was a life to return to, but the Jackboots were waiting. When I arrived, the agents attacked us. They killed my family attempting to recapture me. My mom. My gramma. My fiancé," he said with a crack in his voice. "I got away, which pissed them off. After that, they got nasty. Friends I'd had scattered throughout my life were used as bait to get me back, then slaughtered anyway when I surrendered. Uno had warned me, but I didn't listen. He rescued me again. Now, I do what Uno tells me. We all do," he said with a quick glance at her. "There are some powerful people in this world who will stop at nothing to get their hands on immortality. Nobody matters but their own greed and their insatiable desire to live forever."

Cinco took a moment to bring his anger under control, staring off into the distance for several long moments before remembering she was there. When he spoke again, his voice sounded clipped and tight. "We feel death like everyone else," he said, trying to remain in the present. Mindlessly, he spun his knife on the tip, gouging a small hole. "All the pain that goes with it, the fear. We suffocate and sizzle and suffer, just like mortals. I remember screaming, crying, begging them to stop. We all did. They ignored us, even laughed. And each time, our bodies betrayed us, resetting after each long, painful death. Dying once is bad enough; over and over is ... ," his voice broke here and he breathed deep, trying again to shake it off. "I stopped aging after my first death."

Pherall stared at the table, trying to imagine any human being possessing the level of cruelty Cinco described but couldn't. She'd never known this side of the government, and it frightened her.

Cinco redirected the topic. "Uno resets the fastest, in only minutes. I guess he's gotten pretty good at it. He'll be back to normal when he wakes. Had that been me last night in the barn, you would have been killed or captured. I take almost ten minutes to reset and then about a week to fully recover."

Pherall looked toward the camper, remembering Uno dying in her arms, a sight she never wanted to see again. The mere thought that it wasn't his first time brought tears to her eyes.

"Blue died in the war," Cinco continued, leaning on an elbow and looking off with his head in his hand. "He woke in a coffin on a plane and started knocking. They called him Number Two, which didn't go well with him, so we call him Blue. They had him the longest. He was Uno's first rescue. By the time Uno reached him, though, he'd gone a bit nuts. He's better now, but he slips sometimes."

The awful stories brought a chill to Pherall, and she shuddered. "Why not use his real name?" she asked, rubbing the goosebumps away and trying to flatten the hair standing up on her forearms.

"Because the person the name belongs to *is* dead," he answered solemnly. "Hearing our old names brings back the memories of a life we can't return to. None of us can stand the walk down memory lane, so we just kept the numbers. Blue prefers the Spanish numbers, so we use them."

Pherall caught the hint about memory lane and knew this talk would not happen again. Vowing never to make him needlessly relive it, she continued the interview. "And Ocho?" she asked.

"We rescued Ocho the same way. His story is similar, except it was his children who were slaughtered. The government wanted to know if they were immortal too," he said softly. His voice dropped to a whisper. "They weren't. His wife died trying to save them."

Hearing that rocked Pherall's insides, and it took a moment before she could speak. "That's horrible."

Cinco's focus came in slightly. "Ocho cried for months," he told her with a sad smile, "and swore he'd never love another mortal again."

Pherall's sigh was heavy and broken. "Why stay? You could leave the country. There has to be someplace to hide."

"We did, but we had to come back."

"Because of Seven?"

Cinco flattened the knife he'd been playing with and drummed his splayed fingers on it, rhythmically tapping the ends in a mindless fidget. "Uno won't stop until all the Immortals are free," he said with conviction. "So far, Ocho is the youngest, and we know of only one death—Six. That leaves Three, Four, and Seven. Trust me, Uno will find them."

"Wouldn't they be at the base where they took you?"

He shook his head. "We checked there. Nothing. We've lost the trail on Seven."

"So, where are we going now?"

"In circles," he said, chewing his lip. "Uno thinks there's a new number, so he's stalling until he finds a direction."

Pherall's eyes went wide. "A new one! What makes him think there's a new one?"

Cinco gave his hair a scramble and grimaced, apparently wondering if he was relaying too much information but then supposed it was too late to stop now. "Because," he hesitated to reposition his knife over a fresh patch of table and dug a design into the wood, "Uno monitors their encrypted conversations. That's why he's always looking at his phone. He hasn't broken all the code, only some. They've begun using a new number."

A wash of emotions crashed through Pherall at the news. Knowledge of a new rare and amazing Immortal sent a thrill through her yet sickened her at the same time. It was a brutal reality these people faced. The thought of going in and trying to rescue someone from the picture Cinco just painted terrified Pherall, but the thought of being left behind frightened her more. Suddenly, she understood Uno, but, more than that, she understood Cinco, Ocho, and Blue's loyalty to him, and she treasured the knowledge. Well, she decided with an inward vow, he had hers now too. The realization made her want to vomit. "So, where do I fit in?" she asked, almost afraid to hear the answer.

Cinco glanced up from his carving. "You noticed us," he said in all seriousness.

The explanation sounded ridiculous to Pherall, but he didn't appear to be joking. "That's why the Jackboots came after me," she snorted, "because I looked at you or—well … the others."

Still bouncing his knee, Cinco gave his head a small shake, indicating that wasn't what he'd meant. "The Jackboots thought you knew something and wanted information. That's not why Uno kept you," he clarified.

"Why did he?"

"Uno wanted to know *why* you noticed us."

"Because you were walking against a current."

Cinco shook his head again, entirely rejecting her dismissal. "Blue said Six once told him she could tell when Immortals were near. It never seemed important before, but you noticed us enough to alert the Jackboots. It made Uno remember that. He thinks if you can detect Immortals, you can help us rescue them. Maybe even help us reach them before the government does. The danger is, once the Jackboots realize this, they'll want you for the same reason. With that skill, they will do whatever it takes to get you."

A moment of raw fear struck Pherall, and she recoiled. The truth was, she couldn't identify anybody. Spotting them had been a fluke, nothing more. She realized, though, that to be captured by these monsters would result in a fate far worse than death and, whether she liked it or not, she was in. The very thought terrified her. "What if it was a mistake," she worried, "a coincidence?"

"The Jackboots won't believe you. You'll die trying to convince them. Right now, they're being sloppy, though, which means they don't suspect anything yet," he assured helpfully. "Doesn't matter anyway. Whether you can or can't recognize Immortals is irrelevant. You're already compromised. You know waaay too much. About us. About our patterns. You'd be useful either way. Once you're used up as a resource, you become bait and bait doesn't survive. Anyway," he increased his octave, bringing his tone to a lighter note, "I'm not going to tell them."

Pherall had heard enough. Before he could go on, she held up her hand and stood. "It's cold out here," she said, shaking off the disturbing conversation. "Come on, let's find something to eat."

*****

Uno woke to the smell of breakfast, took a quick shower with the last of the water, and staggered into the kitchen. His wet hair was brushed straight, but otherwise he looked normal. Pherall stood at the stove. With Ocho gone, she had taken over cooking, a task Number Eight guarded jealously. Today she was glad, though, because it gave her something to do.

Right away, she felt Uno's presence in the room. The memory of the previous night flashed in her mind, and her ears warmed in response. Slightly mortified over the incident and rather annoyed at her silly pitter-pattering, she concentrated on looking busy. She did notice, however, that he was running low on clothes, evidenced by the fact that he was wearing the faded green shirt Cinco had worn the day before, still wet from its hand-washing. It just so happened she was wearing one of Blue's old brown shirts today.

"Anything?" he asked Cinco, referring to Blue and Ocho.

"No."

A bit awkwardly, Pherall handed him a steaming cup of coffee and fixed him a plate. Their fingers brushed when she gave him a fork. He didn't notice; she felt an electric jolt. Startled, she turned away, rubbing her fingers for a moment before shaking the sensation off. Whatever was going on, it was getting worse, not better. Soon, she'd fall into a dead faint when he walked into the room, she thought, picturing the scenario with a look of disgust on her face: Uno steps into the camper. She falls forward all aflutter, breaks her nose and wets herself—all because he's cute. At this rate, she wouldn't be able to hide her reactions much longer either. Hell, Blue already knew. Checking to be sure Cinco hadn't noticed, she returned to the stove and busied her hands.

Uno plucked his phone from his pocket, entirely ignoring her, and fooled with it while he ate. A few minutes later, he shook his head. "No messages," he said quietly and frowned. "Something's wrong."

Cinco took the last of the coffee, tight-lipped and a bit irritated after his previous conversation.

"Who were those men last night?" asked Pherall. "Were they Jackboots?"

Uno took a bite. "No," he answered without looking at her. "They were bounty hunters."

Pherall turned in surprise. "You have bounties out?" she asked. "I assumed you guys were classified."

"The bounty hunters were after you, Pherall, not us," Cinco told her, swirling coffee in his cup.

Her eyebrows lifted. "Me?"

Uno shook his head pensively and sipped his coffee. "That's how it was supposed to look. It was a distraction," he corrected to Cinco. "Only the Jackboots knew about Pherall. The bounty hunters were set up."

About here, Pherall noticed that Uno wouldn't look at her and paused for a moment in confusion. He seemed just as uninterested and withdrawn as always, as if nothing had ever happened between them, while she had become a quivering mess. So, why *did* he try to kiss her? She tucked a lock of hair behind her ear and curled the hem of her t-shirt. Maybe it was just the adrenaline after the fight, she reasoned to herself, or perhaps last night had simply been her imagination or, worse, a terrible prank. Actually, strike that, she decided, facing the stove again. Uno didn't come across as the prank and tease type. Perhaps he tended to be emotional after dying. That would be a much more reasonable explanation. Either way, it was over and, according to his body language, he still didn't care much for her. The silence, however, was uncomfortable. She needed to keep them talking. "Set up how?" she prompted, cracking an egg into the pan.

"They were used to find our location, for one," Uno explained in a distracted tone, "and probably to see how we behave around you. The bounty hunters knew nothing about us, or they would have approached differently. The Jackboots knew those men would die."

"Buttheads."

Cinco replayed the events of the previous evening in his head with a frown. "Do you think the Jackboots were there?"

"Probably," Uno muttered, his tone leaning more toward the affirmative. He moved to another webpage. "They were either collecting Ocho and Blue while we were busy or recording us, which seems to be their new hobby. The bounty hunters' deaths are being reported as a territorial dispute between disgruntled hunters," he relayed, reading a local news article as he spoke.

Pherall straightened her shoulders. "Are you serious?"

"Found her," Uno said thoughtfully and showed Cinco a webpage. He still wouldn't look at her. "Pherall is listed on the site as Jane Doe," he said, making a face.

Pherall leaned to see a recent photo of herself taken at a coffee shop. "How'd they get that?" she wondered, pausing to notice the ridiculous reward amount below her picture. A sick feeling twisted her stomach. No wonder the bounty hunters wanted her.

Cinco stood and threw his paper plate away. "It smells like a trap."

Uno didn't answer.

"So, where are Ocho and Blue?" she asked a minute later, filling another gap of silence.

Uno and Cinco looked at each other.

"Hopefully running," said Cinco, though he clearly didn't believe it. "They know where we are."

"If they come here," Uno said calmly, "they'll lead the Jackboots right to us."

"Maybe that's why they're not here," Pherall suggested.

Uno considered that and flicked a glance toward her without actually looking at her. "I won't risk it. We're going back," he said, finishing the last of his breakfast. "We need to ditch the RV first. They know we have it."

Pherall sat down across from Uno with her own plate.

Cinco gave the RV a scan. "I kinda like having a camper," he admitted. "It's homey."

Pherall imagined all five of them snuggling together in the jeep and wrinkled her nose. "Can't we tuck the camper into a cave somewhere?"

Uno stood up and threw his plate away. "There's an abandoned rock quarry in the mountains near here. There might be somewhere to hide it in there. They know we have the jeep too," he said directly to Cinco. "We need a new one. Pherall, eat quickly," he said, reaching for a backpack. "We leave in five minutes."

CHAPTER 9

As dangerous as it was to go back, Uno insisted they return to the marketplace where Ocho and Blue had gone for food, just as soon as they were free of the camper. It was hidden off a dirt road in a tight grove of bushes deep in the forest on the backside of the rock quarry. The lightly used hunting trail proved Uno was indeed familiar with the area, though nobody mentioned the observation. On the way back to the historic town, the decision was made to ditch the jeep. They would park it somewhere near the old-town marketplace and find another vehicle once the sun went down. Almost immediately, they found the red, super-cab pickup near the market square, still parked where Ocho and Blue had left it—not a good sign.

Pherall, wearing a green baseball cap with her blond ponytail dangling through, nervously got out. Long tendrils escaped from the hat, framing her face and catching on her dark lashes. Quietly, she walked between Cinco, who was dressed in a gray hoodie, and Uno, who also sported a black ballcap, only his was backward. The look would have been cute as hell on him if Pherall had taken the time to notice, which she absolutely refused to do. She also didn't notice the light scratch in his voice, quiet as it was, or the charming shift of his brows when he concentrated on something. She entirely failed to notice how steady his gaze was when someone had his attention or the way he closed his lips when he was finished talking. She damn sure hadn't noticed how often she snuck peeks at him or the fact that he was still avoiding eye contact with her.

As soon as they began to look around the marketplace, neither Uno nor Cinco paid much attention to Pherall, but the other men certainly did. Several even stopped to stare. She ignored their appreciative glances and scanned the crowd, searching for anything to help find Ocho and Blue, which was not an easy task a day late. Uno and Cinco seemed to know what they were looking for, but Pherall really wasn't trained to track, so she concentrated on keeping up and not bothering them while they searched. Besides, she was having fun. She loved markets and couldn't help enjoying herself. The people here were friendly enough, or at least not generally rude, which made the outing a rather nice one despite the cool air. It was a large marketplace with an open courtyard that formed a cross. The food court was in the center with other goods extending outward. Produce and farm animals went one direction, disappearing down a crowded road, while crafts and handmade goods filled the opposite street. People milled about, eating, talking, and buying. Strains of music blended with the throng, casting an uplifting feel to the place.

Occasionally, Pherall slowed to look at the items in a booth or to pet a friendly dog. Animals seemed drawn to her for some reason —they always had been—so she responded with good manners. To ignore them would be considered rude and rudeness to a polite animal was unacceptable.

To Pherall's delight, there were plenty of polite dogs at the market.

To Cinco and Uno's irritation … there were plenty of polite dogs at the market.

Pherall squealed and bent to pet another one.

"Come! On!" Cinco groaned, crossing his eyes toward the heavens as she scratched more fuzzy ears.

Cinco stayed a few steps ahead of Pherall while Uno lingered a bit closer. Probably because he didn't yet trust her alone, she mused, pausing to look at a rack of crystal necklaces.

Uno slowed to a stop and scanned the row of vendors. "We don't have time to browse," he said, glancing behind them. "Let's go."

Pherall touched a necklace shaped like a turtle. "They aren't here," she said, admiring it.

Uno looked at her.

Ha! First time that morning, she thought in amusement and touched another one. "I love frogs," she smiled, showing him.

He glanced absentmindedly at the trinket, then motioned to Cinco, who had gotten to the end of the row. "We're leaving," he said, leading them to the parking lot.

Uno hot-wired the red pickup and backed out, sloshing the heavy water filling the tank in the back of the truck. After a moment of perusal, he turned toward the old campsite but didn't take the dirt road. Instead, he pulled off the road behind a row of unkempt hedges and turned hesitantly to Pherall.

She paused. Was he asking for her opinion?

Pherall blinked toward the hill blocking the campsite, a bit caught off guard by his attention. She supposed this was as good a place to check as anywhere else, so she gave him a shrugging nod, doubtful that she could be of any real help.

Flat-lipped, Uno killed the engine and lifted his backpack off the floor.

Cinco slid out of the truck and eased the door shut with a click.

Slinging his backpack over his shoulder, Uno opened the gate on the truck and pulled the plug on the water tank, letting the stream splash out onto the ground. Pherall was about to ask why he'd done that, but he stepped over the stream and took her hand in a secure grip, surprising her again. Eyes forward, he pulled her along behind him. They hurried through the tall brush, stepping in hard mud until they reached the base of a hill. Uno dropped to a crouch there, tugging her down with him, and crept up through the brown grass. Near the top, he elbowed his way to the crest and peeked down at the open field below—their old campsite.

It looked very different now.

The barn was almost entirely burned to the foundation and still smoldering in a steaming mass of charcoal. There were flags, body outlines sprayed on the ground, and police tape all over the area. Of course, the camper was gone, but in its place and filling almost the entire field were government vehicles, green tents, and tough-looking Jackboots in uniforms and shiny black boots.

Uno bit back a curse and scanned the field for signs of Ocho and Blue.

Cinco shook his head. "I don't see anything," he whispered over Pherall's head. "We have to check the tents."

"No, there's too many," said Uno, squinting at all the trucks parked haphazardly throughout the field. "We'll have to wait until tonight."

A couple of Jackboots strolled into view near the tree line, looking back and forth as they patrolled the perimeter.

Uno pulled Pherall down the hill and eased beneath the branches of a fat bush with her. Cinco ducked behind a low rock, visible to Uno, and waited for the agents to pass.

While they waited, an old memory flickered in Pherall's mind— a moment in time she hadn't recalled in years. In a flash of nostalgia, she twisted her neck around and peered up into the tree towering over them. There was nothing in the branches above her, so she scanned the nearby area. The contour of the ground blocked her view after only a few feet, but trees outlined the entire field. Again, she looked up, remembering a time long ago when she and Korbin had gone camping. In her mind, she could clearly visualize a disappointed Korbin poking his blond head out from the perfect hiding place—a hollow tucked inside the trunk of a fat tree. Without knowing why, she knew one of the boys was in a tree now.

Surprised by her own certainty, Pherall turned to whisper to Uno, who was watching her, and nearly crashed her face into his. She jumped back with a start and he grabbed her wrist, stilling her. Silently, he put his finger to his lips. Pherall, inches from his nose, moved her eyes up, gesturing to the tree above them. Uno made no indication that he'd received a message or had any idea that she was even trying to communicate. Instead, his gaze shifted back to the agents passing by.

Why had she done that?

Pherall felt like an idiot and instantly regretted the gesture. She knew she shouldn't be playing into this. It would make them think she could detect the others. They wouldn't take it well when it was revealed that she couldn't. Right then, she decided to tell Uno it was simply a guess … just as soon as the Jackboots were out of earshot. Naturally, they took their time. When they were clear, she leaned her head close to whisper, but Uno was already crawling out toward Cinco. He spoke to him and crawled back.

Cinco nodded hesitantly, then hurried away, skirting the outer ring of trees and ducking the low branches.

Pherall face-palmed, certain this wasn't going to end well.

Twenty minutes later, Cinco returned.

Ocho ran at a crouch behind him, looking haggard and pale with tree bark in his hair and a large patch of dried blood on his back. In his hand, he held a miniature crowbar. "Uno!" he hissed in unbridled relief.

Uno waved him silent and backed down the hill to talk. At a safer distance, they huddled together.

"I was stabbed in the back. I woke in an alley," Ocho whispered frantically, tripping over himself in his haste. "Blue was gone. We were waiting for food. I wasn't even near an alley but woke up in one. I've searched everywhere. I can't find him. He's not at the market. I came here but can't find him!"

Uno nodded, calming him. "What have you seen from the Jackboots?"

"Nothing!" he hissed. "They're just walking around. Not even investigating anything. Not doing anything. I've been here all night."

Uno and Cinco passed a quick look, silently agreeing that something wasn't right.

Pherall touched Ocho's arm and leaned close to whisper. "Can you tell me what—"

"Don't touch me!" Ocho slapped her hand away.

She flinched sharply.

Like a snake, Uno caught Ocho's wrist and jerked it back at an awkward angle, twisting him sideways with a pressure point. "You're pissing me off," he warned quietly.

Ocho hissed in pain.

"Where is Blue?" Uno asked him.

"I don't—ahh!—I don't know," Ocho managed through his teeth, trying to stay quiet. "I can't find him."

Uno didn't blink. "Pherall can. If you aren't going to help," he said, staring Ocho down, "go wait in the truck."

Ocho made no effort to resist.

After another moment, Uno released him with a snap and waited for Ocho to decide.

Cinco leaned his head toward Pherall. "What were you going to say?"

Pherall gave her head a quick shake. "Nothing," she assured, flashing him an embarrassed smile. "It was nothing."

Ocho glared at her.

Cinco inched closer, frowning at her response. "If you know where he is, say so," he demanded.

"I don't."

Uno flicked an irritated look at her, then pulled her back to the top of the hill on his elbows. At the top, they lay on their bellies and peered again through the grass at the crowded field. Cinco and Ocho crawled up beside them, but Uno ignored the men. "Where is he, Pherall?" he asked, positioning himself close alongside her.

Pherall was all too aware of his nearness, his shoulder bumping hers, his thigh against her leg. It was nerve-wracking and made it hard to breathe. Growing flustered, she turned to face him and nearly bumped her head against his. "That's what I wanted to tell you," she insisted emphatically. "I don't know."

Uno held her gaze, his eyes intense. "Find him."

"I was just guessing under the tree."

"Find him."

"Uno." Pherall imagined those same eyes glaring hatred at her when she failed to produce, and her heart trembled. "I have no way of knowing if he's even—I mean—Ocho was a coincidence," she insisted, scanning helplessly out at the field.

"Find Blue."

Pherall exhaled angrily. There was no way she could find Blue in that mess down there, and Uno was refusing to listen. "I can't detect Immortals," she insisted.

Uno tilted his head closer, well into her bubble. "Find him, Pherall," he whispered, following where her gaze pointed.

Pherall swept her eyes around the haphazard camp, shaking her head at the clutter. There were numerous structures and a variety of vehicles scattered about but nothing stood out. There was a food tent and government vans parked in a row. Green military trucks.

Port-a-potty. Food tent. There was no way Blue was down there, she thought in annoyance. Everything looked legit. Vendor trucks. Government SUVs scattered. Muddy tracks. Dirt road. There was nothing. Nothing below her radiated with the essence of Blue. Somehow, she had to make Uno listen. "I–I can't."

"Find Blue," he murmured.

Ocho snorted. "What the hell is—?"

Uno jerked his fingers up, silencing him. "Where is Blue, Pherall?"

Pherall continued to shake her head. Military trucks. Burnt barn. Muddy tracks. Vendor trucks. Food tent. Twisting her brows, she scanned faster. "Uno."

"Find him."

Vendor trucks. Yellow tape. Burnt barn. Vendor trucks.

Pherall's gaze traveled a smaller pattern until it stopped on the food tent. She studied it for a full minute before her breathing began to slow.

"Where is he?"

Muddy tracks. Food tent. Vendor trucks.

Vendor trucks.

Uno looked where she looked. "Which one?" he asked, his voice barely audible.

White truck. Yellow truck. Muddy tracks. White truck. Muddy tracks.

"Which one?"

Pherall frowned at the muddy tracks, then pointed to the white truck. "He's in there."

"Oh, come on!" hissed Ocho in disbelief.

Cinco snatched the crowbar from Ocho's hand and backed down the hill to find a better entry point. Ocho scowled at Pherall, then hurried after him with a curse.

"Stay here," said Uno.

He vanished, leaving her peering through the grass with a sour stomach and Ocho's scowl dancing across her mind. Imagining the worst, she exhaled and covered her face. Clearly, these guys had too much faith in her. What if she'd just picked the wrong truck? she worried. There was no tingle, no psychic wa-wa-wa buzz, no magnetic sensation. It was a guess—plain and simple. Behind her, Uno opened a small case and began snapping a rifle together. Groaning inwardly, she pinched her temples, bracing herself for the disaster that would follow. Moments later, she felt Uno return to the top of the hill and slide onto his belly beside her.

With skilled hands, he zeroed in on the truck in the clearing below, then cut his eyes to the side to wait. "Cover your ears," he said, watching the edge of the clearing.

Cinco appeared a few minutes later at the tree line and crouched low behind the parked trucks. With skill and precision, he moved from one hiding place to the next on silent feet, ten feet at a time toward the white vendor truck. Ocho crept behind him, mimicking his every move, only with much less grace. Halfway there, Cinco doubled backward and darted out of sight behind a military jeep. Ocho slipped and scrambled behind a nearby bumper.

Cinco adjusted his feet beneath him and waited.

Seconds later, an agent strolled around the nose of the jeep.

Cinco covered the man's mouth, silencing him, and heaved him off-balance. In one motion, he smashed his elbow down hard beneath the Jackboot's skull and violently jerked his chin up, breaking the dude's neck with a sickening crunch.

Pherall, watching from the hill, clapped her hands over her face and turned her head away.

Silently, Cinco eased the dead man to the ground and rolled him beneath the jeep. Without a shred of remorse, he peeked around the front bumper, then ducked back again, flattening himself against the wheel-well. Two Jackboots walked by moments later, talking quietly together.

Neither noticed Cinco.

They jerked their doors open and climbed in. A rumble shook the vehicle as it started and it pulled away, maneuvering carefully through the maze of cars. Cinco clung to the moving bumper, allowing it to shield him as he snuck closer to the white vendor truck.

Ocho lagged behind, stuck where he hid.

Another small group of Jackboots exited the food tent, laughing and meandering toward the burnt barn. Cinco, twenty feet from the vendor truck, ducked back, watching. Ocho used the sound of their footsteps to hide his own and ran, scurrying up to the rear tire of the black van where Cinco hid. Clutching the crowbar, Cinco peeked around the bumper, hid for a couple more seconds, peeked again, then darted through the muddy tracks toward the back of the white vendor truck. In one swift motion, he hooked the claw of the crowbar, yanked down hard, and snapped the lock off.

Uno raised the rifle.

Pherall covered her ears.

Ocho moved to the front tire of the black van.

Cinco jerked the large door open and went rigid. "Jesus!" he cried, charging into the back.

The front door of the cab opened, and a man in a uniform stepped out, reaching for his weapon.

Uno fired.

Ocho charged forward, leapt over the falling man, and jumped into the driver's seat. A passenger fell out the other side, screaming. Ocho threw the transmission into gear and floored it.

Uno followed the passenger with the rifle for a moment, then jerked his head up and watched the truck plow through the tangle of vehicles, crashing front ends and ramming refreshment tables. Engine screaming, it raced toward the dirt road. Jackboots shot out of the food tent, running in every direction, scrambling for their vehicles and swallowing their mouthfuls.

Uno jerked Pherall up and threw her toward the base of the hill, grabbed his rifle case, and charged after her. Thirty feet from the pickup truck, he shoved the rifle into her hands, raced around to the driver's side, and yanked the red pickup into reverse. In a splash of mud, he fishtailed onto the pavement, his brown gaze focused forward. A mile down the road, he saw the white vendor truck and floored it.

Pherall understood then why he'd drained the water tank.

Ocho saw him coming and screeched the stolen vendor truck to a stop, waited for him to pass, then turned sideways to block the road.

Uno squalled to a stop beside him.

Ocho ran to the back just as Cinco appeared, dragging something out. "Shit!" he cursed, rushing around to help.

Black vans, military trucks, and police cruisers appeared at the end of the road.

Uno glanced calmly into his mirror, then shifted his gaze the other way, watching Ocho and Cinco appear with their burden.

Pherall twisted in her seat to see and paled as Blue's frozen solid body appeared. Horrified, she clapped a hand over her mouth. Cinco and Ocho crawled into the bed of the pickup with him, moving carefully in their haste, and slammed the gate up. As Ocho side-armed the truck keys into the ditch, Uno took off.

*****

Pherall warmed a pot of water on the stove while the guys worked to get Blue into bed. He lay in a half-curled, half-twisted position on the open sofa bed. Cinco rushed to find something to prop him with while Ocho stripped down to his underwear.

Weeping softly, Ocho crawled in beside Blue, who was actually that color now, and wrapped his arms around his friend. Over and over, he apologized for letting him down, for not watching out for him.

"Uno, the water's ready," said Pherall after a bit.

Uno pulled off his shirt and handed it to her. She soaked it in hot water, wrung it out, and handed it back to him. He laid it over the top of Blue while Cinco searched for anything else that would fit in the pot. Soon, he was completely covered beneath warm, wet rags, which were covered again with the blanket from the back room.

"I'm out of water," she said, turning off the stove.

Uno exhaled loudly and backed away from the sofa bed. Cinco did the same. Pherall watched them both stare down at Blue with agonized expressions, helpless and afraid. The only thing they could do now was wait. It surprised her to realize that the guys were indeed afraid for Blue, afraid that he wouldn't wake up, terrified that he would.

Uno dragged his eyes away from the sofa bed and turned them to Pherall with a flicker in his expression. He held her gaze for a long time before severing the connection. Without a word, he went into the bedroom and slammed the door shut. Cinco, his face contorted in hatred, spun toward the door and stormed out, barely clearing the doorjamb with his shoulder.

Pherall went after him.

Cinco charged for the truck and jerked the door open.

Pherall threw herself inside the door of the pickup before he could close it and, as he started the engine, reached through the steering wheel to grab the gearshift. "Cinco!" she said sharply, refusing to let go when he tried to put it into gear. "It won't help him."

"Let go!"

"No."

"Let go!"

"Cinco."

"Let it go, Pherall!"

"No."

"Gaaaaah!" he roared and slammed his fist into the dash, cracking it.

Pherall flinched but held the gear.

"What did we ever do to them!" he bellowed at her. His voice cracked, and he dissolved into tears. "Why won't they just leave us alone?"

Careful to keep a solid grip on the gearshift, Pherall wrapped her free arm around his head and hugged him to her. She didn't shoosh him or tell him it was okay because it wasn't. She just held him and watched a flock of birds fly overhead.

After a minute, he hooked his arm around her shoulder and rested his forehead against her collarbone. They stayed like that for a long while before he shifted his head. "I'm good," he murmured softly.

Pherall scratched her fingernails against his scalp. "There should be some food in the kitchen. Why don't you fix dinner tonight?" she said softly.

A bit reluctantly, he nodded and got out of the truck.

It took Pherall a minute or two to get the hot-wired engine shut down, but she managed it with a sigh and closed the door. Never in her life had she imagined coming face to face with such cruelty, such evil, but she was undoubtedly facing it now. Worse than that, now that she had seen it, she was recognizing it everywhere. As the sun went down, she stared out at the thick canopy of trees and listened to the crickets chirp while her brain rewired itself for her new awareness. Somehow, these Jackboot monsters had to be stopped. She didn't know how, but if she had to die trying to do that, she would.

CHAPTER 10

The distinguished gentleman pressed his fingertips into a point and leaned back in his leather chair, waiting somewhat patiently while his guests seated themselves. His pristine white hair was swept back in a thick wave that blended neatly into a curl at the base of his expensive haircut. His chemically bleached skin boasted a youthful glow that belied his age, as did the stark white veneer on his perfect teeth. With the confidence of a man proud of his appearance and station in life, he acknowledged each polite greeting with a slight tilt of his regal head but waited to speak. When they were finally seated, he lowered manicured fingers and entwined them in front of his unnaturally fit belly. "Good morning, gentlemen," he said with a haughty purr. "My name is Rigori."

"Rigori, the billionaire?" squealed a wild-haired scientist in a lab coat and coke-bottle glasses.

Rigori inclined his head, guilty as charged. "I can imagine you are all quite curious as to why I have summoned you here," he said, flashing something of a grin, then continued in a noble tone. "Before I explain why we are here, let's go around the table for introductions so that you will know who your colleagues are."

He faced the man directly to his left, pointedly stilled, and waited.

The excessively poised blond man glanced around the table with a stony expression and a single elevated eyebrow. He didn't fidget. Clearly uncomfortable among the others, he inclined his head politely to the group. "I am Dimitri," he told them in a strong, clipped Russian accent, "from Russia."

"Oh! You're KGB," decided a curly-haired American to his left.

Dimitri paused, annoyed by the rude assumption. "Actually, no. Zat organization is not called KGB anymore. Now zey are called —"

"I really don't care what you call yourselves, Dimitri," the American said, waving the Russian silent. "Russian spies are KGB. It's common knowledge."

"Spy?" Satirical amusement flickered in the light smile that resulted, though it didn't reach the Russian's piercing eyes. "You are very presumptuous," noted Dimitri.

The American ignored him. He wore the rough, weathered skin of an active forty-something with deep lines that accented rugged features. His curly hair was dark and neat, his manner assertive. "My name," he informed his listeners in an important tone, "is

Maxim Blackwood, commander of the Jackboot Quick Reaction Force."

The antique scientist smiled. "Dr. Hyde von Stein, United States. Employment location, classified. Job title, classified. Favorite pastime, classified," he announced proudly, leaning forward and folding restless hands together. He stared at them. "I am familiar with all of you and your work. You can call me Dr. Stein."

Rigori smiled, a gesture that stayed at his lips, and retook the conversation. "All of you have a direct interest in and advanced knowledge of the Immortals," he said, coming right to the point. "That is why you have been called here."

"This topic is classified," Maxim informed his host. "My government—"

"Your government takes bribes," interrupted Rigori.

Maxim sputtered appropriately at the accusation.

Rigori's sharp blue eyes shifted to the curly-haired man. "Who do you think funds this operation?" he said haughtily. "I have been investing in the Immortals since their discovery nearly twenty years ago. However, I grow tired of watching you circus performers bumble around and waste my money. It was my decision to unite the three branches and collaborate, thereby pooling our knowledge, so let's do away with the phony outrage, Maxim. With a single phone call, I can have your position eradicated and all records of your existence deleted."

Maxim sat back, reconsidering his virtuous position on the matter.

"What is your interest in ze Immortals?" asked Dimitri.

Rigori reached into a bowl of macadamia nuts and cracked one. "For years, I have sat quietly by watching all of you make asses of yourselves. It is an embarrassment."

Maxim pointed to himself. "My organization—," he began.

Rigori's vexation was evident in his tone. "Your organization is as fucked up as a football bat," he railed. "All you do is run around squalling tires and shooting shit. You're idiots! You have manpower but no brains. While you were on your way here, I took over your hunt for the Immortals. In a few moments, I'll show you what I accomplished in twenty-four hours of your absence."

Maxim drew his head back in offense but wisely held his tongue.

"And you, Dimitri," he continued, turning on the Russian. "You horde all your data but don't have the manpower to do anything with it. How are you supposed to benefit from what you've learned if you don't share it?"

Dimitri didn't answer.

Rigori faced Dr. Stein.

"Will you fund me?" the scientist exhaled, ready to crawl over the table.

"Your lab is downstairs."

Dr. von Stein shoved his fingers into his wild hair, beside himself with delight.

"From this moment on," Rigori told his company, "I oversee the Immortals. All data will be shared openly. Everything you say, everything you do, every decision regarding them will go through me. I will decide which moves to make, and you will follow my orders exactly. Like pieces of a chessboard, we will work together as one impenetrable force until we reach checkmate!" he declared, smashing his fist into the table. "Only then will the Immortals be brought under control."

A servant brought refreshments and hors d'oeuvres.

"Maxim." Rigori faced him again. "Bring us up to date on the Immortals in your area."

Maxim tugged at his collar and reached for his glass of wine. "Well—*Ahem*—we have four that we are working to bring in. Uno, Blue, Cinco, and Ocho. One, Two, Five, and Eight," he explained for those who couldn't understand Spanish. "Uno is their leader. Without him, the others are unorganized. To date, we know of no weaknesses for Uno. We can pick the others off one at a time, but he always comes for them. He's killed plenty of my men. Until you find a weakness, you aren't going to catch him."

Rigori slid a snapshot of a webpage with a photo on it to Maxim. "Who is this?"

The Jackboot glanced at the page. "A civilian. We discovered her assisting Cinco during the movie theater capture. She was filmed communicating with the other three using eye contact, which proved recognition. We aren't certain yet how they are associated, but we suspect it's through Cinco. We feel she may have information we can use. She can also be used as leverage."

"I see you have a bounty out for her."

Maxim proudly indicated the large number beneath the image. "That'll find her."

"That is an impressive reward amount," noted Rigori in disapproval.

Maxim chuckled and wrinkled his brow at the older man in personal satisfaction. "It attracts the hunters."

"That number puts her in danger," Rigori countered using a common sense tone designed to disguise his irritation.

"I am not worried about the girl. She is unimportant."

Rigori smiled, glaring at the Jackboot. "She is traveling with them. I'd say she is quite important."

Maxim wasn't at all impressed. "I've been dealing with these Immortals for years," he said arrogantly. "They're violent and skittish. If she's traveling with them, trust me, they aren't going to let a bunch of bounty hunters hurt her."

"You are correct. I want to show you something." Rigori purred, then glanced sharply at a servant by the door. He signaled, and the lights were lowered. On the blank wall behind him, a video projector blinked on, and he stood. "It just so happens, Maxim, Uno does have a weakness."

Using a clicker and a telescoping pointer, Rigori introduced the video. "This footage was taken seventy-two hours ago. Seven bounty hunters," he said with a glance at Maxim, "arrived at the Immortal's campsite with instructions to capture or kill the girl. This is Uno, yes?" he asked, extending his pointer at a figure squeezing through missing slats in the barn.

"Yes," said Maxim. "He's slightly smaller than the others and the most dangerous. Tactical minded. Extremely intelligent. His parents were KGB too."

Dimitri slow-blinked and reached for his drink.

Rigori pointed to a second figure running away from the camper, firing a gun and ducking behind a pile of rocks. "And this is?"

Maxim squinted at the replay. "That's Cinco. Very astute. Prior Special Forces. Counter-terrorism."

They watched for a moment before the pointer shifted to a bounty hunter entering the barn. "This gentleman here aims to shoot the girl. Watch right … bah, bah, bah … here. Uno takes the bullet, and we have the opportunity now to watch a death. Please note the time. Here, the girl is struggling with the bounty hunter. Pardon the shaking. The videographer was moving in for a better angle. There. Here's the girl again, still struggling, and look," he thwacked the screen, "right there. Uno is up. You'll notice the reset happened within ninety seconds."

Dimitri gasped. "Ninety seconds!"

Dr. Stein bounced in his seat. "Bring him in!" he squealed, pulling his fluffy hair.

Rigori pressed a button. "You said, Maxim, you suspect an association through Cinco, but I disagree. It's Uno who shows interest in the girl. Fast forward to the next day," he said, stopping at a clip of the threesome at a crowded market. "Cinco is over here but watch Uno. He acts aloof but notice his position around the girl."

A silent clip played through.

"He's guarding her," the billionaire explained, facing his audience. "Uno is very aware of what she does, where she looks. He's hiding it. Without looking directly at her, he sees what she sees, stops when she stops, turns when she turns. Gentlemen, the boy has a weakness. Uno is in love," he thwacked the wall again, "with her."

"It's irrelevant," Maxim insisted. "We can't get him. They pick us off like flies."

Rigori advanced the video. "While you were in route, Maxim, I had your men conduct a reconnaissance mission with my head of security. Forty-eight hours ago, we killed this man," he prompted expectantly, "with the sole purpose of studying their behavior. Who is he?"

"Ocho," offered Maxim. "A newer Immortal, not much intel."

"While Ocho was down, we captured this man." Rigori thumped the image on the wall.

"That's Blue," injected Maxim slowly, "or Number Two. Volatile, unpredictable, unstable. Most recorded resets. You captured him?"

"Indeed," Rigori boasted. "We hid him in a maze and then sat back and waited to see what would happen."

Maxim leaned forward.

"Ocho we left dead and watched," he finished, looking around for dramatic effect. "We didn't see the Immortals come into the camp nearly twelve hours later, but in one strike, they chose Blue's hidden location and broke him out before we ever knew they'd arrived. Gentlemen, I want to know how."

"You let them get away?" Maxim asked in disbelief.

Rigori put his nose in the air. "It was an opportunity to study the Immortals in the wild."

Maxim face-palmed himself.

Dimitri frowned thoughtfully and raised his fingers. "Play ze footage."

The video played, but the angle was poor. A distant view of the white vendor truck crashing out of the field was unimpressive. When the video stopped, all eyes turned to Dimitri, waiting for some explanation.

"Ze girl," he said pensively. "What do you know about her?"

"Very little," said Maxim. "Why?"

Instead of answering, Dimitri signaled to his secretary. "Prepare Number Four. Send a plane for him," he said quietly, handing the woman the printed photo from the website. "Zis girl will be his target," he ordered, "and send for my files."

Rigori signaled again, and the lights came on. "Enlighten us," he said in interest.

Dimitri nodded. "Oh, I will," he smiled, leaning back in his chair. "I will. In ze meantime, I want any information you can find on ze girl. Anything."

CHAPTER 11

Once the warmth of the heated blankets faded, Blue was uncovered and allowed to thaw overnight at room temperature. By morning the others were able to peel his clothes off. There was no more water in the camper tanks and the group was reduced to a few water bottles for drinking. Without electricity, there was no heat, so that had to be generated the hard way. Cinco and Ocho took turns lying beside Blue to offer body heat. There was enough propane in the tanks for a few more meals, which helped warm the camper, but that was it. The hours were long, but the men spent every moment beside Blue, worried sick that he wouldn't survive the death. Pherall helped pass the time by playing cards with Cinco, who looked like hell. Her ponytail sat low in a charming sag and lazy tendrils framed her face. She wasn't in the mood to fix it, though. It would just fall again. Ocho, who was nearly naked, sat reading Cinco's book, refusing to move from Blue's side. Uno stayed to himself and rarely spoke. He kept his head down and busily worked on his small phone, brows furrowed and knuckles curled over his lips.

Blue was completely thawed by the next evening and slowly began to warm. Ocho and Cinco hovered around him, waiting with white knuckles for his heart to restart. Every few seconds, one or the other of them would touch Blue's neck with two fingers. After a while, Cinco snapped his head up. "He has a pulse!" he said. "It's weak."

While the others fussed, Uno, wearing the brown t-shirt today, set his phone aside on the kitchen table and waited.

Pherall sat apart from the group, giving them their space while they held their breaths. As the camper darkened, she set out the solar lights she'd charged earlier in the day. She'd found them while exploring one of the closets and was thrilled to see they still worked. The camper wasn't bright, but they could see clearly inside. In boredom, she began organizing one of the dimly lit kitchen drawers. Busily. Meticulously. As she worked, her mind wandered to Mia, who had been so full of spirit. She missed her friend's super cute giggle and witty comebacks and was sorry that such a promising life had been so unfairly ended.

Uno paused at her back, interrupting her thoughts, and gave her shoulder a squeeze. "Where are you?"

Pherall blinked back to the present and gave a sheepish smile. "I was just thinking about Mia," she said softly. "I miss her."

"You were close?"

Pherall nodded. "We were study buddies in college, then got hired on at the same elementary school."

Uno took the seat beside her. "Tell me about Mia," he said, leaning back and getting comfortable.

"What would you like to know?"

He shrugged. "I don't know. Just tell me about her. Do you have any funny stories?"

Pherall's eyes lit up. "Oh, do I!" she laughed, curling her legs beneath her. "There was the freshman dorm scavenger hunt disaster that almost landed us in jail after we snuck into the science lab for a leech ..."

Uno smiled and settled in to listen.

The sun was fully down before Blue twitched for the first time. More time ticked by.

Ocho jerked upright a little while later, eyes rounded, voice choked. "He just squeezed my hand!"

Pherall closed her eyes in relief and hung her head, but her response was nothing compared to the emotional shouts and hesitant celebration around the bed. Ocho was usually the one who fixed meals, but tonight he was making no move to do that. Quietly, Pherall eased her ridiculously organized drawer shut and dug out some canned vegetables. Those were added to quick-cook noodles they'd purchased from a convenience store, and a pot of soup was born.

Ocho sat beside Blue and rubbed his cool arm. "C'mon, buddy. Come back to us, man," he said softly.

This additional stimulation increased Blue's breathing. After another ten minutes of coaxing, he began to shiver violently. He hissed loudly through clenched teeth, struggling to draw a full breath. Ocho curled up beside him beneath his blankets. When that didn't help, Cinco crawled beneath the covers on his other side.

The violent shivers turned to thrashing and nightmarish grunts. "Uno," he shivered through his teeth, "... brr gr ... amb ... cold ... mm n mmbl ... Uno, I'mmm ... mm cold," he muttered pitifully. "Dnnnn ... don't like it."

A few minutes into this, Uno moved calmly to the bed. Patiently, he stood beside the mattress and waited, his expression stoic.

"Uno, I want out ... I'm cold ... Come get me out!" Blue wailed, struggling miserably against Ocho and Cinco. "Unooo!"

A tear rolled down Pherall's cheek. In silence, she watched Blue relive his death.

By now, he was crying. "Uno ... please find me."

Uno waited.

When Blue started speaking in coherent sentences, Uno shouted, starting him. "Blue!"

Blue went still, listening. Tears glistened on his pale cheeks. "Uno?" he dared in a shaky whisper.

Uno spoke in a firm voice. "I'm here, Blue. What's the matter?"

Blue's breathing increased, but his panic calmed. "I'm cold. I want out," he panted and shifted in the bed.

"The door is unlocked," Uno said, still using a sharp tone. "You can come out."

Blue calmed visibly and relaxed on the bed, breathing heavily and clutching his hands in tight fists. Pherall expected him to open his eyes, but he didn't wake right away. After lying still for a few minutes, he began tossing again.

"Open your eyes, Blue," Uno instructed. "Wake up."

Blue's lashes fluttered briefly. Another minute passed before he opened his eyes, just enough to see Uno standing over him and closed them again in relief. Weak and exhausted, he almost smiled. "You found me," he whispered, cracking his lids and working to hold them open.

"You knew I was coming," said Uno.

Blue nodded and tried to chuckle. "Where's Ocho?"

"I'm right here."

Blue peeked at him, then spotted Cinco on his other side and smiled, his lids still heavy.

Pherall waited until Uno looked up at her, then lifted a cup. At his nod, she turned to the stove and, using the last of the water bottles, made hot broth for Blue. While it was heating, she recited the ABCs quietly to herself, struggling to maintain her composure. Witnessing that had rattled her.

"Did they freeze you too?" Blue asked Ocho in a tired voice.

"No. They left me. I didn't know where you were." Ocho shouldered his eyes dry and glanced toward the kitchen. "Uno and … and Pherall found you," he admitted in shame. "I lost you."

Blue shook his head. "Don't beat yourself up over it. They got you first," he argued weakly. "I never saw them coming either."

Uno moved to the foot of the bed, so Blue didn't have to turn his head, and shook the hair from his eyes. "How did they attack?"

"From behind. I was hit with a tranquilizer. They knifed Ocho in the back. They were dragging him toward an alley when I passed out. When I woke, I was in a freezer. A truck, I think. They broke my glasses."

Uno frowned and returned to his seat at the kitchen table.

Cinco's expression matched. "Why didn't they take Ocho?" he wondered. "They had them both."

"That's what's bothering me," said Uno. "We found him too easily. The whole rescue. It was too easy."

Pherall came through with a warm cup of broth and handed it to Blue. "Welcome back," she smiled. "They've been wringing their hands for days."

"Days?" he said, sitting up to take the cup.

She nodded. "You've been thawing for two days. They weren't sure you'd come back this time."

Blue took a drink, then snorted and wiped his chin. Wide-eyed, he gaped at Ocho. "Are you naked!"

Ocho drew up in offense. "No. I'm in my underwear."

"Get some damn pants on."

"I'm dressed," Cinco offered from Blue's other side. "Just in case you were wondering."

Scowling, Ocho threw the covers back and got up.

"Oh, shit!" gasped Blue. "Come back. I'm cold."

Ocho pulled his pants on, not at all concerned that Pherall was in the room, then returned to the bed. "Are you tired?"

Blue nodded and took another drink. "But I don't want to go to sleep yet."

"Wanna play cards?"

"I could play cards," he smiled and rested his head back on a cushion.

Pherall, listening from the kitchen, took the playing cards from a drawer and brought them to the open sofa bed. Standing by the side, she handed them to Ocho and turned to go. Instead of taking them, Ocho caught her wrist, stopping her.

Uno looked up.

"Play with us," said Ocho.

Pherall paused in surprise, then gestured awkwardly toward the stove. "I'm cooking. I will after I'm finished."

Ocho released her wrist and took the cards.

Uno's eyes lowered and followed Pherall's feet back to the kitchen as she passed.

Back at the stove, she braved a peek at Uno and found his steady brown eyes on her. Warmth crawled up her neck, and she quickly busied herself adding salt and pepper. Listening to the chatter behind her, she turned to the cabinet and began counting plastic cups, which is how they would eat their soup tonight. As she counted, she sensed movement from Uno behind her. Right on cue, her heart started banging, indicating he was approaching. This made her forget what number she was on. The number she was trying to get to was five. Doing her best to ignore him, she started over.

He stopped directly at her back.

Slowly, she lowered her hand and slid her eyes to the side, wondering what in the hell he was doing.

Uno's arm stretched past her head, removing the cups she'd been attempting to count, and set them down in a stack. "I've got this," he murmured into her ear, leaving his arm extended past her on the counter.

Was he … ?

Pherall looked over her shoulder with a start, then turned to face him, bumping his chest when she did. He was standing too close! Why was he standing so close? She noticed a vein pulsing in his neck, matching the tempo visible in the fabric of his shirt. His heart was racing. Too surprised to speak, she blinked up at him. His brown eyes pinned hers, locking her there.

Pherall's knees knocked, threatening to throw her on the floor, and she eased a hand to the edge of the counter behind her. The world spun around them. Would he try to kiss again? The very thought terrified her.

His lips came no closer.

Disappointed, she looked up.

Their eyes held.

This time, something was there, turning Pherall to jelly. He wanted to kiss her, she was sure of it, but he was stopping himself. Why, dammit? It occurred to her, at that moment, that he was very aware of the reaction he was causing in her and was likely doing it on purpose.

Playboy.

From the other room, a playing card crashed loudly onto Blue's blanket.

Staring up at Uno, she realized suddenly that the only sound she could hear was the stumbling of her heartbeat in her ears. The chattering from the other room had stopped. Pherall's gaze shifted past Uno's shoulder to three unblinking faces on extended giraffe necks, and she nearly died of embarrassment. Mortified, she flicked her gaze back to Uno's.

"I'll finish," he said in a low voice, barely audible despite his nearness. "Go play cards."

Without another word, he slid past her to the counter, leaving her wide-eyed and breathless. And just like that, the chatter resumed—a bit hesitantly at first, then with forced naturalness beneath a chorus of lifted eyebrows. Awkwardly, Pherall wiped her hands on a paper towel and crossed the small floor to the bed, her cheeks flaming. She sat on the foot of the mattress, unable to make eye contact with any of them, and waited to be dealt a hand.

A few minutes later, Uno passed out cups of steaming soup and sat beside her on the foot of the bed with his knee against hers. Cinco, Ocho, and Blue shared quick looks, then quickly re-dealt the cards to include Uno.

Uno won.

The cards were passed out again.

Pherall was careful not to look directly at anyone, though she could totally feel their eyes on her. Actually, even without confirming, she was pretty sure the gazes were regularly shifting back and forth between her and Uno. Heat seared through her, lighting her ears up and ending in her toes.

Other than the faintest hint of amusement in his expression, Uno behaved normally, speaking only when necessary and moving with his usual deliberate precision. Nothing about him suggested loss of composure. Pherall, on the other hand, was lucky not to fall off the bed. She played cards with jittery fingers, dropped entire hands, and babbled incoherently—behaviors not missed by everyone else in the room.

Uno won again.

CHAPTER 12

A week later, Pherall woke to the sound of violent shivering and sat up. Careful not to disturb Uno, she slid out of the bed and padded to the tiny kitchen table-bed. Uno's previous warning not to startle Blue danced through her mind, reminding her to approach carefully and touch lightly. Blue's head was freezing cold and drenched in sweat. He lay curled in a tight ball, shivering air through his teeth. Using the pale moonlight peeking in through the window blinds, she quickly collected hoodies and t-shirts and draped them over him.

He startled violently, and Pherall jumped back. Patiently, she gathered the clothes he'd just spilled and covered him again, then brushed his hair from his face to slowly wake him. He caught her wrist in a severe grip, but the sound of his breathing shifted. "Blue," she murmured softly, scratching her fingernails over his wet head, "open your eyes, hon."

They opened but didn't focus.

Pherall brushed messy hair from her face. "Look at me, Blue."

Gray eyes shifted to her. "Cold," he hissed.

When she was sure he knew where he was, she knelt beside him. "I'm going to warm some broth," she murmured. "Does that sound good?"

He nodded.

She stood, tucking the clothes tightly around him, then hurried to the stove. Using only a small battery-powered light, she put some broth on to heat. While it warmed, she found a clean tube-sock in Cinco's bag of belongings and took it to the counter. There, she dug out a bag of rice, dumped the contents into the sock, and tied off the end with a knot. Using a dry pan, she set the sock on the stove, covered it with a lid, and heated it.

During the day, Blue was pretty much back to normal after his ordeal. The evening lessons had even resumed, but at night he struggled. The incident had scarred him badly. He woke nightly now, sweating, shivering, and believing he was back inside the freezer dying that horrible death. Though he didn't say so outright, he had developed a fear of cold. This was significant enough that he no longer wanted ice in his drink or to touch anything chilled. He wore his hoodie around, oftentimes zipped up despite the warmth of the day, and kept his hands in the pockets. Almost every night since his return, Pherall had woken to the sound of shivers and a nightmare. Seeing him this way made her want to slap the

Jackboots, who seemed to have forgotten that these guys were human.

The broth was done.

Blue propped on an elbow and took the cup. "I didn't mean to wake you again," he apologized softly.

Pherall shook her head. "Don't worry about me. I'll be fine when you warm up. What were you dreaming about?"

"I keep seeing the truck."

Pherall crossed her arms over her knees. "It took a long time?"

He nodded. "Hours," he said, gripping the steaming cup with both hands to warm them. "It was locked. I couldn't get out. When I banged on the walls, they banged back."

Pherall sighed. "I wish we would have found you sooner," she whispered.

"I'm just glad you found me at all," he said, finishing the broth. "I was afraid you wouldn't."

In the silence that followed, Pherall stood and crossed to the stove to see if the rice bag was warm. After giving it a moment to cool, she tucked it into Blue's arms. "Don't tell Cinco," she whispered, earning a smile. "It's his sock."

"This is clean, right?"

"I hope so," she teased, "or you won't be nightmaring about the cold anymore. It'll be dirty laundry."

He chuckled quietly.

She was about to stand when he caught the bottom of her shirt, stopping her.

"I'm glad you're here, Pherall."

Pherall felt a warm glow spread through her.

"I've missed having a family," he admitted and let her go. "We all have. I mean … we were always a family, me and the boys, but you've brought life back to us."

She smiled. "And we're glad you're home safe."

Relaxed, at last, he lay down on the hard cushion and hugged the sock. "I like this," he beamed, reminding her of a child with a brand-new teddy bear.

"I thought you might," she whispered and tried again to stand.

"Don't leave yet," he pleaded.

Pherall covered him with his makeshift blankets again and lowered her knees back to the floor. He closed his eyes. Kneeling beside him, she scratched her fingernails through his hair until his breathing grew steady and then for several minutes longer. She just wanted to be sure he was asleep before leaving his side. This time, he didn't move.

When she returned to her own bed, Uno was propped on an elbow waiting for her.

"I didn't mean to disturb you," she apologized quietly.

Uno folded the blankets back, inviting her in, and covered her. "I don't mind," he murmured. In the dark, he edged closer, sliding an arm around her waist, and folded his knees into hers.

Pherall was surprised at first but quickly relaxed, enjoying the sensation of being in his arms. Content where she was, she sighed softly and closed her eyes, thinking about what Blue had said. A light smile touched her lips, and she drifted back to sleep.

*****

Standing over the coffeepot the next morning, Pherall smiled to herself. She'd woken that morning to the feel of Uno's arm around her, guarding her from the evil world. She wasn't sure what had happened between the two of them during the last week, but something had. The physical reactions hadn't changed, but now instead of avoiding each other, the opposite was occurring. They couldn't stand to be apart. When opportunity allowed, he stood too close, brushed his fingers across her hand when she took something, held her gaze when he caught it. Pherall was reduced to a blushing schoolgirl every time she felt him approach, which he was doing now.

Noticing the familiar tingle, she bit her lip and turned just as Uno stepped out of the bedroom. Despite his youthful appearance, he seemed older now that she knew him, ageless and wise. There was nothing young about him. He took care of the people who relied on him and absolutely deserved the position he held within the group. He had earned her respect just as he had the others. That she was attracted to him was entirely understandable.

With purpose in his step, he walked into the room and thumped Cinco, who lounged lazily in his bed reading a book. "We've been here too long," he said, tossing a pillow at Blue. "Shut the camper down."

Pherall handed Uno a cup of coffee. "Can we go back to the campsite by the lake? I want a good shower."

Uno nodded and took the cup, letting his fingers interlock with hers for a long moment. "We leave in thirty minutes," he said, gazing leisurely at her over his coffee cup. "Bag everything."

Thirty-five minutes later, Ocho pulled the camper to the waste dump and drained the sewage, while Blue filled the water tank by pretending he was peeing into it. Cinco and Uno tossed the garbage and then gathered their own clothes for a shower. Men's showers were on the left, women's on the right. Pherall couldn't wait and quickened her pace. Two feet from the door, however, she slowed to a stop and turned back toward the trees surrounding the sleepy lake.

Uno followed her gaze.

"What?" called Cinco.

Pherall spun to face him, smiled happily, and disappeared inside with her soap. Her shower was a hot one. Standing beneath the spray, she soaped her clothes clean and rinsed them out, humming to herself. The wet bra would be uncomfortable for a little while, but it would dry, she thought, slinging soggy hair aside and snapping the clasp. She bent to pick up her shirt, the next in line to be cleaned, and paused her song.

Frowning, she poked her head out of the shower stall.

The front door was closed, and the restroom was empty, just as she'd expected it to be. Irritated by her own paranoia, she went back into the stall and pulled on her jeans. They were wet but clean now, which made it okay.

Suddenly, a gust of cool air hit her and she spun, quickly securing the buttons. Warily, she opened the stall door and peered out again. The bathroom was empty. "Uno?" she called softly.

The front door opened, and he poked his wet head in. His brown hair was brushed straight, with the front dangling lightly in front of his eyes and the back brushing the tops of his shoulders. "Are you finished?" he asked.

She yanked the shirt up, covering her bra. "Um … y–yeah, I just … have to get dressed."

Uno moved to close the door again and glanced up at the window high above her head.

It was open.

In the next instant, he charged into the room, grabbed her, and slammed his shoulder hard against the open stall door, scattering his neat hair.

There was an 'oof!' and a scuffle of feet.

Uno threw Pherall into the stall against the shower knob, turning it on, and spun around the door into the man standing behind it. He crashed into the guy, jerked a heel out from under him, and took him to the ground. An instant later, he and a very large man with wavy blond hair crashed through the stall door together, knocking Pherall to the floor beneath the shower spray.

A large hand grabbed for Pherall.

Uno knocked it aside.

A moment later, a knife appeared.

Uno jerked her away from the blade with one hand, caught the knife wrist with the other, and twisted, throwing his weight backward. Dropping her on his other side, he spun around on his back, holding the arm straight. With a yank, he torqued the thick arm backward.

The blond grunted, and the knife clattered to the watery floor just outside the shower stall. To free his arm, the man lurched sharply, flipping himself and Uno around, and landed on top. Growling angrily, he seized Uno by the throat.

"Cinco!" Pherall shrieked, scrambling past them to get the knife.

Uno got his foot between them and kicked hard, knocking his opponent into the walkway. As the brute stumbled, he bumped Pherall and sent her to the floor. Uno grabbed an ankle, bringing him down, and leapt on top again, reaching for the knife. The blond jerked his hips up, sending Uno flying, and grabbed for Pherall. Uno twisted his legs around, hooking a knee around the man's neck, and jerked himself upright, yanking the blond head back and smashing it to the floor.

Pherall wiggled free.

Blondie swung a meaty fist, connecting with Uno's cheek. Uno grunted and fell backward into Pherall, knocking her across the wet floor toward the sinks. As he landed, the blond snatched the knife and stabbed down towards Uno's stomach.

"No!" Pherall tackled him with her shoulder, knocking him into the broken stall door. Flailing his arms, he slashed the knife upward, catching her in the ribs. She shrieked and fell onto the man.

Uno dove over the top of Pherall with a shout, straddling her on his knees, and punched the bastard twice in the face. The assailant grabbed Uno, and the two rolled away from Pherall.

Just then, the door crashed open, and Cinco bolted through. Before Blondie could make another move, Cinco grabbed him by the head and the belt and ran him face-first into the cinderblock wall.

The man shouted and fell.

Pinning him there, Cinco slammed his fist into the man's kidney, buckling his knees, then grabbed the blond head. With a powerful crack, he rammed his elbow down into the back of the man's neck and snapped it. Gritting his teeth, he dropped the body and stepped back.

Uno shot to his feet. "Pherall," he hissed, landing on his knees beside her.

Pherall lifted her hand away from her wound to see it. Right on cue, she was struck with a wave of nausea. "I'm okay," she said breathlessly.

Cinco hooked an arm around Pherall's bleeding middle and jerked Uno to his feet. "He isn't alone," he said, hauling both out the door. Clutching Uno's arm, he charged toward the pickup, which sat idling without the camper. Blue opened the door and slammed it behind them.

"Is she okay," Ocho asked, squalling out of the campground.

Uno pulled his shirt off and pressed it over the wound. "It's just a cut," he said, looking behind the truck. "Where's my backpack?"

Blue passed it back and stretched upright onto his knees to watch. "I got most of our stuff," he said, folding his arm over the seat. "Was he trying to kill her?"

"No. She got in the way." Uno took the bag and dug in it. "How many were there?"

"Five," said Blue. "Carrying zip ties, tranquilizers, and duct tape."

Uno pulled a sewing needle from a pocket of his backpack and threaded it. "Turn around, Blue."

Blue jerked wide eyes away from the needle and spun forward in his seat, breathing deeply.

"You can't be serious!" she yelped, wincing in pain. When the threaded needle was ready, Uno pushed Pherall over Cinco's lap and shook messy hair from his eyes. "Hold her," he instructed, folding one knee into the seat and hooking his other leg tightly around hers.

Cinco pinned her arms, and Uno bent over her.

Pherall cried out in pain at the prick of the needle and tried to get away, nearly unseating Uno. "Stop! Stop! Get off me!"

"Knock her out," Uno said without looking up.

"No! No!"

Cinco's hand slid around her throat. She felt a sharp pinch, and the stinging pain faded to black.

*****

When Pherall awoke, the sun was angling toward the ground, and the tires were rumbling over the open road. She blinked her eyes open and found her head bobbing around in Cinco's lap. Her ribs were killing her, pounding with every bump in the street. Carefully, she sat up, favoring her side, and glared at Uno. "That hurt, you asshole."

Uno almost smiled.

106

"Hungry?" Cinco handed her a cold fast-food burger.

While she ate, she twisted in her seat. "Where's the camper?"

"We had to leave it," said Cinco.

Pherall took a bite, mourning the loss of their little home, and curled her legs into the seat with her. Golden wheat stretched into the distance as far as the eye could see. She watched the mesmerizing breeze roll over the fields like ocean waves on their way to nowhere. "Where are we going now?"

"Coast," said Uno.

"We need to lay low for a bit," Ocho said into the rearview mirror.

"But what about your mission? Seven?"

Blue leaned his head back against the headrest. "We lost the trail. We didn't locate Seven in time. They moved him once they discovered we were looking. We'll try again. We can't do anything until we find another lead, though."

Pherall looked at Uno. "Have you ever found a bad Immortal?"

"No," he said, handing her a clean shirt from his backpack.

About then, Pherall realized she was wearing nothing but a bra and quickly pulled the shirt over her head. "What about one who didn't want to be found?"

"No."

"Has one ever tried to find you?"

Uno turned his attention to her, curious now. "Why?"

"That man," she began.

"Have you seen him before?"

"No, but ... ."

Blue rolled his head to the side to look at her. "Are you talking about the big blond bastard? We don't believe he was after us," he said in brilliant British accent, "but rather that he was after you."

"Me?"

Cinco knuckled her thigh. "Don't worry about him," he said with a wink. "He's dead."

Uno was watching her.

Pherall shook her head. "No. He's not dead," she corrected a bit hesitantly. "He's an Immortal."

Uno frowned at her for several seconds, at a momentary loss of words, then glanced toward the rearview mirror. "Ocho, you said you heard his name. Was it a number?"

Ocho's eyes flicked away from the road. "No. It was a weird name. Foreign, I think. Cha Tee Dee or something like that."

Uno lifted his brows in surprise, holding the driver's gaze. "Che-**tir**-dee?" he corrected, adding inflection to the second syllable.

Ocho nodded. "Yeah! That's it."

Uno stared at him.

"Why? Do you know of him?"

"No. Chetireh is a Russian word," Uno said heavily. "It means Four."

CHAPTER 13

There was no telling which day it was. Pherall had long since ceased caring. Fridays didn't matter anymore, so there was no reason to celebrate them. Mondays held no meaning and, therefore, required no dread. A Thursday was no more important than a Sunday, and five o'clock in the afternoon merely meant that the sun would soon set. In truth, the loss of such meaningless milestones seemed like a blessing, and the energy she'd wasted on them unimportant now. Pherall had come to realize, looking back, that she had been well on her way to becoming a robot. For the first time in her life, she was truly experiencing freedom. Constantly being chased sucked, yes, but the thoughts that wandered leisurely through her head seemed so different from those she had been used to. It was nice. Creativity had made a presence. When she studied the scenery, she saw art in nature and longed to draw it or paint it. The song of the birds grew musical, and she imagined colors to go with the sounds. She'd begun to hum to herself. Wind, once an inconvenience whose only purpose was to mess up her hair, now carried scent and personality. It felt good on her skin and made her smile. She'd never seen this beauty before, and she liked it.

This luxury had its drawback, however.

Living on the road was hard, and she couldn't help feeling a pang of longing for some of her old comforts. Besides family, it was the food she missed most—melted cheese and salad dressing, cheesecake, sautéed mushrooms, silverware. She missed hot showers and perfumed soap, her warm bed, her soft pillow, and her nappy old bunny slippers with the floppy ears. A random thought questioned whether she would delete all she'd learned with the boys and return to her old life if she could. Oddly enough, the answer to her own question wasn't 'hell yeah.'

Would she?

Pherall glanced at Uno, who stared mindlessly out the window, and felt a tug toward him. No way could she give him up now— ever, she thought, shifting her feet in the floorboard. His focus returned at that moment as if sensing her stare, and he blinked out of his daydream. His gaze shifted her direction, but she dodged the connection before he could catch her gawking yet again.

Tires rumbled over the road, lined tight with fir trees.

Outside the truck window, Pherall watched the rays of the sun glow across the horizon and wondered for the first time which life she preferred—a notion that rather surprised her. The comforts of her old life were missed, yes, but she'd actually begun to enjoy the sound of her unscheduled thoughts, the charismatic voice her mind used, and the new personality she'd discovered hiding within herself. What else had been hiding behind the distractions of technology and the mad rush to work for money? Maybe there was a way to combine both, she mused absentmindedly.

Without warning, Cinco lurched forward in the seat beside her, interrupting her thoughts, and pressed his nose to the glass. "Ocho, pull over!"

Ocho jerked quickly off the road, and Cinco pushed Pherall out of the way in his rush to get out the door. Puzzled, she stretched her neck as he jogged into the middle of the road and watched him approach a rather large turtle.

It was an ugly turtle.

Uno's brows flickered, and he snatched the front passenger side door open. "Cinco, no!" he shouted, nearly falling out of the truck in his haste. "That's a—!"

Snap!

The turtle's head rocketed out and snapped at Cinco, missing his reaching fingers by inches.

Cinco jumped back with a yelp. "Holy shit!"

"Don't touch it."

"It tried to bite me!" Cinco complained with a point.

Uno folded his elbow over the open door. "That's a snapping turtle," he called in amusement.

"Yeah, I was just figuring that out," Cinco grumbled, holding his hands well out of the way of the sharp beak.

"Leave it, and let's go."

Cinco angled his head at the disgusting suggestion and scowled at Uno. "I can't just leave it in the road," he scolded. "It'll get hit by a car."

"If you touch it, you'll lose a finger."

"I believe we've covered that," Cinco said dryly.

A car drove by.

Ocho rolled down his window and poked his head out of the truck. "We can't stay here, Cinco. We're out in the open."

"I'm not leaving the turtle, even if he is an asshole."

Blue unbuckled in the seat beside Pherall and leaned out his window. "Just pick it up. You'll grow the finger back," he hollered helpfully.

Cinco sliced an unamused hand through the air. "Not if I don't die," he argued. "I can only do that if I reset."

"That can be arranged," offered Blue, ducking back into the truck and reaching forward for Uno's bag.

Uno slapped the idiot's hand away from the bag and got out of the truck with a noisy sigh. After a quick trip to the side of the road, he joined Cinco clutching a long branch.

Another car went by, honking as it passed.

They ignored it.

Ocho flipped the driver off.

Uno stuck the branch in front of the turtle's open mouth. "Don't start shit, Ocho," he said over his shoulder. "We don't need trouble."

The turtle snapped the branch and held the cracking fibers in its jagged beak.

Cinco jumped behind Uno and peered around him. "Geez!"

Uno lifted the stick. The turtle, refusing to let go, held on. "Now pick him up," he said to Cinco.

"That driver was being a dick," Ocho fired back, determined to argue his point. "There was plenty of room on the road. He didn't have to honk."

Cinco, a bit timidly, grabbed the temperamental turtle's shell and hurried with Uno toward the side of the road with it. Together, they set it in the grass near a ditch. Once it was down, Uno fixed Ocho with a look. Clearly, he had no intention of arguing with the mechanic.

Ocho tossed his hands in the air. "Fine!" he snipped and rolled his window up. "I don't see why everyone can treat us like shit, and we have to be nice about it," he ranted to whomever in the truck was listening. "I'm tired of being nice. It doesn't matter where we go, we have to put up with people pushing us around and bullying. Why can't we teach some of these pricks a lesson? It's not like …"

Pherall suppressed an irritated sigh and ignored his griping as best she could.

Outside the truck, Cinco sniffed his hands and wrinkled his nose at the smell, then slid in beside Blue. The odor that came with him was impressive. "Wow. That thing stunk."

Pherall made a face, agreeing, and covered her nose with a laugh.

Uno climbed into the front again, effectively silencing Ocho's complaints.

Cinco held his hands out. "Find a station quick," he told Ocho. "I need to wash my hands."

111

As Ocho pulled onto the road, sunlight shifted across the windshield. "Good," he grumbled, lowering the visor against the evening sun. "I'm hungry."

Blue agreed. "Me, too."

The smile faded from Pherall's face at the thought of more road food. An urge to voice her complaint appeared, but she bit it back, certain Ocho would have something to say about it. The last thing she wanted to do was get him started again. Still, she couldn't help noticing that she was no longer hungry. Swallowing another sigh, she faced the window in disappointment and imagined a home-cooked meal with sauce, dinner roll, and dessert.

Uno frowned to himself, then turned pensive eyes ahead. When Ocho pulled into the gas station, he held up a hand halting the group before anyone could unbuckle. "Just fuel," he murmured to Ocho. "When Cinco gets back, find a grocery store. We'll barbecue tonight."

"Where?"

"I saw a city park sign a few miles back," Blue offered with a jab over his shoulder.

*****

An hour later, Ocho pulled into a run-down city park and stopped beside a picnic table spray-painted with ugly graffiti. Uno scowled at the lousy art and foul language scattered everywhere over every surface. After a moment of hesitation, he ignored it and unbuckled.

"Here?" Ocho scowled, noticing the ominous symbols.

Uno adjusted his backpack on the floor. "Did you see anywhere else?"

"No ... but this place is a dump."

Blue snorted. "The whole city is a dump."

Uno frowned again at the symbols, entirely agreeing, but he had already made his decision. "Either we do this now or we throw the groceries away and go back to the convenience store."

That did it.

All four doors opened simultaneously and the chattering bunch piled out, their arms loaded with supplies—raw meat, salt and pepper, veggies, foil to cover the grill, paper plates, and a lighter for the fire.

Pherall shut the door, noticing the instant change in the men's demeanor. Glad to be out of the truck, she gathered her board-straight hair into a quick ponytail and examined the park. She would never have come to a place like this before, but now it seemed so normal. In truth, she was thrilled. A hot meal? Oh, yeah! The evening was comfortable, though growing cooler as the sun set. Thick green trees surrounded bare patches of dirt along the road with stained concrete picnic tables and well-worn grills. Smooth pebbles, which made up the ground around the eating area, were surrounded by thick railroad ties. Litter and spray-painted threats marred the pleasant view, but otherwise it was a nice enough park. Neglected, but nice.

Ocho grabbed the foil and rolled up his sleeves. "I need wood!" he barked, covering the rack. "Hurry up before it gets dark."

The group scattered, eager to do his bidding.

"We can have a lesson," Blue called eagerly to Pherall.

"Knives," she said quickly.

"Blocking, disarming, or throwing?"

"Throwing!"

Blue gave her a thumbs up and rushed away.

Pherall headed off to find broken branches, moving a bit slower than the others. Her stitches were still tender and didn't appreciate any sharp movements, but they were healing nicely. Carefully, she bent for sticks and bundled them into her arm. She could hear the others nearby, each busily doing his own thing. Behind her, Cinco gathered fallen branches near the shore of a small pond. Blue had found an old, rotten branch and was heaving it backward toward the grill. Uno was dropping his first bundle of sticks off with Ocho and organizing a pile of wood on the ground.

"Oh, look!" she heard Cinco mutter, his branches forgotten. "Geese."

Pherall picked up a long stick from the darkening ground and broke it into usable pieces. She found more branches closer to a line of trees bordering the picnic area. These she stacked neatly before going back for more.

"Ooh! There's a nest of them. Well, hi there, little fellas," crooned Cinco. "Where's mama goose?"

About then, an arm slid around Pherall's waist, startling her, and she felt Uno step up behind her. She'd been so focused on her task that she'd missed his approach.

"That's far enough," he murmured into her ear.

Pherall's heart did a backflip, partially from the start, partly from the rush of warmth rocketing through her. She smiled dreamily, enjoying the feel of him against her, and bit her lip. Her heart hammered against her ribs, pounding a broken tempo that rang in her ears. "You made my heart skip," she whispered.

His head leaned close. "Made," his lips said, pressing against her temple, "or make?"

A goose honked angrily behind them, and Cinco yelped. "Aaah!"

Pherall giggled. "Both," she answered softly.

Cinco danced backward, trying to escape the angry goose. "Oh my God! She's mean!"

Uno's arm lingered, holding her lightly against him. "How are your stitches?"

"What stitches?" she sighed.

"The ones that hurt."

"You're such an asshole."

He chuckled, satisfied, and the two shared a look. "Blue is waiting by the grill with throwing knives," he said softly, then loosened his arm and turned away. "Stay closer. It's too dark over here."

"Hooonk!" shrieked a second goose. "Honk! Hooonk!"

Cinco yelped again. "Oh, damn! There's two of them!"

Blue, standing near the grill, slapped his knee and barked in laughter. "It's the daddy!" he offered, enjoying the show.

Pherall sagged in disappointment, empty without Uno's arm around her, cold without him against her back. No question about it—she had it bad. She turned to follow him with her bundle and smiled at the commotion beside the pond.

"Shit!" Cinco raced along the bank, flapping his arms and bulging his eyes. Hot on his tail was an angry daddy goose, neck stretched, beak chomping. "Get him off! Ow! He's biting me!"

Mama goose joined in, honking and flapping indignant wings. "Honk!"

"What the hell?" cried Cinco, running the other way.

Pherall dropped her load of branches into the woodpile with a giggle and crossed to Blue for her lesson, but he was too distracted to worry about her. Cinco leapt onto the lower branch of a large tree and hung there, legs wrapped, butt hanging.

The geese snapped at him.

He shouted, lifting his rear-end out of reach and shimmying further up the tree.

Blue adjusted his new glasses on his face and laughed merrily. "That's it. I've seen everything. Here," he said, handing Pherall his pack of throwing knives. Smiling wide, he hurried off to help Cinco with the geese.

Uno rolled his eyes in amusement and lounged lazily atop the picnic table with his arms folded behind his head. "Idiot."

Ocho pursed his lips with an air of importance and busily added food to the grill. "Never a dull moment with that moron," he grumbled, gathering empty wrappers and torn meat trays. "Go throw this stuff away, Pherall. There's a garbage can over there by the road."

Pherall took the wadded pile and crossed to a garbage pail, holding Uno's gaze as she passed.

He smiled at her.

Pow!

A pistol shot rang out, and goose feathers went everywhere. "What you muthafukas doing in my park!" screeched an angry voice.

Pherall froze.

The men whirled.

Uno cursed in exasperation.

At the edge of the clearing, a gang of sneering thugs emerged from the trees, one holding a lifted pistol. Unkempt men in mismatched clothing and an assortment of weapons strolled toward the picnic area with menacing scowls and finger symbols that matched the graffiti. Each wore a black bandana, either around his head, over his mouth, or on his clothing. The bandanas were sloppily applied and goofy-looking, consistently enough throughout the bunch to imply intent. One's bandana flopped over his eyes so thoroughly that he had to hold his head back at an ignorant-looking angle to see past the flap.

Pherall noticed around ten gang members but quickly lost count because more were filtering out of the trees. Unsure where to go, she started to move toward Uno, whose back was to her, but he opened his hand to stop her from approaching.

The group was scattered.

Cinco slid out of the tree and stood over the dead goose, his movements smooth and deliberate. Blue stood near the shore of the pond, furthest from the invaders. His steel-gray eyes cut to Uno, watching for a signal. Uno, grumbling beneath his breath in annoyance, stepped warily off the picnic table and eased himself between Pherall and the thugs.

This prompted one gang member to fire off a warning shot that struck the concrete table. "Where you going, white boy?" barked the thug, who was white.

Uno looked at the shot crater, then slow-blinked his gaze to the shooter.

The young man thrust the gun forward, talking tough. "Sit your scrawny ass down."

Uno stayed where he was.

Ocho held up his hands to diffuse the situation. "If you want us to leave, we'll leave," he offered.

The pistol shifted from Uno to Ocho, who was the closest, and the gang leader advanced his men into the picnic area, calling out insults and threatening slurs. The others moved with him, several with weapons. While their attention was diverted, Uno motioned to Cinco and Blue to hold, then flicked a finger behind his leg. He gestured toward the pistol at the small of his back, telling Pherall to get ammo from the truck, which was a good distance away—but not yet.

Aggressive shouting increased as part of the gang circled Ocho and Uno, berating them for using their grill. In their tough-guy frenzy, the gang members lost sight of the other two. While they were focused on Ocho, Uno made a subtle gesture and Cinco dashed into the woods. Blue sidestepped to follow.

He was spotted.

At a signal from their leader, the gang, eager for a fight, attacked.

Uno snatched his pistol from his belt. "Pherall, go!"

Gang members charged forward, dog-piling onto Uno and Ocho. Some went after Blue.

Blue rocketed forward to meet them. Pherall ran for the truck. Uno delivered a violent kick to the closest thug, then shot two holding guns. With a shout, he disarmed another of his weapon and used it on someone else before vanishing inside a circle of flailing arms and legs. After a short struggle, Ocho's entire pile moved, and he fell against the grill. He landed hard on the hot metal, burning his hand and forearm with a shout.

"Aaaah!" An animal scream pierced the park, but not from Ocho.

It was Blue.

Blue saw the burnt flesh and freaked, charging past bowed-up gang members in a mad dash to reach Ocho. Eyes wide with insanity, he leapt, chicken-kicking one in the head, landed, and punched another without slowing his stride. Two more had their skulls cracked together before he got to the melee. Ocho, favoring a burnt hand lined with grill-marks, came up swinging. He wasn't as refined as the others in a fight but landed a few good strikes before vanishing again inside the squirming dog-pile. Blue leapt toward the center, bellowing like a madman. Wild-eyed, he jumped over heads, landed beside Ocho, and began slamming thugs to the ground like a crazy man, screaming and biting chunks of flesh.

Pherall, almost to the truck, stopped suddenly as Ocho and Blue appeared briefly in their fight. In that instant, she saw a thug with a bandana sticking up stupidly from his ear yank a metal pipe high with both hands, his focus on the back of Ocho's head. Without pausing to think, she snatched a knife from her training pack and hurled it.

The pipe fell to the ground with a *twang!* and the attacker sank to his knees, choking on his own blood. Ocho saw him fall and whirled to look at Pherall, who stood gaping, then grabbed a nearby thug and punched him in the face. Blue was still screaming, crushing noses and breaking knees.

Gang members grew angry, and their shouts got louder.

Snapping out of it, Pherall charged for the truck and yanked the door open. Uno's bag was too heavy to lift, so she pulled the five-thousand pound bag onto the seat with a grunt and caught it before it could roll out.

Running feet scattered rocks behind her. "Oh, no, you don't!" shouted a deep voice.

Pherall spun inside the door, clutching Uno's bag, and spotted a thug running straight for her. She shrieked and braced for impact. Before he could tackle her, Cinco darted out of the woods and crashed into him. They slammed together in the open door of the truck in a violent tangle, smashing her backward into the seat. In the chaos of their struggle, Pherall felt Cinco's hand curl into her shirt, and she was thrown sharply away from the fight. She fell hard with the bag.

More gunshots ripped through the park.

Quickly, she scrambled backward, dragging the heavy thing with her, and yanked at the zipper.

Someone screamed.

Another gang member scrambled into Cinco's fight, and the group toppled to the ground together. Cinco grabbed a thug by the back of the head and slammed his face into the frame of the truck, denting it. The gangster dropped and two more approached. Cinco took a strike to the kidneys that knocked him to his knees, giving his attackers the advantage.

"Cinco!" cried Pherall. Warm from adrenaline, she lurched upward with her second knife, reacting on instinct, and stabbed one. As he recoiled from the piercing, she got the next one and jumped back, leaving Cinco with only one opponent, who was proving to be a problem.

"Move!" grunted Cinco.

Pherall scrambled backward, angry now, and heaved the bag toward the rear of the truck. Glancing at the larger fight, she shoved her arm inside the inner pocket and withdrew two magazines. Uno appeared, pistol-whipping the thugs around him, which meant his clip was empty. "Uno!" she shouted.

A man's knee buckled backward. He screamed in response and went down. In the next moment, Uno faced her.

Pherall threw a magazine and reared back to throw the second.

Uno caught the magazine and body-slammed a man trying to tackle him. He was unable to take the second clip, but he had the one. His pistol was about to be loaded. Satisfied, Pherall turned back to Cinco, who landed on the ground atop his opponent, their fists flying. More gang members rushed in to assist, knocking Cinco to the ground.

He needed help.

Pherall snatched her knife up and shoved the handle into Cinco's momentarily outstretched hand, then quickly got out of the way. It wouldn't take him long now to regain control of his fight. In the surge of excitement, random gunshots erupted from the brawl by the grill, startling her. Breathing heavily, she stood up in time to see Blue fall to the ground, bloody and unmoving. "Blue!" she cried out in horror.

Just then, Ocho, beaten and disoriented, stumbled free and fell from a strike, landing just short of the pipe on the ground. Pherall shoved the bag under the truck and took off, determined to get the weapon for him.

"She's arming them!" someone shouted.

Several violent sneering faces charged toward her.

"No!" Ocho lurched to his feet and tackled Pherall, taking her to the ground.

Pherall collapsed under his weight with a cry.

Crawling on his hands and knees, Ocho stuffed her beneath him seconds before the swarm arrived and covered her head with his. An instant later, violent pounding crashed down on his backside—fists, feet, weapons—coming from every direction, ramming him into her, smashing her into the ground. He wrapped his arms around her and squeezed, grunting in pain as he took her beating. She could hear his bones breaking.

Pow!

Pow!

Pow!

Earsplitting shots rang out, slow and methodic.

Pow!

Pow!

Pow!

Moment by moment, the pounding slowed and bodies fell to the ground, each wearing a fresh bullet hole.

Pow!

Pow!

Pow!

As the beating stopped, Ocho's weakened arms loosened and he sagged over Pherall, gasping for breath. "Ocho," she cried, struggling to face him.

Glassy-eyed, he slid off her and rolled onto his broken back, choking on blood.

"Ocho!" Pherall knelt over him. "Oh my God!"

"Pherall!" Uno, still shooting, walked toward her, his hand opened wide.

Pherall threw the second magazine.

The empty clip landed on the ground beside Uno's feet. With a click, he was reloaded.

"Drop the gun," ordered a punk with a weapon trained on Ocho and Pherall, "or I shoot the motherf—"

Pow!

Uno shot the pistol from the thug's hand, then pointed his weapon at Ocho and fired, killing him himself. He kept walking.

The guy blinked at Uno and scrambled backward. "He's crazy," he cried, suddenly frightened. "He's crazy!"

"Run!" someone else shouted.

Rough hands seized Pherall by the arms, and she was hauled backward into a small crowd of remaining gang members. She stumbled against unfamiliar bodies, which quickly pinned her.

"I'll kill the bitch!" one shrieked, trying to put a pistol against her head.

Pow!

The pistol exploded from his hand in a splatter of shrapnel.

As he screamed, Uno rocketed forward and leapt, running sideways against the trunk of two trees, and landed on the man clutching Pherall. Both landed on the ground in a heap.

Uno fired twice, killing him, and lurched backward, knocking Pherall into a tree trunk behind him and pinning her there. Cold eyes and a smoking pistol leveled on the group, which was no longer advancing.

Behind the staring bunch, a sneaky hand retrieved a pistol from the ground.

Uno fired, knocking the gun and a finger from the man's hand. Both went flying. "I win," he said calmly to the remaining few. "Get your asses out of here."

"Who are you?" asked one in a shaky voice.

"Scrawny white boy," said Uno, his weapon trained on the speaker.

Carefully, the men backed away, finally seeing the ground, finally realizing the carnage scattered around the picnic area. They stumbled over the writhing bodies of their friends and quickened their exit. "You won't get away with this," the new leader cried, running now. "You just wait! I'll be back to pop a cap in your ass! You crazy motherf … !"

The insults faded.

In the quiet that followed, Uno turned to Pherall and stood against her with his hand on the tree, unmoving and lost in his own thoughts. She gathered a wad of his shirt in her fist, relieved to have him there. After a moment, he gripped the back of her head and pressed her face against his shoulder but quickly released her. "Are you hurt?"

Pherall shook her head. "They killed Blue," she began with difficulty, "and Ocho—"

"They'll be fine," he promised, lifting his head to look at her.

A glow of moonlight outlined his messy hair. He had a black eye, and his clothes were torn, but he was alive. Pherall was sure he'd never been more handsome, even with the filth, scratches, and blood.

"We have to get out of here," he said, breaking the spell. "Go find my clips and get in the truck. You can drive until Ocho resets."

Pherall nodded.

Behind them, Blue sat up in confusion and saw the bodies lying around him, some moaning, some dead, then touched the muddy blood coating his shirt. "Really!" he barked in irritation.

Uno tucked his pistol away and headed for the well-cooked meal sizzling on the barbecue grill. "Cinco, get Ocho into the truck," he said and quickly gathered their dinner. "They'll be back any minute with more ammo. I want to be gone before they get here."

CHAPTER 14

Rigori looked up at the sound of light knocking on his hotel room door. "Come in, Chetireh."

Chetireh entered slowly. "Mr. Rigori?"

The billionaire reached for a macadamia nut and cracked it. "You let them get away," he said, dropping the shells into a small wastebasket and dusting his fingers, "twice, actually."

Chetireh's eyes glossed in fear, and he hung his blond head. "I vas unable to get past Uno," he answered, near tears.

"You do remember what I said would happen if you failed?"

Chetireh's lip trembled. "I von't fail again, I swear it."

"How many sisters do you have left?"

A tear rolled down his freckled cheek. "Mr. Rigori, please," he whispered.

"Two. Is that right?" Rigori glanced up at him but didn't give him a chance to answer. "You're running low on siblings," he noted, wiping the glossy table free of nut dust. "You started with quite a few."

Soft sobs shook Chetireh's shoulders. "Mr. Rigori."

"Pick one."

Chetireh's knees nearly buckled. "Please!" he cried. "I'm begging you, please! I von't lose her again. I know how Uno fights now. Maxim has scheduled me for training in the morning. I'll be ready next time. I swear I'll be ready. I'll train until I'm ready. Please."

Rigori chewed a nut. "Explain to me why I should be lenient?"

Chetireh, barely able to speak, lifted wet lashes and took an eager step forward. "The mission vasn't a failure. I got the girl's blood," he choked. "They've taken her shirt to the plane and vill analyze it immediately after you land. Dr. Stein is already preparing the lab."

Rigori reached for another nut. "Then, let's hope for good news, Four," he said, cracking it. "Pray for good news."

"Yes, Sir."

"So," continued the old man, "how are you going to find them next time?"

Visibly in check, Chetireh answered with forced calm. "A Jackboot patrol spotted them in an altercation with a gang in a city park. Vhile they vere distracted, the Jackboots vere able to get a low-radius tracker on the truck. Once Uno gets into range of a receiver, it vill signal."

Rigori was impressed. "Good," he smiled. "Get me names, and I'll see that our Jackboot heroes get a bonus."

"They did not survive, Sir."

"Ah. Well, a penny saved is a penny earned, I suppose. Keep me posted."

*****

After the gang attack, Pherall changed her attitude about Ocho. No matter how hard she tried, she couldn't delete the memory of him taking her beating. It played with vivid clarity, over and over. Worse, it took him nearly twenty minutes to reset, which scared her. He was still the same as before, griping and complaining about everything, but now she didn't care. He was Ocho, and she liked him just the way he was, even if he still didn't care much for her. She understood the bond the men shared now. She thought about this for several hours before she fell asleep that night. The next morning, just to pass the time, she thought about it again. By afternoon, she had relived the whole scene from the beginning, passing many more miles recounting the attack before boredom finally set in.

Years and years into their long-ass drive, Pherall could stand it no more and threw herself across Uno's lap. "I'm bored!" she announced dramatically.

It was unusual that Uno sat in the back, but after days and days of staring out the side window, Blue wanted a change of scenery and asked to sit in the front so he could watch impatient cars pass the slower semi-trucks struggling up the hills. Cinco had snuggled against the door for a nap, which placed Pherall in the middle, right beside her beloved.

Uno's brown eyes dropped to hers.

"I'm boooooored! I've got to get out of the truck. I'm gonna die! I'll die if I have to listen to another mile of those awful tires," she crooned, throwing an arm over her forehead.

Ocho checked the rearview mirror. "What the hell is going on back there?"

Blue rolled his head to the side but didn't bother craning his neck to look back. "I dunno," he said in ultimate boredom, "but it sounds serious."

Cinco, who ceased pretending to nap, lifted his brows and peeked at Pherall. "Are those the acting skills you were bragging about?" he wondered with mounting concern. "Because that is awful."

"That's normal. It happens when you have the hots for someone," argued Ocho. "It'll pass."

"No!" Uno said with a jab. "I've had the hots before. This is different. I don't have a damn crush on her."

"What, now you're in love?"

"Yes. I mean, it–it's more than that. It's way beyond just … that," Uno answered, then exhaled to regain his composure. "It's … magnetic or something too. Physical."

"What are you talking about?" demanded Ocho.

Uno shook his head in irritation and gave up trying to explain. "I don't know. I can't describe it," he said, gesturing to shut down the conversation.

"I know what you're talking about," said Blue. "I feel it. When she walks into the room, I can feel it. It's like a buzz or something. I mean, it doesn't make my heart pound, but it's there."

Uno looked at him.

"Me, too," admitted Cinco. "That first day. I noticed it in the alley. I've never felt anything like it. That's why I couldn't leave her with the Jackboots," he said with a small shrug.

"Did it stop?" asked Uno.

Cinco shrugged and made a face. "Mostly. It got better when she got into the truck … when she met you. I barely notice it now."

"That's when it started," said Uno to himself.

A silence passed between them as unexplained pieces fell into place. One by one, they all turned to Ocho.

"I'm immune to witchcraft," sniffed Ocho.

Uno flicked a dry look at him.

Blue's eyes grew wide. "She's a witch?"

Ocho spread his hands matter-of-factly. "Sounds like a hex to me."

"She's not a damn witch, you dumbass. She's a good-looking woman," Cinco told Ocho dryly. "We're a bunch of horny men. It's not hard to figure out what's happening."

Ocho sliced his hand through the air, regaining their attention and negating the pointless argument. "I don't care how she did it. Voodoo witchcraft. Love Potion Number 9. It doesn't matter. Pherall needs to go," he insisted, determined to talk some sense into Uno. "Staying with us will just get her killed. If you love her that damn much, Uno, then you need to hide her somewhere. We have a job to do," he said, emphasizing his point. "You can't rescue Immortals with stars in your eyes."

Uno shook his head, refusing to even humor the idea. "She stays with me."

"Uno!"

Uno's brows snapped high. "Where am I stuttering, Ocho?"

A look of horror stiffened Blue's features. "But what about the other Immortals?" he asked in a small voice.

Uno's eyes cut to the blond. "What *about* the Immortals?"

"They need you," Blue argued. "We have to rescue them."

"I'm not giving up on the Immortals," Uno said with finality. "Pherall is going to help. Keep training her, Blue, especially with the knives."

Blue nodded.

Cinco made a face and shook his head. "Ocho's right, Uno," he admitted reluctantly. "The Jackboots will get her eventually. They'll use her against you. What then?"

"You should have thought about that before rescuing a civilian, Cinco," Uno admonished. "You knew better."

"I'm not the leader," Cinco shot back, pointing to himself. "She was supposed to be my liability, my risk—not yours. If something happens to me, so what? You guys would be fine. It's different for you, Uno. If they use her against you, we're screwed."

Uno acknowledged Cinco's concern with a squint and a nod. It was a serious concern and, for the first time in a long time, he felt doubt. He pondered the dilemma for several seconds, tapping his thumb on his thigh while he considered a solution. His mind was made up, though. "If something happens to me, Cinco, you're in charge," he said, twisting his brows decisively. "Find the other Immortals. Give them a life. Kill anyone who threatens them."

Uno walked away.

Cinco sputtered after him. "What? Wait … Uno. Uno!"

But Uno was done talking. Ignoring him, he strolled across the grass and motioned for Pherall to get into the truck. "Time's up. Let's go."

CHAPTER 15

Pherall didn't know what had transpired among the men, but the ride after that was silent. Only the radio broke the sound of the monotonous rumble of tires humming over the highway. They didn't speak. They didn't look at each other. And Uno kept his hands to himself. Leaving them to their thoughts, Pherall closed her eyes and tried to ignore her stitches. They were almost healed and had begun to itch.

A million miles into their trip to nowhere, the clock struck midnight. It was time to get out of the truck. By unanimous vote, which finally broke the tense silence, they selected a sleepy gas station and made a B-line for the restrooms. Pherall finished quickly and hurried back out. Cinco was there alone, digging through his bag of clothes in search of something clean. "There's nothing!" he complained and flopped down on the seat beside her. "I'm so tired of traveling."

She agreed. "I used to love traveling," she said, leaning her head back on the seat and smiling in recollection. "My brother and I used to travel with our parents. My daddy would go on business trips. If it was someplace cool, he would sneak Korbin and me along, which meant we had to have a separate room. He would pretend he didn't know us, and we got to play grown-up. Oh, the trouble we got into," she laughed. "Korbin was never boring. I could tell you stories."

Cinco sighed in irritation and flopped down in the seat. "Tell me one."

Pherall checked to be sure he was serious, then thought about her favorite. "Well," she began, losing herself for a moment in the memory, "one trip in particular ended up being, like, two weeks long. We kept having to move hotels because daddy was going all over for some inventory thing or whatever, so after a while the hotel rooms started blending together. One night, Korbin and I got into this really stupid argument, and he refused to room with me anymore. So, I got my own room. That night, he gets up out of bed to go to the bathroom and forgets which hotel he's in. He opens a door, thinking it's the bathroom, and finds himself standing in the hallway. He's in his underwear, and that's it," she giggled. "He turns around and *wham!* The door shuts in front of him. He has no idea which room I'm in. So, there he is. No phone. No key. No pants."

Cinco smiled, visualizing.

"So, to get back into his room, Korbin has to go to the lobby, which is conveniently busy, to get a key. The lady at the counter sees him in his underwear. Before the other guests realize he's there, she quickly calls the maintenance man to put him back in his room just to get him out of the lobby. Never checked his name, nothing."

Cinco rolled his head toward her in amusement, watching her tell the story. "Did that really happen?"

Pherall nodded. "Yep. So then, several nights later, at a different hotel, we get into it again over some television show. It's, like, the middle of the night, right. So, all mad and pissed off, he slams down the remote, precedes to remove all but his underwear, and stomps down to the lobby."

Cinco started laughing.

"He knew the room next door was vacant, so he moseys to the maintenance office, tells him the room number, and gets his own room. It was funny until our father found out."

Cinco laughed with her, appreciating the tale, then spotted the others heading for the truck. "Oh, good. They got food."

Ocho slid behind the wheel. Blue and Uno shut the doors and began divvying heat lamp-dried convenience store food. Pherall took an unappetizing-looking chili dog, and Cinco took the microwave burger wrapped in hot plastic. As the meal began, Ocho pulled onto the road toward the crowded interstate and headed for a large city.

About two miles down, Cinco pointed toward an exit. "Pull off here, Ocho," he said without explanation.

Ocho did.

"Take a left. That parking lot there," Cinco said with a point. "Pull in and go around the back."

Pherall's eyes went wide.

As Ocho crossed the back lot, Cinco pressed his nose to the glass and studied the building. He stared intently at a dark room with the curtains pulled open, then sat back in his seat. "Park over there on the side," he said a minute later.

Uno peered out the window at the towering hotel, trying to figure out what in the world the madman was looking at, then frowned at Cinco. A police siren wailed in the distance. Ocho stopped and peered into the rear-view mirror, waiting for an explanation. Beside him, Blue busily recited bad poetry, ignoring everyone.

Without a word, Cinco handed Pherall his hamburger and began removing his clothes.

128

Uno's chewing slowed.

Cinco popped his shoes off and yanked his pants down over his feet, leaving his socks on, then tossed his pants onto Pherall's lap. "Be right back."

She rolled her eyes in amusement but said nothing.

Uno blinked at him, a partial frown twisting his brow.

Wearing only his underwear and a pair of dirty socks, Cinco stepped out of the truck and entered the hotel from the side. When he was gone, Uno turned dubious eyes to Pherall, the only one who was laughing. Five minutes later, Uno's phone rang. After another questioning look at Pherall, he clicked it on and put it to his ear. "Yes?"

Uno's brows flickered, and he handed the phone to Pherall.

"Hello?" she smiled, taking it.

"It worked," laughed Cinco. "Room 304. Bring my pants."
Click.

Pherall laughed aloud and handed the phone back to Uno. "Find a parking spot," she told Ocho. "We're going in."

Cinco, dressed only in his underwear, opened the door with a bow when Pherall knocked. She handed him his pants with a giggle and stepped inside the hotel room. The room was orange and blue, with two queen-sized beds and a small table. It had fat pillows and fat comforters on the beds and fat bathrobes. Everything was clean and smelled nice and, best of all, it wasn't rumbling down the street.

Heaven!

"What in the hell are you two doing?" Uno asked, eyeing them suspiciously as he stepped into the fancy hotel room.

"Taking a break from the road," said Cinco. "I'm going to take a shower."

"I'm next," called Pherall, marking her place in line.

Blue and Ocho hurried inside and flopped onto a bed.

"Third."

"Fourth."

Uno faced her, waiting for an explanation, so Pherall told the story she'd told Cinco. He rolled his eyes at the utter ridiculousness, then sat down on the second bed. "I've seen everything," he muttered to himself and turned on the television.

Five showers and one black and white television show later; it was bedtime.

Ocho and Blue crawled beneath the covers, claiming the bed they were in. Uno and Pherall occupied the second, leaving Cinco standing at the foot of both beds. "You bunch of pigs," he grumbled, scowling at them. "Where am I gonna sleep?"

Blue poked his butt out, and Ocho sprawled his arms and legs, taking up all of the bed space.

"You can sleep with us," Pherall said, fluffing a pillow beside her.

Uno reached across her for the pillow and tossed it to the floor between the beds. "You can sleep on the floor," he said, clicking the television off.

Cinco snatched the pillow up and hit him with it. "I am not sleeping on the floor, asshole," he retorted and marched around the end of the bed. "Push over, Pherall."

Pherall scooted to the middle. Cinco slid in beside her and snuggled in with a satisfied moan. Uno turned off the lamp. The soft hum of blowing air filled the room, filtering the occasional sound of a passing truck or noisy muffler. In the next bed, someone shifted beneath the covers, and the room fell peacefully silent.

A minute or two later, Cinco let out a long sigh of contentment and draped his arm around Pherall. "Oh, wow, you're soft," he muttered dreamily. "I could get used to this."

Uno's eyes popped open in the dark, and he reached for the lamp.

Click.

Light flooded the room.

Cinco cracked an eye open and found Uno sitting up in the bed, lips flattened in annoyance. "What? I'm not gonna touch the important stuff."

Uno lifted Cinco's arm off Pherall and dropped it. "Don't touch anything."

Ocho, who hadn't fallen asleep yet, blinked his eyes from the other bed as if woken from a deep sleep. "You three cut it out over there," he grumbled, not fooling anyone. "We're trying to sleep."

Uno reached for the lamp.

Click.

The light blinked off, and the room fell quiet once more.

Another minute later, Cinco's arm slid around Pherall again and inadvertently touched Uno. "Oops. That wasn't me, Uno. That was her."

Uno's eyes opened again.

"You guys shut up," muffled Blue.

A truck rumbled by, and the silence returned.

Cinco purred a low rumble and folded one arm beneath his pillow. "You smell good," he smiled, nuzzling his nose into her hair.

Pherall yipped and tucked her ear away from him.

"Cinco!" snapped Uno.

"Sorry."

Ocho shuffled beneath his covers. "What in the hell is going on over there?"

"It's all good now," said Cinco sleepily.

The air clicked off.

In the hush that followed, Pherall thought about Number Seven, wondering what he looked like and how long he'd been in captivity. Did he know Uno was looking for him? She hoped so. How horrible it would be to think he didn't know. She imagined what it must be like either way. If Seven knew, he surely wondered what was taking Uno so long; if not, he would certainly be overcome with hopelessness and despair. But Uno was trying. She wished she could let Seven know just so he had something to carry him through his lonely days.

Cinco's voice cut the silence. "No, seriously. Do you have any idea how long it's been since I've slept with a woman?"

Pherall's eyes blinked open.

Click.

Light rocketed through the room.

Uno sat up in the bed and draped his arm over a knee. "Really, Cinco?"

Pherall giggled.

"It was just an observation," Cinco assured, squinting at the bright light and snaking his arm tighter around her.

Uno removed Cinco's arm for the second time and pulled Pherall away from him, intending to position her against himself.

Cinco reached for her. "She was mine first, you thief," he said in accusation and tried to pull her back. "You've had her long enough. From now on, she sleeps with me."

Uno flashed an I-don't-think-so smirk. "You're smoking crack," he accused, then threw the covers aside and got up. With one hand, he took Pherall by the arm; with the other, he hooked her thigh and slid her, squealing, to the outside of the bed, then crawled into the middle between them. "Goodnight, Cinco."

Pherall reached for the lamp.

Click.

The room went dark.

Smiling like a cat, Cinco snuggled close and wrapped an affectionate arm around Uno. "You're not as soft, Unee, but you'll do," he murmured with a deep, shampoo-appreciating sigh.

Uno jabbed an elbow. "Get the hell off me."

Cinco chuckled. "You don't smell as good as Pherall, but you do make a good snugglebunny—oof!" he grunted in pain.

Pherall smiled.

Uno scooted closer to Pherall and draped an arm around her.

Cinco scooted closer to Uno.

The air clicked off, and the room went quiet again.

"That better be your fucking knee," Uno's low voice warned in the darkness.

"I'll take that as a compliment."

Pherall giggled again.

Blue snorted in amusement from the other bed. "Yeah, put that away, Snuffleupagus."

Uno started laughing. "Cinco! Get off me!" he grunted, scrapping with the larger man.

"Will you guys *please* shut up," Ocho grumbled into his pillow.

Pherall tried to hold onto the flailing blankets. "Do I need to separate you two?"

Cinco jerked his head up. "Yes. Let me just get him out of the way."

"No!" Uno countered in amused irritation and slapped at Cinco through the covers. "I don't want Pherall anywhere near you … or your knee. Scoot over, you jackass."

"But Unee."

Click.

Light flooded the room again.

Ocho propped on an elbow, glaring in irritation. "If I have to come over there—"

Blue stood up with a fatigued grunt. "I got it," he sighed and jabbed a thumb at Cinco. "Switch!"

Cinco raised his head, the epitome of innocence, and blinked into the bright light. "What?"

Uno slid backward, pulling Pherall back into the middle, and knocked Cinco out of the bed with a thump. At the same time, Blue slid beneath the covers in front of Pherall.

Cinco stood, clutching his pillow, and pointedly looked at Pherall snuggling comfortably into Uno's arms. "Just so you know," he informed her and sliced his hand through the air, "it's over between us."

Pherall laughed and watched him flop indignantly into the other bed. Amused by their ridiculous antics, she shared a smile with Uno, realizing now why he and Ocho had been so quick to throw a roadblock at Cinco and the sleeping arrangements in those first days. They were right. It would have been bad.

CHAPTER 16

Early the next morning, Pherall gathered everyone's clothes and headed down to the hotel laundry room to start a load of laundry. Humming happily, she checked pockets and dropped everything into the bucket. The machines were industrial strength and, fortunately, washed hard and finished fast. Fifteen minutes later, she was loading the dryer, smiling to herself over the ridiculous antics of the night before. She'd really begun to like all her new companions. They'd gotten off to a rocky start but she knew them now, understood them, and loved them completely. An image of the first moment they'd met played in her mind, but this time the memory warmed her. Just this morning, she'd woken with Uno's arms around her, and just the thought sent a tingle of warmth through her body. She didn't know what it was about him, but she couldn't get enough.

"What in the hell are you doing?"

Pherall whirled in surprise at the sound of Ocho's irritated voice and found him standing in the doorway wearing only a five o'clock shadow and a bathrobe. "Oh! Geez, Ocho," she wheezed in relief and started the machine. "You scared me. I was hoping to be back before you guys woke up."

His cobalt blue eyes narrowed on her. "You left us with no clothes!"

"I know," she said with a point. "They stink. I'm washing them."

He put his hands on his hips, comically stretching the fabric of the robe to look like a dress. "How long is that supposed to take?"

Pherall giggled, but wisely kept her thoughts to herself. "About thirty minutes," she said, taking a seat beside the machine. "The breakfast buffet is open. While this is drying, help me gather some food and bring it up."

Ocho spread his hands, indicating his ridiculous garb.

"Oh, fuss and stuff. Nobody cares," she said, pulling him to the buffet bar.

There were fruits, cereals, bagels, eggs, fried potatoes, and bacon, cartons of milk, yogurt, and biscuits.

Pherall quickly piled food high onto three separate plates and stacked them. Ocho had the same idea. Loaded with food, Pherall turned to bring the plates up to the room and found herself face to face with the hotel maintenance man just strolling into the buffet kitchen.

The man, a forty-something salt-and-pepper dressed in a navy blue uniform and sporting a bushy, graying mustache, stopped short looking past her to Ocho who was adding more bacon. Instantly, his face paled. "Jayce?" he whispered in surprise, staring hard at Ocho. "Jayce Ruxton?"

Ocho went rigid.

"Jayce," the man repeated in breathless hesitation, moving to Ocho's front for a better look, "it *is* you!"

The bacon crumbled in the tongs. Not breathing, Ocho flicked a glance at the man, then quickly snapped his panicked gaze to Pherall, clearly caught off guard.

The gentleman shook his head in utter disbelief. "Jayce … I don't understand. You–you died," he said in confusion.

Pherall blinked at the maintenance man, then at Ocho in surprise. "¿Alejandro, quién es este hombre? Lo conoces?" she asked in quick Spanish, wondering who this guy was and if Ocho knew him.

Ocho lifted a shaky shoulder. "No lo conozco, pero piensa que me conoce," he replied in obvious difficulty, claiming he didn't, but the man thought he knew Ocho.

Batting baffled lashes, Pherall leaned to look at him. "¿Hablas español, señor?"

He shook his head at her, then frowned at Ocho. "I've known you my whole life, Jayce. You can't tell me—"

"Lo siento. Esto es Alejandro," she apologized, insisting Ocho was Alejandro, not Jayce. Smiling politely, she took Ocho by the hand and pulled him toward the elevator.

The maintenance man stared. "I miss you, Jayce," he said with a crack in his voice. "Every day … I miss you."

Ocho stared back.

Pherall pushed the elevator button, selecting the third floor, and the silver doors slid shut.

Safe inside the elevator, Ocho jerked his head away and exhaled heavily. "Dammit!" he cursed in English, visibly shaken.

"Do you know him?" she asked softly.

Quick, jerky hands scraped at the tears on his cheeks and he faced the elevator wall in embarrassment. After a moment, he nodded. "That was Chet. We grew up together," he choked, snapping his head away and his eyes up in attempt to stop a flow of tears, but it didn't work. "He was my best friend. I thought they killed him."

Pherall pushed the button to stop the elevator and gave him a minute to compose himself. "You miss him?"

Ocho exhaled heavily and laughed, a sour sound. "I miss them all," he corrected in a thick voice.

"At least you know he's alive," she said gently, "and he still loves you."

Ocho flashed a sad smile, then shook his head. His voice was resigned. "It makes it worse. Knowing he's alive makes … ," he thumped his heart and exhaled again as a fresh round of tears rolled down his cheeks. "I want them back."

Pherall left him alone. While she waited, she thought about her family and the friends she would never see again and felt a pang of sadness. This was a hard life. She was just getting started, but Ocho had lived it for years. To say he was homesick was an understatement. The shock on his face upon seeing Chet was all the proof that was needed. Suddenly, she understood why he painted himself so mean and unapproachable. He wasn't like that at all, and it made her heart hurt.

After a couple minutes, Ocho shook himself and cleared his throat, his composure in check once more. When he was ready, he gave a small nod indicating he was again in control. Pherall pushed the button and the elevator continued to their floor. When they arrived at the room, she shoved the food into Blue's hand. "Wake the others."

"What's going on?" he asked, noticing Ocho's red eyes.

"We're compromised. I'll be right back," she said, slinging fine, blond hair over her shoulder, and hurried to the laundry room to get their clothes.

Ten minutes later, they were in the battered red pickup truck and on their way again, buffet food in hand.

Ocho was quiet the rest of the day.

*****

Rigori stumbled into the conference room in his bathrobe and slippers and shuffled to his overstuffed chair at the head of the table. His usually pristine white hair stood on end, giving his head a lopsided look. With a loud groan, he took his seat and scratched his head. "What in the world is so important that I have to be dragged out of my warm bed?" he demanded with a crooked sniff.

Dr. von Stein slapped a drumbeat onto the table, bright-eyed and energetic. A large smile split his skinny face. "Love the lab! Love the lab," he announced. "Just throwing that out there."

On the table sat a monitor with a small image of Maxim who was busily adjusting the video screen from his location hours away, also looking shaggy and unshaven.

Dimitri sat forward in his seat, as fresh and bright-eyed as if he'd just stepped out of the shower. "Can you hear us, Maxim?"

"Yeah," yawned Maxim. "I can hear."

"Can you see ze video screen behind Rigori?"

"Yes. Yes."

"Good." Dimitri stood and reached for the pointer. "I will get right to it. Ze blood sample Four collected from ze girl has been analyzed and found to be positive for ze protein."

Rigori sat up straight. "She's an Immortal?"

"Yes and no," said Dimitri with a slight bow. "Females are very different from ze males. I will show you video."

The lights lowered and an old experimentation video flickered on. Muted screams and thrashing from a gagged black girl strapped to a table filled the room. Dimitri spoke over her. "In ze twenty years we have known of ze Immortals, only one female has ever been found positive for ze protein. Needless to say, zey are extremely rare."

Rigori jerked forward in his seat and gripped the arms. "What! You have a female!"

Dimitri shook his head and gestured towards the screen. The video resumed playing and the audience watched the medical procedure with rapt attention. However, in the middle of the operation, the screams and thrashing came to a stop and the medical team stared at the patient—at first patiently, then in alarm.

The girl was dead.

A time stamp at the bottom corner sped up, showing progression of time, but the patient didn't reset. Clearly panicking, the medical team frantically tried to revive her. Despite all their efforts, she remained unresponsive.

A voice on the video screeched in outrage. A man with a gun shouted at the Russian medical team as the videographer circled the dead body. The bloody operators whirled in horror, pleading and throwing out their hands. Screams and gunfire blended together and faded, and the video blinked off.

Dimitri continued. "Ve expected her to reset after death, but she didn't." He clapped his hands together and altered his tone for the explanation. "With our first female, ve immediately became interested in reproduction of Immortals and stem cell research. Her eggs also proved positive so ve extracted some. Ze extraction process destroyed ze protein, so we tried again using a different procedure. Ze second procedure failed, so ve tried putting some eggs back. As you can, see she did not survive zat operation. We made every effort to bring her back, but we lost her. Ze only female specimen ever found did not reset. Ze female Immortals are not immortal."

The audience listened in unblinking silence.

"Ze good news is in ze short time she was in custody, we learned a lot about Immortals. Ze males were strongly attracted to ze female, not necessarily sexually but more as an awareness of her, whereas ze female could actually detect ze males from a distance. Both subtle connections entirely undetectable by our equipment … until," he emphasized with a point, "ze alpha padonak appeared," he said, using the Russian word for scum. "Ze connection between ze two was instantaneous and quite physical. Once zey came in contact, an unbreakable, physical bond formed. Ze purpose of zis bond is still unstudied; however, it is significant enough zat when she died, her Immortal mate died too. We called her a Queen." He paused, looking around at the others, then lowered his voice to indicate the significance of his point. "Uno's female is a Queen."

Maxim fumbled clumsily with a phone, his shoulders rising and falling with each breath. "Wake up! Get up!" he hissed, holding it to his ear. "I don't care what time it is. Shut down the bounty on the girl! Do it now," he ordered. "Move her to classified."

Doctor Stein squealed and jumped out of his seat, clapping his hands. "I want her. Oh! Bring her to me! Rigori!"

Rigori could barely speak. He pointed at the small monitor, shaking his finger. "Maxim," he exhaled, his eyes bulging with excitement. "Who is she! What is her name?"

Maxim's face pressed against the screen. "Ten," he said breathlessly.

A frown darkened Dimitri's light features. "A tracker was placed on ze truck, right?"

Rigori nodded. "Those were part of the instructions."

The Russian gestured, pleased. "Where are zey?"

Maxim, distracted by the amazing news, shuffled around his desk for a moment, then picked up an electronic tablet. After a few moments, the screen he wanted popped up. "According to this," he said, taking a moment to study the screen, "they're heading west toward the coast. In fact, they're right down the—Oh, shit!"

CHAPTER 17

When Pherall woke the next morning, the sun was rising, but clouds blocked the view. They were deep in rolling mountains covered in thick, broad-leafed vegetation. Red, orange, and yellow leaves blended with persistent green, creating a panoramic painting that opened at the top of every hill. Thick clouds hovered in the valleys in mystical puffs. All that was missing were dragons and hobbit huts. This amused her for a while until a rogue turn into a wooded forest snapped her from fantasyland. The road darkened. Now, they were heading for a witch's shack made of candy. By the time Uno, Cinco, and Blue woke another hour later, it was drizzling. Ocho, looking haggard and tired, pulled over to the side of the road. "The sky is about to open up. If you gotta go, go now."

Pherall made quick use of a bush and hurried back. Unable to find a ponytail holder, she twisted her hair up into a sloppy bun. It was cool out, so she dug a large blue shirt from Cinco's bag and pulled it on over her clothes to warm up. Moments later, heavy rain drops pelted the windshield, blending a pitter-patter with the scrape of the wipers.

Cinco, whose hair always looked freshly brushed, yawned and peeled an orange left over from the hotel buffet. "So, what's the plan for tonight, Unee?" he asked, stretching his long legs and popping a wedge into his mouth. "Want some?"

Uno took a chunk of Cinco's orange and opened his atlas. Today, he wore Pherall's long sleeve t-shirt. His hair was a disaster, but it worked well on him. "I saw this spot marked on a wall map at the last base, but there's no compound listed in this area," he said, touching the page. "There may be a secret Jackboot base around here somewhere. I think that's where they're holding Seven. I want to take a look."

"How's our ammo," asked Cinco with his mouth full.

"We're low, so it'll have to be a low-key operation," said Uno.

"Either that or we steal more."

Uno nodded. "The easiest way would be to get a few Jack suits and search at our leisure."

"Or raid another weapons cache."

Uno made a face. "We hit this one once before," he said, tapping the page. "It won't be as easy the second time."

Bored silly, Pherall allowed the sound of their voices and the unbelievably boring conversation to lull her into a daydream. She'd been building daydreams for a few days and had gotten pretty good at it. Focusing her creative mind, she summoned a new daydream and pictured it clearly:

She and Uno sitting over a romantic, candle lit dinner ... spaghetti—no! lasagna ... gazing deeply into each other's eyes. Gently, he takes her fingers in his and stands ... he's wearing a tux —gasp! They've just gotten married—and pulls her to the dance floor in her wedding gown. To soft music, they sway lightly back and forth, more in love with each step.

Pherall sighed.

Sweet music envelopes them in a world of their own. Nobody else exists. Only them. They were on a beach now—their honeymoon! Waves crash against their feet. With love in his eyes, Uno lowers his head and ... and ...

Pherall blinked out of her daydream, frowning, and sat up sharply. "Uno," she began uneasily and scanned the trees blurring by.

Uno lifted his head, letting his attention linger on the map. "Mm hmm?" he frowned, then looked at her.

"Someone's nearby."

Uno flicked a glance at Ocho through the rearview mirror, gesturing for him to halt. "Someone?"

The truck bumped off the asphalt and jerked to a stop in a rocky puddle.

"Yes." Pherall sat forward in her seat and peered across Uno into the thick woods. They were in the middle of nowhere, she reminded herself, but the sensation remained. "I'm positive," she whispered.

Uno pressed his nose to the rain-dotted window, scanning up and down the soggy road, and stopped on a set of dirt tracks not far behind the truck. The tracks, bare stripes in the grass, curved away from the asphalt, and vanished behind a thick patch of bushes, so subtle it was barely visible. With quick hands, he dropped the atlas to the floor and unzipped his backpack. "Ocho, hide the truck. Pherall, put your shoes on," he ordered, digging weapons out. He shoved a snub-nose machine gun into Cinco's outstretched hands and pulled a rolled ammunition belt out after it.

Ocho drove over brush and nosed the truck behind some trees, careful to position it for a quick exit.

Part of the ammunition belt, which was heavy as hell, thumped across Pherall's lap and she gaped at it. Frowning, she scowled at the backpack, wondering how in the world all of Uno's whammy kablamy stuff fit inside. It was like a weaponized clown car. Baffled, she put on her shoes.

Cinco quickly draped the belt around his shoulders.

Uno strapped blades to his ankles, wrists, and waist, then shoved spare ammo magazines into one pocket and a grenade in the other. "Someone has to watch Pherall," he said, glancing up at Ocho and Blue. "The other fights. Choose."

Blue snatched the pistol from Uno's hand. "They froze my ass. I'm fighting," he growled, grabbing clips from the backpack. "Gimme grenades too."

"Are you serious!" Ocho exclaimed, snapping furious eyes to Pherall and twisting around in his seat. "I have to babysit?"

Uno handed him a very long rocket launcher and ammunition for his pistol. "Stay out of the fight," he instructed. "Don't lose her."

"Uno!"

Uno shoved an RPG into Ocho's hands, knocking him backward into the steering wheel. "*Don't* lose her," he repeated.

Ocho cursed quietly and motioned Pherall to follow. "Come on," he grumbled, getting out.

Embarrassed to be the focus of such an argument, Pherall slid out of the truck after Cinco, who reached past her to the floorboard for his hoodie. "Let me help," she said, waiting for him to stand so she could close the truck door.

The rain was cold.

Cinco yanked the hoodie down over Pherall's head. "No," he said simply, ignoring the rain soaking his clothes. "You'll get in the way."

Pherall straightened the hoodie and scowled at him.

Uno came around the truck, his black ballcap pulled low over his eyes, and stopped in front of her. "Stay out of sight," he said, then pulled his pistol from his waistband and handed her the gun and a spare magazine. "If you need it, use it. Let's go."

The group darted into the rain in the direction of the tracks, keeping several feet apart, their expressions drawn with focus. Maintaining low profiles, they moved through the soggy woods for about a half mile before a small, fenced compound came into view. A double razor-wire fence lined the top, one side leaning outward toward the woods to keep people out, and another leaning inward toward the compound to keep people in.

Hot adrenaline burned through Pherall's veins, giving her a small taste of what the others must have felt. It was a sensation she was unfamiliar with, but feeling it made her want in on the action. Ocho found a high point in the ground near the tire tracks and pulled Pherall down into the mud. Buried among the grass and brush, he readied the rocket launcher. Uno, Cinco, and Blue eased toward the compound.

"How are they going to get through the fence?" she asked, trying unsuccessfully to clear water from her eyes.

Ocho sighted in the launcher with a squint, then raised his head. "As secret as this place is, I'd imagine they already know we're here. If not, the moment our boys touch that fence, alarms will go off, whether we hear them or not. Best way to get in is to just ring the doorbell."

Uno threw a grenade and ducked.

Pow!

The magnetic gate shattered and swung open.

"Ding dong," Ocho sang and peered through the scope.

Instantly, machine gun fire erupted from the compound, preventing Uno, Cinco, and Blue from entering through the massive hole in the fence.

"Yep. They knew we were coming," Ocho said and fired a rocket.

The rocket took off, struck the front face of a building, and exploded in a fireball of debris. A fog of black smoke billowed out, engulfing the compound. Jackboots scattered for new hiding places, giving the gunfire a momentary break. Uno, Cinco, and Blue charged in during the lull and vanished into the smoke. Pained screams and rapid gunfire erupted moments later from inside the compound.

*****

Drab buildings with no distinguishing characteristics were clumped together, each with a metal front door and locked round knob. Narrow foot-trails crisscrossed back and forth between them. Agents poured out of one, keeping Cinco busy and indicating it was likely the barracks. Blue darted to the next building and blasted the lock off. Uno leapt over a slump of dying bodies and moved in the direction the Jackboots defended the heaviest. From both sides, soldiers flanked the building.

Blue hummed happily, firing off shots. "That's for putting me in the freezer, assholes."

144

Uno saw a figure drop into position on the roof of the building he was heading toward. As he ran, he wiped slippery blood from the hilt of his knife and threw it, earning an 'Oof!'

The body fell into a puddle and Uno charged toward it.

More Jackboots piled around the farthest building, peppering the muddy walkway between buildings with bullets. Uno felt a sharp sting on the left side of his ribs and grunted through his teeth. The Jackboots were too thick to break through, forcing him to find cover. In a flash of blinding pain, he redirected his charge to the edge of the nearest building and fell against the wall. Grimacing sharply, he pressed his hand to a wound on his side.

There was a hole in his lung.

Uno sucked in deep breaths, giving his body a moment to heal. He could feel his ribs and lung trying to repair themselves, which really freaking hurt.

The sound of helicopter starting hummed through the gunfire.

"Dammit." He didn't have time to heal. "Blue!" he called. "Get me in there."

Blue, singing opera as he fired, shot in random patterns around the building, allowing Uno to advance. Uno took off, clinging to his side and breathing in shallow breaths. Behind him, he could hear Cinco in a fistfight, which meant he was out of ammo and needed to gather more.

With a flying kick, Uno smashed his foot beside the already busted lock, gasping a foul curse at the pain that resulted, and flew through the door. Clutching his knife, he hurried into the small building and skidded to a stop, slinging rainwater. Inside, he found an active lab, a table with leather restraints, and an open cell with a breakfast food-tray spilled on the floor.

Thud!

Somewhere ahead, a door slammed, echoing across the empty building.

Hauling ass, Uno charged toward the back exit and burst out in time to see a helicopter lifting off the ground. "Seven! Goddammit!" he roared, watching it go. "I'll find you!"

A sharp voice shouted and, suddenly, the entire bunch of Jackboots scattered and dove to the ground.

Before Uno could react, the building he had just exited exploded, knocking him forward in a splash of debris. Seconds later, another building blew, and then another, sending Cinco backward and burying Blue in a thunderous blast.

"Move, move, move!" shouted a commanding voice.

Jackboots climbed to their feet and raced forward to apprehend the temporarily dead Immortals.

On the hill, Ocho snapped his head up and jumped to his feet, his eyes widened in horror. "Pherall!" he choked in alarm. "Stop them!"

Without further instruction, Ocho tore off in the direction of the torn gate.

Pherall, reacting entirely on instinct, darted forward to a tree just outside the fence and lifted Uno's pistol. Without thinking, without remorse, she began firing at anyone wearing a black uniform. From where she stood, she could see the mounds of debris covering Cinco and Blue and guarded both. One by one, she picked the thugs off.

At the second wave of attacks, the Jackboots, unsure how many snipers were present, ceased their attempt to reach the dead Immortals and took defensive positions. From new hiding places, they fired their machine guns toward the perimeter fence, searching for the sniper.

Pherall ducked behind the tree, trembling violently and wiping rainwater from her eyes.

Moments later, new gunshots erupted from the other side of the compound, meaning Ocho was coming around through the gate. Pherall leaned her head out and fired again, backing the few remaining militants away, while Ocho dug Cinco out and dragged him from the rubble.

The Jackboot commander called an abort, taking the opportunity to flee while the Immortals were still down.

Pherall watched, pistol high, for any trying to sneak back. During a short lull, she reached into her pocket for a fresh clip and, her eyes pinned on her targets, dropped the clip and reloaded it with a snap.

Thwak!

A sound from behind startled her and she whirled in time to see a Jackboot stiffen and fall forward, a knife in his throat, a syringe in his hand. He flopped to the ground at her feet. She jolted in surprise and spun toward a bloody Uno, his wet hair muddy from dust and debris. He was coming around a corner of the fence, another knife poised to throw in his filthy hand.

Stepping carefully, he watched a spot past her head, his expression dark. A silky thread of warning softened his tone. "Walk away and I let you live," he said to a point directly behind her shoulder, so close it seemed as if he was speaking to her.

Careful not to move, Pherall slid her eyes to the side and saw a black figure shift. With precision slowness, the Jackboot lowered his weapons—a pistol and a burlap sack—to the ground and stood with his hands up.

"Get out of here," said Uno.

Sloshing footsteps indicated the man was retreating.

Keeping dangerous brown eyes on the Jackboot, Uno took the pistol from Pherall and gestured to the clip at her feet. Quickly, he gathered weapons from the scene and pulled her through the open gate. Inside, he directed her toward a parking lot full of black trucks. "We need a vehicle," he said, stuffing a key-fob into her hand. "This goes to one of those. Push-button start. Find it."

Pherall hurried to the jeeps, pushing the start-switches until she found the correct one and backed it out. By the time she reached the drive, Uno was dragging Cinco and Ocho was fireman-carrying Blue, whose leg had been blown off. Mimicking Uno's prior behavior during the vendor truck heist, she remained in her seat and waited for them to load the bodies. Both left for another trip. Uno ran into the compound and came back within minutes, his arms full of munitions. Ocho darted for the mound where he'd left the RPG and came back with the launcher and the one remaining round.

Pherall drove the jeep to the road.

When they reached the red pickup truck hidden behind the patch of trees, Uno motioned to Ocho, who jumped out and ran to the driver's side. He watched from the passenger mirror as Ocho pulled forward, then gave Pherall a nod to go. Traveling together, both trucks were taken to an empty gravel lot and, under Uno's watchful eye, all the loot and both bodies were transferred into the red pickup truck.

They were all soaked.

Ocho reclaimed the steering wheel and pulled out, leaving the jeep. In the passenger seat, Uno restuffed his backpack, loaded empty magazines, and quickly organized their weapons with practiced hands. While he was busy, Pherall crawled into the backseat with the two dead bodies and tended to them, cleaning them off and positioning them more comfortably. She reached down to adjust Blue's budding new leg, which was twisting beneath the seatbelt strap. At the touch, Blue startled sharply awake and lurched forward with a shout, knocking Pherall into the back of Ocho's driver seat.

In one motion, Uno whirled over the bench seat, grabbed him by the throat, and slammed him backward. "Blue!" he barked.

Blue jolted in surprise and recoiled. "Uno!" he cried, breathing through his teeth and passing glossy eyes at his unfamiliar surroundings. "Where am I?"

"In the truck," said Uno, still holding him. "It's over."

Blue looked at Pherall, angled awkwardly against Ocho's seat, and made a face. "Aw, shit—are you okay?" he began, helping her off Cinco's lap.

Uno let him go and returned to his weapons.

Blue's leg tried to thicken against the seatbelt strap, and he grunted sharply in pain.

Pherall helped him loosen it. "I'm fine," she said, shaken but not angry. "I was just cleaning you off. You lost your leg."

"Damn that hurts!" Blue hissed, watching the leg reform. When it was finished and had gone through a thorough motions check, he glanced around, then peeked into the back of the truck. "Did we get Seven?"

"No," said Uno.

"The helicopter was out of my range," Ocho said apologetically. "I should have moved closer."

Uno shook his head. "That wasn't a planned attack. It is what it is. We'll find him."

Pherall fussed over Cinco next. His eyes had closed, finally, which meant he was alive again, but he still didn't respond when she wiped his face dry. "How long until he wakes?" she asked over her shoulder.

"Another minute or so after he starts breathing," said Uno without looking up. "He's pretty slow."

"I'm awake," Cinco mumbled painfully without opening his eyes. "That broke my spine. It's still mending. It hurts."

Blue nodded, knowing all about what hurt. "I'm hungry and I'm cold."

Uno dropped a handful of empty magazine clips into the side pocket of his backpack and placed the loaded ones inside with the other weapons, then zipped the bulging bag. "Detour north away from this road," he said to Ocho. "Find food and a thrift store for clothes. We need to get the hell out of here before they retaliate."

*****

Maxim seethed in outrage. "How did they find that base!" he shouted, glaring at the video camera and thrusting his finger. "That location is classified! I want to know what asshole—"

"Maxim." On the tiny screen, Dimitri adjusted a pair of glasses on his nose and smiled. "I told you," the Russian said haughtily.

148

"Zey have a Queen. With her, it is only a matter of time before zey locate all ze Immortals. If you have any more hidden, you should relocate zem now."

Maxim drew himself up angrily. "Seven wasn't hidden from you," he retorted, offended by the accusation. "I've been entirely upfront about him."

"Zen why is he not here on ze island?" demanded the Russian. "It seems to me as if you wanted to keep him for yourself."

Maxim's eyes narrowed and his voice lowered to snake-speak. "How many do you have hidden, Dimitri!" he demanded.

Dimitri didn't answer.

Maxim sat forward in disbelief. "You have more Immortals!" he accused incredulously. "You do, don't you!"

Rigori interrupted the men in irritation. "Gentlemen, this argument is irrelevant at this point. I am not interested in listening to it further," he said, waving the men silent. "Seven's previous location has been discovered—"

"Destroyed," Maxim corrected angrily.

"—and he is in route now. Let's move on," said the billionaire.

"But he has more Immo—"

"Maxim! Is Four in your custody?"

"Yes."

"And you are still tracking the location of Uno's Immortals?"

"Yes."

"Good. Stand by for instructions …"

*****

Before they could go anywhere to get food, the group needed clothes. A thrift store was located and Ocho and Pherall, the only two who weren't bloody, got to do the shopping. For Cinco, Pherall was unable to find a pair of jeans in his size, but she did find a black athletic suit with a string tie at the waist and a matching jacket. Blue scored a pair of baggy black sweats, another thick hoodie, and a pair of shoes. She and Uno wore new jeans, simple t-shirts, and light jackets.

Dressed in their new digs, they found a hole-in-the-wall convenience store with a concession booth and filed in for something to eat. A chalkboard sign near the counter boasted fresh fish as the sale item of the day. The man behind the counter, wearing a stained apron stretched taught over an enormous belly, faced them with a grunt. "What can I do fer ya?" he said heavily and reached for a dead fish lying on a cleaning tray. With the other hand, he picked up a cleaver and *Whack!* chopped the fish's head off.

They all saw it.

Blue jumped violently, toppling a display rack, and snapped. Eyes bulging, he slapped for his weapon and charged the man, breathing loudly through clenched teeth. Ocho jerked Pherall out of his path, nearly throwing her into a set of shelves. Cinco caught Blue in a headlock and jerked him sharply toward the floor. By now, Blue had the gun. Uno dropped to a knee and twisted, disarming him with a strike and quickly stood out of reach with the pistol. Blue, hissing loudly through his teeth, struggled wildly to reach the wide-eyed cook with the cleaver.

"Take him outside," Uno told Cinco, tucking the pistol into the waistband of his own pants and looking up again at the menu board. "Pherall, we're gonna need another bag of rice. Use that microwave," he said, gesturing to his left.

Cinco hauled the purple-faced Blue backward through the door, leaving a trail of debris behind them.

The man slowly set the cleaver down. "Sorry … about that," he said in apologetic embarrassment.

"PTSD," Ocho explained with a nonchalant wave. "We'll take one—wait—two of everything you have on the menu, five sodas— no ice—and that box of cookies."

"Not the fish," said Uno, stepping toward the register to pay.

Blue was better once he got a cookie and a warm rice sock.

Pherall had never seen anyone eat the amounts of food that these men put away after a death. All of them gorged themselves silly and licked their fingers clean. And there Pherall sat with her puny little burger and her small pile of fries, which were still threatened by a glance from Blue.

"You gonna eat those?" he'd wondered, sliding one from the package.

Fed and clothed, they moved quietly down the road, too tired even for the radio. They were all drained of energy, including Pherall, and eager to find somewhere to sleep.

"Where should we stop?" asked Ocho.

"It doesn't matter where," yawned Uno. "Just find a parking lot or something."

An hour later, Ocho pulled into an industrial area and nosed the pickup behind a massive warehouse surrounded by work trucks. Slipping between some, he cut the engine, leaned his seat back, and closed his eyes.

Uno looked over the bench seat at Pherall.

Cinco hooked a possessive arm around her and tipped her over, so she lay against him. "Good night," he groaned happily.

Uno's smirk lacked amusement.

Blue drew his hood tight around his head and stuffed his rice socks into his pockets. "Wanna trade with me, Uno?"

To Cinco's disappointment, Uno got out, switching seats with Blue, and dropped his backpack into the floorboard. "Get off her," Uno said, giving him a knuckle-thunk on the head.

In the manner of someone who had done this before, Uno leaned diagonal between the seat and the door and stretched his legs across to the opposite floorboard. Pherall snuggled against him in the seat with Cinco's head in her lap. It was the most uncomfortable arrangement she'd ever snuggled into; nevertheless, she was happy. Wrapped tight in Uno's arms, she went still, smiling to herself as the men fell sleep.

CHAPTER 18

The next day brought the group closer to the coast. It was raining again and chilly outside. Blue was driving while Ocho attempted to doze in the passenger seat with his arms folded over his chest. Everyone else was sprawled across the backseat in an uncomfortable tangle of knees and elbows.

"How much longer?" asked Pherall with a yawn.

"We'll be there in an hour," Blue said, switching the irritating radio off. "It's on the other side of these mountains."

Uno adjusted his legs with a groan and brushed messy hair from his face. "Start watching for an impound lot," he said over the squawk of windshield wipers. "We've had this truck too long."

Blue gave a backward glance at Pherall through the rearview mirror. "Next vehicle," he told her matter-of-factly, "I'm teaching you to remove the ignition switch. Then, once we get where we're going, it'll be hand to hand combat."

Pherall sat forward and folded her arms over the bench seat. "Ooh," she smiled, looking forward to it, "and in exchange, I'll teach you Pig Latin."

Blue made a face and snapped a dirty look at her. "What?" he scoffed in disgust. "I already know how to speak Pig Latin. Everyone knows how to speak Pig Latin. Teach me to dance."

Pherall brightened, absolutely thrilled by the idea, and gave him a shoulder bump. "I know several styles of dance. What kind are you interested in?"

Blue blinked into the rearview mirror at all the eyes shifting his way and gave Pherall a sidelong glance. "I'm not gonna say," he grumbled, giving the extremely interested Cinco a scowl through the mirror.

Ocho, who was doing a terrible job of pretending to sleep, tossed a knowing look to the backseat. "He wants to learn ballroom dancing!" he blabbed, then folded his arms and resumed trying to get comfortable.

Cinco hooted in hilarity and slapped his knee. "Ballroom? No way! I will pay money to see Blue tango. Hahaha!"

Uno smiled. "I insist he have a flower in his mouth."

"Hey!" Blue barked, adding manly baritone to his offended retort. "There is nothing wrong with ballroom dancing," he informed the snickering idiots. "Ocho, *you* are an ass. From now on, I'm not telling you—"

Ka-boom!

An explosion blew a hole into the asphalt beside the front tire, nearly knocking the truck from the road. The truck fishtailed, spilling everyone violently into locked seatbelts.

"Shit!" Blue cursed, stomping on the gas and squalling the truck around the crater. Massive chunks of asphalt and dirt pummeled the pickup, caving part of the roof in and shattering all the windows on the driver's side. "Lord, what fools these mortal Jackasses be!" he recited, loudly misquoting Shakespeare and ducking the blast of cold air. "This is very early morning madness."

Cinco, tangled in his seatbelt, crawled up from the floorboard. "Helicopter! Six o clock!" he shouted, twisting to pull his pistol from his waistband.

Uno grabbed his backpack. "They were waiting at the base too. There's gotta be a tracker on the truck. Get off the road, Blue."

Blue jerked the wheel, angling the vehicle down a steep hill, and eased into the woods in search of some cover. Uno pulled a pointed grenade from his backpack and thrust it on Pherall's lap, while Blue swerved between trees and bounced over bushes. Flopping in his seat, Uno pulled the long RPG launcher out from behind the seat and loaded it.

Rapid machine gunfire peppered the forest behind them before striking the bed of the truck.

Everyone ducked.

Cinco grabbed Pherall and yanked her beneath him, but the gunshots stopped before reaching the cab. "Why'd they stop?" he asked in hesitant alarm.

They'd all noticed.

"That's unusual," Ocho agreed, trying to peer up from the intact passenger side window.

Uno busted out the back glass with the butt of his weapon, knocked the broken cubes away, and crawled into the bed of the truck with the grenade launcher.

"What light through yonder back windshield breaks?" Blue wondered in Old English accent.

Lying on his back, Uno aimed as the helicopter circled around. "Hold, Blue!"

Blue slid the truck to a stop.

Squinting into the rain, Uno launched the grenade.

It exploded near the rotors.

"Blue, go!" called Uno. "To the right! To the right!"

Blue jerked the truck forward and to the right in a spray of mud.

The helicopter sheered sideways to the left and spun over the trees to the other side of the road. There was a spray of leaves and —*Crash!*—the mangled helicopter tumbled down the side of a mountain.

Blue regained control of the pickup near the edge of the hill overlooking the colorful valley. Through the trees, a panoramic view opened up before them, and what a sight it was! Stretched out in the cloudy valley below were military trucks, another helicopter, police cars, and Jackboots on motorcycles—all waiting for them.

"Shit." Blue skidded the truck to a stop, smashing Uno against the cab in a clatter.

"Oh, damn," Ocho murmured hesitantly, his arms braced wide against the seat and dash. "That's … a lot of Jackboots."

Ka-Blam!

The downed helicopter reached the bottom of the hill and exploded in a fireball, announcing their arrival and setting gigantic offensive into motion. Shouts and the roar of engines erupted from the valley.

"Back up! Back up!" shouted Ocho.

Blue threw the gear in reverse. "These violent delights have violent ends," he continued, bending his neck to look backward beneath the very puckered roof. "Methinks this will not end well."

"Give me the C4!" Uno said, smacking his palm against the truck cab to encourage haste.

Cinco pulled partially built explosives from the bag and passed them back through the missing window.

Working quickly, Uno wired a bomb with expert hands. "Stop the truck. Everybody get out," he ordered. "Blue, pop the hood."

The doors opened.

Uno ran to the front of the truck and lifted the lid. Shaking rainwater from his eyes, he set the plastic explosives deep inside, armed them, and slammed the hood shut again. "I'll take this to the road and meet you at the bottom of the hill," he instructed, grabbing a football-sized rock and running towards the driver's side.

Ocho caught him. "I got this Uno. Get Pherall outta here," he said climbing behind the wheel.

"Don't get caught." Uno snatched his backpack from the truck, grabbed Pherall's hand, and bolted down the hill with the others.

Ocho squalled the truck to the top of the hill, set the rock on the gas petal, and jumped out. The truck raced down the sloped road, speeding straight for the oncoming army, and crashed into the mass of moving vehicles.

The explosion was enormous.

A massive concussion knocked the wind out of Pherall, sending her to the ground with Uno tumbling down beside her in the mud. He slid to a stop on his hip, scrambled back to his feet, and snatched her into a run beside him. The chop of rotor blades cut the air overhead as another helicopter sped toward them. Uno motioned the group toward a thick patch of trees. "Scatter!"

A valley full of boulders and rocky drop offs stretched out before them. Just beyond the hill, angry voices and pounding footsteps grew louder. The rain increased, blocking the view of their pursuers. Uno slid around the base of a boulder, spotted a gap beneath it, and scraped to a stop. With all the grace of a bulldozer, he shoved Pherall inside the crack. Once she was hidden under the rock, he snapped the base of a nearby bush and squeezed in beside her, covering the gap with the plant. From his hiding place, he saw Blue follow suit in a nearby crevice. Within moments the entire mountain side was covered in Jackboots.

"Find her!"

"What about the men?"

"If you can find one, tranquilize him, bring him."

"Targets are on foot," shouted one voice. "They can't be far. Find them!"

"I want sniffing dogs and thermal imaging set up. Now!" barked another.

"Four! Where the hell are you?" a voice shouted from a distance, then cursed loudly in Russian.

"I think Chetireh was killed in the explosion, Sir."

The officer slung a point toward the top of the hill. "Bullshit! He doesn't die," he shouted. "Go find his big ass."

Beneath the rock, Uno and Pherall looked at each other.

Shiny black boots marched through the mud, mere feet from where they hid. "I can't find them."

"Where are those thermal cameras?"

"It's raining too hard to use the cameras, Sir."

"Find an umbrella, you imbecile! Hold it over the cameras!"

"Yes, Sir!"

Lying motionless, Pherall peered out at the muddy black boots, sick to her stomach from adrenaline. As they clopped by, she felt something run across her neck and jerked instinctively. Something else ran across her leg and she flinched. Uno clapped a hand over her mouth and held her still while whatever it was crawled down her back.

"Is that a gun! Is that a damn gun?" shouted an authoritative voice. "I said use tranquilizers. They don't die! I sound like a broken record. No bullets! God, I'm surrounded by idiots. If that stupid helicopter had waited like I instructed, they would have driven right into us. But, no! They had to be heroes!"

"The Immortals aren't here."

"Yes! They! Are! They're on foot! Check the other side."

"They're hiding somewhere," another voice said from a distance. "Look over there."

The mass of boots moved away.

On the sharp slope between boulders where Uno and Blue hid, a Jackboot stepped wrong on a wet rock. It rolled out from beneath his foot, and he slid down in the mud, slapping at the ground until he caught a root. Embarrassed, he climbed to his feet. "It's getting too slippery over here. Let's go check the other side."

The rain increased again making it hard for the Jackboots to open their eyes. Eagerly, they cleared the area, preferring the protection of the trees past the ridge. From where he hid, Uno could see the top of the trees just beyond a drop off but could not see up the hill behind them.

Blue could, though. Easing his blond head forward, he peeked up the slope, then frantically waved Uno and Pherall out of their hiding place. Uno shoved the bush aside, hauled Pherall unceremoniously out into the rain, and threw her with a gasp off the side of the drop-off. At the same time, Blue scrambled out of his spot, dragging spiderwebs with him. Too far away to join Uno, he disappeared instead over a rocky outcropping.

Pherall hit the steep ground with a grunt and rolled down a grassy embankment. Uno slid down beside her, yanked her up, and took off with her. Drenched from head to toe and covered in mud, they reached the base of the mountain at a hard run and charged through the wide leaves of a bush, right onto a winding street. Surprised to be out in the open, they skidded to a stop.

Twenty feet away, an old farmer in overalls and a red hat tightened the last lug nut of a donut onto the rear tire wheel of an antique pickup. He stood up, spotting them and startling Uno.

Uno grabbed his gun.

"They went this way!" someone shouted. "Down there!"

Dripping wet, the old man heaved the flat tire into the back of his truck piled high with loose hay, entirely unconcerned about Uno's weapon, and glanced past them to the helicopter circling the mountain. Whistling brightly, he lifted a large section of hay and waited.

Uno hesitated warily for a moment, then pulled Pherall toward the truck. They climbed quickly into the bed and squeezed between the wheel-well and the enormous stack of wet brown grass. Continuing his tune, the elder covered them, opened the squeaky door, and climbed inside.

*****

In the narrow space, Uno and Pherall squeezed together. He lay atop her, propping his head on his elbows, while the truck rattled slowly beneath them, meandering its way down the mountain. Minutes later, they stopped at a rundown gas station. The old man climbed out, still whistling, and took his time gassing the truck. The sound of whistling faded, and he disappeared inside the convenient store with the tinkle of the bell. Uno's eyes shifted uneasily as they waited, and he held his pistol ready. He was just about to peek out of the truck when the sound of an approaching vehicle stopped him. The bell tinkled again, and the whistling returned.

"How's it going, old timer?" asked a voice through the heavy patter of rain.

"Hello, officer," the man said pleasantly. "Sounds like you got yourself a mess up there. That was a nasty explosion."

"Just an exercise drill," lied the Jackboot. "Have you seen anybody walking along the roads?"

"Nope. Coulda used the help. Had to fix that flat by my dang self. I'll be lucky to get this old girl home. Good luck out there."

The driver's side door slammed and the truck rattled back onto the road.

Pherall, who'd been holding her breath, peered up at Uno's handsome face, mere inches from hers, and exhaled in relief. She could have stared into his eyes forever but opted instead to start up a conversation. "How did you know where to look for Seven?" she asked.

"Jackboot emails. The leader Maxim uses a poor encryption. It takes time, but sometimes I can get enough of the message to make sense. That's how I found Ocho," he said, bouncing above her. "Maxim had an argument by email the other day. Someone wanted him to relocate Seven. Maxim got pissed and referred to the mountain range once by name."

The truck hit a bump, knocking Uno sideways and earning a wince from Pherall.

"The night I met you," he continued, straightening himself, "I saw an aerial map with a circle on it, but didn't know where it was.

I only broke the encryption the other night. The name Maxim used was a cluster of mountains in this region, so I headed this way and had Ocho drive around. You did the rest."

Pherall turned her hand and touched his shoulder. She'd always wanted to but never had the chance. Now, she couldn't help herself. She ran a finger along the well-defined contour of his arm. It was slender and corded, his muscles as rock hard as they appeared. Satisfied with her inspection, she looked up and found him watching her fingers. "Where will they move him now?"

Uno hesitated, caught off guard by the touch, then shrugged. "Who knows?" he answered, peering down at her.

Pherall moved a blade of hay from his lashes and took her time doing it. She hadn't intended to be so forward with him, but his reaction to her simple touch was funny. He was so awkward it was cute, and she was enjoying herself. "At least now he knows you're looking for him."

The look in Uno's eyes intensified, passing over her features and lingering on her. "I hope so," he whispered.

Pherall slid her fingers over his cheek to brush some mud away, which actually made it worse. He went quiet, though, so she pushed her fingers into his hair and raised her head to kiss him. Her heart thumped at her own boldness, but she was more than ready. She'd waited long enough.

Their lips met sweet, tender, unhurried … and—*Smack!*—the truck hit a bump, clacking their teeth together. Both winced, holding their mouths, and started laughing.

"Where will we go now?" she muffled around her fingers.

Uno shook his head. Lightly, he trailed his finger over her lip where he'd smacked it. "I want to lay low. They're awfully interested in you, which is pissing me off, and they keep catching me off-guard, which … is pissing me off."

The truck sped up.

"How will the others find us?" she asked.

"I'll leave a message. They know how to check it."

They rode for a long time before the truck pulled off the pavement and bounced along down a narrow dirt road. Deep in the woods, the rickety vehicle came to a stop beside a ship graveyard, and the driver stepped out. "Come outta there, boy," he said in a gruff voice. "Ain't nobody gonna hurt you here."

Uno crawled out from under the haystack with his backpack and a fat lip and helped Pherall out of the truck bed. The rain was lighter now, but still cold. She shook grass from her wet hair as best she could and scanned seagulls swarming the shallow cove. It was isolated and filled with leaning cargo ships, tankers, and barges. Rusted hulls and mangled equipment bobbed against the ground in the receding ocean tide.

Thunder crashed above them.

The old man scooped fallen hay from the ground. "You kids'r in a mess of trouble if those asshole Jackboots is pulling their helicopter out to look for ya," he said, squinting at them through the rain.

"Why'd you help us," asked Uno.

The gentleman took on a wistful expression, remembering some moment that darkened his features, and set his chuckle to sour. "I hate everything about 'em. I was an agent once, when the Jackboots was still the good guys. They ain't the good guys no more. I ain't seen 'em do a decent thing in damn near twenty years. Destroy everything they touch. Slaughter innocents with their big guns and loud trucks. I'm too old to do anything about it myself, but dammit I can support those who can. Anyway, you know what they say: Enemy of my enemy is my friend. So, I reckon you and I is friends," he said, eyeing Uno. "You set off that bomb?"

Uno studied him for a second before giving a small nod. "Yes, Sir."

"So, you're the real deal, huh?"

"I'm afraid so."

The old man eyed Pherall through the rain, then shook away the unpleasant topic. "I don't wanna know nothing about you, boy. Either o'you. You can call me the old man, and I'll call you a bunch of kids. How's that?"

Uno smiled, clearly surprised. "Sounds good."

"Thank you," said Pherall.

"Is there more of ya?"

Uno nodded. "Yes, Sir, Three. A bit older than us."

The old man bobbed his head, satisfied, and pointed. "There's a paddle boat under that there tree," he said with a point. "Go find the red cargo ship, she's rusty and don't float no more, but she'll keep you safe. There's food and fresh water. I go there to hide from the missus. She's a cranky ol' bat." He handed Uno a key. "I'll go find your friends."

*****

Still a bit stunned by the turn of events, Uno paddled out through the old, abandoned ships until he found a rusty red cargo boat sitting cockeyed near the center of the shallow bay. It's algae-stained hull sat heavy in the mud, visible two-feet below the water line. He hooked the paddle boat to the anchor chain and helped Pherall up the side of the leaning hull. The lock clicked with the turn of the key. Warily, Uno pushed the door open and peered skittishly inside. It was empty. Inside the dry cabin, he sagged heavily against the door and closed his eyes.

"Are you okay?" Pherall asked, concerned by his rare show of weariness.

Uno brushed messy hair from his face, snapping out of it. "Yeah. That was just … really close this time," he said in a whisper. "This isn't just about bringing us in anymore. They're after you now. They've stepped up their efforts and I want to know why."

"They just want me for bait," she said, turning to look at the cabin.

Uno put his arms around her wet shoulders and set his chin on top of her head, holding her there just a little longer. "They've never gone to this much trouble over bait before. It's bothering me."

Pherall leaned against him, enjoying the feel of him holding onto her, and admired the decor in the small boat. The cabin was brown and red plaid with shuttered windows and a covered skylight. Ship wheels and anchors appropriately accented the room. It was musty inside but clean and warm. The floor tilted slightly beneath them, and the vessel occasionally rocked lightly back and forth with the waves.

With a heavy sigh, Uno turned on a light and crossed to the refrigerator. To his delight, there was food inside. Plenty of it. During a quick meal, he left a message for the others then stood up to take a tour of the place. There was a small bedroom at the back with a cot inside. A blanket lay folded on one end and a pillow sat on the other. Beyond, was a small bathroom with a shower adjacent to the bedroom. On the other end of the ship, they found solar panels, filtered rainwater tanks, which were filling nicely, and radio equipment. The radio equipment immediately attracted Uno's attention.

"Here's an atlas," she said, sliding a large book from a cubby and opening it on a worktable.

Uno flipped it to the correct page and tapped it with his finger. "Seven was there. They attacked us here. Now, you and I are here. I think there was a tracker on the truck," he said, pulling his phone from his pocket and checking the screen. As he scanned, his brows flickered. He fooled with it for a minute, then leaned forward on his elbows and showed her a page full of nonsensical characters. "He just sent another email."

"I can see why it takes so long," she said, scanning the gibberish.

Next on the screen, he brought up a page of links. "There are different algorithms to help break encryption. The trick is finding the right one. Sometimes, I get partial text back. Then, it's like a puzzle," he explained, looking at the newest email. "Other times, I get nothing. Lots of guesswork. I'll work on this one tonight," he sighed, sounding weary again. "Maybe it'll tell me where he's gone."

Pherall gave his shoulder an encouraging squeeze. "I hope so," she said, then looked over her shoulder toward the bedroom. "If you don't mind, I'd like to take a shower."

He nodded at her and then tried to focus on the screen again, but he couldn't. Her voice was ringing in his ears. After a minute or two, he turned the phone off and gripped his head. She was driving him nuts.

*****

It was a small shower, less than three feet square, and the water had little pressure, but it was clean and inviting. Pherall found a bottle of men's shampoo on the floor of the stall and smelled it. Smiling, she lathered it into her hair and rinsed it clean, loving the scent. When her hair was clean and most of the hay removed, she soaped herself silly with the soapiest smelling soap ever and purred beneath the warm stream. It smelled so much nicer than truckstop shower soap and she took the opportunity to sniff the bar a few times before soaping again.

Without warning, the cargo boat shifted, throwing her sideways with a shriek. The soap went flying and struck the shampoo bottle. She landed low on the far wall with hygienic shrapnel raining down on her head.

A draft of cold air bowed the shower curtain as the door flew open.

"Pherall!" Uno yanked the curtain aside and grabbed her.

A wave of embarrassment pinked Pherall's cheeks as he stood her up on the tilted floor.

"Are you okay?" he rushed, giving her a once-over to check for injuries.

She was naked!

"Er ... uh," she managed.

Uno shifted away abruptly, stammered something incoherent, then picked up the soap and shampoo. Standing fully dressed beneath the warm water holding the soap in his hand, he cleared his throat. He stood inches from her, his clothes soaked through, his hair dripping wet. Awkwardly, he handed her the bar. "Sorry," he said in a breath.

Pherall took it.

Carefully not looking down, he set the shampoo aside and tried to pass.

The floor rocked, spilling them again.

Uno hooked her waist and braced for the boat to correct itself, but it only swayed with the waves. "I'm afraid to leave you now," he huffed in amusement.

"Then don't."

Uno glanced at the curtain he held pressed against the wall, unsure he'd heard her correctly. "You want me to shower with you?" he asked quietly.

Pherall wasn't sure she'd heard herself correctly at first, either, but that's what she'd said. Mortified by her own boldness, she nodded. "Stay with me."

Their gazes locked.

Water beaded on his black lashes, but he paid no attention. Ignoring the spray, he passed his brown eyes silently over her face. "Is that what you want?" he whispered.

Blushing furiously, Pherall nodded, sending her pulse into an erratic tempo. A vein at the base of his neck thumped visibly with his heartbeat, matching the thunder of her own. Naked and unsure exactly what to do next, she drew the curtain shut behind him.

Uno kicked off his shoes, then stepped, fully dressed, beneath the stream. Gently, he slipped the soap from her wet fingers.

She watched it vanish with wide eyes.

Taking his time, he slid her hair away from her back and rubbed the bar across her shoulders. She stiffened at the intimate touch but made no move to stop him. His hands, hard and calloused, caressed her neck and slid lightly over the contours of her slippery back. Pherall couldn't help but enjoy the sensation and closed her eyes, wishing he would continue forever.

But he didn't.

When her shoulders were clean, he slid a soapy hand behind her neck. This time, when he lowered his head to kiss her, he didn't stop himself. At long last, his lips made contact, turning her insides to jelly and sending a spicy shiver through her. Lightly at first, they touched hers, paused, then touched again, leaving Pherall warm and dizzy. His lips were firm and full, his mouth warm and inviting … better than she'd imagined.

Pherall lifted shaky hands to his shoulders. This was unfamiliar territory for her, but she wasn't about to let him stop, not this time. Securing her grip, she parted her lips and felt the light brush of his tongue. His kiss was slow and intimate, his touch personal.

Just then, the floor shifted sharply and the boat rocked the other way, setting them both off balance again.

Uno caught the wall, knocking the shampoo back to the floor, then peered down at her with an unreadable expression. For a split second, he almost looked unsure of himself. "Do you want me to leave?" he asked again in a low voice.

Pherall's voice actually failed just then, and she answered without it. "I want you to stay."

The boat shifted back, rolling the shampoo bottle past their feet.

With trembling hands, she lathered the soap and slid her fingers under his shirt to return the favor.

Holding her gaze, he pulled the wet shirt over his head and tossed it to the floor.

Brazenly, she slid soapy hands up his contoured chest and around his corded shoulders and neck. She could feel his heart beating against her fingers. "And I want you to kiss me again," she continued, looking into his eyes as she bathed him, "but this time … don't stop."

That was all the signal Uno needed. Gripping her head with both hands, he backed her deeper into the stream and covered her mouth with his. No longer hesitant, no longer uncertain, this kiss was different—greedy and demanding, urgent and curious.

Pherall dropped the soap. It hit his bare foot with a crack and slid across the shower floor. Uno grunted, then smiled against her mouth.

Pherall giggled.

The spray of water ran down over them but neither noticed.

Turning up the heat, he eased his arms around her waist, pulling her against him and sliding his hands freely over her.

Pherall let out a soft sigh at the intimate touch and raised to her toes. There was no turning back now. She fumbled the clasp of his jeans open and slid them down over his hips. With a toss, the jeans landed on the floor by the door.

The boat shifted again.

With a slap, Uno shut the water off, then slid his arm beneath her knees and carried her to the bedroom.

The shower was over.

164

*****

In the wee hours of the morning, Uno felt a breeze and opened his eyes. Pherall lay snuggled against him, naked and warm. Careful not to disturb her, he slid his hand beneath the pillow and withdrew his pistol. The floor rocked lightly beneath his feet as he stood. Without a sound, he pulled his jeans on and peeked out the bedroom.

A shadow moved in the darkness.

Like a shot, he crashed into the dark figure, shoved his forearm against a man's throat, and smashed the pistol in his face.

The light flicked on

It was Ocho, his arm extended to the wall switch.

"Uno!" Cinco blurted happily, coming in behind Ocho. He was wet and had hay in his hair. "This *is* the right one."

Uno released Ocho and lowered the pistol with a scowl. "You can't knock?"

"We wanted to surprise you," teased Cinco.

"Nailed it," Ocho grumbled without much humor and rubbed his tender throat.

Blue entered last. "You should lock the door," he said, demonstrating his suggestion with a click. He, too, had hay in his hair. "Anyone can just walk in here."

Uno tucked his pistol into the back of his waistband. "I don't recommend it."

Cinco gave Ocho's shoulder a smack. "That's why I sent Ocho in first. I'm not as dumb as I look," he assured, checking the place out.

Ocho wasn't amused.

Stepping lightly, Uno padded barefoot across the cabin and eased the bedroom door shut, then turned to face them. "Anyone know how to kill an Immortal?"

"Freeze him to death," Blue snorted and found a space on the floor. "That just about worked for me. Why?"

Uno crossed into the kitchen and opened the refrigerator. "Number Four is after Pherall," he said, pouring a glass of orange juice.

Cinco took the carton and reached for his own glass. "Yeah, what's up with that?" he asked, pouring. "I don't understand why the authorities want her so bad. For as long as I can remember, it's always been us. Now, suddenly, we're chopped liver."

Blue crossed his ankles and cocked his head at the larger man. "You actually sound jealous," he chuckled.

Cinco gave him a dry look.

"I don't know," said Ocho, "but Four is definitely Russian."

Uno leaned against the counter and folded his arms. "I heard that," he said tossing hair from his eyes.

"He's helping them." Cinco searched the cupboard for some food and found a box of crackers.

Blue drained the last of the carton. "Of course, he is. This is what happens when we don't reach an Immortal in time," he said, wiping his mouth. "Four doesn't need to be killed, Uno, he needs to be rescued."

Uno took a handful of crackers and popped one into his mouth without answering.

"Well, we're safe here for now," Ocho sighed, exhausted after a long day. "The old man said we could stay as long as we need until the heat dies down."

Uno indicated the tiny living room. "This is it."

Ocho took his wet shirt off, yanked a cushion off the teensy sofa, and dropped to the floor with it. "Works for me."

Blue pulled the ponytail out of his hair, which spilled into his face, and flopped down beside him. "Goodnight," he muttered into the carpet.

Cinco took the tiny sofa, only wide enough for his torso, and left his legs hanging off. He yanked his muddy shirt over his head and left it balled on his stomach. He was asleep before he got both hands out.

Uno, wide awake now, closed the thin bedroom door and crawled onto the cot beside Pherall. Propped on his elbow, he brushed a lock of blond hair from her face and watched her sleep. She would be the death of him, he was certain of it, but it was too late to remedy that. He'd already fallen in love, dammit, and hard.

*****

Maxim adjusted the screen and squinted into the camera. "Mr. Rigori!" he said in surprise, giving his uniform a yank and brushing his hair into place with his fingers. "I just got your message. What can I do for you?"

The billionaire's face appeared on the screen, hard and unamused. "I just received a report regarding a rather large offensive I recently funded," he said, foregoing formalities, "and learned that the girl got away yet again. I wonder," he said, forming his fingers into a temple, "was Four part of the operation?"

Maxim glanced past the camera to Chetireh frozen in horror against the opposite wall. Frantically, the Russian shook his blond

166

head and waved his hands, his expression pleading for denial. Maxim agreed. He wasn't finished with the Immortal and, therefore, wasn't in a hurry to hand him back over to the old man. "No," he lied. "My men scoured the mountain, but Uno is an expert on evasion."

"Four should have been there. Where was he?" the older man demanded.

Maxim leaned back in his office chair and fitted his fingers together over his stomach. "Uh, w–well, he arrived with one of the squads during the initial formation," he said, adding convincing inflection to his tone, "but our location was attacked before we began our mission. We suspect Uno obtained prior knowledge about the operation and set up an ambush," he said, rocking the chair back and forth. "A vehicle-born explosive device wiped out half my vehicles, a helicopter, and twenty-three of my men while we were assembling. Four was killed in the initial explosion and accidentally removed from the scene before he woke up."

Rigori didn't care. "Is he there with you?"

Chetireh looked ready to vomit.

"N–no," Maxim said quickly. "I sent him to the barracks with the others."

Rigori scowled. "I told him to get that girl."

"And he will."

"You seem awfully chipper after such an expensive defeat."

Maxim spread his hands matter-of-factly. "I've been after Uno for years, Rigori," he said, producing a smile. "This is the first time he's had a weakness. It's only a matter of time now. I personally believe we should have kept Blue and Ocho before since we had them, but—"

"The information we obtained from that footage is what clued us into the presence of a Queen," Rigori interrupted hotly. "Gathering intelligence is just as important as military tactic. If you want to catch Uno, you must learn about Uno. You find his weaknesses, study his patterns. His weakness is the girl. That is how you catch Uno!"

Maxim inclined his head politely. "That information was invaluable, yes, and I thank you for it. I just wanted to impress upon you how difficult it is to capture one Immortal, much less two," he grinned. "Anyway, my men are working out a new plan of attack—"

"No," Rigori interrupted again, his tone clipped. "I've had enough of your fighting. War is getting us nowhere. We will make the girl come to us," he said, popping a macadamia nut into his mouth. "I'll prepare Number Nine and send instructions. Tell Four to expect him."

"Before you do that," Maxim said apologetically, "we may need a bit more time."

"For what?" growled the old man.

Maxim tamped down his own temper and remembered to be cordial. "As I mentioned," he told the billionaire with a cheerful smile, "the Immortals are quite adept at escape and evasion. Unfortunately, the pickup truck with the tracker was destroyed by Uno's bomb. We have to locate him again before initiating another mission. We are quite certain he had help off the mountain, but we believe he is still in the area."

Rigori scowled in disgust.

"My investigators are studying satellite footage and interviewing local businesses as we speak," the Jackboot assured with a flippant wave. "I will notify you the moment we find them."

"You do that," Rigori growled, leaning forward to sever the connection.

CHAPTER 19

Living on a small cargo-ship-turned-houseboat with four grown men definitely made life interesting for Pherall, especially considering her developing relationship with Uno. In the last twenty-four hours, a significant shift had occurred among the men as well. After coming to terms with Uno's decision regarding her, they threw their support behind him. They were certainly aware that something had advanced between the two and ogled both to the point of ridiculousness in hopes of catching something worth gossiping about. Oh, and there was plenty of that any time the three men were alone. Hushed whispers and meaningful looks made their way around the eensy weensy cabin. It amused Pherall, but she pretended not to notice. Uno made it a point to behave as he always had, much to their dismay, and remained level-headed and cool … mostly. The only difference was that now he sat by her, watched her openly, and occasionally smiled.

A full week after arriving on the small boat, the group had fallen into a new routine. Every other day, the old man left a bag of fresh vegetables on the shore and waved as he drove away. He also left them fishing line, bait, and hooks. When the tide was high, someone would paddle the boat to the bank and pick it up. When the tide was low, it was possible to walk across the muddy bed all the way to the bank. Every day, they went fishing. The group, it turned out, loved to fish and the diet of fresh fish and vegetables instead of convenience store crap helped all of them regain their strength and color. Even Pherall felt better.

One night beneath a full moon, Uno, Ocho, Cinco, and Blue strolled out together, enjoying themselves and exploring the dark, squishy ground. At first, Pherall was apprehensive about going into the mud, especially at night. There was no way to rinse it off and she wasn't about to allow mud in the old man's cabin; however, once the boys started exploring, there were simply too many things to discover for her to pass on the opportunity. To her inexperienced eye, the mud flat was really neat. It was smelly and the mud sandy, but it was alive with bubbles and creatures. There were ripples in the mud, shells, and snails. The muck was soft and gooey, making navigation somewhat difficult, but eventually she discovered a method and was soon slogging through slimy algae with the men.

Cinco stuck his head inside the hull of a sunken fishing boat, which made no sense because it was too dark to see inside anyway. Ocho and Blue were nearby trying to climb up onto an old barge, and Uno was pulling a rusted anchor out of the mire. Pherall found tide pools with trapped fish and clams burrowing down beneath patches of bubbles. Above the bubbles, disturbed seagulls squawked and swarmed and pooped on everything. Tree trunks and swollen branches, rocks, anchors, tires, engines, broken fishing equipment, and trash littered the bay. And there, all by itself, floated a slimy orange football.

Pherall picked it up and squeezed it. Not too flat, she decided, then tossed the ball playfully into the air.

Uno noticed as she turned to find the others. "You like football?" he asked, taking it.

Pherall shrugged modestly. "I used to play some."

"Did you now? Let's see how good you are." He gave the ball a squeeze, then zeroed in on Cinco's exposed rear-end. "We'll start you on defense," he warned and launched it with a sharp spiral.

Blap!

Cinco grabbed his butt and whirled. "What jackass … ?"

Uno put a surprised look on his face and pointed at Pherall. Her mouth popped open.

Cinco grabbed the ball and thrust a threatening finger at her. "You're dead!" he shouted, charging after her.

Pherall yelped and whirled to run.

Clomping through the mud, Cinco reared back to throw.

Pherall ducked behind a large engine just as the ball reached her. It hit the engine, ricocheted toward Ocho and Blue, and smacked the barge with a splat. Ocho snapped his head back with a startled curse and Blue whipped a mud-splattered face around, their surprised gazes pinned on her.

"Oh, hell no!"

Cinco pointed to Pherall. "Get her!"

Glaring impending revenge, Ocho bent down for a handful of mud and slung it. Blue took off after her.

Pherall cried out in outrage and ducked out of the way. "I'm innocent!" she shrieked, dodging mud balls and rounding the end of a rusted fishing boat.

Cinco tried to grab her, his arm extended. "Liar!"

Pherall spun away from him, and he fell.

Ocho leapt in the air, hurdling the fallen Cinco and reaching for her. "I got her!"

Pherall slapped his hand away, spun behind him, and darted the other direction. Blue, moving too fast to stop, ran past, watching her giggle by, and skidded to a halt. His feet slid out from beneath him and he toppled, flapping his arms wildly before landing on his hip in the mud.

170

Pherall laughed.

They all passed horrified looks among themselves and scrambled to their feet with renewed determination.

Pherall grabbed the muddy football as she passed, heading back toward Uno with hell in her eyes. "Traitor!"

Uno looked past her head and pointed. "She's got the ball," he called out to the three slipping and sliding behind her in the mud.

"Oh, now it's on!" growled Blue.

"You're on offense now," Uno informed her helpfully. "You should run."

Pherall sloshed through deep mud, desperate to keep her distance.

Amused, Uno, standing fifty feet away, frantically waved his arms at the boys. "Go around that pit," he shouted to them. "It's deeper than it looks."

Pherall sloshed to a stop, digging her feet down in the mud, and turned, twisting away from their clawing hands. Cinco, Ocho, and Blue splashed by with surprised looks on their faces.

All three fell again.

Uno tossed his hands in the air in disgust. "What was that?" he scowled.

Squealing with laughter, Pherall ran toward a ferry, rounded a sunken piling, and leapt over a gnarly tree carcass that resembled like a large grasshopper in the moonlight.

Cinco scraped wet mud from his face with the last clean patch of skin on his forearm. "What the hell?"

"What is she, a retired football player?" demanded Blue with an accusing look at Uno.

"My brother was a quarterback. I was his practice receiver," she boasted. "He would hand me the ball, then tackle me."

Ocho used his fingertips and scrambled back to his feet. "That's what I'm going to do when I get my hands on you."

The men came around the tree, leaping over debris to pick up speed in the mud.

"I got her!" called Cinco, arms extended.

Pherall slapped Cinco's arms away, redirecting him and dropping him to a knee, then thrust her shoulder into Ocho's ribs, knocking him backward. Toe to toe with Blue, she faked left, then spun right, sending him down onto Ocho's back with an outraged shout. This time all three stayed down in the muck and stared, blinking muddy lashes at her.

Uno dropped his arms. "Oh, come on!" he railed at them. "This is embarrassing."

"You get her!" Cinco yelled, slinging an arm.

"I'm the coach," said Uno with a self-important point.

"We can't catch her."

Uno shifted his brown eyes to Pherall.

Laughing almost hysterically, she slogged through the smelly mud toward Uno. "Don't you dare!" she warned and stopped to throw the ball at him. Rearing back, she wound up, bracing to give it all she had, and hurled the football.

It landed twenty feet in front of her with a splat.

Uno watched the ball land and set his hands on his hips. "She definitely wasn't the quarterback," he clarified to Blue.

Mortified in front of her audience, Pherall hurried to the ball and tried again. It landed twenty-two feet in front of her.

As she picked up the ball for another throw, Uno charged.

"Aah!" Pherall shrieked and hauled ass. "No! No!"

A quiet shout went up from the crowd. Cinco, Ocho, and Blue threw their arms high and jumped, cheering Uno on. "Get her! Get her!"

The sound of their riotous encouragement struck fear into Pherall's heart. She ran screaming softly through the mud, flapping her arms in a desperate attempt to gather speed.

Uno's foot-splats grew louder.

Squealing in anticipation, Pherall grabbed a corner of the upended engine, sling-shotted herself around it, and—*Oomph!*—landed face-first in Uno's arms. He tackled her backward, taking her down into a small tide-pool with a splash. Filthy water soaked Pherall's hair and filled her mouth. She came up sputtering in outrage, gasping in laughter.

Shouts and whistles erupted from the three swamp-things behind the fallen grasshopper log. "Touchdown!"

Uno popped the football from her hand and caught it in the air. "I win," he laughed, then grabbed her algae-slimed hair and splatted a muddy kiss onto her mouth, earning a shriek of disgust. "I always win."

*****

By the end of the second week, Pherall was content to stay in the shipyard forever. Quarters were cramped, but the five of them had fun. Meals were served on the floor with plenty of laughter on the side. There weren't any more football games in the mud because of the mess and lack of clothes to change into, but there were plenty of exploration expeditions around the mud flat at low tide and inside the old ships at high tide. After one such afternoon adventure, Pherall rinsed her shoes off and set them out to dry, while Ocho and Blue went to collect a bag of goodies from the old man pulling up to the shore. After a nice chat, they were back with fresh potatoes, bell peppers, and a chunk of meat.

"This is the fixins for stew!" squealed Pherall.

Uno's face brightened with interest. "I can help with that," he said and picked up the bell pepper. "I want to learn how."

Pherall nearly melted at the sight of enthusiasm spreading over his handsome features. This was the hidden side of Uno she never expected to see. He had a sense of humor and a quick wit about him she was only just now discovering. He was very careful to conceal his charismatic personality outside the group, keeping it carefully buried deep beneath his preferred stone-cold exterior. To be honest, she hadn't been positive it existed at first, but now that he'd opened up and shared it freely with her she fell in love with it. It made her wonder if this resembled the real Uno and the personality he had before he died the first time. Now, every time their eyes met, she felt an eager affection coming from him. Best of all, he loved to learn. The very idea warmed her.

"Help me peel potatoes," she smiled. "You'll be amazed how easy it is to make stew."

He joined her in the kitchen.

Suddenly, a long, dramatic gasp filled the cabin.

Everyone turned to see Cinco, wide-eyed and breathless, clutching a large frozen tub. "Ice cream!" he announced, his voice two octaves high.

"Holy shit! All we need is music and we have a party," said Blue.

Uno pulled his phone from his pocket and turned on some upbeat music. "How's this?"

Blue bit his bottom lip and bobbed his head to the beat. "I can dance the pigeon," he boasted, demonstrating a fantastic impression.

Pherall laughed and danced her shoulders playfully, joining him.

"Okay, seriously. Cinco looks ready to swoon," teased Ocho.

"I am," Cinco nodded. "I'm going to swoon."

Blue took a seat nearby so he could watch the show. "I've never seen Cinco swoon," he said, getting comfortable. "I've gotta watch this."

Cinco demonstrated his most impressive swoon. Throwing his arm over his forehead, he staggered around, 'Ooh, ooh, oohing' in a high-pitched voice.

"Damn. That's worse than Pherall's acting," Ocho observed with a cringe.

Pherall spun in outrage. "I can swoon!" she informed him haughtily and set her potato down.

Ocho waved toward the floor, inviting her to demonstrate, then crossed his arms for the judging process.

Everyone waited.

With a delicate sigh, Pherall folded her knees beneath her and slumped to the floor.

Blue started laughing. "I think they both need lessons," he said, stretching out his long legs. "That was awful, Pherall. I'm not convinced at all."

Pherall, lying flat on the floor, rolled her head back to look at him. "That was a good swoon," she argued, without bothering to get up.

"Naw. You need to bump your head going down," he insisted. "Show her, Uno."

Without hesitation, Uno buckled his knees, slapped the counter, and threw his head back as he went down in an extremely convincing swoon. With a thud, he fell face-down onto Pherall and lay still, putting all his weight on her.

She laughed loudly. "You weigh a ton!"

A brown eye peeked up at Ocho from the floor. "How was that?"

Ocho shook his head and emptied his hands. "Actually, you're all wrong," he informed them. "Observe."

He cleared his face of expression, rolled his eyes back in his head, and fell forward toward the growing pile of fainting victims, stiff as a board.

Pherall screamed, bracing for impact, and Uno scrambled to get to his knees. Ocho crashed onto Uno's back, flattening him onto Pherall with an 'oof' of laughter, and sagged atop them both.

Blue clapped his hands. "We have a winner!"

Pherall squealed and wriggled to get out from beneath them. "You two are getting the fat free stew," she grunted, crawling to her feet.

The table was too small and there weren't enough chairs for everyone, so when the stew was ready, all five sat on the kitchen floor, as was their tradition, and ate together.

"This is awesome!" Blue declared with his mouth full. "Oh my God!"

Ocho blinked bulgy eyes at Pherall. "You knew how to do this all along and said nothing?"

"Oh, there's more where that came from," she bragged.

174

Cinco dug into the pot for more. "If you aren't going to propose, Uno, I will. Are you available, Pherall?"

"Nope," said Uno.

Pherall leaned close to Cinco. "Uno did all the work," she whispered loudly and gave him a meaningful look, implying the marriage proposal should go to the appropriate party.

Cinco wrinkled his nose and declined the romantic offer. "It's not that good."

The ice cream came out a few minutes later.

Blue moved to the sofa, preferring to sit this course out.

"There's one more serving of stew, Blue," Pherall said, reaching for his bowl. "You can clean it up while we have ice cream. It's still warm."

Blue, who no longer had any interest in anything cooler than lukewarm, quickly took her up on her offer. "So, what will we do after dessert?" he asked, returning to the stove.

Uno shrugged. "We could play cards."

"No!" the others said in unison.

"You always win," accused Ocho.

Uno licked the ice cream off his spoon. "I can go easy on you a few times."

"Where's the fun in that?" Ocho complained, scraping his spoon around the empty ice cream container in search of drips.

Pherall clapped her hands together. "We could play Uno. There's a deck of Uno cards in that drawer."

They all looked at her and laughed.

"He'd win that too," grumbled Ocho. "Let's play charades."

Blue scowled and pointed with his fork. "I want to see Pherall act again. That shit is funny."

"No, really," she persisted. "Seven-O-Uno! If you play a seven, you switch your hand with Uno—the good-looking one—and use his own cards against him."

Cinco shook his head. "I'm confused."

"You can take anyone else's hand," said Ocho.

Pherall nodded. "If you play a zero, we all pass our hands to the right and confuse Uno—the good-looking one."

The protests fell silent and blinky eyes bounced around the room.

Blue scratched his chin. "Using the Seven-O-Uno method, Uno —the ugly one—might actually be defeated," he marveled.

Not a hint of concern flickered across Uno's amused features. "Sounds like a challenge," he chuckled. "I accept."

"The odds are against ya this time, shweetheart," Pherall teased with a click and a wink. "Good luck."

Cinco draped his arm around Pherall's shoulders. "If I win," he announced to everyone present, "I sleep in the cot with Miss Pherall."

Blue jerked upright. "Oh! I could sleep in the cot," he said, rubbing his hands together and blowing kisses at Pherall. "This one's for you, baby."

Ocho gave the others a fist-bump. "It's on! We can take Uno."

Clearly beyond intimidation, Uno smiled, finding their collective show of confidence amusing. Calmly, he took the cards from the drawer and removed Cinco's arm from Pherall's shoulder. "You guys are gonna have to work together," he said, passing them out.

"We'll use hand signals," Blue announced, blowing his cheeks out to psych himself up and rubbing his hands together.

Uno won.

*****

Late into the night, Pherall and Uno left the sleepy group in the main room and crawled into their tiny cot. Alone at last, Uno propped on an elbow and peered down at her. "Are you still afraid of me?" he asked quietly.

Pherall brushed messy brown hair from his eyes and watched it fall right back where it was. "More now than before," she murmured, wrapping a lock of his hair around her finger. "I'm afraid that you'll come to your senses and realize how much trouble I am."

"I already know that."

"I'm afraid that I'm the butt of some ridiculous prank. You're not immortal. You don't really like me. We have millions of viewers."

He laughed.

She trailed her fingers to his chest where he'd been shot. "I am afraid that one day your enemies will find a way to make you not wake up," she whispered.

"It won't be them that takes me down," he said, passing his eyes over her face.

She slid her fingers behind his ear and around his jaw, trying to tuck his messy hair. "That I'll grow old without you, then you'll move on and forget me."

He shook his head. "I don't care how old you get. We'll stay together," he vowed, draining her doubts and fears. "I feel it. I did the moment we met. That's why I couldn't kill you."

"I thought you hated me."

"I wanted to, but I couldn't," he admitted. "What I hated was watching you laugh and play with Cinco and Blue and not me. I was afraid you would fall in love with Cinco. I didn't know how to stop it."

Pherall tickled her fingernail over his ear. "It was always you. It always will be."

"Promise me."

"I do," she vowed. "I'll go anywhere you go, Uno—wherever that takes us—for as long as you'll have me."

A thumb brushed over her mouth, and he shifted his weight toward her. Warm lips pressed against hers, then gently covered her mouth, sending her pulse into a tailspin. He kissed her slow and intimate, tracing her tongue with his until goosebumps puckered her skin. Gathering her close, he eased his fingers beneath her shirt, taking his time, and slid it over her head.

CHAPTER 20

Over coffee, Uno sat at the minuscule table and poured over a map. He wore a blue t-shirt and jeans. It was late in the morning. Everyone had slept in after the ice cream bash the night before. Blue, fresh from a shower and wearing his blond hair loose, took the seat across from Uno and accepted a plate of food from Ocho, who was dressed in black, while Cinco moved around the small cabin gathering and bagging their few belongings.

"Time to go already?" scowled Blue.

Uno nodded. "We've been here too long," he said and gestured to his phone. "Another number has come up in the encrypted Jackboot emails. It's bothering me."

"Bothering, why?"

"Because it's out of order."

Blue's chewing slowed. "What number?"

"Ten," frowned Uno, "and they're behaving differently about him. Like they're excited."

"But no Nine?"

"No."

"What about Number Seven?" Blue asked, taking another bite. "We still haven't located him."

Uno shook his head and curled a finger beneath his lip. "He dropped off. They aren't mentioning him at all in the emails anymore," he said thoughtfully, "and it has me worried. I don't even know where to begin looking for him."

Blue took the news hard and picked at his food. "It must suck to be so close to rescue from those monsters and not make it out," he said softly. "So now what?"

Uno looked at him, then transferred his gaze to Pherall, humming at the stove and busily stealing another sausage. "We're going home. I don't have a location on Ten yet, but something doesn't feel right. We need to lay low until I find out why," he said, glancing over his shoulder at Ocho, clean-shaven after his morning shower. "Ocho, you and Blue will go to town for supplies, including some tents. I want this cabin restocked for the old man and some money left on the table. Cinco, you'll go boat shopping, something big enough to get us all the way home. Pherall, clean up your mess and get showered. I'll get the weapons ready. We need to be gone in two hours."

*****

179

Clean and dressed in a white t-shirt and jeans, Pherall stepped over the pile of weaponry Uno was organizing and stuffed her meager belongings into the bags on the table. Today her hair was down and fanned across her back, not because she'd planned it that way but because she'd lost all her hair ties again. She was ready, Uno was almost ready. Once the others got back, they would leave. A glance at the clock told her the two-hour mark was fast approaching. Behind her, Uno busily stuffed his backpack and counted magazine clips. Suddenly antsy, she unlocked the door and stepped out onto the narrow deck, letting the salty wind blow her hair around her shoulders.

The tide was out, causing the old red cargo ship to list slightly in the soft, stinky mud. Screeching seagulls spiraled overhead, noisily doing whatever seagulls did. She smiled, watching them, and scanned the beautiful shore one hundred yards away.

As she scanned, her smile turned to a frown.

Suddenly, the call of the seagulls faded and the warm breeze went still, leaving her alone with nothing but an odd sensation crawling over her skin. Focusing hard on the shore, she paused, wondering if the old man had returned but couldn't see the dirt road through the brush. Hesitantly, she eased down the ladder and stepped into the soft mud, knowing she'd regret ruining her shoes later. Staying close to the next unsailable vessel, she stepped around the broken stern until she could see the patch of ground where he usually parked.

It was empty.

A lump tightened her throat and she leaned further out, watching the spot until she saw a familiar face step into the clearing. The blond hair. The slender build. Instantly, the wind left her. "Korbin," she exhaled a short gasp. Extending a trembling hand, she took an abrupt step, then cried out in disbelief. "Korbin!"

Her brother froze at the sight of her, his expression drawn with surprise.

"Korbin!" Pherall ran to him, moving as fast as she could through the mud.

The cabin door crashed open behind her. "Pherall!" shouted Uno. "Pherall, no!"

Korbin hurried to the shore, meeting her there.

Pherall crashed into her twin brother. "Korbin!"

With a grunt, he threw his arms around her and squeezed. "I'm so sorry," he wailed, burying his face in her neck. "I'm so sorry!"

"Pherall!" cried Uno.

Pherall pulled back in Korbin's arms and frowned. He was crying, not at all happy to see her.

"Get away from him!" Uno yelled, racing through the tangle of broken ships.

"Korbin?" she squeaked and glanced back.

"They threatened Mom," Korbin said through his tears.

From the bushes to her left, a familiar large blond stepped out, clutching a tranquilizer gun. She recognized Chetireh instantly.

"Number Four!" Pherall's stomach dropped. She'd walked into a trap. Cold black fright seized her, and she whirled away from her brother in alarm. "Uno!" she cried. "Run!"

Seven darts struck Uno as he came around a barge, dropping him. "Pherall!" he grunted, crawling.

Pherall screamed and tried to run to him, but Chetireh hooked her around the waist, pinning her with his massive arm, and spoke into a wire tucked behind his ear. "Uno is down. Ten in custody. Move in," he said in a strong Russian accent.

"Korbin, what have you done?" she shrieked, sobbing wildly. "What have you done! Oh my God!"

Instantly, two black SUVs appeared on the dirt road. Jackboots spilled out, raced for Uno lying prone in the mud, and carried him quickly toward one of the vehicles.

"How could you!"

"Get in the truck, Nine," ordered a sharp voice.

Korbin angrily scraped a tear from his cheek, watching Pherall flail wildly in Four's arms.

"How could you!" she choked, barely able to form the words. "Nine!"

Obediently, Korbin turned to enter a third vehicle pulling into view, his face contorted in shame. At the last second, he lurched toward Four. "Let her go!"

The Jackboot shot him.

Korbin grabbed his chest and sank to the ground.

Pherall's cries lodged in her throat, for a moment silencing her horrified screams.

Uno disappeared inside the first truck. The doors slammed shut and the engine roared into motion.

"Cinco!" Pherall sobbed.

Chetireh hauled Pherall, screaming like a crazy woman, to the next truck in line.

She kicked as they reached it, trying to prevent him from stuffing her in. "I'm Ten!" she shrieked, drawing her cry from deep within. "I'm Ten!"

Chetireh's fingers clamped sharply around her neck and pinched, silencing her.

Pherall's world went black, and she sagged limp in his arms. Carefully, he climbed in with her, letting a nearby Jackboot slam the truck door shut, and both remaining SUVs drove away.

*****

Blue tightened his elbow around Cinco's throat, straining to hold him, while Ocho clamped his legs around the larger man's knees. Cinco thrashed violently, throwing his weight and struggling wildly to free himself. Tears streamed down his muddy cheeks, purple from Blue's snug headlock.

When the black SUVs vanished, two long gray vans pulled up and the side doors slid open. Very calmly, twenty Jackboots carrying tranquilizer guns stepped into the clearing from their hiding places and climbed inside. Blue waited for the last van to vanish before loosening his hold on Cinco.

Cinco shook them off angrily and sagged to the ground in despair. "Aaaah!" he roared, giving the wet ground a thump with his fist.

"They would have caught all of us," Blue panted quietly, trying to shake blood back into his arms, "and then there would be nobody to rescue Uno."

Cinco gripped his head, letting his elbows sink heavily into the mud. "She was calling for me," he managed in a strangled voice, then shouted. "They needed me!"

"There were twenty Jacks in those bushes!" snapped Ocho, who had added a bit of distance.

Blue wanted to fix his messed-up ponytail but couldn't because his hands were too muddy. Awkwardly, he lowered them and adjusted his position in the mud. "We're gonna find them," he vowed, slinging a tuft of hair from his eyes. "Uno's backpack is still on the boat. There's a Jackass station a few hours away. If we leave now, we can blow it up—"

Ocho shook his head. "No," he said quickly. "That's exactly what they'll be expecting us to do. We'll be walking into another trap."

Blue slung mud from his hands and scowled at the empty shore. "Then we have the advantage."

Cinco, struggling to compose himself, raised his muddy head and forced his mind back into the game. "Pherall is Ten," he whispered in a low, tormented voice.

"Yeah, and that was her brother Korbin on the beach," said Blue. "Korbin must be number Nine."

Cinco was calmer now, but the acute sense of loss tightened his throat making his voice sound unnaturally calm. "That explains the attacks, but what does that mean for us?"

"I don't know," said Ocho, "but I think shit's about to get real."

"It wasn't real before?" asked Blue in sarcastic disgust.

"It was," Ocho said soberly, "but now that they have Pherall, they can force Uno to do anything."

Blue didn't think so. "It'll backfire. This is going to piss Uno off, not make him cower."

Cinco exhaled heavily, better now. "Blue's right, Ocho, but the game just changed," he said quietly. Angrily, he wiped his cheeks and got up, oblivious to the mud covering him. "The rules we played by before no longer apply."

"Right," said Blue. "If we're going to rescue Uno, we have to think like Uno."

"No." Cinco shook his head. "No. I'm in charge, now. If we intend to get Pherall back alive, we have to move fast, which means we're about to play dirty. My way."

"So … when are we going to rescue Uno?" Ocho asked.

Cinco looked restlessly around the empty shore, composed at last, and shouldered his eyes dry. "We're not," he said in a thick, broken voice and motioned them to the boat. "They're going to let him go. I have an idea. Let's get our things. We don't have much time."

*****

Uno woke to the sound of blood pounding through his ears. Cold concrete pressed hard against his cheek and handcuffs attached to rough iron chains pinned his wrists, connecting him to a bolt in the floor. He could feel the effects of several gunshots fading in his chest along with the lingering sedative from the tranquilizers. Over and over, they killed him, laughing and making bets. He'd been heavily darted many times after coming to in the vehicle. After that, he'd awoken in this clear-walled room, heard an alarmed voice, and felt the hammer of a bullet to the ribs. This was the eleventh time he'd woken since arriving in this room, but something had changed. Now, when they shot him, he had only to wait for the shock of the strike to pass before all systems functioned again. He wasn't losing consciousness. Puzzled, he stayed still, paying attention.

"He's getting weaker," said a voice thinned by an intercom. "Every time we kill him it takes longer for him to reset. We're past two minutes now."

"Interesting," responded another voice.

The deafening report of another gunshot set Uno's ears ringing and he felt his body jerk. This time, however, he swallowed the pain and clamped his teeth in anger, but he didn't die. Breathless, he tensed, feeling the indescribable pain radiate outward with staggering intensity. Sharp stabs crisscrossed throughout his chest as the tissue mended itself. Familiar with the unpleasant sensation, Uno remained absolutely still, taking note of his body's response. As he lay there, the bullet fell out of his skin and dropped to the floor inside his bloody blue shirt. There was a pile of them there now.

Was he not dying anymore?

His stomach growled mercilessly, his body demanding payment for working so hard. Nearly sick from hunger, he shallowed his breathing and waited a full two minutes before moving again.

"This is amazing!" someone said.

Another shot.

The crisscrossing sensation returned but worked faster this time. His pain receptors were shutting down. Uno was careful to wait longer before taking a full breath, which notified his audience that he was awake. "Fucking quit it!" he growled, turning deadly brown eyes to the Jackboot with the weapon.

His audience laughed.

Four men stood guarding the outside of a glass wall with one holding the tip end of a machine gun on single shot in one of air the holes drilled through the ridiculously thick glass. Others lined the hall beyond, craning their necks to watch.

"That's enough," said an amused, familiar voice.

Uno glanced the other direction toward a two-way mirror with an intercom below it, then hung his head over his elbows. He really felt like shit now.

"Well, well, well," said the familiar deep voice. "Boy Wonder can be caught."

"Fuck you, Maxim," Uno grunted, adding a convincing crack to his voice.

"Not so tough now, are you?" he taunted.

Uno smiled and looked out of his curtain of messy hair. "You're the one armed and hiding behind a damn mirror," he noted in good humor.

"You have a very pretty girlfriend," said Maxim, effectively removing the smile from Uno's lips.

"Be careful, Maxim," warned Uno.

Maxim chuckled. Beeping sounds, indicating he was dialing, came through the intercom and his voice moved away from the speaker. "Uno's awake," he said to the person on the other line. "Yes, Sir. Hold on, Sir."

Uno braced for what was to come. Encouraging himself to keep a level head, he focused on the background noise, movements, tones of voice, and the posture of the jittery Jackboots in the hall. Nearly beside themselves with accomplishment and curiosity, a group of them watched with unblinking eyes, hanging on every echoey word escaping the holes in the glass. He needed to get the handcuffs off, but they were tight. If they caught him trying, they would shoot him again.

Less than a minute later, a section of mirror flickered with light, revealing a rectangle of live video footage.

"Uno," purred a voice Uno was sure he'd never heard before. "You look younger than I imagined you would."

Uno glared at the screen. "Who are you?"

"I am Rigori," said the older man. "Someone here wants to see you."

Pherall was dropped to the floor in front of the camera. Groggily, she lifted her head, and tried to focus glossy eyes to a point past the screen. "Soy desyat uno," she babbled incoherently. "Orbin–Cay neun ..."

Uno frowned, certain she was acting, and focused on her mumbles. It sounded like she was speaking in a blend of several different languages—Spanish, Russian, Pig Latin, and German. His brain kicked into high gear, piecing the string together. I am Ten, Uno. Korbin, Nine. Flying over water. Sun starboard. Seven is there.

Rigori returned to the screen, interrupting her. "She's very pretty, Uno. You have exquisite taste," he smiled, touching her, then hardened cold blue eyes. "I wonder if she's immortal."

The camera shook with movement, then positioned for a better angle. A Jackboot stepped into the image and pulled Pherall's head back by the hair, exposing her neck. From his belt, he produced a large knife.

Uno shot to his feet and charged toward the screen. "No!" he screamed, snapping backward at the end of the chain. He fell hard to the amusement of his audience. "No!"

The knife pressed against Pherall's throat.

185

"Not her!" screamed Uno, climbing to his knees and frantically twisting his wrists. "Not her! Stop!"

A drip of blood rolled down over her collarbone.

"Rigori!" Uno yanked frantically at the chain, writhing and twisting his wrists in the cuff, as if reaching the mirror might save Pherall. "I'll destroy you!" he roared in a cracked voice. "I'll tear you to pieces! I swear to God I will!"

Rigori lifted his hand, halting the execution. "Your reaction is concerning, Uno."

"Your entire bloodline," Uno threatened, his voice trembling now. "Every goddamn one."

The billionaire smiled. "It looks like you and I require negotiations."

Uno glared at him, visibly shaking. "Don't piss me off, Rigori," he warned with difficulty.

The old man stuck his face in the camera, producing a distorted image of his unnaturally youthful features. "Deliver your friends. All four of you surrender or the girl dies," sneered the billionaire. "Your move."

The screen went blank, leaving Uno staring at his own reflection in the two-way mirror. Blood soaked his hands, but the cuffs were almost off.

A slow clap broke the heavy silence that followed. "*That* was worth every moment I've spent chasing your irritating ass," Maxim marveled. "*That* was beautiful."

Uno's unblinking gaze fell out of focus. "I need a phone," he whispered in surrender.

A murmur passed through the agents standing outside the glass and an argument quickly followed. A moment later, a firm, angry voice shouted in irritation. "Ames!"

A curly-haired Jackboot stepped forward in alarm. "Me?" the man said, pointing to himself.

"You have a weapon, Ames!" barked the leader's voice. "Use it!"

Ames looked back and forth between Uno and the owner of the voice just out of Uno's line of sight. Warily, he eased away from the others and carefully approached the glass, as if Uno might attack him through it, then put the end of his weapon into a hole in the wall.

Uno faced him.

All the Jackboots backed up.

Ames jolted hard, shrinking from the cold, steady gaze locked onto his. Swallowing a lump, the Jackboot aimed nervously, struggling to hold his machine gun steady. A bead of sweat rolled down the side of his face. Breathing heavily, he zeroed his sights in, exhaled, and fired.

The bullet missed.

Horrified, the Jackboot yanked his head up. Uno was still watching him, his features hard and unafraid. Trembling visibly, Ames wiped his palms on his pants, scraped his sleeve across his nose, and tried again. In a gush of air, he blew out his cheeks and aimed, focusing carefully on his target, breathed again, and fired.

The bullet struck Uno in the chest. Wincing in pain, he dropped to his knees, coughed up a mouthful of blood, and fell forward. As he landed, he jerked the cuffs toward his wet knuckles, ripping the skin from the base of his thumb.

"You have two minutes, Ames," the stern voice continued. "Unlock the door and put the phone where he can reach it."

The door lock clicked.

Uno opened his eyes.

A faint breeze stirred inside the room.

Careful not to move, Uno slid the cuffs off his bloody fingers.

Wary footsteps shuffled toward him.

A little closer.

Very carefully, a cellphone was placed on the floor five feet from Uno and kicked forward.

It skittered toward his hand.

Uno caught the phone and launched into the man.

Ames screamed.

In one motion, Uno disarmed him, taking a bullet point blank in the stomach. Stunned only for a moment, he hooked a foot behind Ames' ankle and threw him to the ground, tearing the man's throat out as he fell.

Ames gagged and choked, writhing wildly on the floor, but Uno didn't stick around to watch. Like a shot, he hurried to the holes in the glass with Ames' weapon and began picking off scattering Jackboots. When the hallway was clear, he stepped out of the open door and strolled calmly toward the room behind the mirror.

A bullet struck him in the kidney.

Uno turned and fired back, killing the shooter.

"The bullets aren't working!" someone shouted. "He's not dying anymore!"

Panicked feet clattered across the floor. "Find more tranquilizers!"

Uno stopped abruptly, cocked his jaw in exasperation, and backed up. Irritated, he fired, killing the one heading for the tranquilizer gun, then continued. With a flick of his wrist, he shot the knob off the mirror-room door, knowing it would be locked, and kicked the door in.

The room was empty.

"Maxim," he sing-songed.

Silence.

Uno followed the hall to the end, killing a few more Jackboots as he went. "Maxim!"

A sign on the door indicated which office was the boss's. Again, he blew off the knob and kicked the door in.

A bullet slammed into his shoulder from inside the office, knocking him back a step. "Dammit," he cursed, gritting his teeth in pain, then rounded the corner shooting.

Maxim poked his head up, planning to fire again, but Uno shot the pistol from his hand, then very calmly strolled around the desk to retrieve it.

Maxim shouted in pain, falling backward, and crab-walked himself into the corner of the office. His dark hair, messy now, stuck up in hair-sprayed clumps. "Uno!" he panted, clutching bloody fingers.

"You don't like it, do you?"

"Uno, listen to me."

The begging didn't work. Uno propped a hip on the man's desk and placed cold brown eyes on him. "Where is she?" he asked in a low voice.

Maxim shook his head. "I don't know," he swore. "Rigori has her."

Uno pointed the weapon at Maxim's ankle and fired. "Wrong answer," he said between screams, then pointed at the other ankle. "Where is Seven?"

"Rigo—"

Pow!

"—aaah!"

Uno waited.

"Please," Maxim sobbed, struggling to catch his breath. "Don't do this."

Uno ignored the whimpering and picked up Maxim's cellphone from his desk. Seconds later, he was reading Cinco's message. In it was a plan and instructions just in case Uno got loose. Still not speaking, he typed out a text message reply, notifying the men he was loose and in place. The plan, already in motion, was a go, and Cinco was in charge.

Send.

"What are you doing?" Maxim wheezed in alarm. "What did you do?"

Uno had to wait.

While the commander begged and pleaded, Uno yanked a flag off a decorative pole and began tearing it into strips, ignoring the bribery attempts and hollow promises. Taking his time, he dragged Maxim up from the floor and dropped him into his plush leather office chair, then tied his arms down with the strips. Satisfied with his handiwork, he propped on the edge of Maxim's desk and looked around for something to do. To his right, he noticed a heavy paperweight with a dead scorpion inside. He played with it for a minute, quite interested in the ugly object, then slammed it down onto Maxim's fingers, crushing two in one blow.

Maxim screamed in pain.

Impressed, Uno set the paperweight down.

While Maxim hollered, he examined other objects around the room—intercom system, metals of valor, photos with celebrities, awards for bravery and heroism, tactical books, and photographs of his happy family. Beside a collage of images, he found a decorative quill pen and inkwell set perched open on a shelf.

Uno plucked the quill from its cradle and eyed the razor-sharp edge. Playing with it, he returned to his spot on the edge of the desk. He was curious whether the 24-carat gold tip would buckle against soft forearm flesh or hold its shape all the way to the arm of the chair. Before he could find out, though, Maxim's phone buzzed in Uno's hand. Disappointed, he turned the phone on and activated the speaker. "Say hello, Maxim," he said, setting the phone on the desk.

A woman's voice came over the line. "Hello?"

Maxim's eyes rounded wide. "Uno, please."

"Maxim?" said the woman.

"Uno!"

"Maxim, what's going on?" she asked in a quivering voice. "Who are these men?"

"Uno, please, I'm begging you."

Uno cocked his head at the man. "Wait, you mean you don't want your family harmed?" he asked incredulously. "That's a bit hypocritical, isn't it, Maxim? How many kids do you have?"

When Maxim hesitated, Uno lifted the gun and blew out a knee.

Maxim screamed in agony.

The woman joined in, demanding to know what was going on.

Uno ignored her. "How many kids do you have?" he asked again, aiming at the other knee.

"Two!" Maxim panted, spraying spittle.

"We'll start with the oldest," said Cinco, who must have been holding the phone.

Uno, twirling the quill on the desk, lifted his brows and gave Maxim a look of surprise, implying he was not in control here.

A moment later, a child screamed in fright and the woman cried out in horror. "No! No! What are you doing? Don't hurt her," she shrieked, sobbing wildly. "Maxim! Do something!"

"Carryann!" cried Maxim.

Uno fixed a deadly stare on the Jackboot commander. "Now, do you remember?"

"They're taking her to Russia. There's a man named Dimitri—"

"He's lying," said Uno.

"Ocho," Cinco ordered in an unamused tone. "Kill the girl—"

"Nooo!" screamed the woman.

Maxim blurted the name of the island and its location. "There's a map in the drawer! With coordinates! Please don't hurt her."

The woman sobbed.

Uno retrieved the map and folded it. "I want to know everything," he said softly, sliding it into his pocket.

"Okay! Okay. I'll tell you everything I know," he vowed, crying. "Just please don't hurt my family."

Fifteen minutes later, Maxim fell silent.

The woman's voice, unsteady and broken, spoke calmly over the line. "Maxim," she said hesitantly, "please tell me none of that is true."

Maxim began a fresh round of tears.

Uno glared at him, barely able to keep his temper in check. "Answer her, Maxim," he said in unbridled hatred. "Tell your wife what happened when we begged for our families. Tell your wife some of the funny one-liners you use when you rape them."

"Uno."

"Tell your kids how old my sister was when you murdered her. I want your family to hear it from your mouth."

When Maxim didn't answer, Uno lifted his weapon.

"Thirteen!" sobbed Maxim.

Dead silence crackled over the phone.

Ocho's voice growled over the phone next. "Tell your pretty daughter how old my children were when you slit their throats," he demanded.

"Four and … seven."

A child began to cry.

Uno snatched Maxim up by the collar and leaned close. "Pay attention you piece of shit," he said through his teeth, mere inches from the older man's nose. "From now on, we play by your rules. If I catch you on my ass again or anywhere near my Immortals, I'll kill your family the same way you killed mine—slow and painful. All of them. Your wife. Your pretty daughters. Your little dog," he vowed slowly. "And when I'm done, I'll let you live, while I delete your friends, your psychiatrist, and your tear-stained teddy bear, and," he peered dangerously into Maxim's wide eyes, "I'll make it look like you did it."

Maxim made not a sound. He knew better.

Uno released him with a snap. "You won't be warned again," he said quietly and left.

CHAPTER 21

Pherall was hauled to her feet in a scatter of blond hair, ushered into a fortress-style mansion, and taken down several flights of stairs to a dungeon-esque laboratory. There were vials and computers and whirring machines everywhere she looked and guards blocking every entrance. On the far wall of the dim room, she saw a glass enclosure with a plush bed, overstocked buffet table, comfortable clothing, and soft music. Halfway into the room, a wild-haired man with a syringe stopped her, insisting she give blood. Before she could protest, she was firmly pinned and her arm extended. While he drew a vial, a Jackboot shoved Chetireh rudely aside and punched a code into a panel. A few buttons later, the glass door of the enclosure clicked. When the man in the lab coat skipped away with his vial, the door to the glass room was opened and she was thrust inside.

Chetireh, the tall Russian she'd seen in the campground shower, remained on the other side of the glass, watching her with pale blue eyes. He had dark, wavy blond hair and freckles. His gaze was haunted and hopeless. To Pherall, he appeared beaten, despite his large muscular build and strong, deep voice. "I am sorry, beautiful lady."

Pherall put her hand on the glass. "Fight them," she whispered, still groggy.

The Russian gave her a sad smile. "I can't," he whispered back. "I have sisters."

"Bait never survive, Four. The only way to save them is to save them," she said, piercing him with a glossy stare. "You can't do that with a leash around your neck."

Chetireh scanned her face, committing it to memory. "It is a tight leash," he said softly. "They make me do terrible missions, kill people, steal things. They made me bad. Vhen I make mistakes, they kill my family." His eyes glistened and fell out of focus. "Your Uno never came for me."

"No. Four. Uno searched for you. Every day he tried to find you."

Chetireh's brows twisted. "Ve vaited for him."

Pherall's heart tightened. "Who?"

"Me, Three, Six, and Seven," he said, frowning in painful recollection, then spread his fingers over the glass as if he might touch her face through it. "In Russia, the vord for ten is desyat. I vill call you Desyat."

Tears rolled down Pherall's cheeks.

"I can feel you, like I felt her."

"Six?"

He nodded. "She vas so beautiful. Three loved her. Six vas his Queen, like you. He died vhen they killed her."

Pherall shook her head, not understanding. "How did he die?"

"A Queen takes her mate vith her vhen she dies."

Immediately, Pherall thought of Uno and her blood ran cold. "If Six was immortal, how did they kill her?"

His pale gaze travelled back in time, reliving the vivid memory. "Queens have immortal babies," he explained, "but they are not immortal. They tried and tried to bring Six back. She vas not strong enough to survive death. Vhen they learned Six already had a child, they found him and killed him. It was Seven."

Pherall closed her eyes, unable to imagine what Six must have gone through before they realized she was mortal and sick they would slaughter an innocent just to see if he would die. Bile twisted her stomach. "Where is Seven now?"

"In the lab," said Four. "They experiment on him because he refuses to cooperate, to train. I already tell him you are here. He believes Uno vill come for him."

"And you?"

Chetireh thought about his answer and gave her a sad smile. "I lost faith in Uno long ago. The experiments stopped vhen I agreed to cooperate. I found you to make them stop killing my family," he admitted heavily, "but now, I have met Uno. I fought him. He was half my size and twice my strength. I could not take you from him," he said with gleaming eyes. "I watch him destroy army, shoot down helicopter, and outsmart the Jackboots. This is the first time in years I have hope," he admitted, "but I am scared for Uno. Rigori is terrified of him. He vill be chained like animal now they have caught him."

Pherall paled. This was her fault.

"This island is equipped with containment security designed specifically to hold him. This place is fortress. It is easy to get in, but impossible to get out. If Uno comes here, he vill not leave."

Pherall rested her dizzy head on the cool glass.

Chetireh put his hand beside her face, again, as if to touch her. "I am sorry to say, Desyat, they vill not kill you. Your fate is far worse."

It was almost too much to ask, but Pherall had to know. "Why? What do they want me for?"

"You carry immortal protein. Alive," he whispered, "you are fertile."

194

Pherall was so startled by the suggestion she couldn't speak right away and, for a long moment, she stared at him. "They … plan to breed me?" she whispered, barely able to form the words.

Chetireh didn't answer, which was answer enough.

His face blurred in her vision. Pherall closed her eyes, streaking tears down both cheeks. "With whom?" she managed, knowing she didn't want the answer.

"Me."

*****

The next morning, Uno, dressed in black Jackboot fatigues, stopped the stolen military truck by a long dock and set the brake. Ocho and Blue hurried to unload the back, while Cinco tied a large powder-blue ferry to the piling. Within minutes, a truckload of munitions, food, and clean clothes were loaded, and the ferry pulled away from the dock with Cinco at the helm.

Uno stood with his brown hair whipping around his face, watching the shore fade. After giving his temper time to calm, he reconnected with the present and scanned the ferry Cinco had found. There were three levels. The middle level, where he stood, was covered, but open on all sides with an old concession stand near its center. Inside, bits and pieces of a kitchen complete with saltwater damage and an empty soda fountain waited to be tested. A staircase at the stern led to the lower deck, which was surrounded by thick plexiglass panes and sported a glass-bottom viewing hole encased by metal railings. Public restrooms took up one of the four walls, while one long continuous bench seat formed a ring around the entire deck. Once Uno had seen the two lower levels, he felt better, at least calm enough for conversation, and headed up to the top deck. This deck was open with a pilot house perched near the bow.

Behind the pilot house, he met Ocho and Blue, both stone-faced, and sighed heavily. "Good work," he said simply.

Ocho snorted and watched the water splash behind the ferry. "That was tough, threatening a kid."

Uno agreed, but that didn't change his mind. "I meant what I said," he assured simply. "I'm done with Jackboots."

"I am too," Blue agreed, gripping the rail and peering out. "If we can't have families, neither should they."

Ocho faced his leader with a heavy heart. "I just pray they got the message. I'll lose sleep over it," he said firmly, "but I'm done running. I won't ever get my family back. At least they have the option to decide."

195

Uno paused to touch his friend on the shoulder. "Their sins do not belong on your shoulders, Ocho. Don't wear them," he said softly. "Let's go see Cinco."

At the helm, Cinco threw an arm around Uno, much to Uno's discomfort, and squeezed him. "Unee!"

"Get off me," Uno laughed, pushing him away, then slapped hands with him. "Where were you?"

"What, while you were visiting Maxim?" Cinco clarified mischievously. "Oh. Well, after you sent that text message, I went to the library and ran a hack search on Maxim's phone number. Found a cloud file backup of his computer and a list of IP addresses he likes to connect to. His backup password was the same as his email password which we already had, so I got right in. His most recent activity was in a video history file, so I disguised you as a robot. Then, came back and gassed the boat. Sorry, it isn't better. I found it at the back of a marina. She hasn't been touched in years."

"It's fine as long as she's ocean worthy."

Cinco gave a grimacing nod. "She's equipped with stabilizer fins, so she's been out before. There's a lifeboat and the engine is in excellent shape. As long as we avoid hurricanes, she should float."

"I'll take her," said Ocho, moving in on the controls. "Show him what you found."

Cinco pulled Uno's cellphone from his pocket and fooled with it for several moments. Finally, he selected a folder, opened it, and handed it to Uno. "You're not gonna like this."

Uno took it and selected the first video.

A grungy, unshaven image of Maxim started the film with him adjusting the screen.

"Can you hear us, Maxim?" said a voice thick with Russian accent.

"Yeah," he yawned. *"I can hear."*

"Can you see ze video screen behind Rigori?"

The video shifted slightly, and a screen appeared.

"Yes. Yes."

"Good," said the Russian voice. *"I will get right to it, zen. Ze blood sample Four collected from ze girl and sent back has been analyzed and found to be positive for ze protein."*

Rigori sat up straight, just visible on the outer edge of the screen. *"She's immortal?"*

"Yes and no," said the Russian. *"Ze females are very different from ze males. I will show you video."*

An old experimentation video flickered into view. Muted screams and thrashing came from a young black woman, gagged and strapped to a table. Uno jerked his head away and closed his eyes, unable to watch as they cut into her. When the gurgled sobs faded and the Russian's voice resumed, Uno's brown eyes shifted warily to the phone again, hooded beneath a deep frown.

"In ze twenty years we have known of ze Immortals, only one female has ever been found positive for ze protein. Needless to say, zey are extremely rare."

Rigori jerked upright in his seat. *"You have a female!"*

The video continued.

Uno's eyes blurred, but this time he watched to the end, which ended with the death of the young woman. The team waited, but she did not reset. When they realized this, frantic, unsuccessful attempts were made to revive her. A voice behind the video screeched in outrage and shouted at the medical team as the videographer circled the dead body. "That was our only Queen," he shouted in Russian. The bloody operators whirled in horror, pleading and throwing out their hands. Screams and rapid gunfire blended together and faded, and the video blinked off.

"We expected her to reset after death," the Russian said when the video ended, *"but she didn't. With our first female, we immediately became interested in reproduction of Immortals and stem cell research. Her eggs also proved positive, so we extracted some. Ze extraction process destroyed ze protein, so we tried again using a different procedure. Ze second procedure failed, so we tried putting some eggs back. As you can see, she did not survive zat operation. We made every effort to bring her back, but we lost her. Ze only female specimen ever found did not reset. Ze female Immortals are not immortal."*

Uno flattened his lips, disappointed by the news.

"Ze good news is in ze short time she was in custody, we learned a lot about Immortals. Ze males were strongly attracted to ze

*female, not necessarily sexually but more as an awareness of her,
whereas ze female could actually detect ze males from a distance.
Both subtle connections entirely undetectable by our equipment ...
until ze alpha padonak appeared. Ze connection between ze two
was instantaneous and quite physical. Once zey came in contact,
an unbreakable, physical bond formed. Ze purpose of zis bond is
still unstudied; however, it is significant enough zat when she died,
her Immortal mate died too. We called her a Queen,"* he said,
pausing for effect. *"Uno's female is a Queen."*

Some vile, sick person in the back clapped his hands, sickening
Uno.

Maxim juggled a cellphone to his ear. *"Wake up! Get up!"* he
hissed, contorting his face in excitement. *"I don't care what time it
is. Shut down the bounty on the girl! Do it now,"* he ordered.
"Move her to classified."
Someone off camera broke in with a high-pitched voice. *"I want
her. Oh! Bring her to me! Rigori!"*
Rigori's voice returned, barely able to speak after the news.
"Maxim, who is she. What is her name?"
Maxim's shaggy face pressed against the screen. *"Ten,"* he said
breathlessly.

Uno's face went pale.
"They're going to breed her," Blue realized in a heavy whisper.
Cinco frowned. "At least we know she's alive."
"That isn't necessarily a good thing," said Ocho from the helm.
"Who will they breed her with, and how? I'm doubting candles
and poetry will be involved. And I can only imagine what they
would do with the babies."
Uno's fingers tightened on the windowsill, whitening his
knuckles. The image Ocho just put into his head nearly blinded
him with fury and he wasn't handling it well. Rage boiled inside
him, and he struggled to contain his temper. "Now, I'm pissed," he
said in a deadly voice. "They aren't breeding my Queen."

*****

Two days later, Pherall jolted awake to the sound of a thump and
sat up in her bed. Her only clothes were a sheer, floor-length white
satin gown with matching panties and robe. The robe, the only
thing not see-through, never came off. Tightening it around her
shoulders, she glared at the ridiculously romantic decorations

around her cage and the fresh cut flowers perched on a small table and remembered where she was. Something had woken her. Frowning, she turned to the front glass and peered out at the horrid dungeon-esque laboratory. It was empty, indicating it was still the middle of the night. Slowly, she got out of bed. Peering into the darkness, she looked for the source of the sound and found her brother's dark silhouette crumpled on the ground just outside the door. A bloody handprint slid down the glass to where his hand rested now, streaked where he fell. His clothes were blood-soaked and torn.

Horrified, Pherall hurried to him in a flutter of satin and lace. "Korbin!" she cried, trying desperately to open the glass door. It wouldn't budge. "Oh my God!"

Devastated that she couldn't reach him, she slid down beside him on the opposite side of the glass.

"Pherall!" he sobbed, pressing his blood-stained, tear-streaked face against the glass. "They keep killing me."

"Korbin."

"Over and over, they kill me. I die and wake up. I keep waking up. I can't take it anymore," he hissed, shoulders shaking. "I don't want to wake up."

"Just a little longer, Korbin," she whispered. "Uno's coming."

"They captured Uno."

Pherall shook her head. "You don't know him."

Korbin's eyes flashed at her. "Uno wants you, not us," he growled angrily.

"No!" she snapped back. "He's been looking for Seven. Every day, he searches. Once he knows where you are, Uno won't leave without you. He won't leave without any of us, Korbin. We're his Immortals."

"Seven screams for Uno when they cut him," Korbin told her, his eyes glossing in acute memory. "Dr. von Stein has no mercy. He's deaf to someone else's pain. He laughs when Seven screams. Now that they have you, I have no purpose here. I can't breed with you, and I'm not trained to fight. They're preparing another experiment block with restraints. For me. They want to learn how to exterminate us."

Pherall lay her hand against his on the glass, trembling as he spoke.

"I thought I was saving mom," he murmured softly. He choked, struggling to form the words. "They swore she'd live if I cooperated."

Pherall covered her mouth, recoiling from the awful news.

"They lied," he said, meeting her gaze at last. "She missed you so much. When she found out about Mia," he paused to exhale, then continued. "The news said you were dead, but the cops couldn't produce a body. The story kept changing. She was told they were searching the water. It was bad."

Tears rolled down Pherall's cheeks. She shook her head, begging him to quit. "Korbin, stop ..."

"I didn't know about the Immortals until they killed me," he said, resting his temple against hers. "I woke, confused and scared. I didn't know where I was, and they killed me again. When I begged them to stop, they forced me to find you. I disobeyed them at your shipyard." He lifted his tormented gaze, making eye contact with her. "They killed mom. It was my punishment. I killed mom."

Pherall's shoulders shook. "No! This is not your fault, Korbin," she cried angrily, wiping her cheeks. "They did this, do you hear me? They did this!"

Further words failed her, and she dissolved into wracking sobs. She'd never known hatred before, but it was an emotion she was quickly becoming familiar with. She remembered Uno's cold eyes when she met him. Cinco, Ocho, and Blue all wore the same look, and now she understood it.

"Dr. von Stein is working on an elixir for Rigori," Korbin said numbly, "so he can live forever, using Seven's blood. They drill holes into him and watch to see how long the tissue takes to repair itself. The protein is in the blood, so Rigori drinks it. No person ever deserved death like that man does."

Pherall agreed, ashamed of herself for wishing so hard for such a thing.

"They plan embryonic studies once you're pregnant," he continued. "I imagine you'll stay pregnant. The babies may or may not survive, but the idea isn't to have immortal children. It's to make Rigori immortal. With you, he can do it."

Korbin looked at his twin, long and hard, with miserable, hopeless eyes, and managed a tender smile. "If I ever get my hands on you again," he swore through fresh tears, "I'll kill you myself."

Pherall closed her eyes and sagged into the glass, snuggling as close as she could to her brother.

Comforted by her presence, Korbin pressed his cheek against hers and closed his wet eyes.

Lying together, they both fell asleep.

CHAPTER 22

The next morning, Pherall sat with her back to the glass, preferring to look inside her room rather than stare into the laboratory. Korbin was gone by the time she woke. She could hear scientists moving back and forth, clacking on computer keyboards, and speaking in muffled conversation as they moved about their day. None of them paid the least bit of attention to her and she had no interest in their business. Only one scientist concerned her.

Dr. von Stein.

She stiffened at the sound of his mousy voice and watched him stroll to his workstation through a reflection in her glass room. Trying to appear to be asleep or merely bored senseless, which she was, she remained still and listened, hoping to glean whatever information she could. It worked. He ignored her, not that it mattered, but it gave her something to do. She watched him scribble notes into a green notebook, then jot quickly into a red one before gathering supplies onto a medical tray. Horrid surgical instruments, gauze, and knives were placed in the bucket and a folded apron was set out. He was preparing for surgery. Nausea sloshed through Pherall's stomach. With vivid clarity, she remembered what Korbin had told her the night before and could only imagine that those things were for him. And there she sat, helpless to do anything about it.

Hot tears rolled down her cheek.

*****

On the island, Uno, dressed in stolen black Jackboot gear, crawled to the top of the hill and looked down into a layered fortress nestled in a rocky valley. The air was hot and humid here, even in the shade, and the sun blazed down from a blue sky. Everything sizzled. Even though his hair was shorter after a barber session with Ocho and fit better beneath the cap he wore, Uno was already sweating. The new haircut was to help him blend in with the guards on the premises, the ones he was about to kill. At the center of the yard rested a dominating stronghold-style mansion with tiered courtyards surrounding it and a very active, reinforced guard shack. On every level, hired guards in dark green battle-gear patrolled in prison-yard style.

"The only thing missing is a moat," said Cinco sarcastically, "and perhaps a dragon."

Ocho cursed quietly. "I wish it was just a dragon," he said, scanning the grounds. "Where does he find all these guards?"

A frown darkened Blue's features. "I don't know about this, Uno. We're way too outnumbered," he said, looking hopelessly at all the guards.

Uno frowned at the mansion, then dug a pair of small binoculars from his pocket. He checked, lowered the glasses to squint, then checked again. "The guards will only be on the outside," he said, examining the stronghold pensively. "The top of this building is designed to resemble a barbican with castle turrets but look there … at those things on the roof," he said, pointing to a series of massive blocks. "They're decorative, to hide the braces crisscrossing the roof."

The others followed his point, then noticed the same thing elsewhere.

"Castle turrets don't have braces and bolts. They're designed to protect the guards from arrows and bullets. Those braces have a different purpose," he said, handing the binoculars over.

Cinco peered first, then passed them on. "What the hell is that?"

"Containment security," said Uno. "A lot of it. Once we get in, there won't be any getting out."

"That's bad," muttered Cinco.

Uno stared down at the mansion and thumped his knuckles against his lips. Running possibilities through his head, he peered down again over his fingers. "If we get trapped inside, it's game over. They win," he said after a full minute, his tone a bit darker than before, "unless we shut the containment system down."

Cinco liked this better. "So, what's the plan?"

Uno surveyed the scene below carefully, his brown eyes narrowed in concentration as he took each section in. "First, we get into those green uniforms. These Jackboot suits won't work." After another moment, he pointed to different positions around the fortress. "Blue," he said, gesturing to the guard shack, "lock that shack down. Dismantle their internal communication. Ocho," he said and pointed to two spots, "you take power. Shut it down. Cinco, radio and external communication, then," he pushed his backpack to him, "set these around the fortress."

"All of them?"

"Every last damn one. I'll go find Pherall and the other Immortals," he said, scanning the grounds for a way in. "Four, Seven, and Nine are trapped inside with her. Kill whoever you have to and get them out. Go!"

*****

Blue ran his fingers through his reshaved blond mohawk, tucking it back, then pulled his brand-new dark green cap low over his eyes. Dressed in his new digs, he adjusted his glasses and peered out over the dead body. The yard between him and the shack was filled with guards. To his right, an electrician stood on a scaffolding working on a section of wire near the eave of the first level. To his left, guards in pairs patrolled the outer perimeter of the enormous yard. Right away, he began searching for patterns in the guards' behavior. The moment he found one, he stepped over his first victim and out of the bushes.

Instantly, he blended in.

As he strolled casually toward the shack, nodding with curt politeness to the other guards, he angled his path toward the scaffolding beneath the electrician. With a quick flick of his wrist, he had a small tool bag and a three-foot grounding rod in his hands.

Armed with his new arsenal, he turned steel gray eyes to the guard shack and quickened his pace.

*****

Ocho fastened the belt around his waist and adjusted the green cap over his dark head. Moving quickly, he stuffed his feet into the dead man's boots and arranged the corpse over the toilet seat. The shoes were too big but would work for now. Eager for fresh air, he stepped out of the sweltering porta-potty and used the tip of a key he found in his pocket to switch the lock back to 'Occupied.'

Careful to match his pace to the others in the yard, he hurried to the electrician's scaffolding. As he passed it, he ran into the corner, knocking a pile of bolts to the ground and stepping on a piece of paneling.

Crack!

"Oh, crap!" Ocho cursed apologetically and dropped to his knees to clean up the mess. "I am so sorry."

The electrician whirled in irritation. "What the hell is wrong with you?" he grumbled, climbing down to assess the damage. "You aren't supposed to be on this side of the yard, you idiot," he scolded, noticing the insignia on Ocho's uniform. "You're supposed to be guarding the outer—uuh!"

Ocho eased the man to the ground, careful to keep his hand over the dude's mouth until he stopped squirming, then emptied every pocket he could reach in search of keys to the power panel. He found the keys and rolled the unmoving body beneath the bottom floor of the scaffolding. As casually as he could manage, he wiped his trembling hands on the grass to remove the blood and tucked his knife away. All he needed now was a tool bag.

There was no bag.

Frowning, he scanned overhead to see if the electrician's tools were on the eve of the roof or maybe on the ground. "Where's his tool bag?" he muttered, looking around, but there wasn't one. The only tool he could find was the reversible screwdriver the man had dropped on the ground and a hand-held radio.

Ocho picked both up with a curse and zeroed in on the power panel thirty feet away. As he strolled toward it, his fingers identified the correct key.

*****

Cinco, dressed in a uniform much too small for him, felt over his head for bricks with good finger-holds and spider-crawled upward until he reached the roof of the fortress. The outer perimeter of the building was reinforced and would withstand an attack from the bottom floor, but the roof, he was certain, was unprotected. He pulled himself up, splitting the armpits of his clothing, and dropped his backpack in a shady corner of the ceiling, intending to come back to it after his first mission. Mindful of the cameras posted around the roof, he made his way toward the antenna block.

"Hey!" shouted a voice. "What are you doing up here?"

Cinco spun sharply, hurling a knife.

The guard stiffened, clawing at the throwing knife poking out of his throat, then sank silently to his knees.

Cinco removed the dead man's radio. "I'm about to jack up those antennas," he answered, yanking his knife from the guard's throat. "You wait here. There's an asshole in the area. You could get hurt."

*****

Uno squatted in the shadows of an air-conditioning unit and took a moment to focus. He was afraid. It had been so long since he'd had something worth losing that he found himself unprepared for the possibility of failure. The very thought terrified him. It was a sensation he'd become unaccustomed to, and he noticed he was making mistakes—running too heavily on his feet, taking too long to silence a guard, and walking in front of cameras. He was rushing. Mentally, he chided himself for being careless. He couldn't afford mistakes, not today. He didn't have time to introduce himself to useless emotions either and several were taunting him. Of all the emotions available to choose from, the one he needed most now was the rage. The others could wait. In his mind, he replayed the video of Six's torture and death, nearly bringing himself to tears. Then he imagined, with rather vivid clarity, what Rigori had planned for Pherall.

That did it.

Hot, black rage surged through his body, numbing his heart and drawing a scowl down over his features. They weren't breeding his Queen. No mercy, he coached himself silently. No hesitation. No fear. He took a deep breath, quieting his nerves, and glared at the fortress.

It was time.

Rage firmly in place, he gathered his weapons, then waited for two female guards patrolling the side entrance of the fortress to find a distraction. While he waited, he opened a small knife in one hand and stretched a thin cord in the other. When they took too long, he picked up a pebble and tossed it behind them. Both turned to investigate, and he slipped down the hill toward them.

They were dead in seconds.

Quietly, he dragged the women's bodies into the bushes and jumped down a low wall to the next level, landing on the back of one guard and stabbing another. Moving quickly, he hid their bodies and dropped down to the last level, then eased toward the recessed door. A guard paced inside the covered walkway. Taking a moment to quiet his breathing, Uno stepped behind a pillar out of sight of a camera and waited. The guard, bored to death at his post, strolled methodically to the end of his walkway, spun with dramatic ridiculousness, and marched back.

As he passed, Uno grabbed him, twisting his head at an odd angle, and shoved the tip of his blade beneath the man's ear. "Open it," he hissed quietly.

A bead of blood rolled down the guard's neck.

Wide-eyed, he fumbled his keys and unlocked the knob.

*****

Inside the guard shack, a uniformed officer with short brown hair frowned up at one of the monitors above her head. The image looked fine now, but she was certain she'd just seen a flash of something unusual. Nimble fingers reversed the film until the blur appeared again.

There.

She stopped the video feed.

205

Frame by frame she backed it up until the distorted image appeared again, then square by square zoomed in. Puzzled, she reached for her phone. "Boris," she said hesitantly, "can you come into the monitor room?"

A minute later, a tall, distinguished-looking officer entered the room with a scowl beneath his red mustache. "Yes! Ms. Onna?" he enunciated irritably.

Onna gestured to the screen. "Look at that," she said, pointing to the dark blob.

Boris lifted his brows at the blob, then shifted his gaze to the smaller woman. "Is this another bug crawling across the lens?"

"I don't think it was a bug," she said backing the film up. "The camera rotates—look. It isn't there, but when it rotates back it's there. On the third rotation, it's gone again."

"It's feedback."

Onna shook her head. "It looks like—"

"I was in a meeting," he interrupted hotly. "This is the second interruption in ten minutes."

She nodded. "Yes, I apologize for the interruptions, but—"

"Rigori is in the conference room waiting for an explanation. Twice you've bothered me. I don't have time for this! Do you have something to show me or not?"

"Yes, Sir. I understand, Sir," she rushed, trying again to get his attention, "but I believe we should have it checked out."

"I sent a patrol the first time. They haven't reported anything."

"You don't find that odd?" she dared.

Boris slammed his hand down on the table. "Onna!" he barked. "I am in an important meeting. I don't have time to go running around the compound every time the video flickers. I have real shit to worry about," he said coldly, "and this is a waste of my time. If you persist—"

"It looks like a body," she blurted.

Boris exhaled in exasperation.

"The patrol never reported back," she continued, then turned to the wide panel of video screens. "Right now in the yard, including the two you sent, there should be twenty-four guards on patrol, but there are only nineteen."

Quickly, she counted the guards to prove her point, then counted again. "Seventeen."

Boris stared at her for a minute, then shoved her out of the way and took control of one of the cameras. Staring up at the screen, he panned the side entrance of the building and zeroed in on the door. "Why is this door unguarded?"

Onna didn't answer. Instead, she moved to a separate panel of monitors and scanned them. After a moment of examination, she pointed at the monitor. "There's something under that bush," she insisted. "That's another body. I'm sure of it."

Boris, staring unblinking at the video, reached for the phone and dialed without looking. "Rigori, it's Boris …"

*****

Uno pushed the frightened guard into the building, taking quick note of the layout, and kicked the door shut behind them. Inside, he pulled the man into a corner behind heavy drapes, the closest hiding place he could find, and pressed the blade firmly against the man's neck. "Where is she?"

The guard pointed. "In the labora—," he said loudly, hoping to attract attention.

Uno jerked the knife, piercing him, and directed the guard's body to the marble floor behind the curtain. Quickly, he stuffed a wad of curtain into the man's mouth to quiet him while he died, then darted behind a piece of furniture. Voices from different distances carried across the hard, ornate surfaces that decorated the mansion. Nothing inside indicated warmth or happiness. It was hospital spotless. Switching weapons, Uno flicked the safety off on his machine gun and peered out over the shiny floors toward the staircase leading downstairs, eager to mow down everyone on Rigori's payroll. He'd found the dungeon. There was no mistake. The smell of chemicals and cleaning solution wafted up, bringing back vivid memories and infuriating him further.

Uno released a shaky breath, struggling to keep a leash on the monster inside him. On silent feet, he crossed the room, machine gun ready, and started down the switchback staircase. When he was almost to the half-turn, increasing voices indicated a group starting up the stairs—two men and a woman—but the silence behind them suggested few occupants on the floor below. He slid the gun onto his back again and pulled his knife.

The three moved up, two side by side, one following behind. They spotted him.

Bypassing the landing, Uno leapt over the rail onto the group of three, crushing one. He lurched forward, slashed one man across the throat and elbowed the female backward. Spinning around, he snatched her head and broke her neck, then dropped his blade between the shoulder blades of the wounded scientist beneath him.

Blood spattered the walls and pooled on the floors, enough now that there was no reason to waste time hiding the evidence. Uno hurried quickly over the bodies toward a drab hallway lined with doors. Vivid memories of his previous captivity flickered in his mind, adding weight to his footsteps and crushing his windpipe. Images clanged through his head—the pain he'd endured, death after death after death, begging them to stop, their cruel laughter. A wave of fear, raw and black, washed through him, compressing his chest, cementing his feet. His mind screamed for him to leave. Run. Escape now before it was too late. If they caught him …

Uno shook the crippling sensation away. "They aren't breeding my Queen," he whispered again, snapping his anger back into place. With renewed energy, he surged forward, taking note of the building's structure. In the entryway of the next hallway, he looked up, noting the containment bars waiting to drop, and forced himself to take deep, steady breaths. Once they knew he was in, steel bars would barricade every wing of the building. If they caught him, there would be no death to relieve the torture, which meant he had to focus.

The monster soothed him, vowing to take over if that happened.

Stepping across the barrier, Uno peered down a long hall and decided it was the wrong way. As he turned, he noticed a fire extinguisher box with an axe inside. He grabbed it. He was down to minutes before his presence was discovered. Any moment, they would realize he was here. Alarms would go off, and he'd be on the run.

He had to find Pherall now.

Following his nose, he ran.

*****

Rigori rushed into the monitor room and stood in the dark glow of video screens. "Show me!" he demanded.

Onna flipped through camera images throughout the mansion, searching for anything out of the ordinary. Pictures flickered by until one caught her eye. She stopped the scan and backed the images up.

"What did you see?" demanded Boris.

Onna turned the camera and zoomed in on the staircase. This time, there was no reason for her to point. Three dead bodies lay piled on each other, blocking the stairs. "Uno's here."

"Find him!" ordered Boris.

Onna's fingers moved expertly over the equipment, her eyes trained on the monitors above her head. It didn't take her long.

Rigori clamped his stark white teeth in seething hatred. "It's him," he snarled. "That's Uno."

Onna zoomed out. "He's in containment level three and heading straight for the lab. Do you want me to drop the outer perimeter gates?"

"No. If you drop them too soon the guards can't get in," Boris told her, his eyes frozen on the monitors.

Uno took off running.

Onna's finger moved to a different button, and he appeared on the next camera. "He's entering the secondary containment level," she said calmly. "I can drop the inner gates and pin him now."

Rigori held up a hand to stop her. "No! That's too close. I don't want him that close to my female. We have to draw him back into the level three perimeter hallway first," he decided, snatching the phone from the cradle. "Get Seven into surgery now! Now! Room Six. I don't care what you do, just make him scream!" he ordered. "Now! And tell that piece of shit Number Four to capture Uno or his whole family dies! I'm on my way."

Slam!

Furious, Rigori stomped out.

Alone in the monitor room, Boris leaned forward on his arms. "Once Uno is back in containment level three drop perimeter gates two and three and pin him there," he instructed.

Suddenly, a shriek erupted from the front door of the guard shack.

Onna and Boris hurried out of the video room in alarm to find Rigori and several other guards rattling the exit door.

"Open this door!" shouted Rigori, banging on it with his fist. "Why is this door locked? Open it up this minute!"

Boris brushed past and tried to open the door himself, but it was no use. Something was barring it shut.

"Knock it down!"

"We can't," Boris said quietly. "It's reinforced steel. A bulldozer couldn't knock this door down."

"Then, get maintenance up here," Rigori barked, throwing a point at a random guard. "You! Call them."

The guard put a phone to his ear, frowned, then tried twice to reset it for a signal. Puzzled, he looked at it, then tried the next phone. "We have no signal."

Rigori's face turned bright red. "Find one!" he barked.

Onna rushed back into the monitor room. "The video is out!" she called. "The whole island. There's no power."

"No!" shouted Rigori, running in after her. "Where is he! Where is Uno?"

Boris rushed into the room behind them. "The cameras have a backup generator line. Onna, help me switch the power feed!"

*****

"Aaaaah!"

Uno stopped short at the sound of a pained scream and turned to face the direction he'd come. The voice was unfamiliar to him, the sound of the cry wasn't. After a moment, he heard it again, this time a higher pitch.

"Aaaaah!" it shrieked, adding a sob to the wail.

The hair on Uno's neck lifted.

A third scream followed by an agonized, gurgling cry danced up the hallway, coming from far away.

It was a trap.

"Uno!" bubbled the faint voice, followed by gagging sounds.

Uno's insides trembled. "I'm coming." he choked.

"Aaaah!" The voice tried to scream, cry, and draw breathe at the same time. "Stop! Stop! Please, stop!"

White-knuckled fingers locked around the hilt of Uno's knife. Before he knew what was happening, he was running. Running hard. Desperate to find the source of the screams before they fell silent. It was a trap. He knew it was a trap. He didn't care. In a blur, he reached the end of the hall, which turned right at ninety degrees, and charged blindly forward. To hell with method. To hell with stealth. He had to reach the voice!

*****

Guards trapped in the shack crowded around the monitors, watching Uno move unimpeded through the corridors. The video quality was poor with the low power and only one monitor could be on at a time, but they were able to watch Uno's progress through the hallways.

"Sir," Boris said in disbelief. "It's working! He's going back."

"It isn't going to matter if we can't get those gates down," Rigori countered impatiently. "Is the security system on generator power?"

A computer technician stepped forward into the dark room. "No, but there may be a way to lower one gate at a time."

"How?" demanded Rigori.

"Through my cellphone."

"You aren't supposed to have cellphones here!" shouted the old man.

The technician stared at him, waiting.

210

"Why are you still standing here! Lower the gates," Rigori ordered, then stiffened. "Wait. Does your cellphone have a signal?"

"Barely. It's very poor on the island."

Rigori flicked his fingers for it. "Give it to me!" he said and snatched it away. Moments later, it was to his ear. "Dimitri … Dimitri! Can you hear me? It's Rigori … Dimitri … We need your militia on the island now! Dimitri? Dammit!" he cursed, waving the phone around the room in search of a signal. "Here," he barked at the technician. "Get those gates down."

*****

Ocho stood on a full trash bin and, balancing precariously on lumpy bags of trash, gripped the disgusting bottom edges of a garbage shoot and heaved himself in. It took effort to slide his shoulders inside, but he managed and looked up.

There were protected fire sensors spaced at even intervals along the metal walls which, if triggered, would produce a spray of water powerful enough to douse any fire inside the shoot. Considering the security in this place, they would likely also register unusual motion as well and trigger a trouble alarm, also resulting in a gush of water. There was no telling how sensitive they were, but a splash of water would send him back down the other way. He'd used the edge of the trash bin to hoist himself up, which meant he would land on it and probably break his back … again. He hated breaking his back. Hated it!

As long as the power was off the sensors slept, but he didn't want to risk it. He needed to hurry.

Far overhead, a trash bin squeaked open.

Ocho stopped.

There was a shuffle of falling … something.

Ocho looked up and—*Splat!*—got a face full of cold spaghetti.

"Dammit!" Gritting his teeth, he shouldered the marinara away and worked himself upward. The smell in the shoot was atrocious —sweet, rotten, bloody, and sour. There was no holding his breath either. All he could do was hurry. After a bit of wiggling and a good yank or two, he was able to get his legs inside the chute bucket. It was a tight fit, but he'd be fine so long as nobody dropped any garbage down.

Involuntarily, he shuddered as he passed the first sensor. Moving only a few inches at a time, he scooted himself upward until he reached a hatch just below a section where the garbage shoot reduced, narrowing to a twelve-inch diameter. Knowing he'd never fit any higher, he gripped the edges of the hatch. By now, he was sweating, but he could feel the cool air seeping through the cover from the air-conditioned building. It felt good. This was almost too easy, he thought. The latch on the thin metal cover was a simple one and easily opened outward with the screwdriver.

The dark room on the other side glowed with pale blue emergency lights.

Good.

With a yank, he slid himself out onto the cool floor and eased the cover down with a click. It took a moment for his eyes to adjust, but when they did, he found himself standing in an eight by ten-foot glass room with two-inch holes in one wall. He turned, looking for a door, but there was no door. He looked up and down and then checked the walls again. There was no door.

Ocho looked at the hole and his mouth went dry. Why was there a hole in a room with no door?

Suddenly, silence seemed wise. Warily, he bent to go back out the garbage shoot, but the door wouldn't open. He tried his screwdriver, but the hatch wouldn't budge. It was locked from the outside. He'd crawled into a trap.

Something scraped behind him.

He whirled to find the tip of a gun poking through the hole. His heart skipped. There was nowhere to run.

The gun angled down toward his knee and quietly fired.

*****

Further down the hallway, the whir of a drill joined the screams, leading Uno to the correct door.

It was unlocked.

Clutching his long knife, he threw the door wide and burst inside.

A blood-soaked boy with jet-black hair and ebony skin, maybe eleven years old, lay strapped tightly to a table. He thrashed around inside his restraints, gasping in agony, while spilled blood dripped along the beveled table at the edges toward a catch-tray and collected in a bag at the corner. Around him stood four technicians, each clutching surgical instruments, a drill, a scalpel, a surgical spoon, and bloody gauze. The one with the drill, shoved down into the boy's eye, whirled and her tool fell silent.

Uno hurled his knife hard, impaling the bitch, then attacked the technician beside her with the axe. As the man dropped, Uno leapt over the boy's legs, kicking the scalpel technician backward into the wall with a crash. Landing, he snatched the surgical instrument from the first technician and thrust it downward into the woman's throat. She crumpled to the floor, thrashing wildly and not at all enjoying being impaled.

The one he'd kicked tried to run.

Twisting around, Uno grabbed a nearby cord and wound it tight around the man's throat, then dropped him to the floor and left him to suffocate. Breathing heavily with emotion, he turned hesitantly around to the table, his unblinking eyes fixed firmly on the child.

The mutilated boy watched him with one eye. "You ca—me," he shuttered, drowning in his own blood.

A hot tear rolled down Uno's face. "Seven?" he whispered in horror.

"Please take … me with … you," the boy choked.

"Damn right, you're coming with me." Breathing heavily, Uno retrieved his axe and yanked the knife from the technician's throat. Angrily, he wiped his eyes, turned the child's mutilated face away, and killed him.

The little black boy jolted and fell still.

With frantic fingers, Uno unstrapped the restraints and jerked the child into his arms, hugging him fiercely. "A fucking child," he hissed into the boy's hair. "God."

In a blink, the power went out, casting the entire mansion into darkness, and silencing the electrical hum that vibrated though the walls.

Uno snapped out of it and jumped to his feet. Quickly, he threw the dead child over his shoulder and hurried back out into the hall. Pale glow-lights lined the edges of the floor, giving him something to follow. As hard as he dared in the dark, he ran.

*****

Pherall lifted her lashes at the sound of a tiny click, then watched in surprise as the lights in the laboratory blinked out. Along the floor against the walls, a pale line of emergency lights glowed to life, giving an eerie feel to the already creepy dungeon. Technicians and scientists dropped what they were doing and followed the lights out, chattering nervously amongst themselves. Not one looked back at her.

"Uno," she whispered.

Hesitantly, she stood and crossed to the glass door. It had an electromagnetic lock, which gave easily when she pushed it. The magnets, it turned out, were entirely worthless without power.

And she was out.

Moving quickly now, she hurried to Dr. von Stein's desk and squinted at the pre-surgical notes he had written. As her eyes adjusted to the low light, the words became legible. Korbin had been right. He was scheduled to begin surgery today to see if the 'Natural Immortals' could be killed.

Natural?

Word by word, she read, covering her mouth with her hand as she reached the bottom. There, it told the location. Room 12.

"Korbin," she worried and hurried to find Room 12.

Running carefully through the dark, she scanned the room numbers beside every door, searching desperately for the right one, but she was in the wrong hall. Quickening her pace, she jogged along the glow-lights until she found a hall starting with Room 16. Almost frantic with urgency, she raced down the corridor toward the lower end until she passed an object glowing on the wall in front of her. She paused to look at it and found a fire extinguisher box with an axe inside.

*****

"Uno has the boy," said Onna.

The blood drained from Rigori's face. "Lower the level one gates. Seal Ten in the lab!" he ordered breathlessly. "Hurry!"

Onna switched the camera view to the laboratory, while the technician worked to direct a signal to the inner perimeter gates. "She's gone. Ten is gone."

"What!" screamed Rigori. "Find her! Find her before Uno does."

"If I look for her, I'll lose him."

Uno blinked back onto the screen, his dark silhouette barely visible in the soft, grainy glow.

Onna switched to a new camera at the end of the hall he was in and watched him run toward her. "He's in Corridor C, almost to B. He's heading for Ground Zero."

Rigori whirled to the technician. "Lower the second perimeter. Corridor C! Lower the gates!"

"We have guards moving in," Boris said, pointing at the screen.

"It's about damn time," railed Rigori, directing his shouts at the monitor screen as if the soldiers could hear him. "Shoot him!"

*****

Up ahead, Uno heard the clank of a gate beginning to lower. With a curse, he took off, racing hard with his burden to get across before it reached the ground. Mere feet away, he dove low and rolled, slamming Seven and the axe into the floor, just as the gate reached the top of the fire extinguisher he'd placed in the track on the way in. The fire extinguisher clanked and buckled noisily before *Ting!* the top popped off.

Pffff!

White fire retardant exploded, casting a cloud in both directions and muffling the already low light.

Gritting his teeth, Uno jerked the limp boy out of the way of the gate on the other side and was on his feet an instant later.

"Uno?" murmured Seven's groggy voice.

As Uno ran, Seven's skinny arms jerked, then slowly lifted and wrapped around Uno's neck. "Uno!" he wept. "I knew you were coming. I saw you from the helicopter."

Two guard silhouettes rounded the corner. "He's in here!" one shouted.

Uno lurched to the far wall, dodging a series of tranquilizer darts.

Seven smacked the wall with a crack. "Oof!" he grunted, then breathed several deep breaths.

Uno caught himself and the boy before they could fall and adjusted Seven in his arms. "Hold on!" he grunted and yanked his machine gun up. He fired, dropping both silhouettes, and took off again.

"Please get us out of here," said the boy, his voice thick with tears.

"I'm not leaving without my Immortals," Uno vowed, turning toward the next hall.

"I can run."

Uno slowed his step at an intersection. "This place is a damn maze," he complained, passing small, dark hallways and confusing dead-ends. "Where are they keeping Pherall?"

The boy dropped eagerly to his feet and ran alongside Uno, wiping tears from his bloody cheeks. "You mean Ten? She's in the lab," he said, pointing to the left toward the end of the long corridor. "She has the protein for trans-differentiation, so they were going to breed her."

"Were?"

"Yeah. She was scheduled to breed with Number Four, tonight, but it turns out she's already pregnant."

Uno slowed. "She's ... pregnant?"

Clank! Clank! Clank!

The gate at the far end of the hall began to lower.

"No! No!" shouted Uno, grabbing Seven's arm and pulling him faster. "Run!"

*****

Cinco found the kitchen. Quietly, he eased the service door shut behind him, then ducked back into the shadow of the short hallway as a woman carrying a tray laden with dirty dishes ambled toward a large industrial sink. Seeming unbothered by the lack of power, she began scraping wasted food into a large garbage pail.

Across the large room, past a row of carts and food storage bins, Cinco saw a service elevator. All he had to do was get there and pry the doors open without being seen.

The woman hummed while she worked.

Cinco glanced at the elevator, then at the woman and readied his knife.

She continued scraping.

On silent feet, he crept out of the hall behind her ... and walked across the room. He inserted the blade into the elevator door and pried it open just enough to squeeze through. On the other side, he pushed it shut, then popped the maintenance panel off and used it as a step to reach the ceiling hatch.

Thirty-seconds later, he was crawling up the elevator shaft. One level up, he came to a pair of doors, but no amount of prying or tugging would open them. This meant to access the floor he needed an access badge, which could only be used with electricity inside the elevator or on the other side of the doors. This was the only way out now, too, because the elevator was blocking anything below. He'd already been to the ceiling, so anything above the locked doors was no good. He needed to get through these. He knew this because someone was screaming on the other side.

Cinco muttered a curse, looking around for a better idea ... and found it.

Fortunately, the doors were so fancy that they required plenty of bells, wires, and whistles to manage all that security. This fanciness required a box to house it. It was a big box—so big that it jutted through the wall in all its unsecured glory. The screws used to attach it to the wall smiled up at Cinco and his knife.

Quietly, he eased the security panel backward and let the whole mess dangle in the shaft. Getting his broad shoulders through the not-as-big hole in the front was a bit more challenging, but he managed and found himself in a dingy hallway meant for service staff. From this hall, the servants could reach several rooms without being seen. There were workstations, closets, and utility rooms. Even more interesting than those, however, was a room with three security guards with their noses pressed to the far wall. One was firing a carbine through a hole.

"Get his other ankle!" laughed one.

Pow!

More screaming.

"Give it! It's my turn," said another.

Cinco grabbed the guard closest to him, removed her throat, and then flipped his knife the other direction. He used it again and the second guard went down with a gurgle.

The shooter spun.

Cinco caught the muzzle and snatched it from the man's hands. "It's *my* turn," he smiled and quietly fired.

Stepping over the man's body, he opened the wall they'd been looking through and found Ocho mangled and bleeding on the floor. "Where you want it?" he asked, pointing the carbine at his friend.

Ocho, trembling in agony, pointed to his heart and Cinco fired twice. One bullet struck Ocho in the chest, killing him instantly. There was no second bullet. The weapon was empty.

Cinco dropped the weapon between the door and the jamb to prevent it from closing and heaved Ocho's dead body off the floor. Beyond the staff entrance stretched an immaculate hall that went on for miles, leading him toward angry shouts and chaotic banging. The noise led to a narrow flight of stairs that reeked of chemicals. Moving as quickly as he could with his dead burden, he hurried toward the sound of gun fire and began zigzagging his way through the labyrinth below. Twice, he encountered guards on patrol and had to put Ocho down to clear the way, which slowed his progress, but it gave Ocho enough time to reset.

Cinco felt him twitch. "Are you awake yet, Ocho?" he asked, reaching a staircase.

"Mmm," groaned Ocho.

"Good, because your ass is getting heavy and we're late to the party. Break time's over."

"My ankle hasn't grown back yet."

"Then hobble," Cinco rushed, dropping him to his feet and giving him a push. "You go that way. I'll go this way. Go!"

*****

Pherall found Room 12 and paused with a start.

The door was open.

Clutching the axe in a trembling hand, she peered into the dark room and eased inside. Hot adrenaline burned her stomach and crawled up her neck, but her focus was steady. There was no sound inside. Terrified, she held the axe like a bat and eased into the room. The air was moist and warm, heavy with the smell of her brother's blood—a sickening realization. On silent feet, she stepped through the doorway, allowing the pale glow of the hall lights to waft in behind her. In the center of the room, she saw a dark block table with a soft silhouette on top. "Korbin?" she whispered, hurrying toward it.

Pale light trickled over him and her knees nearly buckled beneath her. A deep gash split his neck, held wide with surgical instruments. Lying around him were knives and scalpels, dropped haphazardly when the lights went out.

"Oh, God!" Sobbing with urgency, she yanked the gadgets off her brother and slung them across the floor, praying she'd reached him in time. "Please don't stay dead!"

Something moved behind her.

With a cry of fright, she whirled, swinging the axe, and clocked someone upside the head with the flat side of the weapon. A technician with a syringe dropped to the floor at her feet, his temple crushed.

A flashlight blinked on.

She swung toward the light, determined to kill these monsters. "Look what you've done!" she screamed and clocked another. "Rot in Hell!"

The flashlight landed on the floor and spun, whirling light across the room.

Another body dropped. She swung the axe at it, not caring what she hit or who it was. "All of you rot in Hell!"

Suddenly, a heavy body slammed into her, taking her to the ground. She screamed and fell, smashing her fingers beneath the axe handle, and landed in a pile of surgical instruments. Her fingers closed around something sharp and she spun on the floor, slashing upward toward whomever had her with a cry.

It was Dr. von Stein, syringe in hand. Her weapon sliced his forearm and the syringe clattered to the floor.

He dove for it.

Pherall scrambled to her feet, clutching the sharp object, and rushed to Korbin again. With all her might, she stabbed it down, praying it would kill her brother, then fumbled wildly to release the straps pinning him to the table.

They wouldn't budge.

Growling in determination, she heaved the axe up and smashed the blade down on the straps. She was on the third one when an object rocketed across the floor, kicked by a moving foot. She jumped, startled, then rushed to sever the last restraint, but Dr. von Stein slammed into her before she could bring the axe down. They flew sideways, crashing into heavy equipment, which shattered against a wall, and landed on a rolling cart.

Instruments went everywhere.

"Aaaah!" she sobbed, half in surprise, half in outrage, and rolled, struggling with him to the floor. The scientist, far more skilled in restraining people, pinned her down and reached hard for the syringe lying just out of fingertip reach. As loud as she could, she screamed. "Uno!"

CHAPTER 23

A blood curdling scream echoed through the building just as the gate crashed down, pinning Uno and Seven in the dark corridor.

Uno skidded to a stop against the bars. "Pherall!" he shouted, giving the bars a shake.

They were sturdy and heavy.

With frantic efficiency, he looked around himself, then up. The walls would be reinforced, but the ceiling wouldn't.

Uno shoved Seven out of the way, taking the axe handle with both hands, and swung at the wall about hip high.

A hole cracked into it, revealing the metal rods inside. The damage was sufficient enough, however, for a toe to fit in. Now, they could climb.

Seven spun to look behind them. "Someone's coming," he warned.

Uno shoved the machine gun into the boy's hands. "Kill them!" he growled and swung again, making a new hole about head high.

Sheet rock crumbled by his feet.

Seven fired. "Take that, you assholes!" he gritted through his teeth.

Uno swung the axe overhead, busting a hole high in the wall near the ceiling, then spun to grab Seven. "Climb!" he ordered, snatching the gun and shoving the boy upward. "Push through the ceiling."

Seven climbed hard, crumbling sheet rock as he moved. His fingers and toes found holds in the metal bracing. The sharp edges cut his hands, but he ignored it and went up. Uno was right behind him.

They reached the ceiling.

With a mighty thrust upward, Uno knocked a panel out. Seven scurried inside. Uno shoved him faster and rolled after to the other side. The ceiling collapsed with their weight, and both spilled through together. They hit the floor hard on the other side.

Uno rolled to his feet with a pained grunt and dragged Seven back into a run. "Pherall!" he shouted, desperate to reach her.

*****

Dr. von Stein stretched for the syringe.

Pherall cracked her fist into his chin, then twisted beneath him, struggling to knock the shot away.

The scientist's fingers bumped the syringe and it rolled out of reach. He roared in outrage and curled his fingers around a scalpel instead. "I'll kill you!" he screeched.

Eyes wide with insanity, the wild-haired man lurched upward on his knees, hands high, and stabbed the scalpel downward toward Pherall's chest.

Before it landed, a violent thud knocked the doctor backward off Pherall and into the rolling cart, toppling it. A tangle of feet scraped wildly over her legs.

"I'll kill you!" Blue screamed, slamming his fists over and over into the madman.

"Blue?" Pherall whispered, crab-walking frantically backward. She bumped into a body, which snapped her back into focus, and leapt to her feet. She snatched her axe from the floor and slammed it down, freeing Korbin's last restraint, and his leg slid free. She shook him. "Korbin, wake up! Please wake up!"

He slid off the table to the floor.

"Korbin!" she cried, trying to lift him, but he was too heavy. She fell to her knees, sobbing, and saw the syringe. Glaring, she snatched it up and dove for the crazy scientist, screeching and bellowing beneath Blue's flying fists. With all her might, she stabbed it down into the man's neck and injected him with it.

Dr. von Stein's swollen eyes went wide in surprise. He stiffened violently, then sagged down to the floor.

A thunder of footsteps crashed through the building.

Blue shoved backward abruptly from von Stein, suddenly frantic and fearful, and grabbed Pherall's arm. The crazy was there, wild in his eyes. "They're coming," he panted, heaving her sharply to her feet. "We gotta get out of here!"

"Korbin!" she rushed, directing Blue to her brother's body.

Blue yanked Korbin's limp body up and slung him over his shoulders in a fireman's carry. Pherall lifted her axe and the three of them piled out of the room into the dimly lit hall.

*****

Uno charged around a corner and crashed into Chetireh, knocking himself and the larger man apart. Chetireh landed hard and scrambled to face Uno. Near panic, he yanked his tranquilizer gun up.

Uno kicked the weapon aside, ducking a dart that missed him by inches. The gun landed on the floor beside them. "Four!" he barked, launching himself onto the larger man.

Chetireh struggled with him, straining to reach the gun. "I have to take you in," grunted the Immortal.

"Fight with me," growled Uno.

"I can't," Chetireh panicked, trying again to dart Uno.

Uno twisted violently, snapping Chetireh's elbow with a crack.

Chetireh shouted in pain and dropped the tranquilizer gun.

"Four!" Uno bellowed, giving the blond a sharp jolt. "Fight with me!"

"They vill kill them," insisted Chetireh. "They vill kill my sisters."

Uno gripped two fistfuls of the man's shirt and snatched him close. "Four, look at me!"

"My sisters are the only family I have left," he rushed through fresh tears. "All of the others are dead."

Uno pierced him with an intense stare. "They're going to kill them anyway. Only you can save them, now," he growled, giving Chetireh another shake. "Rigori is going to kill them, now or later, unless you do something about it."

Chetireh locked his gaze.

"If you're going to save your family," Uno told him quietly, "you're gonna have to go save them."

"Help me?"

"I can't from here," Uno said, putting his nose inches from the other man's. "You can't."

Chetireh's breath broke. "Uno."

"Fight!"

A lone tear rolled down his cheek. "Please don't leave me, Uno," he said in a broken whisper.

"If I get out, you're coming with me," Uno promised, "but I can't do it alone! I need you."

"Vhat if you don't get out?"

A thunder of feet crashed through the building, vibrating the walls and pounding through the floor. "Go save them," barked Uno.

"I'm scared."

"Then fight!" Uno growled, jerking Chetireh to his feet.

Shouts erupted behind them. "There they are!"

"It's Uno!"

Chetireh fired two darts behind them and pulled Uno into a run beside him. "Ve must hurry," he warned. "Dimitri's men are already on their vay—the Iron Squad. The ones he uses to control the Unnaturals."

A guard dropped.

"Unnaturals?" Uno grabbed Seven, shoving the child forward and fired his machine gun at the dark silhouettes coming into view.

"Dimitri has created an army of Immortals," said Chetireh. "He created them in a lab, but the experiment went bad. They're aging and cannot regenerate tissue. He needs Pherall and her baby to fix this. Once he does, they vill be unstoppable. Dimitri and his Iron Squad are on the way now to get her."

"If the Iron Squad are Immortals, we'll make them join us," said Uno.

Chetireh shook his head and fired again. "These Immortals are different from us. They have no compassion, no reason, and grow meaner vith each death. Their insides are rotting and diseased. Only Dimitri can control the Iron Squad guerillas."

Uno frowned at the larger man. A sickening feeling thudded deep in the pit of his stomach, but he forced himself to concentrate and fired another round of bullets toward a group advancing from a different hall. As he fired, a gate lowered from the ceiling at the far end of the massive corridor, backing them toward the laboratory.

Darts peppered the wall beside them.

*****

Pherall and Blue turned down a large hallway but skidded to a stop.

Bars blocked the far end.

"How did you get in?" she asked, turning to run down a different hall in a swirl of white satin.

Blue swung around with his burden. "I'm wearing their uniform," he panted, his eyes wide and darting. "I walked in."

The metallic clank of a gate rattled in front of them, closing the end of the hall. There was no way they would reach it in time. Blue and Pherall reversed quickly and found themselves facing an onslaught of approaching guards.

"Go!" Blue shouted, turning the only direction left to go.

Pherall hesitated and tried to stop him. "Blue, no! They're directing us back to the lab," she cried, searching desperately for another way out.

"Shoot them!" shouted a voice.

Blue shoved Pherall into a run. "Go!"

Pherall stumbled forward, dodging a series of darts with a yelp, and ducked. Gunshots erupted behind them, hitting Blue in the thigh. He shouted in pain and stumbled hard, nearly dropping Korbin. Pherall caught him with a cry and shoved her shoulder beneath his arm. He limped beside her, leaving a trail of blood on the floor behind them.

This was it, Pherall realized. The horror movie she never wanted to watch. She was living it now. They would never get out of here alive. As they rounded the last corner into the lab, she crashed hard into a body, knocking herself free of Blue, and whirled, bringing her axe around in panic.

Uno caught her arm instinctively, his elbow braced to strike such a close target. They froze for a split second, then threw their arms around each other.

"Uno!" she cried.

He kissed her mouth, hard and sincere, and tucked her head against his shoulder. "I found you," he panted, gripping her hair in a fist and kissing her temple.

Just then, the power surged on and lights blinked on overhead, illuminating the laboratory in brightness. At full power now, the gates slammed down, crushing anyone standing beneath them and pinning the guards on the other side. The unlucky went down, screaming as they died.

Uno shot the few who'd made it through, but it was no use. Every exit was blocked. Clutching her firmly, he backed Pherall and Seven away from the gates. As he moved, his heavy gaze locked with Chetireh's. They'd failed. There was nowhere to go now. Uno saw Ocho across the bars to his right, pushing and shoving his way through the guards. In his hand, he held a detonator. In the wide entrance to Uno's left, Cinco shoved his way forward toward a different gate, clutching two detonators in his hands.

The fortress was rigged to blow.

"Shoot them!" shouted the guards pressed firmly against the blockade. The ends of numerous weapons appeared through the bars—pistols, tranquilizers, and stun gun darts—and went off.

Laboratory equipment exploded and shattered to the floor. Uno and Pherall ducked behind a desk, dodging the projectiles. Blue staggered in beside them and tripped over debris, dropping Korbin.

"Blue!" Pherall cried and spotted the detonator in his hand.

Two more bullets struck Blue, knocking him hard into a cabinet. Blood spewed from his mouth, and he hit the floor. "Go!" he grunted, waving them forward. Bleeding profusely, he dragged Pherall's brother deeper into the lab and peered beneath heavy lids at the guards moving in from every direction. The laboratory was surrounded.

More weapons appeared.

More thundering footsteps.

More guards.

Chetireh pushed Seven behind him to shield the boy from the flying darts and ducked behind a metal workstation. "We're surrounded," said he darkly to Uno.

Pherall looked first at Uno, then at Cinco and Ocho. The two of them also had detonators in their hands which meant they'd wired explosives. "Blow it," she called out calmly.

Cinco's eyes widened. In horror, he shook his head. "But Pherall —"

"No!" shouted Uno. "Not an option!"

"Blow it!" she repeated.

Ocho shoved forward and landed against a set of bars. "Uno, don't listen to her! Get her out of here first," he shouted through them.

Rigori's voice carried through the hallways and he rushed into view, surrounded by guards with metal-melting thermite. "Clear the way!" he barked, slinging his arm. He had a cellphone in his hand. "I want those bars melted! Get those tranquilizer guns reloaded! Now!"

"Blow it!" screamed Pherall.

Neither Cinco nor Ocho obeyed her order.

"We have Immortals with detonators in here," someone shouted. "They're gonna blow the place. Grab 'em!"

Uno and Pherall shared a look.

"I'm not making it out of here, Uno, and you know it," she told him firmly.

"Yes, you are!" he argued, looking frantically around. "I'll find a way. I always find a way."

The high-pitched whirr of a saw indicated someone was about to cut through the bars.

Rigori shouted into his phone. "Dimitri! Where is that damn helicopter? I need Iron Squad here now! Dimitri! Hello?"

"Iron Squad?" echoed Pherall.

A blade screamed against the metal and sparks sprayed toward the ceiling.

Uno backed her up. "Dimitri has created the Iron Squad, a team of Unnaturals. Apparently, they're on their way," he relayed quickly.

"He made Immortals?"

"Bad ones. He calls them guerillas." Uno flicked his gaze over her head toward the glass room, then dropped his eyes to hers with a heavy heart. He didn't want to admit it, but she was right. He

226

couldn't get her out. "That's why he wants you—to fix his mistakes. We have to get you out of here. I can't let them take you," he said in a broken voice. "You or my baby."

"Baby?" Pherall whispered, realizing right away what he meant. She'd wondered about the delay with Chetireh. Stunned, she blinked up at him. "I'm pregnant?"

Uno's fingers tightened around her hand. "Where's the panel to lock the door?"

A tear rolled down Pherall's cheek. Kicking her brain back into gear, she looked at the control pad and inclined her head toward it. "There."

"Chetireh!" Uno called, backing Pherall into the open glass room. "Destroy the panel!"

Blue dragged himself, struggling wildly to reach Uno. "No!" he gurgled, hobbling frantically on his bad leg to reach Chetireh. "Four, no! Don't do it!"

Cinco slung guards away and hollered over the din. "We can do this, Uno! We can get her out!"

"Blow it, Cinco," Uno ordered, almost desperately.

"Uno! You're gonna win," argued Ocho. "You always win."

Guards seized Ocho and slammed him against the melting bars. They clawed at him, struggling to get the detonator from his hand. He gritted his teeth, fighting them, watching Uno with pleading eyes.

"Do it!" Uno shouted back. "Do it now! Cinco!"

Cinco was rammed into the bars from behind. "I can't kill you," he said with a crack in his voice.

"Don't leave us," begged Seven.

Uno faced the little boy. "I'm not leaving you, Seven. I'm saving you."

"Uno!" Cinco bellowed, sobbing, slamming himself against the bars. "Not her! Don't kill her!"

Guards melted through one of the gates. Heavy bars clanged to the floor and rang loudly. Ocho was shoved through and tackled.

"Kill him," ordered Rigori, pointing to Ocho as he passed. "Take off his head."

Uno pulled Pherall into the glass room with him and yanked the door shut behind them. "Four!"

The magnets clanged sharply.

Rigori shouted and ran for the glass room. "No! Unlock the door!"

Chetireh rushed forward and, using his empty gun, smashed the butt down on the control panel, destroying it.

Guards opened fire on the Russian.

Uno and Pherall watched him fall into the panel and strike it one last time before sliding to the floor in a pool of blood.

Rigori crashed against the glass. "Uno! Don't hurt her!"

Uno backed Pherall away from the madman.

Blue fell, dying. "Stop!" he cried, crawling pitifully across the floor. "No!"

"I just want you and the girl," negotiated Rigori with forced calm. "You two stay with me and the others go free. You have my word."

Uno ignored him. Sweaty and trembling with adrenaline, he turned to face Pherall, his damp brown hair scattered across his forehead and around his neck. "I don't want to do this."

Eyes swimming, Pherall touched his cheek. "I know," she whispered, gazing into his brown eyes, then eased herself into his arms. "They won't detonate it unless you do."

He squeezed her tightly to him, clutching her head in one hand, her waist in the other. "I love you," he whispered into her hair. "I love you both."

Behind them, guards poured into the laboratory and pounded on the glass.

"Unlock it!" screamed Rigori. "Get her outta there!"

The second set of gates were melted and crashed down. Angry guards shouted, finally making it into the laboratory. They joined Rigori, pounding their fists on the glass.

"Get him away from her!" the billionaire railed.

Uno ignored the commotion behind him and Pherall didn't bother looking. Gripping her cheeks with shaky hands, he kissed her lips, slow and sweet. In his chest, his heart thumped hard against his ribs, begging him not to do what he was about to do.

Cinco crashed his shoulder against the door, rattling it. An instant later, he was brought down. "Uno, don't kill her!" he sobbed, vanishing beneath a pile of guards.

Thumps and grunts erupted next, indicating a struggle.

"Uno!"

Ocho cried quietly, pinned to the floor across the room with a knee in his back. "This isn't happening," he murmured, over and over. "This isn't happening."

Seven elbowed his way to the glass. A restraining strap hooked around his throat and yanked him backward, but he didn't care. In silence, he watched.

It was time.

When Uno lifted his head, he was the one crying.

"I'm scared," Pherall whispered, peering up into his beautiful face.

Rigori slapped his palms against the glass. "Uno!"

Uno kissed her again, this time quick. "We go together," he murmured, pulling her gently into his arms. Closing his eyes, he tucked her head into his neck, pressing her face there, and tightened his hold on her. Tighter and tighter he squeezed. "Hold onto me, baby," he whispered in a broken voice and slid the blade from his wrist.

Rigori beat on the glass, hysterical. "Uno! No! No!"

Pherall's breaths broke into short gasps. Trembling, she locked her arms around Uno's neck and held on tight.

Rigori screamed. "Aaaah!" he railed, flailing his arms and throwing his weight into the glass.

Machine gun fire splattered the bulletproof wall and ricocheted off.

More crashes.

Uno buried his face in Pherall's hair. "We go together," he whispered again and thrust the knife deep into her heart.

Pherall opened her mouth in a silent scream and stiffened.

Uno felt the pierce in his own heart and gasped in pain. He yanked the bloody knife free with unsteady hands and dropped it. It clattered to the floor. "What have I done?" he choked, locking his arms around her and holding her while she died.

Outside, the staring faces fell silent.

Pherall's arms loosened around Uno's neck.

"I'm sorry," he wept.

Her knees buckled and her head sagged backward.

Sobbing quietly, Uno fell to his knees, fighting to draw breath as he sank to the floor with Pherall. He dropped with her, struggling desperately to keep her in his arms. She lay beside him, her unblinking eyes open in death.

He'd lost.

With the last of his strength, he pulled her body against his and felt his heart go still. She was taking him with her. As he relaxed, he watched her beautiful face fade into the darkness, and he exhaled his last breath in regret.

Ringing silence filled the mansion.

*****

Slowly, Seven crawled to the glass and touched it. With trembling lips, he peered inside at the dead bodies, then rested his forehead against the glass. Tears dropped from his eyes as they closed.

Purple-faced, Rigori whirled. "Lock them up!" he bellowed, slinging his arm toward the Immortals pinned around him. "I want these animals in cages!"

Chetireh snatched a pistol from the floor and stood, a frown of disgust contorting his face, and—*Pow!*—shot Rigori. The old man gripped his ribs and slammed backward into the glass wall. "You killed Uno, you piece of shit," the Russian spat in hatred and shot him again.

Rigori jolted, gurgled a mouthful of blood, and slid to the floor. Silence.

Dimitri's voice broke over the radio, loud in the continuing silence. "Dimitri to Rigori," called the thin voice over the sound of helicopter rotors. "Iron Squad in route. ETA … (static) … Do you copy?"

Cinco's voice split the quiet. "Blow it, boys."

The guards, suddenly fearful, whirled to face Cinco and Ocho, then looked in horror at each other. The math was easy. Uno was dead. Pherall was dead. There was nobody left for the Immortals to protect. In a flash of realization, the entire bunch broke out in panic, screaming and trampling each other to get out.

Cinco grabbed Seven by the shirt and shoved the child to the floor beneath him. "All of you, go to Hell," he snarled and pressed the buttons, detonating the first of the explosives.

The explosion was massive.

Screams erupted from the trapped guards as rubble rocketed into the laboratory.

Blue slammed into something. Gasping for breath, he closed his eyes and pressed the button.

Bars and debris obliterated the lab.

Ocho slid wildly across the floor, rolling into the chaos. Barely alive, he pressed his detonator, finishing the job.

CHAPTER 24

Blue woke first and slapped the ground for his glasses, but they were shattered. "Dammit," he grumbled, climbing to his feet and favoring his left leg as it regenerated. He found Ocho right away and the two started piling bodies outside the rubble. "Cinco," he said, shaking the larger man when he found him. "Wake up."

Cinco, coated in powdered mortar and fragments of flesh, blinked his eyes open and groaned in pain. "Give me a minute," he managed, waiting for his pelvis to reset.

Seven woke next. Groggily, he climbed to his feet, still regrowing part of his face, and took a pistol from a dead body. Moving carefully through the debris, he limped through the laboratory, now bathed in hot sunlight and billowing dust, in search of anyone who'd managed to escape the fortress explosion. He spotted a few of Rigori's employees trying to hide in the yard. "Oh, no, you don't," he said, aiming the weapon.

One by one, he shot them.

Korbin blinked his eyes open, startled by the sound of gunshots, and looked around in alarm. He grimaced in pain as his belly and the entire left side of his body mended itself. Puzzled, he dragged himself to wobbly legs, not entirely sure what had happened, and tried to stand. Last thing he remembered; he was lying on a table. Now, he was outside and the building was gone. He paused to breathe.

"Nine, Dimitri's on his way with reinforcements," Seven told him over his shoulders. "We have to get the Immortals off the island."

Korbin searched the ground for familiar bodies and spotted a fragmented section of the glass wall. "Pherall!" he cried and, after a short hobble, began digging frantically through the rubble. "Where's Pherall!"

With panicked hands, he dug down until he found her, still wrapped in Uno's arms.

Both were dead.

"Oh, God!" With a cry of anguish, Korbin pulled his sister into his arms and brushed blond hair from her face. "No, no, no! I didn't mean it!" he sobbed, rocking her body in his arms. "I don't want you to die. Please don't die!"

"We don't have time for that, Nine," shouted Seven, sounding far more mature than his age implied. "We gotta go."

"I'm not leaving her!"

"Then bring her," snapped Seven. "We gotta go!"

Sobbing quietly, Korbin took a minute to compose himself before wiping tears from his cheeks. With a deep breath, he slid his arm beneath Pherall's knees and carried his sister out of the ruins.

Several feet away, someone moaned.

Seven recognized the sound of the voice and whirled sharply, his face contorted in boyish hatred. "Rigori!"

The old man, trapped beneath a broken cabinet, saw the child and froze in alarm. He looked frail and wrinkled now, like an old man. "Seven, listen to me."

Seven aimed at the monster's knee and fired.

Pow!

"I'm listening," the boy said, approaching with a snarl.

Rigori screamed and tried to scoot away.

Seven aimed at his other knee. "Still listening," growled the little boy.

Pow!

Rigori wailed in agony.

Korbin hurried back to the rubble for Uno and pulled him free of the broken glass panels. Gingerly, he cleaned his face off, then carried him out of the debris.

Chetireh got up, limping sharply on the stub of a new leg, and picked up a black box. "Nine, hurry. Ve have to get out of here!" he called urgently and pointed to the sky. "They'll be here any minute."

"I'll kill anybody who shows up," warned Blue vehemently.

Chetireh shook his big, blond head. "They're Dimitri's men," he said quickly and shoved the heavy box into Cinco's hands. "They are brutal and they won't die. Take this. It's one of their backup hard drives."

"You mean there's more Jackboots?" asked Blue.

"These are worse than Jackboots," said the Russian. "Much worse."

Cinco pointed. "The boat is docked on that side of the island," he shouted, struggling to get up. "Load it."

Chetireh lifted Uno's body into his arms and took off toward the boat with him. Korbin heaved Pherall up and followed. Blue tossed Ocho over his shoulder and staggered over the uneven ground.

Seven glared at Rigori who lay twisted and moaning, his shattered legs twisted into grotesque contortions. He tried to fire again, but his pistol was out of ammunition.

Cinco stopped. "Seven, we have to go," he said, gathering weapons and ammo.

232

"I'm not done!" Seven scanned the ground in search of a weapon and spotted a broken axe handle to use on the monster. He picked it up and stomped toward the old man.

Cinco stopped him. "I'll kill him" he said, raising his weapon to kill the billionaire.

"No," Seven said sharply and gripped the wooden handle. "This piece of shit doesn't deserve a peaceful death. I want him to suffer like he did to my mama!" he shouted angrily at the whimpering Rigori. "To lie in that useless body and rot. You deserve it!"

Scowling in anger, the child heaved the axe handle at the old man, striking him in his side with a nonfatal thud.

Rigori cried out in fear.

"Cinco, they're coming!" shouted Chetireh.

Before Seven could find something else to throw, Cinco, still clutching the harddrive, hooked the kid's skinny waist and took off with him.

"You're gonna live, you bastard!" Seven shouted at the writhing figure. "I hope you choke on a macadamia nut! You're an asshole!"

*****

Cinco raced through the waves with Seven, threw the seething boy aboard, and gave the ferry a shove. "Go! Go! Go!" he shouted, jumping on.

In the pilot house, Blue threw the throttle forward and the engine screamed to life.

Panting with fatigue, Cinco scrambled across the lower deck to Pherall's and Uno's dead bodies and pushed his way through the weeping crowd. Seeing them, he dropped hard to his knees. Gently, he stroked his fingers down Pherall's cheek, then gripped Uno's hand. Overcome with grief, he lowered his head over his friends and closed his eyes, grimacing hard.

Blue's alarmed voice shouted from the pilot house. "Cinco! We got incoming!"

"Dammit!" Cinco climbed to his feet with a curse, refocusing his anger, and grabbed a weapon. "Ocho! Get your lazy ass up," he shouted, running to the back of the boat. "Where's the grenade launcher? Ocho!"

Ocho groaned and opened teary eyes. "In the pilot house," he grunted, then rolled slowly to an elbow. He paused when he saw Pherall and Uno and let out a guttural curse. Fat tears rolled down his dirty cheeks. Wincing at the sight, he crawled to the unmoving bodies and wept openly. "What are you doing!" he shouted angrily, gripping Uno's shirt with his regrowing hand.

Gunshot popped overhead.

Miserably, Ocho pressed his face into Uno's chest. "Why are you doing this!" he squeaked. "We need you. I need you."

Seven scooted up behind him, unused to the bobbing floor, and looked at them. With a heavy heart, he touched the smooth satin of Pherall's gown. "I can feel her."

Ocho reached an arm across Pherall and gripped her filthy shoulder, hugging them both. "This is our fault, my fault. Next time we find a female, we'll take better care of her," he swore to Uno. "I'll take care of her."

Pherall's unblinking eyes stared back.

Seven touched her face. As he did, the tip of his finger felt the faintest buzz. Startled, he snatched his hand away, frowning at her, but when he touched her again it was gone. After a moment of confusion, he bent forward to listen by her lips. She wasn't breathing. Scowling hard, he boldly placed his young mouth over hers and blew. When he did, a sharp jolt cracked through him and he jerked back. His heart skipped hard, and his breath caught. A sensation he'd never felt before zipped through him in an electric buzz, warming him from the inside out. He stiffened sharply, remembering the reaction Chetireh had described upon meeting his mother Six. Hesitantly, he watched her unmoving face. "Ten?" he murmured, then edged closer on his knees.

With dirty fingers, Seven turned her face toward him and blew again. The sensation struck him hard, knocking him back this time. Trembling now, he put his fingers to her throat. There was no pulse, but he knew. "She's trying to reset," he said quietly, then shouted. "She's trying to reset!"

Ocho raised swollen eyes, then peered down at the unchanged faces. "What?"

Seven lurched across Pherall's legs and climbed rudely onto Uno, trying to reach his throat. There was no pulse there either. "Help me!" he shouted at the others. With a violent fist, Seven pounded on Uno's chest, shouting at him and slapping his face. "Uno, reset! Help her! She can't do it alone."

"What are you doing?" Ocho asked, pushing up. "Females can't reset."

A blast struck the water beside the boat, shooting a spray across the deck. It bobbed sharply, spilling everyone to the left. The group caught themselves and blinked at Seven scrambling wildly back to the bodies on the floor.

"They're dead," said Ocho.

Seven pounded hard on Pherall's chest. "How do you know?" he grunted, stretching to bang on Uno's chest next. "There's only been one other!"

Chetireh and Ocho looked at each other, then down at the bodies.

Chetireh inched forward hesitantly. "He's right. Ve don't know," he said. "Dimitri believed that the physical union between the Queen and the King is the key to female immortality. He believed they vere trying to synchronize but didn't know how or vhy."

"They died together. Why wouldn't they come back together!" Seven barked, switching impatiently back to Pherall.

Ocho couldn't argue with the logic. In the next instant, he was on his knees, bending over Uno. Chetireh positioned the unmoving bodies for CPR.

Ocho urgently pumped Uno's chest, barely daring to believe. "You hear that Uno?" he demanded, grunting to the tempo of his compressions. "You're not done. Wake up!"

Korbin rushed forward and skidded to a stop, his blue eyes rounded wide. "What's going on?" he asked hesitantly.

Seven blew in Uno's mouth. "Females have to be paired to reset," the little boy said between puffs.

"Paired?"

"I'll explain later. Help us!" the child ordered, jabbing a point at Pherall.

Korbin dropped to his knees beside his sister's head and blew into her mouth while Chetireh compressed her chest.

Another blast from the helicopter rocked the boat.

Cinco fell on the upper deck and rolled to the roof of the second level, shouting in outrage. Lying where he'd fallen, he loaded the grenade into his brand new launcher. "A little closer, you choppy bastard," he growled, aiming at the helicopter.

On the deck below him, Ocho continued compressions. "Uno, c'mon, you son-of-a-bitch!"

Seven blew into Uno's mouth. "I'm not giving up on you," he vowed quietly, paying no attention to the tears streaking down his dirty cheeks. "Please come back, Uno. You can bring Pherall back. She needs you to bring her back!"

Seven bent to blow again, but Ocho stopped him.

Uno's eyes were closed.

"He's trying!" cried Seven.

Ocho gripped his friend's throat, feeling for a pulse, and shouted. "Uno!"

A leg twitched.

Seven blew into Uno's mouth again. "He's resetting!" he cried, grabbing Ocho's sleeve in excitement.

Cinco darted the other way and rolled. "Where in the hell is everybody!" he shouted, returning fire.

The ferry jerked hard to the right, spilling the Immortals the other way, and bobbed ... but nobody cared.

Korbin and Chetireh scrambled back into their positions and continued working on Pherall whose eyes had closed.

Korbin shouldered sweat from his dirty face. "It's working!"

Moments later, Uno lifted an unsteady hand, stopping Seven's next mouthful of air, and breathed on his own. His arm dropped.

Seven shook him. "Hurry, Uno!" he demanded, trying to rattle him back to his senses. "Ten is trying to reset! She needs you."

Uno opened his brown eyes, dizzy and disoriented, but the echoey words registered. In his chest, his heart thudded a puny beat. After a few blinks, he turned his head and saw Pherall lying dead beside him. He struggled clumsily to an elbow and, with Ocho's help, rolled to her. Too weak to hold himself up, he fell into her and lay suffocating. His body wanted to die. If she didn't wake, it would.

Another heartbeat.

Breathing in shallow breaths, he put his mouth to her ear. "Come back," he wheezed, trying to find his voice so she could hear him. "I can't breathe ... unless you do."

Korbin gave Pherall another breath and set his fingers against her neck. "She has a pulse," he squeaked, then hung his head in relief.

"Give her more air," ordered Ocho.

Tat-tat-tat!

"Helloooo!" shouted Cinco from the upper deck.

Korbin puffed twice.

Uno winced through another beat. "Pherall," he said in a breathy whisper, "heal ... yourself. I can't breathe."

On the next breath, she moved.

"She's trying!" encouraged Chetireh. "Blow again."

Uno sagged onto her in exhaustion. "Come back, Pherall," he whispered, closing blurry eyes. "Bring ... our baby with you."

Pherall's moan was barely audible.

While Uno murmured softly to her, Korbin lifted her shoulder and exposed the back of Pherall's bloody satin robe. The knife wound puckered angrily in her flesh, but the hole was gone. "It's healing," he shouted. "She's an Immortal!"

Korbin breathed for Pherall again and, this time, she inhaled a weak breath of air, trying to take over. After a few puny breaths, she grimaced at the sharp pains shooting through her heart. Stabbing fibers threaded themselves back together, sending bolts of electricity down her legs and through her arms. Struggling to control her heavy limbs, she blinked to wet her dry eyes and squinted at the brightness of the sun. A zap went up her spine, giving her an instant headache. Breathing through it, she focused glossy blue eyes on two blurry silhouettes bending over her until she recognized Chetireh. Confused, she shifted her gaze to the other blob and saw her brother.

Breathing in shallow gulps, Uno lifted his dirty head to look at her, then laid it down again.

Pherall touched him with an unsteady hand and closed her eyes. Flickers of memory flashed through her mind—Uno's tears, the banging, the pierce of his blade. Ever so lightly, her fingers tightened around his. "Uno," she winced.

Uno wrapped his arms around her, drawing his first full breath, and looked at Ocho with tired brown eyes. "Where are we?"

"We just left the island," Ocho said with a crack in his voice. "Dimitri's Iron Squad is attacking us."

Right on cue, the boat rocked and water splashed across the deck.

"When I'm done killing these assholes," Cinco's annoyed voice shouted down over his running footsteps, "I'm going to come down there and kill all of y'all. Just putting that out there!"

"Why aren't they helping!" demanded an angry Blue from the pilothouse.

"They're doing CPR," Cinco growled back, shooting.

Uno took a moment to gather strength and worked to get to his elbows. "Where is Seven?" he asked, trying to find him.

"I'm right here."

Ocho gestured around him and motioned Seven forward into Uno's view. "We're all on the boat," he sniffed. "All but Six and Three."

"CPR!" Heavy footsteps pounded down the stairs and Blue rocketed onto the deck, his eyes bulging. "Uno?"

"Hi, Blue," Uno smiled, twisting to look at him, then frowned. "Wait … who's driving the boat?"

"Uno!" Blue cried again, rushing forward. "You're alive!"

"Blue!" Ocho got to his feet and raced up the stairs. "You idiot!"

Gunshots erupted all over the ferry, clanking and pinging around them.

"Aaah!" Cinco cried in pain. "That! Hurts!"

Uno pushed wild hair from his face. "All of you," he said, gaining strength in his voice, "go help Cinco. I've got her."

Blue, Seven, Korbin, and Chetireh hurried off, eager to obey.

Uno, growing stronger by the moment, bent over Pherall and touched her face. "Look at me, baby."

Through dusty lashes, she peeked up at him, still struggling for air, and curled her fingers into his ugly green uniform. "I can't brea ..."

Gunshots erupted from the upper deck. There was a metallic clank overhead and the chop of helicopter rotors switched to a high-pitch whir.

"Got 'em!" sang Blue.

An enormous splash soaked the ferry as the helicopter hit the water. The vessel bobbed, tossing Pherall and Uno into a nearby bench.

Ignoring that, Uno leaned over her and blew into her mouth. "Don't fight it," he coached, speaking louder. "Your body is repairing itself."

The throttle revved, vibrating the floor, and the ferry pulled away from the bobbing helicopter.

Struggling to handle the pain, Pherall let out a choppy breath and tried to relax.

Uno blew again, giving her more air. Lightly, he stroked her arm, trailing his fingers over her skin until she tensed again. "Relax," he coaxed, allowing time for her breathing to stabilize. "It'll fade."

As promised, the pain eventually began to ebb.

Pherall felt the thump of her heart grow stronger. The stabbing pain decreased in intensity, then faded into an irritating tingle, leaving her tired and hungry.

Uno smiled down at her. "Welcome back, my Queen."

Pherall, breathing in long, slow breaths, glared up into his handsome face and smiled. "That hurt, you asshole."

www.dcsargent.com

238